Jabberwock's Champion

Looking Glass Chronicles
Book 2

R.V. Bowman

Northern
Estates
Faelands
Pearl
Mountains
Pearl Palace
The Hollow
Labyrinth
Kingdom
of
Wonderland
Sackleperny's Home
Gilded
Mountains
Red Palace

Chapter 1

"I CHOOSE TO BE Prince Zander's champion." Alice's voice echoed in the high-ceilinged library in the Pearl Palace.

Time ground to a halt and everyone froze in their seats, except Citrine, who beamed an encouraging smile. Alice swallowed as half a dozen pairs of eyes drilled into her and the silence stretched.

Finally, Lord Beecher's cane thumped on the floor, cracking the quiet, and time rushed back in. "I say! This is highly irregular." He waved his cane in the air. "She's a girl. We can't have a girl as the champion."

The Duchess lifted an auburn eyebrow, her sharp green eyes glittering. "You've said that already, Wilfred."

"But... but..." The older man's face mottled in furious red splotches. "It's not done."

The Duchess's lip curled as a spray of spittle landed on her arm. She wiped it away with her handkerchief before she spoke. "How would you know? There hasn't been a challenge for the crown in a hundred years, at least." She paused and her eyes traveled from Beecher's wispy white hair to his thick-soled shoes. "Well, perhaps you do remember."

The older man's face turned an alarming shade of purple. "Why... why... you..." Unable to come up with a suitable insult, he shook his cane in the air again, forcing Lady Perma to duck so as not to get smacked on the head.

"Really, Lord Beecher! Do control yourself!" Lady Perma sniffed and leaned forward, her bosom straining at the neckline of her dress. Her eyes darted toward Prince Zander and the Commander. "Does anyone even know what the challenge is?"

Zander straightened in his chair. "It's been such a long time since this has happened." He spread his hands. "I'm not sure..." His voice trailed off, and the Commander spoke into the awkward pause.

"It's the labyrinth."

Everyone's gazes swung from the Commander back to Alice. She forced herself not to shrink away from the questions that hung, invisible, in the room.

The Duchess broke the tension. "Not that I doubt your word, Commander, but how did you come by this information?"

Alice's shoulders loosened as the group's attention refocused on the Commander.

He shrugged. "Our father told me and my brother when we were boys. He thought we should know—as a precaution, I suppose."

Lady Perma wrung her plump hands. "Oh, dear."

Zander shot to his feet, his chair teetering before the legs slapped back onto the floor. Several cats on the library shelves hissed, and an enormous bird dozing in a corner took flight, swooping over the table, causing Lady Perma and the Duchess to cover their heads.

Zander ignored the commotion and turned his focus on Alice. Which, of course, meant they were all staring at her again. She pressed her spine straight and lifted her chin. She had a good notion of what Zander was getting ready to say and braced herself. He didn't disappoint.

"I'm sorry, Alice. You can't be my champion." His gaze flickered to Citrine but then zeroed back in on her. Determination settled over his features like armor. "You'll have to marry me, whether you want to or not."

The Duchess rolled her eyes. "Didn't we already have this conversation?"

Alice gripped the edge of the table, and her voice came out smaller than she intended. "But... I thought I had a choice." Her desperate gaze found Sir Lapin Blanc's. "You said I had a choice."

The big rabbit ran a furry paw over one white ear. His nose twitched several times before he spoke, his tone measured. "Prince Zander, I appreciate your concern, and I think I speak for all of us when I say that we don't want anything to happen to the young lady. However, it's only fair to give her a choice in the matter. Her life is the one most disrupted, after all."

Zander swept his arm out. "It will be even more disrupted if she's dead."

Lapin took off his spectacles and polished them with his handkerchief. "I understand your fears, Sir, but it still does not change the fact that the young lady does not want to marry you and stay here. It would be highly unethical to force her to, as she isn't even a citizen."

Zander slammed his palm on the tabletop, and Alice flinched. "Is it more ethical to lose the Kingdom? There's no way she can get through the labyrinth, never mind beating the other champion. Not only will she be dead, but we'll all be in danger of losing our heads."

Alice's breath hitched at the betrayal. She couldn't believe this was happening again, that someone else was trying to dictate her future as if she were nothing more than a piece on a gameboard.

Lapin set his spectacles on his nose. "Ethics aren't determined by outcome. They are determined by what is the right thing to do, regardless of what happens."

Zander's face flushed. Either from embarrassment or anger, Alice couldn't tell until he spoke. "Those are lofty words coming from someone who isn't carrying the weight of this Kingdom on his shoulders."

Lapin held up his paws. "I am on your side, Prince Zander. I realize you carry a heavy burden, but is it fair to ask Miss Alice to share it with you when this isn't even her world?"

The question dropped into the room like a rock in a still pond. Zander's nostrils flared as he visibly brought his emotions to heel. The tension in the room squeezed until it was suffocating.

Alice gripped the edge of the table and pushed down the hot words that wanted to burn her lips. She had considered Zander a friend, an ally, but he was as bad as Hadley. Sure, the prince had different, more noble reasons, but it didn't change the fact that he was kidnapping her future.

Her temper bubbled near the surface, but she kept an iron grip on it. She would gain nothing if she lost control here. If she wanted any chance at being the champion, she had to present her side logically, make them realize she was the best choice. Even as she told herself this, doubts crept into her thoughts, strangling her resolve. What if...

Something brushed against her leg, and she startled before she realized it was the black-and-white cat from earlier. A large ginger tom dropped from the shelf and sauntered to her other side. Both leaned against her ankles, purring. Renewed determination welled up in her. This *was* the only choice.

Unless she wanted to marry the prince.

Which she didn't.

She tried to herd her thoughts into some semblance of a logical argument, but her internal wrestling had cost her. The Duchess spoke into the stillness of the room, her tone cool.

"The prince has a valid point. This affects everyone, Lapin. While I don't hold to Lord Beecher's antiquated views of females"—she grimace—"from everything I've heard, getting through the labyrinth is no easy thing. And the girl isn't even from our world." She looked at Alice, her expression troubled. "I agree it is unconscionable to force her to marry against her wishes, but what is one girl's preferences against the good of the entire Kingdom? And it isn't as if we are asking her to wed an ogre." She gestured to Zander. "He's young, handsome, and from all appearances, well-tempered."

There were murmurs of assent around the table. Alice gritted her teeth and resentment stabbed through her. She had almost died breaking that blasted curse, and now she might be stuck here forever? Well, if they thought they could bully her into this, they were mistaken. She straightened her shoulders and spoke over the other voices.

"Excuse me, but I'd like to remind you all, I defeated the Red Queen *and* broke the curse. I chose to help. I chose to put myself into danger for the prince." Alice met the gaze of each person in the room, ending with Zander. "And you promised me I could go home."

Zander's glance fell to the table, and he ran a hand through his hair. When he finally raised his eyes to hers, his expression was weary but resolute. "Alice, I don't like this any more than you do, and I feel terrible about pushing you into something you don't want. If there were any other way I could see forward..." He lifted his arm and pointed at the brown tattoo that twined around his wrist. She sported its twin on her own wrist. It had appeared when Alice had broken the Jabberwock's Curse at the ball three days ago. "This changes things. I want what's best for you, but not at the expense of my Kingdom. I'm sorry."

Alice wanted to pound the table and scream at him, but she knew it wouldn't change his mind. So instead, she forced herself to keep her voice even, reasonable. "Before I got here, you had all but given up. Without my help, you'd still be a jabberwock, and likely as not, you'd have lost your humanity too. Lyssandra would be the Queen. The only reason you even have a chance for your throne is because I helped you. Do I really deserve to be forced into a marriage neither of us wants?"

Zander looked as if she had slapped him, and Alice silenced the small voice that wanted to sympathize. Lady Perma leaned forward, her hands clasped in front of her. "She has a point."

Lord Beecher slammed his cane on the floor. "Poppycock! She got lucky, and let's not forget, she didn't do that all alone. The prince here and that Felinas fellow helped her." He stopped and blinked owlishly. "Where did he go?"

The Duchess sighed. "Sir Chess was never here, Wilfred. Do stay focused."

Beecher harrumphed and then looked back at the rest of the Council. "It's the prince's choice who he wants as his champion, not this chit of a girl. I say we vote on this and go home."

Alice wondered what the penalty would be if she punched Lord Beecher in the nose. Before she could follow that thought, Zander rounded the table to where she stood.

A lock of bronze hair had fallen over one eye, and his expression twisted with regret and guilt. Her own defenses softened, and she wished they could have this conversation without the audience.

He reached for her hand, and she let him take it and turn her so they faced each other.

"You're right. I wouldn't be here if not for your help, and I know what I'm asking of you is monstrously unfair." He paused and swallowed. "But, Alice, you have no idea what you'd be facing in that labyrinth. I don't want to downplay what you did for me, and if I thought you could win..." He looked away from her. "But I can't gamble the Kingdom. I just can't."

She bit her lip. He was right. She didn't know what was in there. And if she failed... it wasn't merely her own neck at risk. She'd take the entire Kingdom down with her.

But the alternative was permanent—for her and for Zander. The whole situation was impossible. As if in tune with her feelings, the tattoo around her wrist prickled.

Then, anger gushed up in her like a geyser. Anger at the Queen for creating this mess. Anger at Chess for dragging her into all this and not even being here when her fate was being decided. Anger at Zander for making her feel guilty.

Part of her knew that wasn't fair. In many ways, he was as much a victim as she was. Worse, he loved another woman and was willing to give her up to save his Kingdom. Her gaze strayed to Citrine, who watched them along with the rest of the Council. While her expression remained serene, Alice noticed the knuckles on her clasped hands showed white.

Zander was right about one thing. This wasn't only about them. She pulled her hand away from him and shook her head. "I can't stay here, Zander. I have a family that needs me. Surely you, of all people, can understand duty." Even as she said the words, the tattoo on her wrist began to burn. She rubbed at it, trying to ignore the painful sensation.

Zander's tattoo didn't appear to bother him as he leaned toward her, his tone earnest.

"I know there aren't any good choices here, but if you go into that labyrinth, you probably won't come out again. You'll be lost to your family forever. At least, if you marry me, you'll still be alive."

Tears of frustration prickled Alice's eyes. "And how does that work? I'm stuck here either way. I'm not sure if it matters if I'm breathing or not."

His brows formed a deep *v*. "It matters to me, Alice. Do you think I want your death on my conscience?"

"Do you think your conscience matters more to me than my family?"

They glowered at each other, and it was all Alice could do to ignore the painful throbbing in her wrist.

The Duchess's cool voice broke into the heated silence. "Do we know who the Queen will choose as her champion?"

"Most likely her brother, Leander." The Commander tapped his index fingers together and frowned. "He's a seasoned swordsman and would be a formidable opponent."

Zander's mouth pressed into a firm line, and he straightened away from Alice to face the Council. "Then, as my right as a challenger for the crown, I choose Chess Felinas as my champion." He didn't even look at her as he made his next pronouncement. "Alice and I will marry the day of the competition, after the challengers enter the labyrinth. Everyone should already be there, and there is no point in putting things off. The sooner this is done, the better. Shall we vote?"

Each *yes* as they went around the table was a punch in Alice's gut. It didn't make her feel any better that the Duchess and the Commander both gave her apologetic smiles before they voted to bind her to Zander forever.

As Lady Perma voiced the last affirmative vote, Alice could no longer feel the table beneath her fingers. Although she hadn't moved, the room and its occupants felt far away, as if she had left her body. Distantly, she noted that the burning in her wrist had stopped, that the murmur of conversation rose and fell. The room telescoped inward as spots danced in front of her eyes. She swayed on her feet, and Citrine materialized at her elbow. She put an arm around Alice, her face creased with concern.

Sir Lapin's voice spoke above everyone else's. "I know I am not part of this Council, and you only brought me here to consult about the aftereffects of the curse. However, I believe a final decision can't be voted upon without the rest of the Council." He looked around the table with raised eyebrows.

Alice might have crumpled to the floor in relief if Citrine hadn't been holding her up. Which was ironic, but she'd think about that later.

Zander frowned at the rabbit. "I believe my word has precedence here. I am the prince, after all. I don't need the entire Council to make a decision."

The rabbit held up a paw to halt the babble of voices. "Under normal circumstances, that would be correct, but—and I say this with the utmost respect, Sir—that is why we are here, is it not? Your crown is in question and there is no ruler at the moment. We are in a kind of limbo. Thus, if you want to force your decision on an unwilling party, you need the entire Council." He winked at Alice before he glanced around at the rest of the group.

The Commander considered Lapin's words before he shook his head. "No, you're wrong, Lapin." He glanced at the rest of the Council. "We only need a majority to cast a vote, even if there isn't a definitive ruler. And we have that."

The spark of hope the rabbit's words had lit sputtered and died in Alice's chest. Her knees gave way as she sank into her chair.

The Commander slapped a hand on the table. "We need to decide on the day of the competition, but we'll need to find the Queen first. She's still missing."

There was a beat of silence, and then a loud rapping on the window caused everyone to jump.

A large raven stood outside, a scroll clasped in its beak.

Citrine rushed over to let the bird inside. The raven dropped the scroll into her hand and tilted its head. Its beady black eyes bored into Zander.

Prince of crimson, your rival has come. Harken, for she has slithered into the maternal bosom. Death trails in her wake. Caw!

Realizing by his blank look that Zander had no idea what the raven had said, Alice distantly thought someone should tell him but a numbness had settled over her.

Citrine handed the scroll to Zander. When he unrolled it, his hand trembled. He stared at the parchment for a long time before he looked up.

"The Queen isn't missing anymore. She and her brother arrived at the palace." His gaze swung to the Commander. "We should go."

Chapter 2

THE COMMANDER STOOD AND moved to the door. The others also rose to their feet, the buzz of their voices rising and falling as they milled about slowly, gathering their things and speculating about the Queen.

Alice let her head fall into her hands, her thoughts galloping around in her mind. Was it even possible to convince the missing Councilmembers to somehow change the vote?

Hopelessness welled up in her. She'd never seen a labyrinth and had no idea how to get through it, never mind beat someone else in the process. How would she ever persuade anyone she should be the champion? A tremor ran through her at the thought of going up against a male version of the Queen.

A pair of boots appeared in her line of sight. She looked up, surprised to see Zander still there. Didn't he have to hurry to the palace?

He crouched in front of her. "Alice..."

Weariness swept over her and she held up a hand to stop him. "Please, you've said enough."

Zander's mouth turned down. "You're upset; I understand that, but will you just listen? I know you don't want to marry me, and I don't want to marry you either." Alice snorted, and his face flushed. "Sorry, that came out wrong. You know I think the world of you."

Alice folded her arms across her waist. "I understood what you meant, Zander. You don't love me any more than I love you, at least not in that way." Her shoulders hunched. "But, I can't stay here. Why don't you of all people understand that?"

His hazel eyes crinkled with concern, and she stifled a sigh. She wished she could hate him like Hadley. This would all be so much easier if she didn't care about the prince—or, at least, if she didn't care about him like a brother.

Why was the fact she needed to go home so hard for him to get through his thick head? Even now, Hadley could have ruined her father. Would he think she had run away to thwart him? Her breathing sped up. Zander's words interrupted the spiral of her thoughts.

"That's what I wanted to tell you. You don't have to. Stay here, that is. Once we marry, you can go home. Right after the ceremony, if you want." She blinked at him and her mouth dropped open.

Realizing she was gaping like a fish, she snapped her lips together. Then, she lifted her wrist and pointed to the tattoo. "But, I have to affect your life. How can I do that if I leave?"

Zander gave a half smile. "Trust me, marrying you will definitely affect my life."

"But..."

The Commander put a hand on Zander's shoulder.

"I'm sorry to interrupt, but we shouldn't delay our return to the palace any longer." The man's stern expression softened as he nodded at Alice. She thought she saw a flash of sympathy in his gaze.

Zander sighed as he pushed to his feet. He absently scratched at his wrist as he looked at her. "I'll get you back home, Alice. You can trust me."

Chapter 3

ALICE WATCHED ZANDER HURRY after the Commander. She knew the prince meant what he said; she just didn't know if he could *do* what he said. She rubbed at her wrist, which throbbed with renewed vigor. When she glanced down, she was shocked to see that the skin around the tattoo had turned a vibrant red.

Alice looked around for Citrine, but she was speaking to Bliss, trying to help him herd the Council toward the hallway.

The seat next to her creaked, and she spun to find Sir Lapin. "You know, this matter isn't completely settled," he said.

"It sure seems settled to me," Alice said, her head drooping. "The Council voted and Zander certainly isn't going to change his mind."

The rabbit crossed his leg over one knee. "Yes, but the entire Council wasn't here." He leaned toward her and tapped the side of his pink nose. "Those members might not be too happy that the rest made this decision without them." He paused. "Especially if you can prove you know how to beat the labyrinth."

Alice's head came up, and she goggled at him. "But how am I supposed to do that? I've never even been inside one."

Lapin leaned back in his chair, and his head swiveled to take in Citrine's bookshelves that covered almost every wall and stretched to the vaulted ceiling. "Well, it's a good thing that you have one of the most extensive libraries in Wonderland available to you, isn't it?" He winked at her.

Hope flickered to life in Alice's chest. Maybe she could get out this marriage yet. She turned to the rabbit. "Do you mean to say there's a book here that could do that?"

Lapin smiled. "Citrine will know. Her parents have all the Key Books, I believe."

"Key Books?" Alice's face scrunched in confusion.

"Yes, they're books that hold the knowledge of how to get through or into a place." He held up a paw and ticked off various locations. "There's the labyrinth, the entrance to the Fae Kingdoms, the Looking Glass, the Rabbit Hole." He paused when Alice clutched his arm.

"Do you truly think I can change the Council's minds about this?"

He smiled and patted her hand, but then stopped. He adjusted his spectacles and frowned. Then he gestured toward her wrist. "May I?"

Alice nodded, and he gently lifted her forearm and leaned in close. After a long moment of inspection, he sighed and let go of her. "Oh dear. That's what I was afraid of."

Alice's heart lurched in her chest, and she almost didn't want to ask, "What do you mean?"

The rabbit took off his spectacles and rubbed the space between his eyes. "Let's wait for the Pearl Queen." He waved a paw and called the other woman's name.

Hearing him, Citrine turned from the butler. When she saw the serious expression on Sir Lapin's face she broke away from what she was doing and hurried over.

"What's the problem?"

Lapin lifted Alice's wrist so the other woman could see. Citrine gasped, her eyes flying to Alice's face and then back to Lapin's.

"Is that...?"

Lapin nodded. "I'm afraid so."

Alice pulled her arm away. "Would one of you please tell me what's wrong?"

Lapin's nose twitched. "I tried to make it clear earlier. You can't fool this spell. I couldn't help but overhear what the prince said to you before he left. His intention of marrying you and then sending you home has..." He paused so long that Alice wanted to shake him. Finally, he continued. "It has triggered some sort of reaction."

Alice glanced between Lapin and Citrine. "What reaction?"

Citrine glanced away, and Alice's heart sank.

"I'm afraid, if you don't take action to affect the prince's life soon, this will spread until it reaches your heart," said Lapin.

"And then what will happen?"

The rabbit's expression turned grim. "Then, my dear, you'll die."

"Die?" Alice's voice came out in a squeak, her body going rigid. She looked around wildly as if there was some way to escape from this news.

Lapin patted her hand. "It is serious, and I won't downplay the consequences here, but you have some time. Don't panic just yet." He smiled at her kindly.

Citrine seated herself on the other side of Alice and looked at Lapin. "How long do you think?"

"I can't say with certainty, but maybe five days, perhaps as long as a week."

Alice bit back a bark of laughter. "A whole five days—you're telling me I might only have five days to live, but I shouldn't panic."

The rabbit pushed up his spectacles that had slid to the end of his nose again. "Of course it's unsettling, my dear."

"You could say that," Alice muttered under her breath.

"But," Lapin continued as if she hadn't spoken, "that is plenty of time to take action. You could marry the prince today, if you wanted to." Noticing Alice's scowl, he continued. "Or you can find the knowledge you need to change the Council's minds."

"Why must your magic always have bloody deadlines?"

Lapin chuckled. "That's the nature of magic, my dear."

"Well, you and your magic can..." She cleared her throat and her face heated. "That is, I would be happy if I never even heard the word *magic* again."

Lapin smiled and pushed to his feet, preparing to leave. Alice grabbed at his arm. "Where are you going?"

Lapin disengaged her hand. "There's nothing else I can do for you, my dear. You must decide and act. That is the way not only of magic, but life too." He nodded at Citrine and moved toward the door. "I'll see myself out.

If I'm not mistaken, the two of you have a search ahead of you."

Chapter 4

CITRINE'S BROW CRINKLED. "A search?" And then her expression cleared, and she snapped her fingers. "Of course, the Key Book to the labyrinth. I should have thought of that myself."

Alice barely heard her friend as she watched Lapin disappear into the hall. Tears prickled at her eyes, and she blinked to keep them from falling. It suddenly felt overwhelming, and doubts clawed at her determination.

"What if I can't do it?"

Citrine tilted her head. "Do what, dear?"

"Defeat the labyrinth. What if we find this Key Book or whatever it is, but it's too hard?" Alice stared down at her hands. "I... I'm not physically strong, not like the other champion will be, and I'm not clever like my sister or you are."

Citrine stood and put her hands on her hips. "Nonsense. You were the one that realized the Queen's necklace held the Jabberwock's Curse, and I don't think the woman's nose broke itself." She grabbed Alice's hands and briskly pulled her to her feet. "You heard Sir Lapin. You must decide and then act."

"But Zander said—"

Citrine rolled her eyes. "As much as I care about Zander, he can be terribly myopic."

"My... what?"

"Myopic. It means shortsighted. All he can see are his fears—losing the crown to that woman."

Alice somehow found herself arguing on the prince's behalf. "But those things *could* happen. Even if this book tells me how to beat the labyrinth, there's no guarantee I can win the competition. You heard the Commander. If this Leander is anything like the Queen, I'll be in real trouble."

Citrine lifted a slim auburn eyebrow. "So, you want to marry Zander?"

"No, of course not."

"It's all right if you do. Nobody would fault you for not wanting to go into the labyrinth." Citrine leaned down and scooped up a white cat that was twining around her ankles. "And that includes me."

Alice crossed her arms. "I would. My family needs me. And, besides, you and Zander love each other. What kind of friend would I be if I ruined that just to save my own skin?"

Citrine buried her nose in the cat's silky white fur. "I've told you before, that doesn't matter."

"How can you say that? You just said you cared about him."

Citrine gave a sad smile. "I do, but we both have our duties." She shrugged her slim shoulders. "I have to stay here and care for the creatures under my guardianship, and Zander has the Kingdom to run."

"But surely there's a way—"

"No. There's not. When my brother never returned from the Mirror World, I knew it would be difficult, but when my parents passed away, I finally accepted the way things were going to be." She gave Alice a long look. "It's not a kindness to convince me otherwise."

Alice dropped her eyes to the shabby rug under her feet. "Oh... I never meant..."

Citrine didn't let her finish. "Of course you didn't, dear." She set the cat back on the floor and turned toward the soaring rows of books all around them. "If you aren't going to marry a prince, then we need to change the Council's mind."

Alice wrinkled her nose. "Do you really think I'll be able to do that? None of them, including Zander, seemed to have much faith in my abilities, and I've never even met the Councilmembers that weren't here."

Citrine's eyes sparked with amusement. "Books always have the answers we need."

Alice looked around at the seemingly endless shelves that were crowded with volumes, some several books deep. "I hope you know where it is. I do only have five days, you know."

Citrine's expression turned apologetic. "Actually, I've never seen the book. I only ever heard Mother and Father talking about it." She paused. "Once."

"Please tell me you're joking."

When Citrine grimaced, Alice wanted to cry. How were they ever going to find that book in time? Without it, she had zero chance of changing anyone's mind.

Alice dropped her head into her hands. "I may as well tell Zander I'll marry him today."

Citrine tsked. "I thought you were more of a fighter than this."

Alice gestured toward the rows of books. "How are we supposed to find a book that you've never seen and don't know the title of? There must be thousands of books here."

"Actually, there are 6,732 volumes in this library. I'm unsure of the precise number once you add in Mother's notebooks and the ones Father kept in our archive, but that's at least several hundred more."

"Going through all of those is definitely going to take us more than five days."

Citrine laughed. "Don't be silly. We're going to have help, of course."

"Even if you get Bliss and his wife to help, I don't see how—"

Citrine held up a slender finger, and Alice stopped talking. The other woman hummed in the back of her throat. Nothing happened for a long moment, and then something brushed against Alice's ankle. She looked down and bit back a shriek.

A silvery-blue centipede as long as her arm scuttled to a stop in front of Citrine. The top half of its body rose up off the floor like a snake, and the antennae on its head waved in the air.

Alice shuddered when Citrine bent down and stroked the creature's head. "What is that thing?" she asked Citrine.

"Hmmm? Oh, this is a bookwyrm."

"It looks like a giant bug to me." Alice backed away from the creature as it turned what she assumed was its head toward her voice.

"He's not an insect. I'm not sure what you'd call it in your world, but this little fellow has a more complex brain than any of your insects. Just watch what he can do."

Citrine walked over to a shelf, the bookwyrm rippling after her, and rummaged around until she came up with a piece of parchment paper and a pen. She ripped off a scrap of the paper and began writing. Then Citrine offered the paper to the wyrm. The thing opened its mouth impossibly wide and sucked in the paper. She could hear a faint crackling as he chewed up the parchment.

"What..."

But Citrine held up a hand. "Just watch."

The crackling stopped and a moment later, a loud sound burst out of the bookwyrm. It sounded almost exactly like the hounds baying when Papa James went hunting—except it was much higher pitched. Almost immediately, a pattering sound like a million feet filled the library. Alice scrambled backward as a silvery-blue wave of the creatures scuttled out across the floor. They seemed to come from everywhere, sliding out of cracks and crevices that didn't appear big enough to accommodate their long bodies.

With horrified fascination, Alice watched the flood of creatures ripple up and over all the shelves of books.

Seeing her expression, Citrine smiled. "Bookwyrms are amazing. They can find any book. You just have to point them in the right direction."

"Is that why you fed him the paper?"

Citrine nodded. "Yes, I just wrote the word *labyrinth*, and once he digested it, that baying sound he made, that's how he shared that information with his friends." Citrine's eyes gleamed. "Now, they will find every book on that topic in this library. Fortunately for us, there shouldn't be many."

Alice hoped her friend was right because she didn't want to think about what would happen if she couldn't change the Council's decision.

Chapter 5

IT WAS LATE, AND the moon was high when Zander and the Commander came within sight of the Red Palace. Even with the griffons' superior speed, it had taken almost eight hours. It would have taken twice as long on horseback.

The two griffons landed almost simultaneously near the front steps. Zander's mount, Verros, tossed his head and screeched when a groom rushed over to them. Zander slid from the griffon's back and patted his feathered neck to calm him. The griffon ruffled his wings, his tail lashing back and forth. The groom was unfazed by the animal's fractious behavior, but Zander felt a familiar rush of frustration. Couldn't one thing be simple?

"He's not used to you yet," the Commander said, his voice quiet. "And he's still young. Your father hadn't completely broken him before... he passed."

Before Zander had time to respond, Chess rushed out to meet them. "I'm glad you're back. How did the Council meeting go? How is Alice taking all of this?" There was an unusual tightness in his friend's expression.

"We've gotten things settled, but what I want to know about is the Queen." Zander gestured toward the Dower House.

Chess glanced at the Commander and then back at Zander. "She had the gall to suggest she and her idiot brother take up residence in her old rooms in the palace."

The Commander nodded. "That's not surprising."

Chess rolled his eyes. "Maybe not to you, but it sure surprised me. The woman tried to kill Zander only a few days ago. That's a lot of nerve for anyone, even her."

"I believe she's proven that weak nerves are not an issue she struggles with." The Commander's tone was dry. "What I want to know is, who did they bring with them?"

"They had half a dozen armed guards," Chess answered.

The three men turned, and Chess fell into step with his father as they approached the front entrance of the palace.

The Commander stroked his chin. "Hmmm. It's more than I would expect her father to send, but Renard's cautious by nature and it is a long journey."

"Should I be worried about this?" Zander asked, returning the salute of the soldiers who stood on either side of the entry. One man pulled the door open, and Zander let Chess and the Commander go through first.

Their boots rang out on the marble floor. The palace was quiet; the lights dimmed at this time of night.

The Commander gave a sharp shake of his head. "You don't need to worry too much. Six men are hardly a battalion. It's a show of strength, but it isn't a warning shot." He turned to Chess. "Did you have to force them to the Dower House?"

Chess shook his head as the three men paused next to a tall golden urn. "When I saw those men, I thought we might have trouble, but Leander was quite reasonable." Chess smirked. "At least, after he gave me an extremely long lecture about all the Queen's rights that we were trampling upon." He frowned. "To be honest, I expected more of a fight."

"Hmmm," was all the Commander said.

Chess turned to Zander. "You never told me how things went with the Council... or Alice."

Zander weighed his exhaustion against going over all of that mess again tonight. With a sigh, he directed his feet toward the hallway rather than the stairs that led to his chambers. "Let's go to my study."

Chess's smile wavered. "Shall I have Anders send you some dinner now?"

A wash of warmth for his friend settled in his chest. "Thanks, but no. I'll have something later."

Chapter 6

CHESS PERCHED ON THE desk as Zander lowered himself into his chair. The Commander sat opposite of him. Something in Zander's manner made Chess uneasy.

"So what did the Council have to say? Where is the competition, anyway?"

Zander sighed. "It's the labyrinth."

Chess's eyebrows winged upward, and he whistled. "I'm not sure what I was expecting, but it wasn't that. How did Alice take the news?"

Zander's head fell back against his chair and he stared up at the ceiling. "Not well."

Chess could imagine. Had she even been in a labyrinth before? Certainly not one like Wonderland's, but Alice was resilient. "I wouldn't worry too much. When it counts, she'll come through." He grinned. "That girl is a real brick."

Zander didn't answer right away. Instead he shifted and then rubbed his palms along his trouser legs. When he finally spoke, his voice was hesitant. "Actually, she won't be going into the labyrinth."

Chess's scalp prickled. After another pause, Zander continued. "That's what I wanted to talk to you about. I was hoping you'd be my champion."

"Me? But what about Alice?" Chess knew his confusion must be clear on his face.

Zander leaned forward and put his hands on the desktop. "The Council consulted with Sir Lapin. He said this"—he held up his arm so the tattoo was visible—"means Alice has to affect my future."

"But if she isn't going to be your champion, then how...." Chess's voice trailed off, and then he stiffened as the pieces came together for him. If Alice wasn't going to be the champion, there were only a few options left. His chest tightened. "You're... marrying Alice? She agreed to that?"

Zander swallowed. "There isn't a choice."

Irritation straightened Chess's spine. "What does that mean?"

The Commander leaned toward him, his expression neutral—as usual. Did the man ever express any emotions? "It means this is a difficult situation for everyone."

Chess looked between the Commander and Zander and narrowed his eyes. He refused to examine why he cared so much about the answer to his next question. "Obviously, but what was Alice's response to all of this? You know she wants to get home as quickly as possible. She's made that clear from the beginning."

Zander said nothing for a long moment. When he did speak, he had to clear his throat. "Look, the Council voted and everyone was in favor of doing things this way." Chess scowled and Zander rushed on. "Alice is a great girl, but we both know she doesn't stand a chance in that labyrinth."

Chess told himself to stay seated, to keep his voice level. "You still didn't answer my question. Did she agree to this marriage?"

His feelings must have come through in his tone, though, because Zander shifted uncomfortably in his chair. A part of Chess's mind registered how his friend dug his nails into his wrist, but he was too absorbed in Zander's answer to think about it. As the seconds ticked by, he wanted to shake the answer out of Zander despite his friend's tightened expression.

When Zander finally spoke, it was through gritted teeth. "It's not like I want this either."

Chess crossed his arms, his muscles rigid. "So, you're going to make it worse by pushing Alice into something she doesn't want?"

"Son, this isn't your—"

His father tried to interrupt, but Chess cut him off. "Yes, it is my business. She saved my hide just as much as his." He jabbed a finger in Zander's direction.

Zander pinched the bridge of his nose, and his deep breaths were audible in the still room. "What would you like me to do, Chess? She can't win—and if she doesn't, *all* of our lives are over."

Chess could understand the logic in that statement, but the idea of Alice marrying his best friend made him recoil. That she didn't want that for herself only made it worse. "You're underestimating her. Alice is a lot more capable than you realize."

Zander pierced him with a sharp gaze. "Are you willing to gamble the Kingdom on that? Because I'm not."

"He's correct." The Commander crossed his arms, and Chess wanted to do something desperate to shock that blank expression off his father's face. "It's not ideal for many reasons, but—"

"I already know you put responsibility before all else," Chess snapped and then turned his scowling gaze toward Zander. "But Alice doesn't have a duty to this Kingdom."

Zander pressed his lips together and the muscle in his cheek twitched. His body vibrated with suppressed tension.

But Chess didn't care. He leaned close to Zander, a question burning inside him. He had always thought Citrine... But maybe he was wrong about that too. "Do you truly want to marry her so much? "

Zander stared at his desk. Emotions warred across his features, and his fingers dug into the wood. Chess's patience wore thin. It wasn't a difficult question, after all.

He snapped his fingers in front of his friend's face. "Wonderland to Zander."

Zander slapped his hand away so hard it left a lingering sting, and his voice dropped into a growl. "Will you just stop? Of course, I don't want to marry her, but what alternative do I have?"

Chess pushed to his feet to put more distance between himself and his friend. He didn't want to do something stupid, like punch the prince. "There's always a choice."

Zander exploded up out of his chair and leaned over the desk. "No, there's not! I'm not sure how to get it into that thick half-flit skull of yours. She. Can't. Win."

Chess ignored the insult as he stared at Zander, unable to comprehend how his friend could be so dense. "How can you say that? She's already proven she's resourceful. And strong."

Zander pressed his hands together, his pupils constricting to vertical slits. A wisp of smoke escaped from one nostril.

The Commander interjected, "She has done remarkably well, coming from the Mirror World, but this is the labyrinth. And the Queen is sure to have Leander as her champion."

Chess looked from one man to the other. "I can't believe neither of you will give her the chance."

Zander held up his hand and ticked off the reasons on his fingers. "Let's see, Chess. She's a young girl, has no fighting experience, and is from the Mirror World. That's only three points off the top of my head. Surely even *you* can recognize she can't win."

Chess resisted the urge to smack that look off Zander's face as if he were explaining something to a dimwit. "What I recognize is that you're going to force her to marry you, and she'll never get home. I hardly see how that's a better solution." His voice sounded sharp in his own ears.

Zander drew in a deep breath and ran a hand through his hair. When he spoke, his words had lost their earlier fire. "I am not the one forcing anything. Putting a trap in that curse wasn't my idea, and if you think I'm happy with this outcome, you're daft." He pointed a finger at his friend. "Besides, you're the one who brought her here! If you remember, I said it was a bad idea. You have nobody to blame for Alice's situation but yourself."

Chess flinched at the accusation, and his defenses came up. "I didn't hear you complaining when she broke the curse."

Zander collapsed back into his chair, his whole body telegraphing weariness. "This arguing is pointless. The decision is made." He rolled his head in Chess's direction. "Will you be my champion or not?"

Chess clamped his lips together. The crown was important, but to trap Alice here... He shook his head. "Alice deserves better than this, and you know it. She stuck her neck out to help us. How can you repay her by forcing her into a marriage she doesn't want and keeping her from her family?"

Zander dragged a hand down his face. "She won't have to stay here. Once the ceremony is over, I'll take her home."

That still didn't make him feel any better. "But, that's—"

A sharp knock startled both of them. Chess spun toward the sound as Zander stood and moved to the door. When he opened it, Anders was revealed.

The man paused as he tried to catch his breath.

"What is it, Anders?"

"It's the Queen and her brother. They wish an audience with you, Your Highness."

That was just perfect. Chess walked over and leaned on the doorframe next to Zander. "Well, they didn't dally, did they?"

Zander hesitated.

Chess pursed his lips. He may want to strangle Zander right now, but that didn't mean he wanted his friend to walk into a trap when he was this tired. "You shouldn't allow her to dictate your first meeting like this."

Anders swallowed but straightened his shoulders. "Shall I tell them you are unavailable, Your Highness?"

Zander hesitated and then shook his head. "No, I'll see them tonight."

"But, Zander..." Chess started to argue, but Zander cut him off.

"The competition should take place as soon as possible. The sooner all this is over with, the sooner Alice can get on with her life. That is what you wanted, isn't it?" Ignoring Chess, Zander turned toward the steward. "Please fetch them."

Anders nodded once, before he sprinted away.

Glancing away from Chess, Zander said, "There's no need to stay if you don't wish to."

Chess swallowed back the hurt and straightened. "Don't imagine you're doing this without me."

Zander's smile was stiff. "Thanks."

Chess hoped this wasn't a mistake.

Chapter 7

ZANDER WISHED THERE WAS time to discuss the situation with the Commander, but Anders appeared a few minutes later at the study door with the Queen and a tall, whip-thin man just behind her.

"Her Majesty, the Queen, and Sir Leander Renard." The steward stepped aside and the pair swept into the room, the Queen clinging to her brother's arm.

Zander pushed to his feet, and dragged his gaze to meet the Queen's. A malicious delight lurked in their black depths. His body flamed, and then every nerve iced over. He was back in the meadow, her cloying perfume fogging his senses, her lips moving on his, pushing him into darkness.

"Good of you to drop by, Lyssandra." Chess's sarcastic voice broke the spell, and Zander pressed his hands into the surface of his desk to still their tremors. He drew in a deep breath and took a firm hold of his emotions. He could not let her detect any weakness. This wasn't like the last time.

"You will speak to my sister with respect, Felinas," Leander snapped.

The Queen tapped her brother's arm, a smile tugging at her cupid-bow mouth. "Oh, don't mind him. He's only being his charming, half-flit self. He can't help himself, isn't that right?"

Zander cringed to hear the unflattering term he'd used only moments ago drip from the Queen's lips like poisoned honey.

She slanted a coy glance at Chess before she stepped away from her brother and toward Zander. He fought the urge to step back. She couldn't hurt him. Not now. He wasn't fooled by her anymore.

She studied him. "You don't seem happy to see us. I would have thought you'd be more eager to settle the details of the competition so you could reclaim your crown." She smiled sweetly. "Or at least try."

Heat burned away the icy chill that had settled over him. His gaze swept over the Queen from her artfully arranged white-blonde hair to the dainty pale-pink slippers that peeked out from the frothy skirts of her matching dress.

His nostrils flared, and he fought the urge to wrap his fingers around her delicate neck and squeeze until the spark in those mocking eyes snuffed out. For a moment, her death was a dangerous temptation. He jerked his gaze down to his hands. Talons tipped his fingers and were gouging grooves in the desktop. A glint of scales peeked out from one of his shirt cuffs. Horror and shame washed over him. He whisked his hands behind his back to hide his slipping control.

Her brother shot Zander a worried look and stepped forward to put a hand on his sister's arm. "I realize it's late, and you must be tired from your trip, but I... *we* deemed it prudent to meet with you as soon as possible." Whatever his true thoughts were, he hid them behind a polite mask.

"You've saved me the trouble of meeting tomorrow." Zander gestured toward the two chairs in front of his desk. When they were both seated, he continued. "I was rather surprised that you both came here so quickly... without an invitation."

Leander's eyes, the same chocolate shade as his sister's, sharpened. "As the competition must take place as soon as possible, you can't expect us to dally about waiting for a summons. It's a long journey from our home." He raised a golden eyebrow. "But perhaps you hoped we wouldn't show up at all?"

Chess snorted. "The prince's integrity is not what you should be questioning. Your sister is the power hungry witch that tried to kill us both. "

Leander's mouth tightened. "My sister is still the Queen, and I will not tell you again to speak to and of her with respect."

Chess smirked. "Or you'll what?"

Leander's icy gaze moved over Chess and then dismissed him, shifting his attention to Zander. "With the crown in question, she has as much right to be here, in the palace, as you do. I hope you will consider our lack of insistence on that matter as a gesture of our goodwill."

Chess barked out a laugh, and the Commander frowned at him. It didn't stop Chess from speaking. "Do you think Zander's stupid enough to invite the person who tried to kill him into his home?"

"That will do." The Commander's tone was stony. He nodded to Zander who picked up the conversation.

"As the Queen did not tell us where she was going when she left"—he ignored Chess's snort—"it would have been difficult to invite you anywhere." He paused and then continued when Leander remained silent. "At any rate, you're settled in at the Dower House now, and I trust you are comfortable. As for—"

"I have a request," the Queen interrupted.

Zander tapped down his impatience and waited for her to continue.

"I miss my flower maidens." She dipped her chin and looked up at him through her lashes. "Once the competition starts, I'll be all alone, as I'm sure you won't be visiting me."

Zander straightened the papers on his desk. "I'll arrange for any of the maidens that are willing to attend you." He turned his attention back to what he'd been about to say before she'd interrupted him. "Now, as for the competition, the Council has decided it should be in three days' time. We had thought to allow the Queen time to get here with her champion. I'm assuming that will be you?" Zander's gaze flicked to Leander.

The man gave a sharp nod of his head. "Where will the competition be held?"

"In the labyrinth, mid-morning." Zander's words made the other man frown.

The Queen leaned forward. "And who is to be your champion, Zander?"

Zander's eyes darted to Chess and then back to the Queen. "I..."

"Don't tell me you're going to let that girl compete for you." Her laughter chimed out, and then she touched her nose. "I'm not saying she doesn't pack a punch, but my brother is a seasoned warrior. She has no chance, especially in the labyrinth."

"She's not my champion." Zander pushed the words past stiff lips.

The Queen brushed at her immaculate skirts. "Will you be sending the girl home, then?"

The flames of anger flickered back to life, and Zander whipped up his arm so his wrist showed. "I think you know that's not a possibility now."

The Queen opened her eyes wide and placed a hand on her chest. "I have no idea what you mean."

Zander's nostrils flared. "Alice will marry me the day of the competition."

The Queen tapped her bottom lip. "That's very interesting. And what does Alice have to say about that?"

Zander's words stuck in his throat. She waved at Chess. "Certainly, it was difficult to tell. I had to leave in such a hurry, but she seemed very concerned about your friend here at the ball."

Zander straightened, his voice stilted. "Of course she was concerned. You nearly killed him."

The Queen examined her fingernails. "That was purely accidental, I assure you." Then she glanced at Chess and wagged a finger at him. "You don't seem to like the idea very much."

Chess crossed his arms. "You mistake me, Your Majesty. What I don't like is you."

Leander started to rise, but his sister gripped his arm. He settled back in his seat but there was a scowl on his face.

Chess smirked. "What an obedient puppy."

Two spots of color appeared on Leander's high cheekbones, but to his credit, he ignored the jibe.

The Queen watched the exchange with bright eyes. "This is all very diverting, but what I want to know is, did you have to coerce the girl into it, or did the notion of marrying a prince persuade her? She does realize if your champion loses, you'll lose all of this too, right?"

"Lyssandra." Leander's voice held a warning.

She gestured toward Zander and Chess. "Don't you see? The prince here is going to marry Alice, but I don't believe his dearest friend likes that idea." She giggled. "What I'm longing to find out is where Alice stands in all of this."

Alice's forlorn expression the last time he saw her flashed into his mind. The Queen's manner turned knowing. "Poor Zander. She's not happy about this, is she? What a shame—for all of you."

Heat swamped Zander's senses and a red haze dropped over his vision. His breath rasped, and the skin underneath his tattoo crawled like a thousand insects were buzzing across it. He was close to losing control, and the glinting amusement on the Queen's face said she knew it too. He latched on to the first thing he could think of to wipe that smile off of her face.

"You're wrong, Lyssandra. Alice and I are quite happy about our coming marriage. We're having a ball to celebrate the engagement." He felt Chess stiffen next to him, and surprise flickered over the Commander's face, but he didn't care. He refused to be the loser in this encounter.

Leander, seeming to sense the danger in the room, stood abruptly, his hand on his sister's elbow. "We've taken enough of your time. Please keep us informed of any updates." He tried to steer his sister toward the door, but she pulled her arm away and moved until her skirts brushed the desk.

Her small, pink tongue touched the front of her teeth and it was only then that Zander realized that her canines had extended and her pupils were slitted. "Are you sure you want to go through with this?"

"How could you even ask that? I would rather die than witness you on the throne." He spit out the words, all pretense of politeness gone.

"Oh, once we win that can definitely be arranged." She leaned forward and covered his hand with hers, looking up at him from under her lashes. "But wouldn't you rather work together? We're so well matched, you and I. We could rule Wonderland and no one would be able to contradict us."

He shook off her touch and wiped his palm on his trouser leg. "And what about Alice?"

"She's a lovely girl and I quite like her." She gave a dainty shrug. "I told her she'd be sorry, but she didn't listen. If she dies, she has only herself to blame."

Zander's lip curled, a shiver of revulsion twitching over his skin. "Get out. I don't want to see you again until I have to."

The Queen's face twisted, her amusement gone. "Just remember, I gave you the opportunity, and you refused it." She whirled in a flurry of pink skirts and swept from the room.

Leander swiveled to follow her, but stopped when the Commander spoke. "I'm surprised your father didn't accompany you both."

Leander's eyes darted toward the door his sister had walked through and then back to the men. "He's dead." His face was a blank mask. "He died in an unfortunate hunting accident right before we set off. Now, if you'll excuse me, I need to attend my sister."

After he exited, the three men stood in silence. The clock ticked off several seconds before Chess spoke up. "Well, it's clear she killed him."

Chapter 8

ALICE STARED AT THE jumble of books scattered across Citrine's large, scuffed desk. "That one isn't it either?"

Citrine, her red hair shoved up in a bun, leaned over the biggest and oldest book. She shook her head and another strand of hair escaped. She blew it away impatiently. "I mean, it mentions Wonderland's labyrinth, but it doesn't say anything about how to get through it."

Alice's shoulders slumped. The bookwyrms had been very thorough in their job, finding dozens of books that mentioned the labyrinth. Unfortunately, none of them were the one Citrine said they needed.

The clock on the mantle chimed, and Alice rubbed a hand over her face. They had been at this for over a day. Her stomach rumbled, and she hoped they would take a break to eat soon, but Citrine's focus hadn't wavered all morning. Alice looked at the soaring shelves that stretched to the high, rounded ceiling. The only wall spaces that weren't covered with books were the fireplace and the large picture window.

"If the bookwyrms don't come up with something by luncheon, I'll set them to Mother's boxes of journals. It's possible it might have gotten in there." Citrine absently ran a hand over a calico cat that had plopped itself next to the volume she was flipping through.

The idea of more books somewhere boggled Alice's mind. "Are you sure there even IS one to find?"

Citrine pushed a stray curl behind her ear. "I'm positive it's around here. Don't look so glum, darling. We'll find it. You won't have to marry Zander." She waved a hand, taking in the library. "Mother said we had all the Key Books, so it has to be here. Somewhere." She wrinkled her nose. "I wish she had written out her organization system, though." Her expression turned wistful. "Of course, she and Father didn't realize how little time they had."

Curiosity piqued, Alice considered how she could ask what had happened without appearing too nosey. She rubbed at her wrist. The throbbing had become a steady drumbeat in their search. She avoided looking at it. She refused to see how far the tiny red lines had progressed up her arm.

"You really should inform Zander about that."

Alice tucked the arm against her chest as if she could somehow protect it. "All it would do is make him doubly determined to get married. He might even move up the date."

Citrine tilted her head. "Perhaps if he sees the risk you're taking not to marry him, he'll change his mind."

Alice's mouth twisted. "You know him better than I do. How likely is he to do that?"

"Hmmm, you're right, I suppose." Citrine sighed and pushed up her spectacles. She tapped a finger on her lip and stared into space. "What I wonder is how is this affecting him. Did you notice anything yesterday?"

Alice shook her head. "No. He never even glanced at his wrist when he talked to me, and by that time, mine was throbbing."

"That's strange. It should affect his tattoo also." Her brow crinkled into a deep *v*. "I don't understand it. When we're done here, I think I'll look into it more closely. We have enough problems without some dreadful effect—"

A large orange tabby made a running leap onto the table and interrupted her, scattering papers and books. One of the enormous silvery centipedes dangled from his mouth. The creature was frantically chewing something. Citrine looked up from her book. "Marmalade, what are you doing?"

The cat dropped the bookwyrm and rumbled an answer that only Citrine understood. Despite her Creature Gift, Alice couldn't always hear the animals on Citrine's estate. She wasn't sure if they could shield their thoughts or if it was their close bond with the Pearl Queen. As Citrine was fond of saying, they weren't pets. They were friends. Alice supposed she could probe into their conversation if she really wanted to, but that would be rude.

Her meandering thoughts cut off when Citrine gave a whoop and scooped up the cat, smothering its face in kisses. Alice stifled a giggle. This time Marmalade's thoughts came through loud and clear.

Piffle and puffs. Put me down, woman!

Citrine set the cat down and turned to the centipede. It rose off the table and waved its antennae wildly, its tiny jaws working at triple speed as the top half of its body bobbed up and down.

Citrine held out her hand, and the bookwyrm shook its head. Citrine raised her eyebrows and pointed at her palm. Reluctantly the silvery creature opened its mouth and released a surprisingly large ball of half-chewed paper. Citrine frowned at the wyrm, and its head drooped before it dropped flat and slithered away.

Citrine unwadded the ball of parchment. Alice wrinkled her nose, glad she didn't have to figure out what was on a piece of paper laden with bug spit. The frown on Citrine's face transformed into a huge grin. When she looked at Alice, her grey eyes were alight.

"I think we may have found it this time." Citrine raced across the room. How she still had so much energy, Alice had no idea. Citrine pushed the ladder on its tracks toward a distant corner and then scrambled up to the very top. Alice squeezed her eyes almost shut as her friend stood on one of the top rungs and leaned over to a far nook of shelves. Citrine was tall, and she used her height to her advantage as she stretched an arm, barely hooking a finger on a book's spine. Alice held her breath as the book teetered on the edge of the shelf before Citrine hauled it into her arms. Unfortunately, the weight of the book unbalanced her, and Citrine swayed on the ladder step for a heart-stopping moment. Then a nearby cat hooked its claws into her skirt and dragged her back. Citrine dropped a kiss on the cat's head before she scurried back down.

The book was enormous, and she was out of breath by the time she reached Alice. She hefted it onto the desk, and a puff of dust rose from its shabby pages.

Citrine ran a finger over the cover, murmuring to herself. As she did, letters slowly appeared. First an *L*, then an *A*, and then a *B*, until the entire word *labyrinth* had unscrolled across the leather surface. Once the last letter appeared, the book flopped open and the leaves started flipping erratically until they finally settled not quite in the middle.

The inside was blank.

"What in the world?" Alice's stomach plummeted.

Citrine squeezed her arm. "Just wait."

A flicker of irritation flared in Alice's chest, but even as she watched, a picture slowly inked itself onto the pages. When it was finished, a surprisingly detailed map of an intricate labyrinth shimmered on the page. Citrine clapped her hands and reached for the orange cat again, who watched the proceedings with a bored air.

He leapt away with a hiss, arching his back, before jumping down from the table. Citrine chuckled. "Such a spoilsport."

Alice thought she heard a distinct *humph!* before the animal sauntered away. Citrine rolled her eyes. "Silly cat. He's just embarrassed because you're here." She turned to the map. "Now, let's see what we have..."

A loud tapping interrupted her. Both Alice and Citrine whirled to stare at the window. On the outside ledge sat an enormous raven. His feathers ruffled, he looked incredibly put out as it had started to drizzle. He held a large scroll in his mouth.

Citrine hurried over and yanked open the window. The raven ducked into the room and fluffed his feathers, sprinkling water droplets onto them and everything around him. He dropped the paper onto the wide windowsill and let out a loud caw. His beady, black eyes zeroed in on Alice.

Eyes like violets, curls like dusk, swing and sway, swirl and twirl. The prince in red awaits your presence.

Alice wondered if the ravens ever relayed a message in a normal fashion instead of making it sound like some dire prophecy. Citrine picked up the scroll and read it as she absently offered a piece of dried fruit to the bird. He plucked it from her fingers, and with a last caw, disappeared out the window.

She turned to Alice, frowning.

"What does it say?" Alice was almost afraid to ask.

Citrine's face scrunched. "It's an invitation—to your engagement ball."

Alice was baffled. "Engagement ball? Why in the world would Zander want to throw a ball, especially if his plan is to take me home right after the wedding ceremony? That makes no sense."

Citrine's lips pursed. "There has to be a reason." She looked back down at the parchment before she handed it to Alice. Then her eyes widened. "Maybe Zander is starting to be affected by the curse too."

"Yes, but why would that make him want to throw a ball with everything else going on?" Alice's eyes ran over the words. "This says the ball is in a couple of days and the competition is the day after that. When will we need to leave?"

"Tomorrow morning, I'm afraid, or we'll never make it. My flying friends are fast, but since we're taking the carriage, they need proper rests."

Alice's shoulders slumped. "That's not nearly enough time to go through this book." She looked at its dusty bulk. It would take a week just to read the thing, and that was if she skimmed.

She rolled the invitation back up and laid it on the table. "How am I ever going to learn enough to convince the Councilmembers in half a day?"

Citrine pulled up two chairs and sat down. Then she patted the seat next to her. "You won't get anywhere wasting the little time you do have worrying about it."

Alice gave a reluctant smile and dropped onto the seat. Rommy and Papa James' faces flashed into her mind. She lifted her chin. She was going into that labyrinth, and she was going to win. Grasping the edges of the book, she pulled it toward her.

Citrine smiled and reached for a notebook and pen. "Shall I take notes?"

Chapter 9

EARLY THE NEXT MORNING, Alice waited in the courtyard of the Pearl Palace and eyed the ancient carriage with trepidation. It sat at a lopsided angle, its traces still empty. The thing didn't look sturdy enough to go anywhere, never mind down a mountain.

Citrine laughed. "Don't worry, dear, it's in better shape than it looks. I promise." She whirled away and ran up the steps until she reached the ugly stone gargoyles that stood at either side of the front doors. She laid a hand on one and hummed softly. Much to Alice's astonishment, it ground to a standing position. Then it shook itself and granite went flying. Alice ducked as a piece narrowly missed her head.

"Sorry about that!" Citrine called. "You might want to move behind the carriage while I wake Ogox." Without waiting to see if Alice complied, she walked to the other gargoyle and repeated the process. Once both gargoyles stood in front of her, Citrine invited Alice to join her. Alice wasn't too sure that was a good idea, but she did it anyway.

Citrine gestured to the gargoyle on the left who was taller and leaner than his (or her? Alice wasn't sure) companion. "This is Stongorr." She turned to the other creature. "And this is Ogox."

"Erm, hello?"

Both creatures bowed their heads, the motion smooth considering they still looked like giant hunks of moving rock. Then, they sprang forward, making Alice flinch. The taller one snickered. Deciding to ignore it, she faced Citrine.

"I'm afraid to ask why we need gargoyles."

Citrine's eyes danced. "Well, how did you think we'd get down the mountain?"

Alice turned back to the carriage and blinked several times. The gargoyles had put themselves into the traces and were waiting patiently. Alice shook her head in disbelief and then snorted. She was getting ready to go into a living labyrinth and face more fantastical creatures than two gargoyles.

Without another word, the two women climbed into the carriage. Alice settled herself on the seat across from Citrine, trying to ignore the ominous creaking.

"Who's going to driving the carriage?" Alice had seen no one else come out, but she still tried to peer out the window to get a glimpse of the driver's seat.

"The gargoyles know where they are headed."

Citrine's answer did nothing to ease Alice's nerves. "But..." Her head snapped back as the vehicle lurched forward. The seat bounced, jarring her teeth together, preventing either of them from talking. Before she could adjust to the situation, the coach gave another sickening lurch before smoothing out. Alice breathed a sigh of relief until she looked out the window.

They were no longer on the ground and the trees were rapidly becoming smaller and smaller.

Alice swallowed hard, her stomach clenching into a queasy knot. Never mind that she'd ridden on a dragon. It was ten times worse to be in a carriage in the sky.

"You look quite green, my dear." Citrine reached across and squeezed her hand. "The air carriage is very safe, I promise you. In all the years using it, Mother and Father only lost one person. And honestly, it was his own fault." She seemed to think this was reassuring.

Alice smiled weakly. She wasn't looking forward to spending over a day in the sky.

They hadn't been traveling long when Citrine started rummaging around in one of the bags she brought. She emerged with a pad of paper and a pen. "We should do some planning while we have the chance."

"I thought we had a plan—to convince the Councilmembers who didn't get to vote."

"Well, yes, that's definitely the preferable idea, but since you don't know them at all, I thought I'd tell you a bit about them and how best to approach each one."

Alice raised an eyebrow. "Maybe I'm the one who should take notes."

Citrine's face brightened. "Oh, good idea!" She dived back into her bag and emerged with another notebook—this one smaller—and a pencil. "I'm sorry. I only brought one pen."

Alice took the items. "You're more prepared than I am."

The whole thing situation still seemed like a bad dream. After spending weeks with Zander, hiding out and trying to break the Jabberwock's Curse, it was unreal that now she was plotting against him. A lump formed in her throat when she realized she might not just be working against Zander, but Chess too. After all, he was Zander's best friend and he'd only known her for a few weeks.

A tap on her knee startled her out of her thoughts. "I said that Lord Dordo is probably your best option. He's most likely to be sympathetic to your plight and also to be unhappy they took the vote without him. You'll have to overlook his unfortunate affliction, though."

"Affliction?"

"Yes." Citrine held up a finger. "And whatever you do, don't laugh at him."

"Erm, all right." Alice couldn't imagine laughing at someone with an affliction. That seemed unkind. "Who else was missing from the meeting?"

"Lord Whistlewaith." Citrine tapped the end of the pen against her lip. "I doubt he'll come over to your side. He's always looking for an advantage and there's really none for him going against the prince."

"Well, how am I supposed to sway the Council if I only talk to one member? Will Lord Dordo have that kind of influence over the rest of them?"

Citrine sighed. "Unfortunately, no." She furrowed her brow, deep in thought. They glided along for several minutes before her face cleared. "You should approach the Duchess again."

"But she was one of the first ones to argue in favor of the marriage."

"I know, but Leticia is the most progressive member and most likely to believe a woman is capable of defeating the labyrinth—*if* you give her enough evidence. We've learned quite a bit from the book already, and"—she patted her bag—"you'll have time to learn more on this trip since I brought it with us."

Alice goggled at her. "You brought a Key Book? Isn't it super important and magical?"

Citrine smiled. "You are more valuable to me than any book I own."

Warmth spread through Alice and tears welled up. She was touched because she knew how much her friend loved her books. "Thank you, Citrine. I... I don't deserve your kindness."

Citrine waved a hand. "Nonsense. We're friends and this is what friends do for each other." She tapped her pen on the notebook page. "Now, the thing we have to consider is the real possibility that you won't be able to bring the Council over to your side."

Alice's shoulders slumped. "But if the Council doesn't change their minds, there isn't anything else I can do—is there?"

"For a former street urchin, you are disappointingly guileless." Citrine bent over her notebook and sketched something. When she finished she turned it so Alice could see it.

Just as Alice leaned forward, the carriage lurched to the side and then dropped. Alice swallowed her shriek.

Citrine frowned. "What in the world? We haven't gone far enough to run into other conveyances." She got on her knees and wrenched open the window. Wind whistled through the opening, whipping Alice's hair across her face and making her teeth chatter. Unperturbed, Citrine stuck her head out and muttered, "Oh, bother!" Then she ducked back inside, opened the door, and before Alice could stop her, stepped onto the running board.

"Citrine! What are you doing?" Panic clawed at Alice's chest and her limbs felt paralyzed.

Citrine peered in at her. "Oh, tosh—I'm fine, darling. I'll be back in a jiffy." With that, she nimbly put her foot on the wheel rim and boosted herself up, disappearing from view.

Alice desperately wanted to see what was going on, but her body stayed glued to the seat as the carriage lurched first one way and then another. It seemed that if she moved at all, it would tip them right out of the sky. She tried to rid herself of the vivid image of plunging into the trees below.

She heard Citrine's say something, her tone sharp, but she couldn't make out the words. The carriage evened out again, but before she could peel her paralyzed limbs from the seat, Citrine reappeared. She wore an annoyed expression.

The other woman flung herself back inside. The carriage bobbed in response, and Alice gripped the seat with both hands.

"Those silly gargoyles decided to chase after some jeuny birds." Citrine rolled her eyes so hard Alice feared she was going to sprain them. "You'd think they were still juveniles." She shook her head. "To be fair, it has been a long time since they've been unpetrified, but still. They should know better."

Alice pried her fingers from the upholstery and risked a look out the window. Only blue sky and a few wispy clouds were visible. If she didn't remember how high they were, it was almost peaceful.

"Now then," said Citrine, breaking into her thoughts, "if we can't convince the Council, you'll have to sneak into the labyrinth."

"We hardly had time to learn much before we left." Doubts clawed at Alice again. Maybe trying to be the champion was a mistake. What if she lost?

Citrine thumped something heavy into Alice's lap. It was the labyrinth's Key Book. Citrine tapped it. "I've been able to skim most of it, and the two things that I found to be the most important were, don't take anything from the labyrinth, and keep turning right."

Alice smoothed a hand over the cover of the old book. Its leather warmed under her touch. "When you say don't take anything..."

Citrine leaned forward, her eyes alight with excitement. "The labyrinth itself has a consciousness and a will. You must only take what it gives you."

Alice rubbed at her forehead. "Maybe I'm tired, but I'm not sure what you mean exactly."

Citrine pursed her lips. "Well, for instance, you wouldn't want to harm or kill any of the creatures in there, or hurt the labyrinth itself by, say, cutting branches down or something along those lines."

"But what if I'm threatened? If there are creatures in there, I doubt they're all sweet and cuddly."

Citrine smiled. "Well, we have a whole day and then some to travel. I suggest you use the time wisely."

Alice bit back a sigh and stared at the thick volume. She hoped it was more interesting reading than her school textbooks had been. Turning to the first page, she started to read.

Chapter 10

ALICE SAT AT THE dressing table in a bedroom at the Red Palace and tried to ignore the knot in her stomach. She'd yet to see Zander. She and Citrine had arrived in the middle of the night, so the fact that his steward was the one who greeted them and got them settled in their rooms was understandable—if a bit odd under the circumstances.

Still, she had expected to see him sometime during the day, but despite going down for breakfast and lunch, and taking a turn around the grounds with Citrine, Zander had been conspicuously absent. The only indication he knew they were there was the ball gown that had appeared in her room a few hours ago.

A part of her was grateful to put off talking to him, but a bigger part felt it only made the anticipation of tonight worse.

Behind her, Citrine fussed with Alice's hair.

"I'm afraid I'm not very good at this sort of thing," Citrine said, as she tried to gather Alice's curls into some semblance of a hairstyle.

"I don't suppose it matters all that much." Alice reached out and ran a finger over the shaggy leaf of the bright yellow-orange flower that sat next to the mirror. It was in one of several pots scattered around the room, adding a splash of cheerful color to the all-white furnishings and draperies. It curled in response, but she when tried to do it again, Citrine stopped her.

"Oh, no, don't touch that."

Alice paused. "Why not?"

"It's a bumblebee flower. They sting."

"Of course they do," Alice muttered under her breath. She put her chin in her hands and closed her eyes as Citrine continued to tug and pull at her hair.

She wasn't looking forward to tonight, and not just because the idea of announcing her engagement to the prince felt like admitting defeat. She hated being the center of attention, and as the prince's fiancée she'd be the focus of everyone's scrutiny. Besides, her arm throbbed and a dull headache had taken up residence behind her eyes. She massaged her forehead with her thumbs.

A knock startled them both. Citrine let go of her hair, letting it tumble back over Alice's shoulders, and bustled over to open the door.

When she did, Buttercup, one of the flower maidens, waited on the other side. Alice turned toward her and smiled, her headache almost forgotten.

"Buttercup! I'm so happy to see you. I thought you might have returned to your people."

The flower maiden's buttery yellow curls wafted around her head, and a smile creased her brown face. "Not yet, Miss Alice, but I am most happy to serve you again." She turned her yellow eyes to Citrine and dipped into a graceful curtsey. "And you as well, Your Majesty."

Citrine waved a hand. "Oh please, none of that formality." She motioned Buttercup into the room and gestured toward Alice. "As you can see, we definitely could use your help. Styling hair is not my area of expertise." As if to reinforce her words, a hank of her own hair fell down from the haphazard cluster of curls she'd piled on top of her head.

Buttercup dipped her head again, a smile hovering around her mouth. "I am pleased to serve you both."

She glided over to the dressing table and directed Alice back to the stool. Once Alice was seated, Buttercup ran her long fingers through Alice's hair.

Pursing her lips, she surveyed Alice from several angles before nodding her head, her own hair waving with the motion. Alice watched her as she deftly twisted various sections up and pinned them into place.

"You said you're here for now. Have you decided to go back home? Are all the flower maidens returning to their families?" Alice still wasn't sure how it all worked. Buttercup had told her serving the Queen was an honor for the flower maidens, but Alice wasn't sure if they came here to serve the Red Queen specifically or the palace residents in general.

Buttercup lifted her eyes from her work, the vertical slits in her pupils a reminder of the fae woman's otherness. Her fingers paused and her gaze dropped. Alice had just begun to wonder if she'd committed some social gaffe when Buttercup answered her.

"Several of our cluster have gone to the Dower House to serve the Queen." She twisted another curl and pinned it into place. "I am returning home soon. I have served long enough, especially now..." She stopped and pinched her lips together even as her fingers continued to shape Alice's curls.

Citrine straightened from where she'd been lounging on the bed. "Has something happened?"

Buttercup's expression shuttered. "It is nothing to trouble you, Your Majesty. Please forgive me for speaking out of turn."

The girl's long fingers trembled as she pushed the next pin into Alice's updo. Alice bit her lip and exchanged a glance with Citrine in the mirror.

She widened her eyes at Alice and then hopped to her feet. "While you're doing that, I'll just nip over to my room to get my dress. It will save you a trip, Buttercup, as I'll need your help with the buttons in the back."

"I am happy to assist however you wish, Ma'am."

Citrine nodded and slipped out the door.

Even though Alice had gotten the feeling the previous time she had spoken to Buttercup that the appeal of the palace was waning, it was clear that Citrine was hoping Alice would find out more. The flower maiden was obviously in awe of the Pearl Queen, but perhaps she'd open up now that Citrine had left the room.

Alice watched Buttercup in the mirror as she worked. There was a crease between her eyebrows, and her mouth was still pinched.

Subtlety had never been Alice's strong suit. She put a hand up to stop the long fingers that fluttered around her head.

"Miss Alice? Is something wrong?"

Alice twisted on the little stool so she could look the other girl in the eye. "I'm fine, but there's clearly something wrong with you. Won't you tell me what it is? Maybe I can help."

Buttercup twisted her long hands together and looked over her shoulder. Indecision warred on her features, and her hair lashed back and forth, betraying her anxiety. Finally, she spoke, her voice soft and halting. "I did not wish my wings to be clipped again." They fluttered behind her as she spoke, revealing the sheared bottom edge of each one in the lamplight.

"Didn't you say it wasn't permanent?" Buttercup nodded, and Alice frowned. "How often do they clip them then?"

Buttercup's hair whipped around her head. "After the first time, the steward has them trimmed about once a year in the autumn. That is enough to keep our magic muted, but not take too much." A shiver rippled through Buttercup's elongated frame.

"I don't understand what the problem is, then. Are you simply tired of not having access to all your magic?"

Buttercup looked over her shoulder again and at the French doors that led out to the balcony. "It's the Queen. She asked that all the maidens attending her be trimmed again. It's not yet midsummer." Her voice lowered until Alice could barely make out the words. "My sister wanted to go to the Dower House, but I stopped her." Buttercup shook her head. "It is best if we both return home before..." She pressed her lips together and then motioned for Alice to turn back toward the mirror. "But you mustn't concern yourself with all of that. Let me finish your hair."

Alice ignored her. "Does the extra trimming hurt you?"

Buttercup remained silent for several moments, her eyes trained on the floor. Alice wondered if she had put her foot in it and was about to apologize when the flower maiden met her gaze.

Her yellow curls lashed at the air and the slits in her eyes narrowed. "The more that is cut, the more it dampens our magic. Some maidens have become weak. I cannot let that happen to my sister."

Alice frowned, her mind churning. Despite her ruthlessness, the Queen had appeared to care for the flower maidens that served her. None of this made any sense. Still, she wanted to reassure the other girl that she'd help, but there was nothing she could do at the moment. As the prince's betrothed, Alice might be able to ask that the maidens return to the palace, but that was only a temporary fix since she didn't plan on marrying Zander.

"I'm so sorry that happened. I can talk to the prince—"

Buttercup shook her head, and her hair whipped into a frenzy. "Please, Miss Alice. I should not have spoken." She put her hands on Alice's shoulders and turned her back toward the mirror. "My sister is not your concern. We will return home and all will be well."

Alice opened her mouth to argue, but the door creaked open. Citrine walked into the room, a bundle of bottle-green silk in her arms.

After that, no matter how gently Alice probed to find out more, Buttercup refused to say anything else. Instead, she finished arranging Alice's hair and helped her slip into the violet dress that the prince had sent up to her room.

When they were both ready to go, Citrine scooped up the clothes she'd been wearing and moved toward the door. "I'm going to drop these in my room before we go down."

Buttercup reached out. "I can take care of them for you, Your Majesty."

Citrine dodged around her and shook her head. "I'm used to doing things for myself, but thank you," she said and slipped out the door.

Buttercup moved to follow her, but Alice stopped her before she stepped into the hallway. "If I can help you…"

Buttercup shook her head. "I appreciate your kindness, Miss Alice, but it is not your concern."

"But if the Queen—"

"It is best if you forget what I have said," said Buttercup, and pulled away. She glided away, leaving Alice to wonder what the Queen was up to.

Chapter 11

ALICE'S STOMACH FLUTTERED WITH nerves as she made her way down the staircase with Citrine. Zander and the Commander waited for them at the bottom. Both wore dress uniforms, the trousers fitted and the jackets double-breasted with a mandarin collar. Zander's was all white with a golden sash, and the Commander's a severe, unrelieved black.

"Breathe," Citrine said. "You don't want to faint or be sick."

"Both are a possibility." Alice gripped her flowing skirts. "Unless I trip on this blasted dress and break my neck first."

Citrine smiled. "I doubt that will happen. Besides, that gown is perfect on you."

Alice had to admit it was beautiful. Made up of varying shades of violet, amethyst-colored crystals edged the sweetheart neckline of the bodice, and a silver band nipped in the waist. The skirts erupted from the waistline in a profusion of tulle and lace, from palest lavender to nearly indigo, which matched her shoes and her gloves.

She'd been worried how she would hide her arm—since the red streaks were well past her elbow and the fluttery sleeves of the dress barely covered an inch of her upper arms—but the gloves came nearly to her shoulders.

Under the men's scrutiny, descending the stairs took an eternity. With every step, Alice imagined herself tripping and tumbling to the bottom. When they finally reached the marble floor, her shoulders inched down from her ears.

They had stopped a few feet from the men, but Zander wasn't looking at her at all. Instead, his gaze stayed glued to Citrine. She did look lovely. Unlike Alice's ensemble, Citrine's dress was a simple column of bottle-green silk with fluttery cap sleeves that suited her tall figure. Her copper curls, piled on top of her head, gleamed in the light from the lanterns. She studiously ignored Zander's obvious perusal.

The Commander coughed and, when that didn't work, nudged Zander with his elbow, and Zander's gaze snapped back to Alice. Under other circumstances, she would have laughed at his dazed expression. But tonight, it reminded her why she had to do whatever was necessary to get out of this marriage.

The Commander bowed to Citrine and offered her his arm. "Shall we?"

Citrine tucked her hand in the crook of his elbow and shot Alice an encouraging glance. Then she turned to her escort. "You're positively dashing tonight, Commander."

Although his stoic expression didn't change, Alice saw a hint of pink in his cheeks as they disappeared toward the ballroom. When she swiveled back to Zander, she was smiling.

Zander's eyes crinkled as his own lips curved upward. "I'm glad to see your smile, Alice." His gaze moved over her. "You look beautiful."

Alice smoothed her hands down her skirt. "You know what they say about fine feathers."

"Your beauty has nothing to do with what you wear, but that dress does make you shine."

A laugh surprised her, and she swatted his arm. "And here I thought Chess was the one with the silver tongue."

He leaned toward her, his voice conspiratorial. "Who do you think I learned it from?" And then he winked.

The nerves from earlier settled into a sense of familiarity. This was the Zander she remembered. She could almost forget what this night was about as she relaxed into their friendship.

Then the smile slid from her face as she remembered her purpose tonight. She didn't want to lose this camaraderie, this closeness. After everything they had been through together, she counted him a friend. Her stomach twisted at the idea of going behind his back to turn the Council against him.

He tilted his head. "Why so serious all of a sudden? I promise, I won't step all over your feet tonight." His tone was teasing, but it was the genuine concern in his warm hazel eyes that decided her. It was only the two of them, with no audience to impress. She might not get this chance again.

She clasped her hands in front of her. "Zander, you realize I care about what happens to you and your Kingdom, right?"

He nodded but his expression turned wary. "You certainly risked a lot to help me break the curse."

She willed him to hear what she was saying. "This marriage—it isn't right for me, or for you or your Kingdom."

His brow furrowed. "But I told you, I'd take you home after the ceremony. Once my champion has beaten Lyssandra's, everything will be fine again."

As if in response to his words, her wrist gave an especially vicious throb, and she swallowed her gasp of pain. She considered telling him right then, of stripping off her glove and showing him the proof that his plan wouldn't work, but she was afraid. Afraid it would only push him in the wrong direction.

"Yes, and that's what I mean. How would your subjects react if you marry me and then I'm gone? Won't that make you look bad if your new bride disappears?"

"We'll come up with a plausible explanation. You're from the Mirror World so people will expect some strangeness."

"Well, that's good to know," she muttered.

He gave her a sheepish smile. "The citizens have some interesting ideas about Mirror World residents, I'm afraid."

Alice waved a hand. "It's fine. I don't care about your people's opinion of *me*. But what about you? If I go back home, how will that color their view of their king? Could you ever marry again?"

He shrugged. "It might garner me some sympathy. As far as marrying again... Perhaps, if you're gone long enough, I could remarry. But it doesn't matter. Unless... that is, I probably won't want to anyway."

Alice's heart squeezed at the pain lurking in his eyes. "Don't you see? This isn't just about what I want. It isn't good for you either. As the future ruler of Wonderland, your well-being is important too."

For a moment, naked hope etched his features and then, just as quickly, his expression shuttered. "What I want doesn't matter. You don't understand, but it's not your fault. You weren't born into a royal family, but I knew from the time I could walk that the Kingdom comes before my feelings. It has to."

She clutched at his arm. "But I can beat the labyrinth, Zander. I know I can. Citrine and I found the labyrinth's Key Book, and it's not what everyone thinks. Getting through it isn't about strength or fighting ability or—"

"Just stop."

The force of his tone startled Alice into momentary silence.

"But Zander, I really think—"

"No, you aren't thinking. You're only feeling." Frustration hardened his features. "Why won't you let this go? I've explained this to you. You. Can't. Win."

"But the book said—"

"I don't care what it said. I'm not gambling my Kingdom on some dusty old book." He paced away from her, dragging both his hands through his hair, making it stand in odd peaks.

Irritation and desperation churned inside of her. "It's not just any old book. Citrine said the Key Books can tell us more than any person—"

He closed the space between them and loomed over her. "Don't. Don't bring her into this."

Anger spiked through her and she ignored the warning voice trying to get her attention. "Why? Because you love her? You shouldn't have to—"

He grabbed her shoulders. "It doesn't matter! The only thing that matters right now is the crown."

The menace in his voice sent ice down her spine, and she cringed away from him. "What's happened to you?"

"Nothing," he snapped, glaring at her even as a wisp of smoke rose from one nostril.

His fingers bit into her skin, and she wondered if his fingerprints would be visible for the rest of the evening. She raised her chin. "Let go of me, Zander."

He blinked. The glaze of anger lifted from his eyes, and he dropped his hands as if her skin burned him. He backed up a step and glanced away from her. "I'm sorry," he said, his voice stiff. "That was uncalled-for."

"I'm not your enemy, Zander. Don't make me into one."

When he finally met her eyes, the defeat in his expression nearly broke her heart. "Then stop fighting me. Please."

It was the *please* that nearly undid her resolve. Her lip trembled, and she blinked back sudden tears. She wasn't sure whether she wanted to cry more for herself or for him.

He blew out a breath and then held out his elbow. When he spoke, his voice held none of its earlier heat. "We should go in. People will start arriving soon."

There was nothing else she could say. He obviously wouldn't listen to her. She slipped her hand through the crook of his arm, and let him lead her toward the ballroom.

"This is best for everyone, Alice. You'll see."

Alice knew he believed what he said, but that somehow made it worse.

Chapter 12

ALICE STOOD NEXT TO Zander as a never-ending stream of colorful guests flowed into the ballroom and out onto the terrace.

Round tables covered in snowy tablecloths, rainbow-hued flowers, and fancy china filled the room's perimeter. More tables were scattered out on the terrace. Floating orbs of various sizes bobbed around the room and out the large French doors, the flickering lights inside them illuminating the ballroom and where the party spilled outside. In the corner, a group of musicians tuned instruments.

A man stopped in front of her and bowed. Alice's mouth automatically turned up at the corners as she greeted him, only half paying attention as she slid another glance at Zander.

While he smiled and nodded and chatted easily, a sheen of perspiration dotted his brow, and whenever there was a lull in the line, he scratched at his wrist. She wished she could get a glimpse of his tattoo, but the cuff of his jacket covered it. She shifted again and craned her neck to check how many people were left in the line.

"What a lovely girl you are." The wavery voice snapped Alice's attention back to the next guest, and she fought not to gape.

Petite and elderly, the woman beamed up at Alice. As she talked, her puff of white hair waved with each bob of her head, but that wasn't what had grabbed Alice's focus. It was the woman's dress. From the neckline to the end of the train that swept several feet behind her, minuscule butterflies—live ones!—covered the garment, their wings fanning gently and their tiny bodies sparkling like multicolored jewels.

The woman preened. "Isn't it wonderful? My seamstress spent a solid week attaching them all. I had a feeling I'd need something special to wear." Her smile got even brighter. "And I was right, wasn't I?"

"But how...?"

"Special thread. My seamstress is a marvel. She's part fae, you know."

"And we all know how perfectly wonderful half-fae are, don't we, Lady Bantham?"

Alice turned at the sound of a velvety voice.

The grin Chess gave her was so familiar, she could hardly wrap her brain around the fact that it was a man standing there and not a cat. A very handsome man. She had only seen Chess once when he wasn't in his feline form, and he'd been crumpled on the ground, half dead. In a distant sort of way it had registered he was good-looking, but her focus had been on whether or not he'd live. Tonight, with his tailored dress clothes highlighting his tall form and his black curls falling over his forehead, Alice suddenly felt self-conscious.

The older woman shook a playful finger at Chess and glanced at Alice. "You have to watch this one. He's a rogue."

"You wound me, Lady Bantham." The woman tittered as Chess bowed over her hand and pressed a kiss onto the back of it.

Alice watched the woman dodder off into the ballroom, still chuckling, her wrinkled cheeks rosy. "Even little old ladies aren't safe from your flirting."

Chess lifted one shoulder. "You and I both know I made Lady Bantham's night. She's probably telling all of her friends right now how cheeky that Felinas boy has gotten to be."

Alice raised an eyebrow. "Your ego isn't any smaller, either."

Chess's blue eyes sparkled. "If you want to keep it in check, I won't mind."

Heat rose on her cheeks, and she hoped the dim light of the ballroom hid her blush. Flustered, she covered her discomfort with a smirk. "I don't envy anyone that job. It would be most time-consuming."

His smile intensified, and energy buzzed over her skin. "I think you'd be equal to the task." Holding her gaze, he bowed over her hand and pressed a kiss on the back of it. Despite her gloves, a spot of heat blossomed where his lips touched and spread up her arm.

She had the sudden desire to fan herself. The sounds of the party faded, and the moment slowed and stretched. In a dim part of her mind, she realized she should look away, that people were watching her, but she couldn't.

And then their connection was broken. Zander pulled her hand out of Chess's grip. "There are enough women here tonight that you don't need to flirt with my fiancée." He chuckled, but his voice sounded too loud, his skin flushed. Alice wanted to disappear as more eyes in the ballroom turned their way.

She fixed a pleasant smile onto her face and murmured, "Chess wanted to say hello." She slipped her hand into the crook of Zander's arm. "This is the first time I've seen him since the last ball." She turned back to Chess. "I'm so glad you've recovered." She forced a laugh. "Hopefully, you won't end up flying through the air at this one."

Chess grinned. "Since the Queen isn't invited, I think my chances are good."

Zander frowned at them. "You can visit later. There are other people in line, and you're holding everyone up."

Chess tilted his head. "'Hello, Chess, how are you?' 'I'm fine, Zander, thanks for asking.'"

The muscles in Zander's arm tensed. "I didn't need to ask. You're obviously in fine form." He bit off the words, his voice hard.

Chess clapped Zander on the shoulder. "I'm not nearly as fine as you are. After all, you've got the prettiest girl in the room." He winked at Alice.

She repressed a groan. How could Chess be so oblivious to Zander's mood?

"Yes. Because she's *my* fiancée." Zander's arm curled around her waist, pulling her close to his side, and she bit back a yip of surprise.

Chess's eyebrows rose as his gaze moved from where Zander's hand rested on her waist to her face. She widened her eyes at him and tilted her head, but he ignored her hint.

Small clusters of people turned their way. Several whispered amongst themselves. The line backed up as the guests waited for Chess to move on.

She kept her smile plastered on her face, but a headache began an insistent drumbeat behind her eyes. The tension between the two men stretched like taffy.

Then strains of music wafted over the ballroom, and Alice sagged in relief.

"I'm glad you're doing so well, Chess." She put a hand on Zander's chest. "Didn't you say we had the first dance to start the ball?"

Zander blinked and then looked at her. His eyes were glassy and sweat dotted his forehead.

"Are you all right?" she asked.

"I'm fine."

"You don't look fine," said Chess, his teasing expression gone.

"I don't need your opinion." Removing his arm from her waist, Zander grasped her hand and pulled her toward the dance floor, leaving the line of guests without even a nod.

A hush fell over the crowd as they glided to the very center of the ballroom. The glittering orbs gathered in a cluster above their heads and spun, casting patterns of light over the floor. The music paused, and a waltz swelled from the instruments.

Alice had a moment of sheer terror as every eye zeroed in on her, and then they were moving. Her feet remembered the steps she'd practiced over and over in their parlor. She could almost hear Papa James's big laugh, and she blinked to clear the moisture from her eyes.

They swept around the dance floor, and she admitted Zander was an excellent dancer. After all his talk about not fitting in, this surprised her.

"You're better at all this court stuff than you led me to believe," she said.

"I had a lot of lessons." Zander's face lost some of its tension.

He spun her out and back again.

"Well, they seem to have worked. I bet you've got even Chess beat." She gave him a teasing smile, only to find him glaring at her. She missed her step and only Zander's intervention kept her from tripping.

"I suppose you'd rather be dancing with him." It wasn't a question. Her headache roared to life again, and the faces of the crowd blurred in and out.

"That's not what I meant."

Zander's expression hardened. "You seemed all too happy to see him tonight." He spun her out and whipped her back toward him before dipping her low. Her head whirled and heat flashed over her body. She stumbled again.

Zander pulled her closer to steady her. Regret clouded his features. "I'm sorry. I don't know why I said that."

Alice didn't either, but she was sure that stupid curse was involved. Instead of saying that, she smiled in what she hoped was a reassuring way. "It's all right. You've had a difficult few days."

The rigidness of his body relaxed. As he expertly guided her over to the dance floor, she studied him. Something was definitely wrong. He had more mood swings than the middle grade girls at Chattingham's.

He spun her out again, more gently this time, and reeled her back. As his hand touched hers, his sleeve rode up. Scales glittered on his tattoo. As if in sympathy, the dull throbbing in her own wrist flared to a bright flame.

"Are you all right?"

When he spoke, Alice realized she had squeezed her eyes shut against the pain. When she looked up at him, his face creased with concern.

She made a sudden decision. She would tell him. He deserved to know what was happening to him and to her. She worried her lip. The dance floor wasn't the best place to do this, but maybe they could slip out so they'd have a bit of privacy.

"Zander, I need—"

"Her Majesty, the Queen, and her brother, Sir Leander Renard." Anders' announcement caused a hush to fall over the ballroom so that the only sound was the waltz played by the musicians.

Chapter 13

ZANDER HALTED SO ABRUPTLY, Alice staggered. Absently, he put a hand on her waist to steady her, and then, without a word, he stalked towards the door.

Alice remained alone in the middle of the ballroom. Heat crawled up her neck, and she wished she had Chess's ability to turn invisible. It took her a few moments to realize nobody was even looking her way. Everyone's eyes were pinned to where Zander stood in front of the Queen.

"Alice." Citrine beckoned to her from the edge of the dance floor.

Alice hurried over.

"Let me introduce you to Lord Dordo while everyone is occupied." Citrine shot a worried look towards the door. "Or at least before disaster strikes."

Before Alice could respond, Citrine pulled her over to a group of three gentlemen near the terrace doors. Alice didn't recognize any of them.

As they approached, Citrine whispered in her ear, "Remember, don't laugh at him."

Alice wondered why she would. As they strolled over, she studied them, wondering which one was Lord Dordo. She put a pleasant smile on her face as Citrine greeted the group. One of them, a large heavy-set man with a head as bald as an egg, leered at Alice. His double chin jiggled as he looked her up and down. He guffawed and nudged the dapper blond gentleman next to him. Although he leaned over to whisper, his voice was clearly audible to anyone in a ten-foot radius.

"Pretty little filly the prince has gotten himself." He waggled his eyebrows. "I heard she's from the Mirror World. Quite exotic."

The dandy next to him edged away, his lip curling under his neat mustache. He appeared relieved when Citrine touched his elbow. "Lord Dordo, may we have a word with you?"

"Of course, I'd be happy to execute myself from these fellows."

Alice covered her giggle with a cough, but the other men weren't so polite. The large man let out a bellowing laugh. "Execute—did you hear him?" He elbowed the man next to him.

Lord Dordo shot his companion a venomous glare before he followed them out onto the terrace.

"Lord Dordo, I'd like to introduce you to Miss Alice Cavendish."

Alice curtsied, and he bowed in return. "It's a pleasure to meet you, my dear. I am so sorry to have missed the meeting, but I had a manifesto of pixiecorns. You know how delirious they can be."

Alice blinked as she picked through his words, trying to figure out what he meant. Was a pixiecorn a real creature, or had he misspoken? She'd have to ask Citrine later. Now, she murmured a polite response.

"Lord Dordo, did you hear about the decision the Council came to while you weren't there?" Citrine gave a slight emphasis on the phrase *you weren't there*.

Lord Dordo frowned. "I didn't hear all the details yet, but as this is your enragement ball, I understand you're to marry the prince."

Alice twisted her hands together. "Yes, but"—she glanced at Citrine, who encouraged her with a nod—"that isn't my choice."

"I'm not sure what you mean, my dear."

"I don't want to marry the prince," Alice blurted out.

Lord Dordo's brow crinkled in confusion. "You don't? Whyever not? Don't tell me you'd like to be the champion." He chuckled.

Alice scrambled to come up with an explanation that wouldn't offend him. Zander was their beloved prince, after all. "Actually, I'd much rather be the champion. You see, I have a family back home that needs me, and they don't know I'm here."

He reached out and patted her hand. "I'm sure the prince would be happy to take you for viruses."

"Vir... Oh, I understand..." She paused. Then an idea blinked into her brain. "Yes, Prince Zander *would* bring me for *visits*—he's so kind—but my father will be quite upset if he finds out I'm already married. Surely, you understand how a girl like myself would want her father's approval and blessing."

The man's smile nearly split his face. "Yes, yes, I'm happy to see a young person with such respite for her parental figure." He tilted his head. "I'm surprised that the Council did not give this due concealment. What did they say when you told them this?"

"I..." Alice's eyes darted to Citrine.

"Once everyone found out the competition would take place in the labyrinth, I'm afraid things were rather chaotic, Lord Dordo. And then we got a message saying the Queen and her brother had showed up at the palace unannounced. There was a bit of a panic."

The man frowned and stroked his chin. "Yes, yes, I can understand why the Council moved quickly, but it doesn't do to rush into big destitutes. I think I need to talk to some of the members. Perhaps we should rethink this."

Alice clasped her hands. "I would be so grateful if you would. Of course, it's a great honor to marry the prince, but..."

The sound of raised voices interrupted them, and they headed towards the ballroom entrance to catch a glimpse of what was happening. While their faces weren't visible, Zander loomed over the Queen, and her brother was trying to push him back.

Citrine and Alice exchanged glances. "I should probably..." Citrine waved a hand in the direction of the prince and Queen.

"No, go ahead. Za— The prince has been feeling..." She glanced at Dordo and then back at Citrine and lifted her eyebrows. "...not quite himself."

Citrine's face turned white and without another word she hurried across the room.

Meanwhile, Lord Dordo's eyes hadn't left the two royals. After a minute, he cleared his throat. "On second thought, maybe the Council *has* made the right choice.

We certainly can't have that woman as our leader." He patted her hand again. "I'm sure your father will understand, and a nice girl like you doesn't want to go into the labyrinth, anyway."

Alice opened her mouth to tell him *this* girl did, but the dapper little man slipped back into the ballroom. Her shoulders slumped. She was no further ahead than before. She raised up on tiptoe, her eyes scanning the crowd.

Then she saw the person she was looking for—the Duchess.

"No, I'm sorry. I can't change my vote." The Duchess's face showed genuine regret as she waved towards Zander and the Queen who were standing toe to toe. "I think it's obvious why. Nobody wants to deal with that woman if her champion wins." She sighed. "While I admire your pluck, my dear, and I do think you have a sporting chance, facts are facts. The Felinas boy's odds are better than yours, and I never take a poor bet."

"But I really believe I can—"

The Duchess held up her hand to stop Alice and gave a sharp-edged smile. "I've given you the opportunity to say your piece, but my answer is still no. Now if you'll excuse me."

Alice watched her last chance at changing the Council's decision walk away. Tears burned in her eyes, and she blinked furiously to keep them from falling. Her headache formed a tight band of pain around her head. The room tilted, and Alice grabbed the back of a chair to steady herself.

By the door, the Queen and Zander were still in a heated conversation. Even from here, the rigid lines of the prince's body were visible. Although everyone had gone silent when the woman had first appeared, people had gravitated towards each other. More than a few were sliding curious gazes at her as they talked in whispers.

The room felt stifling, and her head was muzzy. She needed to get some air, to catch her breath. She veered towards the terrace and the soft darkness outside. With a last look over her shoulder to make sure nobody was looking for her, she slipped out the French doors and ran down the steps. Weaving through the tables that sat ready for the guests, she passed by the row of lanterns that marked the border of the party.

Following the curling path that led off to the side of the palace, she kept going until she reached a series of humps that reared out of the shadows. The hedges outlined the edge of a garden. She slipped inside and caught her breath. Her arm throbbed in time with her headache. She walked deeper into the bushes, farther from the lights of the party.

After making several turns, she spotted a stone bench nestled in the shadow of a large tree with sweeping branches. The leaves swayed in the night breeze, and the moon glinted off their iridescent surfaces.

Alice sank onto the seat, her knees weak. Even sitting, the garden and flowers swirled around her. The throbbing pain in her arm had reached her shoulder. She looked down and squinted.

A tiny vein of red showed past the edge of her neckline. Alice blinked at it and her heart sped up. Did she even have until tomorrow? Breathing became difficult.

The world spun crazily, and then someone pushed her head to her knees.

"You know, love, everyone will blame me if you pass out." Chess's familiar velvety drawl eased the knot in Alice's chest so she could breathe again.

Chapter 14

ZANDER CLENCHED HIS HANDS at his sides to keep from squeezing the Queen's neck. It was becoming an alarming inclination.

He was dimly aware of the Commander next to him, and the soldiers that had stepped in a loose circle around them.

"I'm sure not inviting me was merely an oversight on your part, darling." The Queen looked up at him through her lashes. "I won't hold it against you. I promise."

"Nobody wants you here." Zander's jaw clenched so tightly, his words squeaked through his teeth.

"Nonsense." The Queen gestured towards the guests. "Look at them all. They're salivating to tell their friends and acquaintances what happened at the prince's engagement ball." She tapped her fan on his chest. "You should thank me for adding such cachet to your little party."

Zander pushed the tip away from him. "What you see is fear, not welcome. They haven't had time to forget the last party you attended."

"Yes, and they haven't stopped talking about that, either." Her eyes danced with malicious merriment. "And just think what they'd say if they found out the entire story."

Zander grabbed the Queen's arm and pushed her towards the door. "You need to leave. Now."

Leander brought the side of his hand down hard enough on Zander's wrist to break his grasp. "Don't touch my sister."

Zander swung around and gripped the collar of the other man's velvet jacket and shook him. Although Leander had a few inches on the prince, Zander outmuscled him. "Then tell her to leave. I don't understand why you allowed her to come in the first place."

The Queen's laughter chimed like a bell. "Allowed me? Oh, Zander, I didn't realize what an antiquated view of women you had." She gestured to Leander. "He doesn't *allow* me to do anything, do you, brother dear?"

Leander jerked away from Zander's grip and straightened his jacket. "My sister is her own person. I only accompanied her because I didn't want her to come alone." He yanked on his waistcoat. "Obviously, I was right about that."

"Gate crashers usually don't get a warm welcome, Renard. I would think even you'd be smart enough to realize that." Chess's arm brushed his own, and Zander welcomed the support, especially after their disagreement earlier.

The Queen tilted her head, and a blonde curl slid over her bare shoulder. Her dark eyes met Zander's and didn't let go. "Now, Zander, don't be like this. I only wanted to wish both you and your lovely bride well. Is that so wrong of me?"

The anger flickered and flared to life, and he could hear the rasp of his own breath. "You've never wished anyone well the entire time I've known you. You only pretended at any kindness or compassion."

"I'm not the only one pretending, now, am I?" Her smiled held a knife-sharp edge. She snaked out a hand and pulled his head down so she could whisper into his ear. "And if I don't win that crown, imagine how everyone will react to your little secret."

Before he could push her away, she stepped back. "I hope we understand one another."

The heat in Zander's chest built, and his jabberwock pushed towards the surface. Her eyebrow rose as she watched him, almost daring him to let go.

Someone touched his hand. "Ignore her, Zander." The familiar voice splashed water on the fire inside of him. It sizzled and went out. He looked down into worried grey eyes...

"Citrine."

"Hmmm, isn't this interesting?" The delight in the Queen's voice scraped over his skin, and he clawed at his wrist, trying to still the insistent itch that was driving him mad. "I thought we had a love triangle, but I see I was wrong. There is more complicated geometry going on here."

"Lyssandra, perhaps we should go." Leander's voice held a warning.

Her lips turned down into a pout. "I suppose you're right, brother, but it's too mean that I can't stay to watch the show."

Leander put his hand under her elbow. "Come, it's clear we've worn out our welcome."

"And I certainly wouldn't want to do that." The Queen spun towards the door.

The muscles in Zander's neck and shoulders loosened.

And then she turned back to him.

Her eyes tracked something in the crowd, and then she flicked her fingers at a spot over his shoulder.

"You should mind your fiancée, though. I believe she just left."

Zander twisted around and caught a glimpse of violet skirts disappearing out the French doors. He only now realized he had abandoned Alice in the middle of the dance floor.

The Queen's chuckle brought his head back around. She reached up and patted his cheek, and he flinched away from her. "It's not too late, you know."

With those cryptic words, she took her brother's arm, and they swept out of the ballroom.

There was a crushing beat of silence, and then Zander started toward the terrace. Citrine put a hand on his arm and stopped him. She lowered her voice to a whisper. "You can't go running out there. Everyone is watching you."

She turned to the Commander. "Get the musicians to start playing again. Something lively. We need people out on the dance floor. Nobody's going to forget the Queen was here, but at least things can return to a more normal footing."

The Commander dipped his chin and strode over to the small orchestra. The strains of a reel filled the ballroom. Then, he made his way over to the Duchess, and soon the two of them were whirling across the floor. Other couples joined them in a dizzying whirl of color and laughter.

Citrine tucked her hand in Zander's elbow. "Dancing is probably the last thing you feel like doing at the moment, but the people need to see that the Queen hasn't affected you."

Zander's stomach churned, but she was right. He let her lead him out among the other couples.

While Citrine kept flicking worried glances at him, he was thankful she for her quiet steadiness. The dance was so exuberant, it would have made talking hard even if he had wanted to. Which he didn't. He was too busy pushing his jabberwock down deep.

As they whirled past the French doors, he caught sight of Chess. He was heading out towards the garden. Zander missed a beat and stumbled, but Citrine found the rhythm again and pulled him along.

He looked into her eyes. "Thanks."

Her smile soothed the frayed edges of his nerves, and he hoped she knew grateful he was for her presence.

Chapter 15

ALICE PUSHED CHESS'S HAND away, and he let go of the back of her head. "What are you doing out here?" She tried to keep her tone light. "Don't tell me I'm interrupting a rendezvous with someone."

Chess came around and seated himself next to her. The bench wasn't very big, so his leg brushed up against her skirt. Reflexively, she scooted away, then flailed her arms as she almost fell off the edge. Chess steadied her.

"Erm, thanks," she mumbled and her cheeks flamed.

He smirked, and her face got hotter. "We don't want you breaking anything, now do we, love?"

Flustered, she took the offensive. "You never answered my question. Surely, you didn't come out here just to embarrass me."

He lifted a shoulder. "I saw you leave the ballroom and wanted to make sure you were all right." He paused. "You looked upset."

She had expected him to flirt and tease. The sincerity in his tone took her off guard. She rubbed her hands over her arms as a chill settled over her flesh.

"I'm fine. I just needed some air." She lifted her face up towards the moon, letting the evening breeze cool her skin.

The sky tilted again, and she swayed. Chess reached out to once again steady her, and she clung to the bench, closing her eyes until the spinning stopped.

"Are you sure about that? You don't look so good."

She peeled her eyelids open and huffed out a laugh. "I thought you were known for your charm."

Chess's mouth curved up. "I didn't say you weren't beautiful, but you seem ready to topple over." He studied her. "Are you that worried about tomorrow?"

Her arm throbbed, and she shivered, her teeth chattering. "I won't marry him, you know."

Chess took off his jacket, revealing his midnight-blue silk shirt. The soft fabric outlined the muscles underneath. He really was a beautiful man.

"Well, thank you," he said, his voice laced with amusement as he draped the jacket over her shoulders.

She clapped a hand over her mouth, mortified that she had spoken those words out loud.

"Did you have too much punch, or do you need one of the palace physicians?" He settled back next to her.

She shook her head and then regretted it as the garden spun again. She closed her eyes. "I'd rather die of thirst than drink any of your party punch. Not after the last time."

He chuckled. "I guess your first experience was unfortunate, wasn't it?"

"That's one way of looking at it." She sighed and wished she could peel off her gloves. The fabric rubbed against her arm, setting her skin on fire.

Chess's expression became serious as he turned toward her. "Look, Citrine told me something in that curse was set off. I'm assuming that's why you're not feeling well?"

Alice touched the red line that peeked out from the neckline of her dress. "I suppose."

He squinted at where her fingers rested and leaned closer. "What is that?"

She angled away from him. "It's my signal that my time is almost up."

"What's that supposed to mean?"

She pulled his jacket tighter, so it hugged her chin. "It means I need to figure out a way into the labyrinth sooner rather than later."

"I'll help you... if you're sure you don't want to marry Zander."

She squinted at him suspiciously. "I already said I don't, but why would you back me up rather than your best friend? I thought Zander was like a brother to you."

Chess's mouth twisted. "He *is*, and I would do almost anything for him. But what he's doing to you is wrong."

She wished the pounding in her head would stop. It made it hard to concentrate on what Chess was saying. "Since when are you the voice of virtue?"

He put both hands over his chest. "Ouch! Tell me how you really feel, why don't you?"

Alice slanted a glance at him. "Well, you have to admit, your actions have been more of the end-justifies-the-means type."

His eyes flashed. "And it *did* justify the means."

"Not for me, it didn't." Alice wished she could suck the words back in, not only because she didn't really mean them, but now they lay between her and Chess like a dead fish.

He drew a hand down his face. "I know you stuck your neck out for Zander—and for me, too. Forcing you into something like marriage... Well, it seems like a rotten way to pay you back is all." He shifted. "I wanted you to know that if you need help, I'm here. In fact, I'll sneak you in tonight, if you want."

"You'd do that for me? Even knowing Zander's wishes?"

Before Chess could answer, a voice called her name.

They stared at each other.

It was as if talking about him had conjured his presence.

Alice's heart surged. She took off the jacket and almost flung it at Chess. "You have to hide." Her eyes darted around the garden, but nothing seemed big enough to conceal a grown man.

Without another word, Chess's body shrunk even as his ears elongated. Fur sprouted along his jaw and his hands curled into paws. She blinked and a familiar black cat, a white tip on his tail, stood in front of her. He winked one eye and scampered into the nearby bushes just as Zander rounded a group of roses.

The prince glanced around the little nook. "What are you doing out here? I thought I heard you talking to somebody."

Chapter 16

A BREEZE TUGGED AT her hair and rustled the nearby roses, tickling Alice's nose with their heady aroma. She shivered. "I... I just needed some air."

Zander peered into the dark garden. "Are you sure that's all it is?"

The band of pain around her temples tightened, and she closed her eyes. "It's just... a lot."

Zander brushed his hand along her arm and took her hand. Her eyes popped open, and she stared at their clasped fingers. She wanted to pull away, but the garden picked that moment to sway drunkenly.

Her knees buckled, and she sat heavily on the bench, her hand slipping from his.

He dropped next to her, alarmed. "Alice, please. I'm still your friend. Won't you tell me what's wrong?"

She shot him a look. "You really have to ask me that?"

He leaned forward, his forearms on his thighs. He jerked at the cuffs of his jacket before he peered up at her. His hazel eyes burned. "I've told you. I will get you home. Once the ceremony is over, I'll take you to the

Looking Glass and you can return to the Mirror World and your family."

Tongues of flame licked at her wrist, and she bit back a gasp of pain. "I know you think that's the answer, but trust me, it's not."

He sat up and turned toward her, frustration etched on his face. "You're making this more difficult than it needs to be. It's not as if…" His cheeks reddened. "That is, it'll be a marriage of convenience. You don't have to worry. You've done enough for me—more than enough—and I won't trap you here. I promise."

She had to tell him. "That's not going to work."

He stiffened. "Why not? It fulfills the curse, and your life can get back to normal."

"No, Zander, you're not listening." She stripped off her glove, hissing as the fabric rubbed against her tattoo. She held out her arm. His eyes widened as he took in the inflamed skin and followed the streaks of red that disappeared under the sleeves of her dress. Small blisters rose over parts of the swirling pattern. She frowned. That was new.

His brows creased as he pulled back the cuff. "That must be why…" Moonlight reflected off the olive-bronze scales that covered almost two-thirds of his tattoo.

"My wrist has been itching like mad, and these showed up, but"—he traced a finger over the scales—"I just thought it was part of it." He gestured towards the markings that matched the ones on Alice's wrist.

Alice leaned over so she could examine his tattoo more closely. "Sir Lapin said the curse knows we're trying to fool it, and it tripped something."

"That's… that's impossible."

She pointed to their wrists. "Apparently, it's not. And if I don't affect your life before these red lines reach my heart... I'll die."

She stared at his arm. "I'm not sure what those scales mean, but I'd guess it's something to do with your jabberwock." A suspicion niggled at the back of her mind, but her head hurt so much she couldn't think straight. "Knowing the Queen, I'm sure it's something horrible."

"So, what does that mean for us?"

She took both of his hands in hers. "It means, Zander, you have to let me be your champion." She swallowed and forced herself to hold his gaze. "Otherwise, you'll have to marry me for real."

Zander stared at her for several heartbeats. Finally, he shook his head and leaned back, his hands slipping from her grasp. "This is such a mess." He barked out a bitter note of laughter. "I thought once we broke that Jabberwock's Curse, everything would be all right. I'm such an idiot."

"This situation isn't your fault. It's the Queen's. She's the villain here, not you." She gave him a tentative smile.

"I'm glad you can still say that." Before she could respond, he braced his hands on his legs. "I should call the priest tonight, then."

"What?"

"Those lines are awfully close to your heart, Alice. If we're going to marry anyway, there's no reason to cut things too close."

"But I thought..."

Realization spread across his face and he grimaced. "Oh, you thought this would change my mind, didn't you?"

"How could it not? This isn't some simple ceremony or a brief inconvenience. This is permanent." Alice bunched her hands in her lap, trying to control the nausea that roiled in her stomach. He couldn't mean this.

He smoothed his expression into a blank mask. "I'm aware of what it means."

Betrayal punched Alice in the chest and black spots danced at the edge of her vision. It was one thing when he believed this was temporary, but now...

She turned stricken eyes towards him. "Then how can you do this to me?"

His face clouded. "You act as if marrying me is a fate worse than death! Am I so awful?"

She touched his arm. "Oh, Zander, of course not! I would feel this way about having to marry anyone in this situation. It's not about you."

"Well, it feels like it is." He jerked his arm away and clenched his fists in his lap. "I wager if it was Chess, your response would be different."

Anger burned away the pain in her head. When she spoke, it was through gritted teeth.

"If it was Chess I wouldn't *be* in this position. He seems to understand my need to go home."

Zander snorted, but Alice continued, her voice rising. "They may not be important to you, but my family is everything to me. I told you about Hadley. He could ruin my father."

His mouth twisted into a snarl. "So, what? You can't marry me, but you can marry some idiot who's blackmailing you? That's better?"

"It's not like that!"

He hit his fist on the bench, and she flinched. "It *is* like that." He got up and paced up and down the path. "We'll go back. Together. Once this is all over, I'll take you home, and we'll deal with this man. I can pay off your father's debts. It'll be fine. You can visit as often as you want."

Alice jumped to her feet, her heart pounding. "Why won't you listen to me? I don't love you, and I don't want to stay here. You can't make me do this!"

Zander loomed up in front of her, his hands biting into her shoulders. "You're wrong about that."

And then his mouth was on hers, and there was nothing kind or sweet about it. Shock froze her as his lips moved roughly on hers. A low growl reached her ears, and Zander jerked away with a yell of pain.

The black cat at their feet rippled upward and Chess stood there, his eyes blazing. He shoved Zander away from her. "What is wrong with you?"

Zander stumbled back a few steps, before steadying himself on the trunk of the tree. His gaze whipped from her to Chess and back again. He sneered and wiped a hand across his mouth, as if her touch had contaminated him. Which was rich, considering *he* was the one who had kissed *her*. "I knew he had to be involved somehow." The violence of his gaze made Alice shrink away. "Maybe you'd like to revise your answer from earlier?" A thin stream of smoke rose from his nostrils.

He stepped toward Chess and poked a finger at his friend's chest. A clawed tip jutted from its end. "And you..."

A small hole appeared in the fabric, but Chess didn't retreat. Instead, he slapped Zander's hand away. "What about me?"

"It all makes sense now." Taking on a more clipped tone, he mimicked Chess. "'It's not fair to Alice.' 'She's so strong.'" Zander's eyes narrowed, and the pupils contracted to vertical slits. "You want her for yourself. The great Chess Felinas, ladies' man, jealous that I got the girl for once, instead of him." He flung a hand in her direction. "Especially one like her!"

All the oxygen sucked from the air, and everything went silent.

Chess's jaw ticked and his hands curled into fists, but his tone was dangerously casual. "And yet, I'm not the one manhandling her."

"She's my betrothed. I can do what I want." Zander spit the words.

"Listen to yourself. She doesn't want to marry you, and I can't say I blame her right now."

Zander grabbed Chess's shirt and shoved him into the tree. "I don't care what she wants! I *have* to marry her."

Alice's feet were rooted into the dirt. How had everything gone so wrong so fast?

Before she could move or speak, Chess's arms came up and broke Zander's hold. In a blur of movement, he reversed their positions and slammed Zander against the tree trunk. Bits of bark floated to the ground. His forearm shoved under Zander's chin, choking him, and Zander grabbed at Chess's arm. Zander bared his teeth, and a growl rippled from his throat.

Alice finally uprooted her feet. She darted toward them. "Stop it! Both of you!"

They glared at her. Scales covered Zander's cheeks. She pulled at Chess's shoulder. "It's not his fault." She pointed to Zander's wrist and the tiny scales covering most of the tattoo. "It's that blasted trap."

Chess loosened his hold, and Zander pushed him off and rubbed at his throat. Alice clutched Zander's arm, and he swung in her direction, elongated canines bared. She fought the urge to cower. Instead, she grasped his face between her hands and looked deep into his eyes. Her palms felt unaccountably warm against his cheeks. "Zander, this isn't you. It's the curse. Please, please come back to us."

Another growl rumbled in his chest, and he gripped her forearms. The clawed fingertips dug into her flesh. Chess moved to intervene, but she shook her head, her eyes never leaving Zander's. "We're your friends. We care about you, and I know you care about us, about me."

His chest heaved once and then twice. Then he blinked and backed away from her. "I'm... I'm sorry." He stared at his hands and then at Chess. He stumbled away from them, shaking his head. "I don't know—" His gaze swung to Chess who watched him warily. Zander's face twisted with remorse. "I'm so sorry.... I didn't mean to.... I don't know why..." He trailed off and ran a finger over the tiny bronze scales.

Alice spoke as if to a spooked horse. "I know why. The trap will kill me, but I think it'll take your humanity."

Chess and Zander stilled.

She blew a curl off out of her face. "This explains so much—why you've been so angry and agitated, not at all like yourself."

"I'm not—" Zander paused and tilted his head. Then his shoulders slumped. "I suppose you're right. The other day..." He glanced at her and then away. "I wanted to kill the Queen."

Chess snorted. "Get in line."

Zander grimaced. "No, I mean truly. The only thing that stopped me was the fact there were other people in the room." He cast an apologetic look in Alice's direction.

She held up her hands. "Don't apologize to me. I certainly wouldn't mourn her."

Zander stepped toward her. "I'm so sorry, Alice. I..." His face reddened. "I don't know what came over me. You have my word that won't happen again..." His face turned an even deeper shade of red before he continued, "...unless you give me permission."

Chess scowled, and Alice's own cheeks heated. "You weren't yourself."

Zander stared at his feet. The only sound was the breeze rustling the leaves. Finally, he lifted his head and drew a weary hand down his face. His gaze held determination, and her stomach sank before he said a word.

"I'm sorry, Alice. I know this isn't what you want, but waiting won't change anything." He held out his hand. "I'll get Anders to fetch the priest." He tried to smile. "After all, we already have a whole ballroom full of guests."

Alice stared at his hand as if it was a snake and hugged herself. The anger that had been sustaining her drained away. Her head throbbed. All she wanted to do was curl up and sleep. Tears shimmered in her eyes when she looked up at him. "Please, can't we at least wait until tomorrow?"

He frowned. "But your arm... We shouldn't take the chance."

"Zander, please." Now the tears did spill over. "I can't do this tonight."

Zander let his hand drop. She could see the anger beginning to build again and panic bubbled up. She'd have no opportunity to get into the labyrinth if he pushed this.

Chess stepped between them. "There's still time. Give her the space she's asking for. It's the least you can do."

At first Alice didn't think Zander would agree, and she wondered if she had the strength to just run. Maybe if Chess distracted him...

Then Zander's shoulders loosened, and he stepped back. "All right, but I'm moving the ceremony up to first thing in the morning. No matter what you believe, I do care about you, Alice. Your death is the last thing I want."

The relief was so strong, she almost crumpled, but Chess steadied her. "Perhaps you should call it a night." His mouth tipped. "You really don't look so good."

Zander pushed between them and pulled her arm through the crook of his elbow. "You don't need to concern yourself. I'll take care of her. She's my responsibility now."

"Zan—"

"No, you've already made it clear you're not on my side."

Chess's eyes narrowed. "If that's what you want to believe."

Zander didn't answer. He simply started walking up the path back to the palace, pulling Alice along with him, and she let him.

At the moment, there was no other choice.

Chapter 17

ALICE FUMBLED WITH THE door handle of her room. Turning it took more coordination than she possessed.

Citrine pushed her aside and opened it. Even in the dim light of the hallway, the concern on her face was clear.

Alice stumbled into the room and plopped onto the edge of the bed gratefully.

"You need to change so we can get you to the labyrinth as soon as possible."

Alice flopped backwards and closed her eyes. She could hear Citrine's skirts rustle as she moved around the room. Something dented the mattress near her head.

"I brought some of my clothes." Alice slitted her eyes open, and Citrine gestured towards a pair of trousers, a linen shirt, and a leather coat she'd dropped onto the bed. "There's no sense in dealing with skirts in the labyrinth if you don't have to. I also...."

Citrine's voice faded away.

And then someone was shaking her shoulder. "Time to wake up, love."

She peeled her eyelids open to find Chess leaning over her. She smiled. "It should bother me you're in my bedroom, shouldn't it?"

He chuckled, but his lips pinched. "As much as I'd like to follow that train of thought, you need to get up." He grasped her limp hands and pulled her up to a sitting position.

Alice slumped there for a moment.

"We need to hurry," said Citrine before she shoved something else into the satchel she'd brought with her. Alice leaned back again. She couldn't, for the life of her, understand why everyone was in such a hurry. The bed was so soft and...

"Oh, no you don't." Chess's arm encircled her waist and urged her to her feet. She stood and swayed.

He and Citrine exchanged glances. "Are you sure this is going to work?" Chess's expression tightened. "What if we get her in there and she..." He trailed off.

Citrine crouched next to one of her bags and rummaged through the contents. Her voice was muffled when she answered. "She'll be fine... if we hurry."

"But what if it's too late? She's so weak. How will she be able to—" He glanced at Alice. "She's in no shape to take on anything right now, never mind the labyrinth."

Citrine stood up, a glass bottle in her hand. "I told you, once she's inside, she'll perk up. It's only too late if she's dead."

They both appeared so worried. Alice wanted to tell them everything was fine. Then the room spun, and she closed her eyes against the throbbing in her head.

Citrine pushed something into her hand. "Drink this."

Alice squinted at the dark green bottle. "What is it?"

"It's a tonic. I only hope it will slow the spread of the curse long enough so you can reach the labyrinth in time." Her lips pressed into a thin line. "Or we might need to get that priest."

Alice wrinkled her nose and turned the liquid sideways. "This won't make me spill all my secrets, will it?"

Chess's hand came under hers and pushed the bottle towards her mouth. Alice mashed her lips together and shook her head.

"We can do this the easy way or the hard way. Your choice, love."

Alice squeezed her eyes shut and shook her head again. The room spun, and she clutched at Chess's shirt, almost dropping the tonic.

Fingers pinched her nose, and she opened her mouth to protest, but cold liquid poured down her throat. The strong licorice taste made her cough and gag, but unable to breathe, she had no choice but to swallow.

Chess held her steady. She could feel the cold liquid snaking a path towards her stomach. Her fingers and toes tingled.

The headache that had dogged her all evening eased to a dull pulse, and the fog in her brain lifted. She blinked a few times.

Then she realized she was clutching Chess's silk shirt in one hand while his arm circled her waist, holding her against his side.

Her face blazed, and she stepped away.

"Are you sure you're steady now?"

"Yes, I'm fine." The reality of the situation seeped into her awareness. She scooped the clothes off the bed and walked towards the screen on the far side of the room.

She peeled out of her dress and slung it over the top, pulling on the trousers and shirt. Then she shrugged into the coat. It was roomy and came past her hips, but the deep brown leather was buttery soft.

"How long do you think that tonic will last?" It was Chess's voice.

Citrine's tone was tight. "I'm not sure, but there's no way you can walk to the labyrinth. It's over two miles away, even if you cut through the meadows."

"We'll ride on Luna, and I'll be back before anyone knows we're gone."

Alice stepped around the screen. The pain in her arm and head had dimmed to a faint throb, and her mind was crystal clear for the first time all evening.

She ignored Chess's admiring glance and cut off his inevitable comment. "I'll ride my own horse."

Citrine frowned. "That could be dangerous if the tonic wears off."

Chess smirked. "I know being so close to my magnificent person might be overwhelming, love, but I promise I won't let my charm out to play."

Alice rolled her eyes. "It's truly amazing."

"What?"

"How you manage to balance yourself with such an enormous head."

Chess laughed, relief flooding his face. "If you're insulting me, I know you're feeling better." He winked and then picked up her satchel. He swung it over his shoulder and headed towards the balcony doors.

Alice turned to Citrine. "Are you coming with us?"

Citrine shook her head. "No, the fewer people sneaking around, the less chance of getting caught. You still have to get in and out of the stables without anyone seeing you."

Alice threw her arms around the other woman and squeezed tight. After a moment, Citrine returned the hug.

"Thank you... for everything." Alice drew back. "You've been a good friend."

Citrine smiled at her but there was a sheen in her eyes. "Remember, if you're not sure which way to go, turn right, and take nothing that the labyrinth doesn't give you."

Alice nodded before Citrine gave her a gentle push. "You need to get going before that tonic wears off."

Alice walked out onto the balcony. Chess had already swung himself over the side and was perched on the trellis, waiting for her.

Now that the moment was here, Alice suddenly realized how high up they were. Grasping the railing with a white-knuckled grip, she climbed over.

Her stomach dropped. She wasn't sure she could peel her fingers from the iron rail. The distance between the edge of the balcony and the trellis wasn't far, maybe two feet, but it felt like two miles. She glanced down at the ground far below and swallowed.

"It's all right, love. I won't let you fall." Chess held out his hand.

Alice screwed up her courage. A measly two feet wouldn't defeat her. With a deep breath, she reached for him with one hand and flung herself at the white lattice. His grip held steady, and her free hand bit into the wood, crushing a vine beneath her palm.

For a moment, Alice closed her eyes and clung to the trellis and tried to calm her breathing. When she opened her eyes, Citrine was leaning over the railing. A new thought made her pause.

"Won't Zander be angry with you?"

Citrine's eyes narrowed and her expression hardened. "Don't you worry about me. I can handle the prince."

The spark in the other woman's eyes made Alice wonder if she should be concerned for Zander instead.

Chess had let go of her hand and climbed down several feet.

"We need to go."

She nodded and gripped the wood with both hands.

As if reading her mind, he called up. "Just reach for the next foothold. It's almost like using a ladder."

She eased her right foot from its spot and stretched her toe downward. It didn't take long to find the next opening. Her chest loosened.

Chess reached the bottom and dropped the last three or four feet to the ground.

Before Alice could worry about doing the same, he grasped her waist, and swung her down next to him.

Together, they ran for the stables.

Chapter 18

CHESS STOPPED ALICE AS the stables came into view. They had to walk across a courtyard exposing them to anyone who cared to look.

Fortunately, that was an easy problem to solve. "I'm going to make us invisible now."

"But it looks deserted," Alice whispered.

Chess lifted a shoulder. "Better safe than sorry, love." He held out his hand.

After a slight hesitation, Alice took it. He'd think about the warm tingle that caused later. They both shimmered out of view.

He led her across the courtyard. His muscles loosened as they stepped into the stable, and he slid the door shut behind them, closing them into darkness.

When he let go of Alice's hand, she shimmered back into view. She frowned and touched her temple.

Concern niggled at him. "Are you all right?"

She nodded, but her face was pale. She waved her hand. "Why are we standing here? We need to go," she said, her tone sharp.

Chess peered at her more closely. In the dim light, a faint sheen of perspiration dotted her forehead.

"All right, come on then," he said.

He led the way down the center aisle to his mare, Luna. She recognized his step and stuck her dappled silver head over her stall door, whickering a greeting.

Alice moved to the horse and put a hand on her nose. "What a pretty girl you are." The horse blew softly against her hand, and Alice smiled.

She patted the mare's neck while she spoke. "Who am I riding?"

He frowned. "I told you, it'll be easier if we ride together, less chance of being spotted."

She looked at him over her shoulder. "Why don't I believe that's the real reason?"

He grinned. "Hey, I..."

A creak froze them both. A slice of light beamed into the darkness.

"Blast," Chess hissed. He grabbed Alice's hand and jerked her into an empty stall. Pulling her towards the back corner, he spoke against her ear. "Don't say a word."

Alice scowled at him.

A cheery whistle pierced the gloom, and his hope withered that it was only a groom fetching a horse for a departing guest. The stables brightened as the person lighted several lanterns.

He grasped Alice's hand again and pulled his invisibility over them both.

Alice's lips grazed his ear. "Who is it?"

"Probably a groom."

Beside him, Alice shivered. He didn't bother to ask if she was all right. He already knew she'd say she was fine.

Even if she wasn't.

Still, this could take a while. She didn't need to use up energy she didn't have. He gently tugged at her hand and slid down the wall. She followed him until they both sat on a mound of clean straw.

The minutes ticked by and still the person continued moving around. The whistling came closer and stopped outside Luna's stall. He held his breath, and Alice stiffened next to him. He squeezed her hand.

"What's you doing with your stall half open, Luna?" It was a youthful voice, and Chess recognized the new stable boy. He couldn't remember his name.

Great. The kid was one of those earnest types who wanted to prove what a good worker he was.

Another shiver passed over Alice, and the wood vibrated as her head fell back against it. Real fear pricked at him now. What if she didn't make it?

The top of the stall closed and the clank of the latch being set interrupted the dark spiral of his thoughts. Alice's body slumped against his. He willed the boy to move back down the aisle so he could see her face.

Instead, the kid peeked around the doorway, confirming Chess was right. It *was* the new stable boy.

He still couldn't come up with his name.

The boy glanced around, his eyes checking the stall. His gaze paused on the corner in which they huddled. Chess held his breath, pushing out his invisibility bubble.

Finally the kid nodded and withdrew. Chess sagged, and Alice's cheek pressed against his shoulder. Although he certainly didn't mind if Alice wanted to use his shoulder as a pillow, he'd give anything for one of her tart remarks.

He let go of her hand, and she shimmered back into view. He frowned. Two hectic spots of color flamed high on each cheekbone. Her eyes were closed, and the pulse at the base of her throat beat erratically. This was not good.

He nudged her, and her eyes slitted open. "I need you to stay with me, Alice," he said, his voice soft but insistent.

"I just want to rest. A little longer." Her eyes slid shut again.

He pulled back the collar of her shirt to check the red lines, afraid of what he'd see. Before he could get a good look, her eyes popped opened again. She pushed his hand away. "Watch yourself."

He couldn't help smirking. "Don't worry, love, I'm only checking your curse lines."

That woke her up a bit. She struggled upright. "Is it bad?"

He forced a smile. "You're not ready to cock up your toes yet."

Her body sagged against him, and her eyelids fluttered shut again.

His smile drained away. They were running out of time. They had to get out of these stables soon or she wouldn't make it. He'd never been the type to wait around, anyway. It could be hours before the boy bagged it in for the night.

"I'll be right back. Sit tight." Chess pushed to his feet and pulled his invisibility around himself. He crept out of the stall and up the aisle.

Movement came from the tack room, and of course, the whistling. He slid into the tiny room. Guilt warred with necessity. He didn't want to hurt the lad, but they had to leave or Alice might die in that stall.

He slipped behind the boy, who stopped whistling and stiffened.

"Who's..." Before the kid could turn, Chess wrapped his arm around his neck and squeezed.

It only took a few seconds for his body to go limp. Chess loosened the pressure and eased the boy onto the ground. He snatched a blanket and tucked it under the kid's head. He probably wouldn't even have a headache when he woke up.

Chess didn't waste any time. He grabbed his own tack and jogged back up the aisle. When he checked on Alice, she lay slumped over on the straw.

Not good. Urgency made his fingers clumsy as he saddled his mare and then slipped the bridle over her head.

He led the horse out of her stall. She stood patiently as he went in and shook Alice's shoulder. She blinked up at him, her face flushed.

"Up we go." He pulled her to her feet, and she swayed.

He looked from her to the horse. She could barely stand on her own, never mind get into the saddle.

Not sure what else to do, he scooped Alice up in his arms and strode over to where his horse stood patiently.

"Hey." She poked him in the chest. "I can walk."

"I know, love, but we're rather in a hurry."

He bunched the reins in one hand, almost drop-ping Alice's legs in the process. Fortunately, Luna was sweet-natured, and she didn't balk at having her sleep interrupted for an impromptu nighttime ride. She am-bled beside him as he walked to the mounting block and positioned herself next to it and waited even after he draped the reins over her neck.

Once up on the block, Chess jostled Alice and her eyes slitted open. "You need to wake up, love. We need to get you onto Luna."

He lifted her onto the horse's back, but Alice needed his help to get her leg over the horse's back so she could sit forward. Once in the saddle, she swayed alarmingly. He quickly swung himself up and got settled behind her before she tipped over the side. Wrapping one arm round her waist, he pulled her against him. She stiffened her body in an effort to avoid touching him.

"I told you I could ride," she said.

Chess frowned. The words she probably meant to snap came out in a weak slur.

He reached around her and gathered the reins in one hand. "Maybe, but we don't have time for me to scrape you up off the ground if you're wrong."

"But..."

He shook his head, a smile lurking on his face. "Always the last word with you."

He squeezed his mare's sides, and they moved away from the block. Once they cleared the courtyard, he urged his mare into a ground-eating canter.

He only hoped they would reach the labyrinth in time.

Chapter 19

THE SCENERY BLURRED BY as if Alice was in a dream—not asleep, but not awake either. The pain in her head kept time with the horse's hooves, and flames licked past her shoulder and onto her chest.

Strangely, her hands and feet felt numb. She tried to sit up straight, but her body wouldn't cooperate. She slumped back against Chess, her head tucked under his chin.

Mother would be horrified, but Alice found she didn't have enough energy to care.

She attempted to pay attention to her surroundings. The stars kept moving this way and that, and her eyelids felt so heavy.

Something tickled her ear. She struggled to move away but her head refused obey.

Then someone called her name.

She blinked her eyes open.

Chess's face swam into view.

"Alice, we're here."

Dumbly, she nodded, and the world tilted. She latched onto something silky. Muscles flinched and bunched under her hands, and she ran one hand over the material.

A chuckle sounded above her head. "I need you to focus, Alice."

"Mm-hmm." Her tongue stuck to the roof of her mouth.

"We're right outside the labyrinth. I can't get any closer unless I ride inside, and I doubt that would work. Do you think you can walk a few feet?"

She patted the firm muscles again. "This is nice. You can carry me."

Again the velvety chuckle. "As much as I enjoy sweeping you off your feet, love, I'm pretty sure you have to walk in there under your own steam."

Alice frowned. Before she could agree or disagree, he set her on her feet. Her knees buckled, and an arm came around her waist and held her upright.

"Easy there. Let's give you a minute to get your bearings."

The world swung crazily, and her heart pounded in her chest.

Finally, things settled.

She looked around. A giant hedge reached towards the sky. It ran in either direction until it was out of view. In front of her, a square opening beckoned.

When she lifted her face, Chess's face was only inches away. He smiled at her in an encouraging way, but his eyes clouded and his brow furrowed.

She tried to smile, but her lips felt strange. His expression pinched. "Are we going in there?" She pointed, and her arm felt like lead.

He nodded. "Yes, we are. I'll help you, but you have to walk on your own."

Alice stared at the labyrinth, and clarity pierced the fog in her brain. Determination settled over her shoulders.

She moved one leg forward. It felt like a weight was tied around her ankle. Chess's arm held her steady.

Sweating, she took one step after another, her legs getting heavier as she went. It was only a few yards, but halfway there she stopped, panting.

"You have to keep going." Chess's voice turned urgent.

Gritting her teeth, Alice moved forward again.

Finally, they reached the entrance. She stepped through and met resistance. The air stretched and then popped.

They were through.

Alice fell to her knees, and Chess knelt beside her. Her eyes found his. "I made it. I'm the champion."

He grinned. "Yes, you are."

She wanted to thank him for his help, but her vision telescoped inward.

Then everything went black.

When she awoke, it was still dark, but twinkling lights spanned far above her.

The first thing she noticed was the blissful absence of pain. Her headache had disappeared, the flames on her arm extinguished. Her heart beat in its normal rhythm again.

Something tickled her palms, and she realized it was grass. She was lying on the ground, a soft bundle under her head.

Her gaze roamed until it snagged on someone lounging next to her—Chess. When he realized she was awake, a big smile washed over his face.

"You're back, love." His voice sounded raspy. "I won't lie. I wasn't sure we had made it in time."

She pushed herself into a sitting position, and he steadied her with an arm against her back. "Don't rush. You were in pretty bad shape when we got here."

She remembered crossing into the labyrinth, falling to her knees, and then nothing else. The entrance hadn't changed, but branches boxed them in on the other three sides.

"I don't remember it looking like this when we got in here."

Chess lifted a shoulder. "The labyrinth apparently doesn't want us cheating."

She scrunched her nose, and he continued, "After you passed out, the walls moved on their own. We can't go anywhere until they move back."

Alice rubbed her arms. "That's not creepy at all."

"The more important thing is, how are you feeling?" Chess picked up her hand and pulled up her sleeve.

They both looked at her wrist. The tattoo had faded, the skin around the markings reverting to its normal shade of ivory. No streaks marred her arm. A tight knot loosened in Alice's chest. She drew up her knees and pressed her forehead against them.

"What's wrong now?" Chess's voice held alarm.

She blinked back tears and lifted her face. "I'm relieved is all. I thought I was going to—"

"Don't say it." Chess smile was crooked. "You didn't, and you're fine now."

Alice pushed to her feet and brushed off her trousers. Chess rose too and stretched his arms over his head. He bent over and picked it up his leather coat that had served as her pillow. He shook it out before shrugging into it.

He nudged her satchel, which sat in the grass.

"I hope you have everything."

She smiled. "With the amount of items Citrine shoved into that, I should be good for a fortnight, at least."

She resisted the urge to straighten her hair and instead gestured towards his mare, who was munching grass out on the green. "You should probably go. It's better if Zander doesn't realize you helped me."

Chess's mouth quirked. "He'll put two and two together."

Alice smiled. "But if you leave, he won't have any proof."

He laughed. Then he reached out and hooked a curl behind her ear. Flustered, she dropped her gaze to the grass.

There was a beat of awkward silence, and she pulled her coat more tightly around herself. "You should go, but I... Thank you, Chess. I couldn't have gotten in here on my own." She shifted.

"I'm sure you would have figured something out, love. You always seem to land on your feet, and you know I'm an expert on that particular skill."

Alice ducked her head. "I don't know about that." She made a face. "I just hope this works, and I don't lose Zander's Kingdom for him."

He drew his knuckle down the side of her face, and she jerked her head up. The smile playing around his mouth wasn't his usual cocky grin. "The champion is supposed to be you, Alice, and I think the labyrinth knows it." His smile widened. "Besides, you're tougher than you look. You'll get that crown, love." He leaned down and pressed a kiss to her cheek.

Heat bloomed across her face, and the words she was going to say stuck in her throat.

He straightened and winked. "For luck." He waved a hand. "You should get some rest while you can. You aren't going anywhere tonight."

With these parting words, he strode towards the entrance. When he stepped through, the view beyond stretched and warped. He made it just past the hedge.

Then he bounced backward.

He landed on his backside and skidded a few feet.

Chess scrambled up, dusting off the seat of his trousers, and tried again with the same result.

They stared at each other, and Chess ran a hand through his hair. "Well, that puts a spanner in the spokes, doesn't it?"

Chapter 20

CITRINE STOOD OUTSIDE OF Zander's door. She smoothed her linen shirt, double-checking the ends were tucked into her trousers. The corridor was quiet and still. The sun hadn't rose yet, but dawn wasn't far off. Somewhere in the bowels of the palace, the staff was already up, but none of them would reach these corridors for another hour or so.

If she turned around now, nobody would even know she'd been here. Before the idea fully formed in her mind, she berated herself for cowardice.

She was doing him a kindness. It would be a hundred times worse if he went out to the labyrinth, only to find Alice was already in there. She pushed up her spectacles and straightened her shoulders. Yes, this was the most logical decision.

She lifted her hand and knocked firmly.

There was silence, then rustling and a creak.

A moment later, Zander opened the door, looking rumpled in his robe and pajama trousers.

When he saw her, he tensed. "Citrine? Is there something wrong?"

Citrine averted her gaze from the triangle of bare chest visible where his robe gapped.

She cleared her throat. "Oh, no. Sorry, I..." She gestured towards his room. "I need to speak with you."

He rubbed a hand over his eyes and yawned. "Can it wait?" He gestured to his robe. "I'm not exactly ready for company."

Her cheeks heated. "Of course, please, get dressed. I'll just wait here."

He hesitated and then shut the door. Citrine leaned back against the wall. She should go check in with Chess after this. Make sure Alice had arrived safely. She had been in very poor condition when the two had left. Citrine bit her lip. Surely, if something had happened, Chess would have told her, no matter how late it was. Or at least he'd have told Zander. That brought her thoughts back to the present. She drummed her fingers against her thigh, wishing this conversation was already over. Zander would be angry. There was no way around that, but hopefully, he'd see...

The door opened again. This time Zander wore a loose shirt and trousers. He'd obviously been in a hurry because pieces of his hair stuck out at odd angles. After looking up and down the hallway, he waved her inside. Her eyes traveled over the room, noting the neatly made bed and the fire crackling in the hearth.

Then she studied him but saw no signs of the curse's effects. This baffled her. It stood to reason if Alice had been struggling so much last night, Zander should have been in similar straits. Although, she didn't know how the trap was affecting him. His room held no clues.

"Citrine, you said you wanted to speak to me."

She started, and her face warmed. She'd been wool-gathering. "Oh, right." She tilted her head. "How are you feeling?"

Zander's face crinkled in confusion. "I'm fine, but... You came to ask me how I'm feeling?"

She lowered herself to perch on the edge of the settee and clasped her hands together. "No, that's not why I'm here, but I'm glad to hear you're doing well. I was afraid, since Alice was feeling so poorly, that you'd also—"

Zander lowered himself into a chair but popped up again. "Is Alice all right? I should have sent for the priest last night."

"Zan—"

He hit a fist against his thigh. "I shouldn't have listened to her and now—"

"Zander!"

He stopped pacing and turned. She gestured towards the chair opposite her. "Alice is fine." At least she didn't have any evidence to the contrary. "Could you please sit down and stop looming over me?"

Zander dropped to the edge of the seat, his body tense and his face expectant.

Now that he was listening, she wasn't sure how to begin. She supposed it was like a bandage. Better to get it done quickly than drag it out.

She squeezed her hands together. "I wanted to tell you..." The words stuck in her throat.

He watched her. His expression puzzled. Then his face cleared, and he gave her a warm smile.

Zander leaned forward and placed his hand over her knotted ones. "This is hard for both of us. I always hoped—that is, I've always been an optimist about our future." He squeezed her hands. "Just because I'm marrying Alice doesn't mean my feelings for you have changed, but I have to put them aside—for both our sakes."

She blinked at him. Why in the world was he bringing that up? Then, realization dawned. She pulled out of his grasp.

"You've misunderstood my purpose. I didn't come here to…" She straightened her shoulders. "I came to tell you that Alice is in the labyrinth. I thought it best if you found out now rather than in front of an audience."

His mouth opened and closed and then opened again. "You can't be serious."

She pushed to her feet and walked over to the mantel. "I am, and"—she looked him square in the eyes—"I helped her."

"You what?" He shot to his feet. "Do you realize what you've done?"

She tilted her head. "Why would you ask me that? I never do anything without thinking it through first."

A flush crawled up his neck and onto his cheeks, and his mouth tightened. "Is this about us? Did you do this to prevent me from marrying someone else?"

"Of course not," she snapped. "It would hardly make sense for me to break our engagement, and then protest if you married someone else."

He ran his hands through his hair and paced back and forth. "How could you do this to me? I'm going be a laughingstock to everyone in Wonderland." He flung out a hand. "The guests will be here for my wedding in only a few hours, but there won't be a bride."

Citrine pursed her lips. "Why do you think I came to see you so early?" Really, he could be so obtuse sometimes. "Besides, you can simply say you changed your mind. There's no way for anyone to disprove that."

Zander frowned. "You act as if it will be as easy as snapping my fingers. And what about the Queen? She'll use this to her advantage somehow."

Citrine shrugged. "Does it really matter at this point? She's been threatening you all along. I heard what she said at the ball."

"It's this blasted Drifter Gene." His hands curled into fists. "I wish I could just get rid of it. All it's ever done is cause problems." He began pacing again. "Of course, it doesn't matter because I'm going to lose the crown, anyway. If Lyssandra wasn't the one to get it, I'd say it might even be better that way."

She rolled her eyes. "Now you're just being needlessly morose."

He stopped and whirled towards her. "I suppose Chess was involved in this too." It wasn't a question.

Citrine pressed her lips together. She couldn't bring herself to outright lie to Zander, but at the same time, there was still a chance Chess's involvement would go unnoticed.

"Your silence is answer enough." He gave a bark of laughter that held no humor. "That's just perfect. The two people I trust most in the world are the ones who went behind my back to ensure I'll lose my Kingdom."

Citrine folded her arms. "We aren't betraying you. We're trying to help you because we care."

He glowered at her. "Explain to me how forfeiting my crown to the Queen shows how you both care so much."

"You're getting ahead of yourself. Alice has a good chance of winning."

Zander pinched the bridge of his nose and visibly struggled to calm his emotions.

"Zander, I know you're upset." He glared at her, but she continued. "However, if you married Alice you'd both be miserable."

His head came up and his eyes burned. "You don't know that. Alice is beautiful, and she's a good person. We could have made it work."

Citrine shook her head. "Even if she had wanted this, she isn't familiar with Wonderland or its politics. If you'd just look past your fears, you'd see this is for the best—for both of you."

He loomed over her again, his face twisting into an ugly smile. "Are you sure this is only about Alice? You don't want me, but maybe you don't want anyone else to have me either."

Hurt shimmered off of him, and she bit back the retort that hovered on her tongue. "Zander, I'm sorry we hurt you, but you left us no choice. You wouldn't listen to anything anyone said."

Zander slammed his fist on the mantel. "Because we'll all be dead if Lyssandra gets the crown." His voice choked. "Don't think you'll be safe, either. She'll come after you and all your precious creatures, too."

Citrine put a hand on his arm. The muscles bunched under her fingers, but he didn't pull away. "The Queen's not going to win. The labyrinth isn't what everyone thinks it is. The Key Book explained how it works, and it isn't about strength—at least not the physical kind. Alice has as good a chance of winning as the Commander or Chess or Leander for that matter."

A flicker of hope flared in his eyes, but then his expression shuttered. "Even if that's true, she's not alone in there. We both know Leander won't play fair, and he'll eliminate her if he gets the chance. I thought you were her friend, too."

Citrine squeezed his arm and let her hand drop. "I understand why you're concerned, but you have to remember, the labyrinth has a mind of its own. It won't allow him to cheat."

Zander turned and put his back to the fire. "Leander has the same Flora Gift as his sister. Surely, he'll be able to manipulate a bunch of leaves and vines, even if they are sentient."

"You're underestimating the labyrinth's power."

"I can't afford to *over*estimate it." He raised his eyebrows. "What if this was the Pearl Kingdom? Would you gamble all those precious creatures of yours on thought and supposition?"

Citrine stiffened. "This is different."

"No, it's not." When he spoke, his tone was bitter. "You should understand putting your Kingdom over your feelings. You were quick enough to do it in our situation."

His words clattered against her heart. "Zander..."

"No, I don't want to hear your reasons again. You've been plain enough, but I thought you'd understand what I had to do. I never dreamed you'd have any hand in humiliating and betraying me this way." He turned away from her.

She grasped his sleeve. "You didn't leave time for another choice."

He whirled back and stared into her face. His body vibrated with anger, but she didn't back away.

"There's always a choice, Citrine. If you'd made a different one, I wouldn't even be in this situation."

Her mouth opened as the words drove the breath from her lungs.

He moved to the door and opened it. "You should go home. I have a lot of things to see to. Someone has to clean up this mess." He gave a bitter smile. "Besides, I'm sure you have your own responsibilities to take care of, and I wouldn't want to keep you from them."

When she got to the door, she paused to look up at him. His face was stony. "Zander..."

"Just leave. You've done enough."

Without another word, Citrine slipped out of the room. The door clicked shut behind her, leaving her alone in the hallway.

Chapter 21

SOMETHING WOKE ALICE. SHE blinked open her eyes. The sun was up, but it was still early. She pushed herself into a sitting position and stretched her neck. Her satchel didn't make a good pillow.

She looked around for Chess. He sat with his back against the hedge, his chin propped on one hand, clearly still asleep. Alice guessed he wasn't the one who had woken her up.

The labyrinth still boxed them in, and a haze hung over the green, visible through the entrance. Alice reached out and tried to put her hand through the space. It stretched forward and then bounced her arm back. She hadn't planned to change her mind, but knowing she couldn't made it difficult to draw in a deep breath.

A soft wheeking broke the stillness. Her eyes searched the shadows to find the source of the sound. A bright spot of color squeezed out from beneath a corner of shrubbery. Alice squinted but couldn't identify the creature. It was tiny, probably not much bigger than her palm. She eased forward, and the small animal scuttled backward. After a moment, it peeked out at her again.

Alice smiled, but otherwise kept perfectly still. "Hello there." It crept out further. "It's all right. I won't hurt you." It took a few more steps. She could see it more clearly now and was enchanted.

Slightly larger than a hedgehog, it had fluffy, bright-turquoise fur covering its body. Enormous dark eyes, just visible under a fringe of hair, blinked up at her.

"Aren't you the most darling thing?"

The little creature chirped and squeaked. The word *Wickle* floated into Alice's mind. Her smile broadened. "Is that your name? Wickle?" she asked.

The animal gave a small hop. Alice glimpsed tiny clawed feet. It cheeped excitedly, and Alice swallowed a laugh as she heard, *Yes, yes, yes*.

"Well, it's nice to meet you, Wickle."

The tiny animal, apparently having lost its fear, scuttled over to Alice. She reached out a tentative finger and ran it over the downy-soft fur. Wickle trilled and hopped onto Alice's lap.

Alice laughed. "I guess we're going to be friends then."

As if in answer, Wickle snuggled against her leg. She stroked the animal and within moments, its eyelids grew heavy. Soon, it was breathing out tiny snores.

The rustle of branches told her Chess was awake, but she didn't want to disturb her new friend, so she remained quiet.

Chess reached his arms over his head and stretched.

"Good morning," he said. "It looks like the games haven't yet begun."

Alice put her fingers to her lips. "Sshhh." Then she pointed at her lap.

"What do you have..." He froze. His eyes glued to the turquoise ball of fluff.

"Isn't he cute?" She grinned at him.

Chess didn't return her smile. Instead, his eyes flew around the square of grass before he spoke. His voice was a hoarse whisper. "Where did *that* come from?"

Alice shrugged. "I don't know. It was hiding in the hedge when I woke up." She rubbed at her forehead. "Actually, I think this little guy woke me up. He said his name is Wickle."

Chess let out a strangled laugh. "It told you its name?" He scooted further away from her. "Alice, do you know what that is?"

She shook her head, confused. She ran a light hand over the creature, and it twittered in its sleep. Chess's eyes almost bugged out his head.

"Don't touch it."

Alice scowled. "What's your problem? It's darling and completely harmless."

"My problem is the thing in your lap may be 'darling' but it's certainly not harmless." Chess ran a shaking hand over his face. "That's a snark, and while it might be small, it's very poisonous." He glanced around the square again. "They usually aren't alone. They live in hives." He looked up into the greenery and shuddered. "One is highly poisonous, but a swarm can decimate anything in its path, including the both of us."

Alice stared at him, and then looked down at the sleeping ball of fluff. "You're having one over on me," she said. "He's so friendly and sweet."

Chess huffed out a breath. "I don't know what witchery you used, but they aren't normally friendly at all.

Generally, they avoid people, and they get irritated if you disturb them or their nests." He shuddered again.

Alice couldn't wrap her mind around what he was telling her. Wickle seemed so harmless. As if he sensed they were talking about him, he blinked open his big eyes and looked at her sleepily. His small mouth opened in an enormous yawn, giving Alice a glimpse of oversized fangs that glistened in the morning light. A cold chill ran down her spine.

He unrolled himself and stood up before he froze, staring up at Chess. He hissed. Chess nearly jumped into the hedge, his head swiveling around.

Alice cupped a hand over the snark's back and spoke softly. "It's all right, Wickle. This is Chess. He's a friend. He won't hurt you."

Wickle let out several clicks and chirps. *Friend?*

Alice nodded. "Yes, he's a friend." The creature shook itself like a minuscule dog. Then it hopped off her lap and trotted towards Chess. Chess jumped to his feet and stepped back, keeping a respectful gap between himself and the animal. Alice clapped a hand over her mouth. She shouldn't laugh but couldn't help it. The sight of a grown man backpedaling from a tiny ball of fluff was ridiculous.

Chess glared at her. "Make it go away," he said. "This will be hard enough without bringing a temperamental thing like that along."

Alice bit her tongue her about who the temperamental one was. No use making things worse. She pushed to her feet. Wickle bobbed after her, letting out a series of alarmed cheeps.

No leave. Scared. Alone.

Her heart gave a pang, and she bent over, holding out her hand. Wickle leapt onto her palm and scrambled up her arm, his tiny claws pricking, and tucked himself into the pocket of her shirt, only his head still visible.

"You can't— That's—" Chess waved at Wickle, his eyes wide.

Alice lifted her chin. "I don't know what snarks are normally like, but Wickle is all by himself. He needs us. If he'd wanted to hurt me, he had plenty of opportunity while I was sleeping." She tickled the little creature under its furry chin. He gave a series of squeaks and rubbed against her fingers.

Chess shook his head. "Just keep it away from me."

Alice rolled her eyes. "I don't think that will be a problem." She squatted and opened her satchel and pulled out a small, wrapped bundle. Opening it, she held out a flat savory cake to Chess. "We should eat while we have the chance. Citrine and her cook packed food, but we'll have to split it."

Chess accepted the cake from her and took a tentative bite, and then he smiled. "Marney is the best. Her cooking never disappoints." Then he frowned. "She wasn't planning on me, though. You should ration this so you have enough."

Alice waved a hand and swallowed. "Hopefully, we won't be in here long enough for it to be a problem."

She looked around and patted a branch. "I wonder when these will move so we can get started."

Chess shrugged. "My guess is when Leander enters." He took another bite and chewed thoughtfully. "I suppose it's a good thing that the labyrinth isn't letting us cheat, so to speak."

Alice rubbed her arms. "I can't decide if that's good or creepy."

The leafy branches around them rustled, and she jumped.

The loud screech of a griffon made her head snap up.

They looked at each other, and then Alice shoved Chess's shoulder. "That's probably Zander. You should hide."

Chess dusted his hands off and pushed to his feet. Then he reached down to pull her up, too. "The time for hiding is over, love. Zander's not stupid. He'll recognize Luna and suspect I've helped you."

"Well, he doesn't know that for sure."

Chess crossed his arms and his eyes glinted. "I'm all for avoiding trouble when I can, but I'm not a liar or a coward either."

"I didn't mean to—" Alice broke off as two griffons landed a few yards from the labyrinth's entrance.

Seeing the thunderous expression on Zander's face, Alice backed up a step and bumped into Chess. His hands squeezed her shoulders. "Steady, love."

Chapter 22

ZANDER'S AND THE COMMANDER'S griffons touched down almost at the same time. Zander took a moment to gather himself. There was still time to salvage things. If he could get Alice out of there before anyone found out, things could go as originally planned.

As he slid off his mount, he caught sight of Chess. All of his good intentions flew from his mind like so much dandelion fluff. He started forward.

The Commander stopped him. "Remember our goal here. You have every right to be angry with both of them, but if this devolves into a shouting match, nobody will win."

Zander gave a sharp nod of his head. "You're right. It's just..." He pressed his lips together.

The Commander let his hand drop from Zander's shoulder. "I know. If you want, I can take care of this on your behalf."

For a brief moment, the offer tempted Zander. He wasn't sure if he could keep his hurt and anger from surfacing. But this was his duty. Princes didn't have the luxury of emotions. "No, I'll be fine."

He strode towards the entrance. He stopped a few feet away from the pair and crossed his arms.

"Both of you, come out right now."

It didn't escape his notice that Chess had his hands on Alice's shoulders or that they were standing close to each other.

Chess stepped around Alice and walked to the very edge of the labyrinth. Less than a yard separated them. "We can't."

"Either you come out, or I'll drag you out. It's your choice."

Chess shrugged. "I suppose you could try."

Zander's muscles tightened. "Don't test me, Chess."

"I'm not trying to be difficult. I'm just stating the facts."

Zander scowled. "Is a pretty face really enough to make you betray me?"

Chess blew out a breath. "That isn't what this is about, and you know it."

"Do I? You went behind my back to sneak her in here, when you *know* what's at stake. What am I supposed to think?"

"You could trust me. Have I ever given you a reason not to?" Chess's expression was carefully neutral.

The lump in Zander's chest threatened to choke him. "Everyone knows you're a half-flit charmer who's biggest concern is his next conquest."

Chess drew his head back, hurt flickering over his features before his expression blanked.

Alice pushed past him and pointed her finger at Zander. "Chess helped me because it was the right thing to do. For *both* of us. It's not his fault you're too pigheaded to listen to reason."

Zander snorted, and her eyes turned stormy. She bit out her words. "I haven't been here that long, but even I can see he's been a good friend to you. He doesn't deserve this." She crossed her arms. "And he was telling the truth. He tried to leave last night, but the labyrinth sealed us both in here." She waved a hand towards the entrance. "If it won't let us out, I don't think it'll let you in either, but you're welcome to try."

"Fine, I will." Zander made it one step inside. The air stretched like a film, and then he bounced out. He stumbled backward into the Commander, who managed to keep them both from falling.

Zander shook his head. "But how..."

Alice narrowed her eyes. "Because the labyrinth is sentient. I've tried to tell you. Citrine's tried to tell you. But you won't listen to anyone."

Heat crawled up his neck, and his defenses rose. "This is still a mistake. You can't win."

Alice jutted out her chin. "Well, I'm in here now, so you better hope you're wrong." She narrowed her eyes. "Or is being right more important to you?"

Her words punched into him. He looked at his boots. "No, of course I want you to win. It's just..." He trailed off. They had been over this ground so many times, he couldn't bring himself to say it all again.

Especially since Alice was already in the labyrinth.

What he thought no longer mattered.

The Commander interceded. "We need to focus on the issue at hand. The competition is set to start in a few hours. If the Queen sees both of you in here, she's going to cry foul." He frowned. "And she might have grounds. There are only supposed to be two champions. I can't imagine having an additional person is in line with the rules."

Chess gestured around them. "The labyrinth seems to have its own ideas about that. It boxed us in here so we couldn't start, and it won't let me out. Surely if it was against the rules, I'd be able to leave."

The Commander tilted his head and the morning sun glinted off its golden waves. "Maybe it's not sure which one of you *is* the champion. Did you go in together?"

Zander saw Alice and Chess exchange glances before she spoke. "I... Chess had to help me." She looked between Zander and the Commander. "I don't think I would have made it on my own."

The Commander tapped a finger on his chin. "That's a possible explanation. Perhaps when Leander enters, whichever one of you starts down the path will be recognized as the champion, and then the other person can leave."

Zander nodded. "But what if it doesn't? What if both of them being in there somehow forfeits the crown?"

Several beats of silence passed before the Commander spoke. "We'll have to wait and see."

It wasn't the answer Zander wanted to hear.

The screech of a griffon broke the morning stillness.

Chess smirked. "The good news is we won't have to wait very long."

The Commander sent him a sharp look. "Stop making jokes and hide yourself."

Chapter 23

DREAD POOLED IN ZANDER'S stomach as the Queen and her brother, along with two of their guards, landed on the green. Had they seen Chess? Would she recognize his horse?

The Queen hopped off her mount and took a moment to scratch the beast's snout while she waited for her brother.

Together, they walked towards the group. Zander wished he could disappear into the wilderness and stay there until this was all over. The responsibility weighed on him, but he squared his shoulders.

"What a surprise to find you all here so bright and early. You didn't start without us, did you?" The Queen's eyes flitted from Zander to Alice. Her mouth curled into a razor-sharp smile. "It appears you've lost your bride. I'm surprised the charming Chess isn't here too." She made a show of looking around.

Zander stiffened, his heartbeat loud in his ears. Did she know? It would be like Lyssandra to toy with him.

He opened his mouth, not sure what he would say, but the Commander put a hand on his arm and stepped forward. He bowed. "Your Majesty, there has been a slight alteration in plans, but it shouldn't affect you or your champion."

Leander gestured towards Alice. "I'm not sure how you can make that claim. First, your champion is already in the labyrinth, and second, she's the wrong one."

The Commander waved a hand towards the hedges that boxed Alice in. "As you can see, she hasn't started yet, and there's nothing that says the prince can't change his mind."

"That doesn't explain why she's already in there." Leander crossed his arms and frowned. "Surely that's against the rules."

"Since she can't start, it really doesn't matter." The Commander's tone was final.

The Queen tilted her head. "But it does beg the question—what happened here?" She wagged a finger between Alice and Zander. "Didn't you two have an enormous ball to celebrate your engagement last night? Don't tell me you had a tiff."

Heat crawled up Zander's neck, and he wanted to disappear. He opened and then closed his mouth. What could he say? Alice *had* run away from him.

Alice spoke into the awkward pause. "We get along perfectly well." She glanced at him. "Of course, I was so flattered to be chosen as the prince's bride. Any girl would count herself lucky to marry him, but after the ball, the prince and I talked. He was very kind, but he made it clear, I'm not prepared for the role of being his wife. He needs someone who understands Wonderland and its citizens." She spread out her arms. "So, we both decided I should be the champion instead."

The Queen studied Alice for a long moment, and then gave a slow clap. "That was an absolutely delightful performance, my dear. You never disappoint." She leaned towards Alice as if confiding in a friend. "But you and I both know our dear prince. He suffers not only from an abundance of chivalry, but an old-fashioned view of females. I find it hard to believe that he would willingly let you risk yourself this way."

"It really doesn't matter what you believe, does it? I don't need your approval to be the prince's champion." Alice smiled sweetly. "I thought we already settled that at your last ball."

The Queen's expression turned ugly for a fleeting moment before smoothing into a smile. "I've always admired your spunk, my dear." She leaned closer, her eyes glittering. "But you must learn when to speak and when to be silent. That old saying that words can never hurt you isn't exactly true. Just ask all the unfortunates who lost their heads."

Zander watched the exchange between the two women. He wished he could talk to Alice without an audience so he could both thank her and warn her.

The rumble of carriage wheels snapped everyone's attention to the other side of the green. The conveyance bounced over the ground until it was a dozen yards away, and then drew to a halt.

For a long moment, nothing happened, and then the door burst open. Judge Foghorn stood in the doorway, a large scroll bundled under one arm, and an ornate wooden box clutched in the opposite hand. He lurched down one step, wobbled, and tumbled out. He landed in a sprawl on the grass, the box underneath him and the scroll unrolling across the ground.

Zander and the Commander hurried over to help him up. Once on his feet, he pulled his arms away and jerked his orange waistcoat down. When he bent to pick up the scroll, his spectacles slid off his nose and dropped to the ground. The Commander scooped up the box.

Silently, everyone watched the judge struggle. Finally, he stood upright, holding the scroll, his glasses firmly perched on his large nose. The Commander offered him the box, but the Judge shook his head, leaving the Commander to carry it.

The Judge scowled at the group. "I don't know why I'm here now when I should be here later, but here I am."

A headache started behind Zander's eyes.

The Commander nodded. "Thank you for coming." He looked at the rest of the group. "I took the liberty of calling the Judge so that we can start the competition. Since everyone is here, there's no reason to delay."

"But what about all the people coming?" Perspiration dampened Zander's back.

The Judge gave a loud harrumph. "I'm here now, and I don't want to be here later, even though I was supposed to be here later but am here now." Seeming to remember who he was talking to, he added in a sulky tone, "Your Highness."

The Queen joined them with her brother. "There's still the matter of your champion," she said.

Zander made his voice firm even though his skin crawled in response to her nearness. "The decision is final."

She raised a blonde eyebrow. "I hope you don't regret it."

Zander swallowed and looked at Alice. He probably would, but he didn't want the Queen to know that.

The Commander turned to Leander. "Are you ready? Or do you need more time?"

Leander patted the long sword at his side and hitched the pack he carried higher on his shoulder. "I'm prepared."

The Commander addressed Judge Foghorn. "Then we should get started."

The Judge peered up at them through his spectacles. "You're sure? Because I don't want to have to come back out here. As I'm already here, and here is not a place I want to be twice."

Everyone nodded.

The Judge took the scroll from under his arm and unrolled it. He had to hold it up high because it was almost as tall as he was.

He cleared his throat. Then he stopped.

"I thought there were two champions."

"There are." Zander pointed towards the labyrinth. "She's already inside."

The Judge frowned. "Tell her to come outside."

"She can't."

"This is highly irregular."

The Commander shrugged. "We should get started."

The Judge tsked loudly and straightened his spectacles. Then he began to speak, his nasally tones echoing over the green.

"Today we gather to witness the Competition of the Crown. Both champions will start at opposite entrances to the Wonderland Labyrinth. At my signal, they shall enter—er, begin. Whomever reaches the center and emerges with the crown first" (here he gestured towards the box that the Commander still held) "shall be the winning champion. If no champion emerges from the labyrinth by the morning of the sixth day the competition will be considered null and void. New champions will be chosen at such time. In the event of disqualification or death, the other champion must still reach the center of the labyrinth and retrieve the crown."

The judge pulled out a large lavender handkerchief and mopped his brow before continuing.

"Will both champions please step forward and place themselves, one at the south entrance and one at the north entrance?" He looked at Alice and frowned. "I guess you, young man, can go to the north entrance, seeing as the young lady is already at this one."

Leander kissed his sister's cheek before striding across the expanse of lawn to take up his place at the north end of the labyrinth.

The Commander reached into his pocket and pulled out a tarnished pocket watch. He handed it to Zander before he unlatched the box in his hands, revealing a gold crown with a small ruby at its center. Zander's throat closed as he looked at the circlet glinting in the early morning light. The last time he'd seen it was at the now infamous ball when Alice had broken the curse that locked him in his jabberwock form. Now she was saving his hide again—or at least she was going to try.

He tore his eyes away and turned his attention to the watch. He flipped the lid open and clicked a button on the side. The watch face folded inward and a miniature brass maze rose. The Commander had told him what he needed to do before they left the palace.

He held it above his head so it was visible to everyone present. "The competition has officially started. The Champion Timepiece has started keeping time. It will let us know when one of the champions has reached the center." He glanced at the Queen. "I'll send a message when that happens."

As Leander entered the labyrinth there was a loud rustling, and the hedges that surrounded Alice folded back, revealing the path. A glow came from the padded interior of the box and pulled Zander's attention away from the champions. The crown inside shimmered and then disappeared from view. The box continued to glow for a few heartbeats before it returned to its normal appearance.

He looked at Alice and their gazes met across the space. She smiled.

He wanted to say something to her, to tell her thank you for covering for him, to say there was still time to change her mind, but the Queen's eyes were watching him. He wouldn't reveal any weakness. He raised his arm in a wave. "May luck go with you."

"I'll get that crown for you," she called back before she turned and disappeared into the labyrinth.

Judge Foghorn rolled up the scroll and snapped his fingers for the box. The Commander handed it to him without comment. The Judge sniffed. "If we're done here, I'm going home. I left a perfectly good breakfast to come out here." He stomped off toward his carriage.

The Commander watched him go and then inclined his head to the Queen. "I'm sure you'd like to return to the Dower House. The prince and I will oversee things from here."

The Queen smiled and patted his arm. "You're always so helpful, Commander."

The Commander nodded and then turned to Zander. "I'll post several men at the entrance to the green. They can turn away any spectators. I also suggest sending out an announcement raven so a crowd doesn't show up."

"Thank you, Commander. If you'll see to that, I would be grateful."

The Commander gave a small bow, and walked over to gather their griffons.

Zander inclined his head to the Queen and turned away, but she put a hand on his arm. He looked down at where her white fingers lay against the dark sleeve of his coat. The muscles in his neck and shoulders tightened. "Yes?"

"I've always liked the girl, but she won't last in the labyrinth."

Zander pulled away. "I don't know, Lyssandra. She's already surprised you once."

The Queen's eyes narrowed. "For your sake, you better hope she doesn't surprise me again."

A surge of anger sparked in Zander's chest. "Don't threaten me. I'm not the callow boy you manipulated a year ago. Alice is going to win that crown, and when she does, you'll pay for what you did to me... and my father."

The Queen chuckled. "I see you do have a spine. Well, good for you, but I can promise you, your subjects won't be impressed with a prince that has the Drifter Gene, no matter how beloved you believe yourself to be." The smile fell from her face, and her mouth twisted into a snarl. "No man will ever have power over me again, not while I still have breath in my body. Your father found that out, and if you're smart, you'd do well to learn from his mistakes."

Before he could respond, she snapped her fingers at the two guards that had accompanied her. "Come along. We need to leave."

She sailed across the lawn to her griffon without looking back. The men trailed in her wake.

A shiver ran up Zander's spine and he locked his knees against their sudden weakness. Even if Alice managed to win, he might still lose.

Chapter 24

CITRINE MADE A SLOW circle around her room to make sure she had forgotten nothing. She jerked her chemise from under the edge of the bed and stuffed it into her bag.

She carefully closed the clasp. She should probably eat some breakfast before she left. She had a long journey ahead of her, but Zander's words played over and over in her mind. A single tear leaked down her cheek. Impatiently, she wiped it away.

How ridiculous to cry. He wasn't even accurate in his accusations. Zander had agreed with her when they broke their engagement. They couldn't both attend their duties in separate places and be together, too. It was monstrously unfair to blame her for the decision they had reached together. Another tear leaked out despite her efforts, and she swiped at her cheek.

Briefly, she considered confronting Zander again, to find out where Chess was, if nothing else. As far as she knew, he hadn't returned yet. Zander's stony expression flashed into her memory. Now probably wasn't the time to bring up Chess. Maybe the curse was still playing havoc with his emotions, making him so pigheaded and foolish and— She caught her wayward thoughts and reeled them back in. This maudlin musing didn't solve anything. She needed to go. Zander had been right about one thing. She'd been gone from the Pearl Palace long enough.

Her creatures needed her.

With one last look at the room, she hefted her bag onto her shoulder and slipped out the door. Once on the first floor, she stopped a young maid.

"Please ask the steward to have my carriage brought around."

The girl bobbed a curtsey and hurried away to do as asked. Citrine leaned against one of the tall marble pillars and closed her eyes.

Despite his recent idiocy, she still wished she could help Zander somehow. Even though he'd never admit it, she knew the Queen's threats frightened him. He bore scars from the past year, which was understandable. What worried her more was that bleak look in his eyes. His normal buoyant spark of optimism had been snuffed out. It was enough to make her commit violence against the Queen. Citrine didn't doubt the horrible woman would use Zander's Gift against him if presented with the opportunity. The question was, would the citizens of Wonderland let her?

She sighed. Of all the Gifts for the Red Prince to have, why the Drifter Gene? And a jabberwock to boot. Too bad you couldn't pick your Gifts.

Suddenly, her eyes flew open. Perhaps you couldn't choose your Gifts, but what if... She whirled toward the front door and nearly plowed into Anders. He hid his surprise behind a low bow.

"Madame, I came to tell you your carriage is ready. I hope you weren't kept—"

"No, not at all," she said, nearly bowling him over in her hurry to reach her carriage.

Anders trailed behind her as she hurried to her carriage and vaulted into the driver's seat.

Ogox turned his massive head up toward her. *Home, Lady Citrine?*

"No, Ogox. We're going to the Hollow. Everyone will have to wait a little longer. I must speak to Sir Lapin."

Chapter 25

As soon as Zander returned to the palace, Anders rushed in, his wispy hair askew. "Your Highness, a few of the Councilmembers are here. I tried to get them to wait in the Meeting Room, but I'm afraid..."

A loud thumping echoed through the entryway. Zander stifled a groan even as Anders spun toward the sound.

"Oh, dear!" Anders hurried to intercept Lord Beecher who was stumping his way toward Zander at a surprisingly swift clip. The old man managed to dart around the steward with more agility than Zander would have credited him with.

His voice reached the prince's ears long before his bulk. "Is it true?" Thump, thump, thump. "When a raven arrived this morning telling me that girl had gone into the labyrinth, I didn't believe it. I had my carriage brought round immediately. I didn't even get any breakfast. How could you let this happen, boy?"

Zander drew himself up. "I understand you're upset, Lord Beecher, but you will address me with respect. I am still the prince."

Beecher pursed his lips. "You may be the King's son, but until this competition is over, you're nothing."

The old man's words stopped Zander in his tracks. He was right—to an extent anyway. With the crown in limbo, the title of *prince* held no genuine power except what the Council granted him. Then his father's lessons stiffened his spine. "Regardless of your feelings, I'm as close to a ruler as there is in Wonderland at the moment." He raised an eyebrow. "Unless you'd like to invite the Queen to step in."

Beecher thumped his cane on the floor. "Don't try to distract me, Sir! I want some answers. Is that Mirror World chit in the labyrinth or not?"

Reluctantly, Zander nodded. "Yes, but after consulting with—"

"I don't care who you consulted with or what that smart-mouthed Duchess has to say, the labyrinth is no place for a girl like that." He leaned forward, his fuzzy eyebrows bristling. "What I want to know is, what are you going to do about it?"

Zander stared at the man, his mind churning. The truth was he didn't have an answer or an excuse. He couldn't very well tell the old grump that his two best friends had conspired against him.

Beecher banged his cane on the floor again, and Zander winced as it left a mark on the marble tile. "Well?"

Zander straightened his shoulders and looked down his nose at the older man. "Lord Beecher, you need to go wait with the others in the Meeting Room. As soon as the Commander returns, I *will* answer everyone's questions. At one time." He tried to make his tone firm and final.

Splotches of red mottled Beecher's face. "I won't be put off. You might think I'm a doddering old fool, but I've been on this Council longer than you've been alive."

Zander attempted to take the man's elbow again and forced himself to smile. "And I'm grateful for your service, Lord Beecher, and the wisdom you've gleaned over the years, but you still need to wait with the rest of the Council."

Beecher yanked away from Zander. The force almost overbalanced him, and he tottered before steadying himself with his cane. "I'm too old to fall for your flattery." He straightened his waistcoat. "I can see I won't get any answers from you, probably because you don't have any." He jutted out his chin, one long hair waving from its end. "If your father were here, none of this would have happened. He wouldn't have let some slip of a girl get one over on him."

Zander reached for him the third time, but Beecher evaded his grasp. He gripped his cane with both hands, and his chest heaved with emotion. "Your father was a fine man and a good leader. He would be ashamed of you."

Zander pinched the bridge of his nose, and reminded himself that Lord Beecher had been a bully long before Zander's time. His father had called the old man a thorn in his side for as long as Zander could remember. "I'm only going to ask you one more time, Lord Beecher. Please go to the Meeting Room with everyone else. Once the Commander—"

"Yes, yes, I know. You'll answer all my questions." He harrumphed and shook a gnarled finger under Zander's nose. "I know you're just going to come up with some cockamamie excuse with that uncle of yours. Heaven knows, we'd all have been better off if he'd been named the King. At least he has some sense. First, you get yourself cursed and almost killed, and now you've as good as lost the crown."

Zander stood stoic as the words rained down on him. He tried to tamp down his temper, but some of it must have shown through. When he opened his mouth to speak, Beecher waved his cane. "I'm going. I'm going, but don't think I'm happy about it."

"As if anyone would make that mistake," Zander muttered.

Beecher stopped and cocked his head, but after a brief pause, he turned and thumped toward the Meeting Room, muttering and harrumphing until he was out of sight.

Once the man had disappeared down the hallway, Zander rubbed at his forehead. This day kept getting worse and worse. He needed some quiet to put his thoughts into order and figure out what he was going to say to the Council.

He turned to address his steward, who stood nearby wringing his hands. "Anders, tell the Commander to come to my study when he arrives. I need to talk to him before I address the Council."

Anders bowed. "Of course, Your Highness." He paused. "Shall I send refreshments to the Meeting Room?"

A trickle of relief soothed Zander's frayed nerves. "That's an excellent idea. Thank you."

"I'll see to it immediately, Your Highness." Anders bowed his head before he whisked away.

Zander's shoulders sagged as he walked in the opposite direction toward his study. Lord Beecher might be ruder than most, but Zander had a sinking feeling that the man was only saying out loud what everyone else was too polite to say to his face.

Chapter 26

Zander dropped into the chair in his study, a wave of weariness washing over him. Between his best friend betraying him, his bride-to-be jilting him, the Queen threatening him, and now having to deal with the Council, it had been a long day.

And it wasn't even noon yet.

He sighed. He had no idea what he should tell the Council. If Alice lost, which seemed likely, would they put the Queen on the throne? Even after all she'd done? Surely, they would bring her to justice for her crimes.

Zander leaned his head against his chair, grateful for these moments of blessed silence. Once the Commander returned, he'd have to clean up the mess this day had become. He flipped open the Champion Timepiece. The color had changed since he'd opened it earlier. A section of the outer ring on either side had turned to gold, showing the champions' progress. Citrine would love to see this.

He snapped the watch shut and squeezed it until the metal edges bit into his hand. Another thing he'd messed up in a long succession of screw-ups. He should apologize, but she'd probably already left. After the way he had spoken to her, he didn't blame her.

But the idea of losing her friendship, after everything else, almost undid him. He needed to fix this. He opened a desk drawer and pulled out a piece of heavy paper. As he reached for his fountain pen, someone knocked.

His entire body tensed. It was probably the Commander. He still wasn't ready to face the Council. He let his hand fall. It didn't matter. This was his responsibility.

"Come in," he said.

He was surprised to see Anders poke his head around the door.

Zander raised his eyebrows. "Are you having more problems with Lord Beecher?"

The steward shook his head. "No, Your Highness, but Baron Belier has arrived and wishes an audience with you."

"Didn't you tell him I was busy?" Zander immediately felt guilty for snapping at his steward. "I'm sorry. None of this is your fault, Anders."

"It's of no consequence, Your Highness. I am only regretful I couldn't persuade him that you were not available." The steward frowned. "He said he'd wait for however long it takes, but he will see you—one way or the other."

The weight on Zander's shoulders pressed downward, and he wondered at what point he'd no longer be able to bear it. He rubbed at the spot between his eyes and tried to think.

The Baron was from the Northern Estates. He should have expected that with the death of Renard, the other landowners up there would be unsettled. He sighed at his own shortsightedness. How had his father kept up with everything? He wished the King was still around to ask.

This had nothing to do with Alice and the labyrinth, but the timing was rotten.

He looked up at Anders who waited for his orders. "Put him in one of the guest rooms and tell him I'll get to him as soon as I am able."

Anders nodded. "I'll make sure he is comfortable, Your Highness."

Zander thought he saw pity in the steward's eyes, and heat crept up his neck and into his face. If he disappeared and they managed to defeat the Queen, the crown would go to his uncle. He would be a better ruler than Zander ever could. It had only been a little over a year since his father's death, and already he was on the verge of losing the Kingdom.

Beecher was right. His father would be ashamed of him and the way he'd messed everything up. He couldn't even get Alice to marry him, and he was a prince, for goodness' sake!

He lowered his head to his desk, the wood cool against his forehead. There were only two people he wanted to talk to. One was in the labyrinth helping his fiancée, and the other one probably never wanted to speak to him again because he'd been so nasty to her.

Despite this, he had a sudden desperate need to see Citrine. Her calm, logical perspective never failed to clear the confusion from his brain. She'd know what to tell the Council.

He stood and called out to Anders. The man reappeared in the doorway as if he'd been waiting just outside.

"Your Highness? Did you require something else?"

"Anders, did the Pearl Queen leave yet?" Zander held his breath. It had been hours since she'd come to his room.

The steward nodded. "Quite a while ago, Your Highness."

Zander exhaled, his shoulders slumping.

He was too late.

Unless... No, he shouldn't just ignore all his responsibilities. The Council was waiting on him and so was Baron Belier. He had a duty to deal with these things.

He couldn't simply leave.

Could he?

Zander did some rough calculations in his mind. If she had taken her carriage, he might be able to catch up to her on Verros. The griffon was far faster than her gargoyles, and she'd have to stop to rest them along the way.

He ignored the guilt that gnawed at his conscience. It would only be for a little while, and besides, Lord Beecher could jolly well wait until Zander decided to talk to him. Maybe then the old goat would realize he wasn't in charge. Hadn't his father told him making someone wait was a good strategy to gain the upper hand?

He'd only be gone a few hours, the afternoon, at most. He'd apologize, and Citrine could help him with how to handle the Council.

His mind made up, Zander strode toward the door. "Have someone saddle Verros for me."

Anders' eyebrows climbed toward his hairline, but his tone was mild when he asked, "What shall I tell the Commander if he asks for you when he returns?"

The question brought Zander up short, and he wavered. He should really stay here and put out the fires that were blazing in his Kingdom right now.

Then Beecher's thumping cane and harsh words echoed in his mind.

No, he needed to talk with Citrine. She'd help him.

"Tell him I've gone on an important errand. I'll be back when I'm done."

Anders bowed. "As you wish, Your Highness."

He backed toward the door, but Zander stopped him. "And tell the Council to go home. When I have answers for them, I'll call for them."

The steward's Adam's apple bobbed in his throat. "I don't want to question you, Your Highness, but—"

"Then don't!" Zander snapped. He refused to feel guilty about the stricken look on Anders' face.

The steward bowed his head and hurried toward the door, but then paused. "Your Highness might find it of interest that the Pearl Queen did not head home."

Zander stopped mid-stride. "She didn't?"

"No, Your Highness. I believe she said she was going to the Hollow."

Zander cocked his head. "The Hollow?"

Anders nodded. "She seemed in rather a hurry, Your Highness."

"Thank you, Anders."

The steward gave another bob of his head and disappeared down the hallway.

As Zander walked briskly toward the stables his mind churned. Lapin Blanc was the only person he could think of that Citrine would be visiting there. The question was, why?

Chapter 27

THE WHEELS OF CITRINE's carriage bumped down on the uneven ground on the grassy knoll. Lapin's cozy burrow lay just ahead. Built into the side of a hill, the chimney poked out the grassy top, sending puffs of smoke into the sky.

Good, he was home! She climbed down and, after a few brief instructions to the gargoyles, she jogged up to the weathered green door and knocked briskly.

When Sir Lapin answered, it was obvious he hadn't been expecting company. He wore a pair of dungarees and had rolled up his work shirt at the cuffs. He pulled the pipe out of his mouth, and a smile lit his face.

"Citrine, my dear, whatever are you doing here?" He moved back to let her in. "Come in, come in. I was just sitting down for a cup of tea."

Citrine stepped inside. She'd visited his home many times as a young girl but hadn't been there in recent years. On the right was the fireplace, plump armchairs, and a small sofa. On the left, shelves full of books covered the walls. A square table with stacks of papers clearly marked it as Lapin's study. She followed the rabbit down a short hallway to a tiny kitchen. Sure enough, a pot of tea and a plate of biscuits sat on a wooden table.

Lapin gestured at a straight-backed chair. "Please make yourself at home. I'll get you a cup." Citrine perched on one of the chairs as he turned to a set of open shelves that held a collection of teacups. After a moment's perusal, he plucked one ringed in violets in his furry paw. Twisting in her direction, he smiled. "Are you hungry? I was only going to have a snack, but I can fix you a sandwich or brown some toast."

Citrine shook her head. "No, I'm fine." She resisted the urge to drum her fingers on the table. He came back and placed the delicate cup in front of her, along with a plate and a pink napkin. "There we go." He laid his pipe on the table and poured tea into her cup and then his own. Steam scented with mint and citrus wafted into the air.

Lapin settled his bulk into his own chair and looked at her expectantly.

Now that she was here, she wasn't sure how to find out what she wanted to know without giving away Zander's secret. So, instead, she asked another question that had just occurred to her. "I was surprised you didn't come to the palace for the competition and ceremony. Are you well?"

Lapin set his cup into its saucer with a clink, his expression turning sober. "I'm in fine fettle, my dear. It's kind of you to ask." He leaned forward. "The Council asked my opinion on this champion business. I told them my thoughts, but they didn't agree." He shrugged. "They're the Council. At the moment, they are in charge of things, at least until we get this royal tangle straightened out, but that doesn't mean I had to watch the young prince and Miss Alice throw their lives away." He reached out and patted her hand. "I know you and the prince were once engaged yourself. I'm sure it was a difficult day for you."

Citrine resisted the urge to roll her eyes. "I appreciate your concern, but Zander and I agreed to go our separate ways years ago. It would hardly be logical to be upset now, would it? I couldn't reasonably expect him never to marry." She set her teacup down too. "And it doesn't matter because there won't be a marriage now, anyway."

Lapin's eyes widened. "Whatever do you mean?" He pushed the treats toward her. "You'd better start from the beginning."

Citrine told him what had happened as succinctly as possible. When she finished, she took a biscuit and bit into it. Then she closed her eyes, momentarily distracted by the taste of almond and vanilla with a hint of cinnamon that melted over her tongue. "These are delicious."

"My Granny's recipe. Now, you say Felinas sneaked them both into the labyrinth?" He shook his head, a smile playing on his lips. "That boy has always been a law unto himself, but even for him, that was a bold move. I wonder..." Lapin pulled one ear down and worried its tip before letting it go. "No matter. I understand why the prince was so upset, though. Your best friend absconding with your bride wouldn't be pleasant for anyone."

"So, you think Alice can do it, that she can beat the labyrinth?"

Lapin snorted. "Anyone with eyes can see the young lady would make a better champion than a queen."

Citrine sat back in her chair with a huff. "I wish Zander could understand that. You wouldn't believe how pig-headed he's being."

"It is a predicament, isn't it?" The rabbit took another sip of his tea and then looked Citrine in the eye. "As much as I love your company, my dear, I don't think you traveled all this way merely to update me on the goings-on at the palace."

"You're right." Citrine gripped her cup between her hands. "I wanted to do more research into the Drifter Gene."

Lapin gave her a long look. "And why is that? That Gift doesn't run in your family lines."

"I'm surprised you still call it a Gift."

"Well, that's what it is, no matter what anyone wants to say. Alchemy can be dangerous, too, but you don't see anyone not calling that a Gift." He took a sip of his tea and set his cup back down. "But that's a discussion for another day. What's your interest in it?"

Citrine put her own cup on the table and gripped her hands together. She didn't want to lie, and she doubted she'd be able to fool Lapin, anyway. But what part of the truth could she share and still find out what she wanted to know? Then it came to her. "It occurred to me that since the Queen obviously has the Drifter Gene, learning more about how it works could be of practical use."

"And that's the only reason?"

Citrine kept her face blandly neutral. "What other reason would I have?"

A smile tugged at the rabbit's mouth. "I was hoping you'd tell me." He placed his elbows on the arms of his chair and tented his paws in front of him. "I'm sure your parents have plenty of books about the various Gifts, even one that has fallen out of favor like the Drifter Gene. You found the curse the young Queen used on Prince Zander, after all. What are you truly searching for, Citrine?"

As she carefully examined and discarded several answers, Citrine became aware of the clock on the mantel ticking off the time. Finally, she said, "If a person who had the Drifter Gene wanted to rid themselves of it, do you think that's possible?"

"Whyever would anyone want to change something so fundamental about themselves?"

"Well, it would make his... their life so much easier. You know as well as I do, people with the Gene have to hide it. Thankfully, the exterminations stopped years ago, but they're still viewed with suspicion, forced to the fringes—especially those whose animal is large or predatory."

Lapin shook his head. "I've never understood this hysteria surrounding the ability to shift into a creature. Of course, what happened with that long ago prince was a shame. Everyone can agree it was a tragedy, but it wasn't the young man's fault. It was the Alchemist who cast the curse, and yet, the only thing we have to do is register. Quite frankly, some boundaries and rules guiding that kind of ability is smart. Making a whole segment of the population deny who they are and persecuting them for it is not."

Citrine blinked at the force of the rabbit's words. She hadn't realized he was a closet Drifter sympathizer. There were several groups over the years that had tried to change things, but nothing had ever come of it. When Citrine didn't say anything, Lapin let out a long sigh.

"My dear, you can speak freely to me." He paused and met her gaze squarely. "I've known for a while now."

"Known what, exactly?" Citrine hedged.

He raised one eyebrow and lifted his cup to his lips. "About the prince's secret," he said before he took another long sip.

Chapter 28

CHESS FOLLOWED ALICE'S LEAD. She set a brisk pace as they moved up the path. The labyrinth, for some reason known only to itself, hadn't let him out once the competition started.

He'd tried several times, both in his human and his cat form, but each time, he didn't make it more than a step past the entrance before being bounced back. He glanced at Alice's profile—the gentle curve of her cheek, the straight line of her nose, the stubborn chin—and admitted to himself it wasn't a hardship to keep her company on this quest.

They'd walked all morning without incident. It felt like strolling in a garden. The sun was warm, and a breeze kept the temperature comfortable. Birds flitted around the tall hedges and insects buzzed among the flowers. It was peaceful.

And it made him uneasy.

He glanced over at Alice, and she smiled at him, her dimple peeking out. She'd probably punch him if he gave into the temptation to press his lips against the small indentation.

Wickle took that moment to poke his blue head out of her pocket and chitter.

Chess veered away and scowled at the little creature. "Can't you keep that thing out of sight at least?"

She coughed to cover what was obviously a laugh and scratched the tiny chin. "He's not bothering you."

Wickle wheeked again and twisted around as if looking for something.

She patted his head. "Can you wait a bit longer?"

Chess edged closer as they continued to walk. "What's wrong with it?"

"He's hungry, but I don't think we should stop yet."

Her stomach chose that moment to growl and Chess chuckled.

"I hate to agree with him, but you'll not get far if you starve yourself."

He could see the indecision on her face, and then her stomach growled again. She put her hand over it. "I guess I'm outvoted."

She let her satchel slide to the ground. Wickle popped out of her pocket, ran down her arm, and hopped nimbly into the grass.

The little creature blinked up at Alice before trundling toward the hedges.

Her brow wrinkled, and she looked at Chess. "What do they eat? Should we try to feed him?"

He rolled his eyes. If he was lucky, the thing would stay in that hedge. "I wouldn't worry about him. He can fend for himself."

As if in answer, the snark scurried into nearby branches. He snapped an unusually large dragonfly from the air. He held it in his tiny jaws and after only a moment of struggle, the insect went limp. Alice turned away as Wickle tore off chunks.

Chess laughed. "You should see what a swarm of them can do."

Alice shuddered. "No, thank you! I'll skip that experience if it's all the same to you."

She opened the satchel and took out the wrapped bundle from earlier. There were still a few of the savory cakes left. They sat cross-legged on the ground across from each other. She set the food between them, along with a canteen of water.

"So, tell me more about Leander. I didn't have much interaction with him." She handed one of the little cakes to Chess.

He took it and stared at it for a moment before he answered. "He's the Queen's twin."

"I thought they looked alike, but I didn't realize they were twins."

Chess lifted a shoulder. "He's not as bad as Lyssandra, but he's no saint, either."

She leaned forward, her eyes bright with curiosity. "Do you know him well? I thought their family was from the Northern Estates."

Chess took a swig from the canteen before he answered. "They are, but there were a lot of court dinners and official events when Lyssandra married the King. I attended most of them. Zander needed my sparkling presence." He raised his eyebrows. "We also had the pleasure of Leander's company."

She tilted her head. "You say that like it's a bad thing."

"Well, it wasn't a good thing. I don't think anyone had ever told him no before." Chess curled his lip at the memory. "I had to extricate more than one of the serving girls from his clutches."

Alice wrinkled her nose. "Oh, one of those."

He tapped her knee. "Surely, a proper young lady such as yourself doesn't know about such things."

Alice snorted. "It didn't happen in our household, that's for sure. One time we had a visiting toff from somewhere." Chess didn't think she realized some of her posh accent fell away when she was relaxed. "I don't remember where, but he cornered a housemaid." She shook her head, her eyes alight with amusement. "Papa James didn't even let him gather his things before he threw the man out of the house. He had to limp all the way into the village to find transportation. Papa James tossed his trunks out after him." She grinned at him. "Come to think of it, I don't think the man ever sent for them. They might still be there, for all I know."

"'Papa James'?" Chess raised an eyebrow. "Why do you call him that?"

Alice tore off a chunk of her cake and shrugged. "It never fit to call him just *Papa* or *Father*. We rather butted heads when I first moved in. For the first year I lived with my adopted family, I called him *Sir*." She gave a rueful smile. "Eventually, though, he became Papa James. To be honest, I'm not even sure when I started calling him that."

Chess smiled. "Your entire face lights up when you talk about them. Your family, I mean."

Alice rolled a piece of cake in her fingers, and her eyes turned shiny. She took a drink from the canteen and when she passed it to Chess, he pretended not to notice her tears.

When she spoke, her voice was choked. "They saved me. I probably wouldn't still be alive without them."

Blinking rapidly, she leaned forward and gathered the empty cloth. Keeping her head turned, she tucked it into the satchel. Guilt nipped at him. He hadn't meant to remind her of what she stood to lose.

Chess touched her hand, and she started, her gaze swinging back to his.

"I'm sorry. The last thing I want to do is make you sad," he said.

She forced a bright smile. "You didn't. I just miss them."

"I'm sure they miss you, too. You're lucky to have each other." She didn't even realize how fortunate she was to have that—but that wasn't a line of thought he wanted to pursue. He stood and held out a hand. "Let's get going. The sooner we finish this, the sooner you can go home."

Alice let him pull her up, and she swung the satchel over her shoulder. Wickle, seeing her ready to leave, scrambled out of the hedge and hurried towards her, his tiny legs churning. She laughed, her face lighting up.

"Don't worry. I won't leave you behind."

Chess couldn't help his grimace when Wickle leaped onto her trouser leg, scuttled up, and snuggled onto her shoulder.

"I still can't believe a snark is acting like that. It's like you've bewitched him." Of course, looking at her glowing face, maybe it was not that strange. He sent her a slow smile and winked. "I understand how he feels."

Alice snorted. "You can't help yourself, can you?"

Chess gave her an innocent look. "I don't know what you're talking about."

She smacked his arm and started walking again. She turned on a pathway to the right.

And halted in her tracks so abruptly he almost ran into her back.

A ribbed brown wall blocked their way. He followed it up and up. When he got to the top, he swore under his breath.

It wasn't a wall at all.

Chapter 29

ALICE STARED INTO TWO black, beady eyes. The eyes were set on top of an enormous oval-shaped body covered with what appeared to be plates of armor. It had seven legs, two of which propped the creature into its precarious upright position. It completely blocked the pathway, and its waving antennae were even with the top of the labyrinth's walls.

She stumbled backward a step, keeping her eyes on the pill bug towering over her. It waved its antennae aggressively.

Humph! So rude, staring like that! It's obvious you learned nothing in your parent's pouch. The low, gravelly voice was somehow feminine.

"I... I beg your pardon," Alice gasped, taking another step backwards. She lowered her lashes, so she wasn't staring directly at the enormous insect any longer.

The creature let out a sniff. *I suppose you can't help it. You are a human, after all.*

Alice wasn't sure how to answer that charge since she was, indeed, human. She glanced at Chess, who was gazing up at the insect.

He waved at the creature and his voice dropped to a whisper. "Why can I understand what it's saying?"

"Maybe because it's part of the labyrinth?" Alice shrugged. She had no idea, but they could figure that out later. She turned her attention back to the bug who stared at her.

"I didn't mean to be rude," Alice finally said. "I was just... surprised, is all."

Why would you be surprised?

Alice gestured at the giant bug, trying to find the right words. "I wasn't expecting to run into—well, you."

The creature waved several of its legs in an agitated manner. *That's ridiculous. I live here. Do you often not expect residents to not be in their residence, or are you looking for non-residents in residence?*

Alice shook her head. "I'm sorry, but I'm not sure what you mean."

The gusty sigh blew Alice's hair back and caused Wickle to dig in his tiny claws. Alice winced.

Simple-minded, too. The insect shook what Alice thought must be its head. It was hard to tell since it didn't have a discernable neck. It spoke each word slowly. *I live here, so you would expect to find me here.*

Alice felt a prickle of irritation at the insinuation she was dimwitted. She crossed her arms. "Of course I would expect you to live where you live. I meant I wasn't aware that you lived *here*, in the labyrinth."

The arms waved even more wildly. *Where else would I live? Such nonsense!*

Alice resisted the urge to roll her eyes. She wasn't sure how well insects could see, but it was obvious they weren't getting down this path unless this behemoth got out of the way. She tried to hold on to her patience.

"I apologize, but I'm new here. I'm not aware of all the residents of the Kingdom of Wonderland."

It crossed two of its legs. *Well, why didn't you say so? Your stupidity makes much more sense now.*

Alice gritted her teeth. Chess touched her elbow, but she moved away from him and kept her eyes trained on the giant bug. She forced a smile.

"I'm Alice, and again, I apologize for my mistake."

I suppose it can be excused since you aren't from here. The bug sniffed again and continued in a more mollified tone, *You can't possibly pronounce my name with your inferior human tongue, but you may call me Inga.*

"I appreciate your kindness." Alice gave a small bow of her head and the bug puffed up its chest. It appeared pleased, but it was impossible to be sure since its face was rather blank. "I and my companion"—she motioned to Chess—"would appreciate your help."

Help? What kind of help? The bug's antennae twitched back and forth.

"We need to continue on this pathway. If you'd let us pass by, we'd be much obliged to you."

The insect tilted its head one way and then another. Finally, Inga nodded her head. *I will do that for you.*

She lowered herself to the ground, shaking the path under Alice's feet. She resisted the urge to back up. Instead she bowed her head again. "We are ever so grateful for your gracious help."

Well, are you going to move? Inga sounded impatient again.

At Alice's confused look, she sighed again loudly. *I need to get back to the crossroad. I'm much too large to turn around on the path.*

"Oh." Alice obediently scrambled towards the intersection. When Chess didn't move, she grabbed his hand and dragged him behind her.

"Do you think we can trust it?" he asked in a whisper.

Alice shrugged. "There's not much choice. Besides, she truly is too big to turn on these pathways."

"That's not a surprise," Chess said under his breath, causing Alice to stifle a giggle.

They stepped onto another pathway to let the pill bug lumber by them. Once she was clear, Alice walked toward the pathway they needed. The last thing they wanted to do was get lost.

She stopped in front of the insect. "Thank you," she said again, meaning it.

The pill bug was still much taller than either her or Chess, even though it was on all six legs now. *You are welcome, newcomer.*

Alice smiled and turned to leave.

Inga's voice stopped her. *You did not say where you have come from.*

"I suppose you'd call it the Mirror World, although I didn't even know about this place until I accidentally fell into it."

The bug's demeanor suddenly changed. Her voice came out in a booming screech, and both Alice and Chess covered their ears and Wickle squeaked in alarm.

The Mirror World? The humans from the Mirror World kill my kind. They have perpetuated a slaughter of my kin. She stomped several of her legs, and the ground shook.

"I... I... I've never killed any of your kin," Alice said, struggling to keep her balance.

I don't believe you. The insect folded two legs protectively over her middle section. *You've come to kill my offspring.*

Alice shook her head wildly. "No, I'd never do that. You must believe me!"

You tried to trick me! You humans are all a scourge, but those from the Mirror World are even worse.

Alice wasn't sure if the tremors in her legs were from the ground shaking or her fear. She stumbled backwards into Chess.

"That bug is clearly not happy," he said into her ear.

Inga shook, the plates on her body shivering with her rage. She stood upright again, and her body curled into itself. Alice stared in shock as the insect became an enormous ball. She might have remained planted there until she was crushed, but Chess grabbed her hand and pulled her toward the closest path.

"Run!"

Chapter 30

VERROS LANDED ON THE grassy knoll in front of Sir Lapin's burrow with a loud screech. It had taken him forever to find the burrow where the rabbit lived. Zander dismounted as the weathered green door opened.

Lapin pulled the pipe out of his mouth and bowed. When he straightened, he was smiling. "Your Highness, it seems my day for visitors. I would invite you in, but I'm guessing you didn't come here to see me."

Zander's mouth opened in surprise. "How did you—?"

"I may be old, but I'm not so ancient that I don't remember what it's like to be in love."

Zander's face heated, and he stood straighter. "I'm not sure what you mean, but—"

"There's no need to be embarrassed. Your constancy speaks well of you." Lapin's voice was matter-of-fact.

"But—"

"You don't have time to dally on my doorstep. Citrine is headed to Sacklepenny's laboratory. It's quite dangerous, and I warned her not to go alone. However, you know the Pearl Queen even better than I do, and patience, alas, is not one of her virtues."

Zander's thoughts scrambled to find purchase, but his brain latched onto one piece of information. "I thought Sacklepenny's home was in ruins."

Lapin took a couple puffs of his pipe before he answered. "The Pearl Queen had made that assumption too, but Sacklepenny's laboratory was underground in one of the many caverns. He accessed it from his home, but the man was beyond paranoid. I told her the place was probably booby-trapped to the rafters, and that doesn't even take into account whether anyone can reach it anymore. Any one of those tunnels could be caved in by now."

Fear formed an icy knot in Zander's gut. "How could you let her go?"

The rabbit shrugged his furry shoulders. "There was no stopping her." He lifted an eyebrow. "She was determined to find a way to help those with the Drifter Gene."

Zander's mouth opened and closed several times, but before he could fully process the words, the rabbit winked at him. "You know how determined a woman in love can be. If I were you, I'd go after her." He stepped back and started to shut the door.

Reality slammed into Zander, and it suddenly became clear to him why Citrine broke their engagement. "But I can't go. I've left a host of problems at the palace."

The rabbit gave him a long, measured look. "Then what are you doing on my doorstep?" He puffed on his pipe as he waited for Zander to speak.

"I... I..." Zander trailed off, not sure how to answer.

Lapin took the pipe out of his mouth. "You know, Your Highness, nobody is meant to carry such a heavy burden all by themselves. If you become King, you'll have to be a strong leader, but strong leaders know when to ask for help, especially when they have two equally important priorities vying for their attention."

"But... shouldn't the Kingdom always be my top priority?"

Lapin looked thoughtful for a moment and then pointed the stem of his pipe at Zander. "Only you can answer that, Your Highness, but you might want to consider another question first."

"What's that?" Zander asked.

"Could you lead at all if something happened to Citrine because you didn't help her?"

Zander heart stuttered in his chest as a chill spread over him.

Lapin smiled. "That's what I thought."

He turned to go back into his home. When Zander continued to stand rooted to the spot, Lapin paused. "And for what it's worth, a jabberwock flies far faster than a griffon." He nodded toward the creature who was currently scratching up his front lawn. "Your boy will be safe enough here with me."

The rabbit didn't wait for Zander's response. He simply shut the door. A million thoughts stampeded through Zander's brain, from the Council he needed to address to the dangers Citrine could even now be facing.

Chief among them, though, was the unmistakable fact that Sir Lapin knew his secret.

And he didn't seem to care.

Was it possible others wouldn't either?

Chapter 31

ALICE'S FEET POUNDED ON the ground. Chess dragged her down another pathway. The ground rumbled beneath her feet, making it hard to keep her footing. A shadow fell over them, and Alice risked a glance over her shoulder.

Then wished she hadn't.

The pill bug was rolling toward them like a runaway boulder, and it was gaining on them. Chess put on more speed and nearly pulled her off her feet. Branches flew by on either side as they ran. The rumbling got closer. Alice's breath came in gasps. The shadow over them lengthened and darkened. Alice pushed herself to go faster.

It wasn't going to be enough.

Suddenly she was yanked sideways. Chess had pulled them onto a connecting pathway. They both gasped for air as the ground became still. Alice heard a loud hiss.

"Can't stop," Chess panted. He grabbed her hand and pulled her onward as the ground shook again.

They ran and ran. Each turn down a new path bought them a few precious seconds. Even when the ground stopped shaking, they continued to run, Chess pulling them down one pathway and then another, going deeper and deeper into the labyrinth. Alice had a horrible stitch in her side, and her lungs were bursting when she pulled to a stop. She bent over, her hands on her knees, trying to catch her breath.

"I... can't... go... anymore." She wanted to lay down but feared she wouldn't want to get up again.

Chess halted, too. He took in great mouthfuls of air, clasping both hands behind his head.

When he could finally breathe again, he looked at Alice. "I guess she doesn't like people from the Mirror World."

Guilt gripped Alice. "I had no idea it would set her off like that."

Chess grinned. "It was a bug. I didn't even know they could hold conversations."

Her chest loosened, and she returned his smile. They both listened, but the birds had resumed their twittering and the insects, their buzzing. Suddenly, Alice's eyes widened. Her hand flew to her shoulder, but Wickle was still there. Granted, he had probably left claw marks in her shoulder, but he had hung on.

She gently stroked him and noticed his small body was quivering. "Poor thing. He's frightened to death," she said.

Chess rolled his eyes. "He's not the one you need to be worrying about. I told you, he's as deadly as the giant pill bug."

Alice scowled at him and cupped a protective hand over the little creature. "It doesn't mean he can't get scared, too."

"You are impossible."

Alice tickled Wickle under his chin and he cheeped. *Safe now?*

"Yes, we're safe now." Alice looked around. "At least I think so."

Her earlier feelings of peace were shattered, and when she looked up she was surprised to see the sun still shining as if they hadn't almost been crushed by a giant insect. It was somehow creepy that the labyrinth still seemed serene and peaceful when they had come so close to death. Alice felt like the sky should have at least gotten darker or the birds stopped their twittering. Alice put out a hand and swayed on her feet, her knees suddenly weak. Chess put an arm around her waist, steadying her.

"Are you all right? Maybe we should sit down." He looked around at the smooth pathway.

Alice drew in a deep breath. "No, I'm fine. It's just I've never almost been squashed by a bug before." A giggle bubbled up in her throat. She clapped a hand over her mouth, but it escaped. Once it did, she couldn't seem to stop.

Chess held her up as she whooped with laughter, a bemused smile on his face. She kept trying to tell him what was so funny, but could only manage a few words before the laughter took over again. Finally, her eyes streaming, Alice wiped at her face and tried to catch her breath for the second time.

"I think you might be a touch hysterical," he said dryly.

She slapped his chest, and realized that Chess was holding her in the loose circle of his arms. She looked up, caught by the blue of his eyes. A different kind of breathlessness assaulted her.

Alice quickly stepped away and ran a shaky hand through her hair. Avoiding Chess's gaze, she glanced around. The path ran in front and behind them. It looked exactly like the pathway they had been on before being chased by an enormous insect. She spun in a slow circle, a horrible realization making her stomach sink.

"Chess, I don't suppose you kept track of which way you turned while we were running for our lives, did you?"

Chess snorted. "That really wasn't uppermost on my mind, so no."

Alice met his eyes. "I have no idea where we are. Do you?"

Chess shook his head. "I'm sure it'll be fine. Didn't you say we had to keep turning right? If we do that, we'll come out in the center eventually."

Alice pushed down her worry and forced a bright smile. "You're right." She rummaged inside the satchel she had let fall when they stopped running and pulled out a canteen. She took a long swig of water and then passed it to Chess. He did likewise and then wiped his mouth before handing it back to her. She tucked the water into the satchel and hefted it onto her shoulder. Then she patted Wickle.

"Ready to go?"

He cheeped in response, snuggling into her shoulder. Alice looked at Chess, who gestured toward the pathway.

"After you." He gave her an exaggerated bow. Despite her worries, Alice couldn't help her smile. She started walking, and Chess swung into step with her. They walked in silence until they came to a fork in the pathway. Alice turned right and Chess followed along.

Maybe it was the near-death experience, but Alice was content in the silence. Chess seemed to feel the same way. After the first right-hand turn, his hand brushed hers. A tingle ran up her arm. Alice didn't look at him, but when he took her hand, she didn't protest.

They had made three right-hand turns, and Alice started to relax when she noticed it. She drew to a halt.

"What is it?" Chess asked.

She pointed wordlessly towards their feet, where a swirling mist seeped upward. She glanced back the way they had come, but the same sparkling blue haze already obscured the path.

Chapter 32

CITRINE WANTED TO PULL her hair out. She'd been over every inch of Sacklepenny's crumbling home, but had found nothing.

"Did you find anything, Stongorr?"

The gargoyle shook his thick head.

She stood in the center of the dilapidated cottage and turned in a slow circle. "If I was Phineas Sacklepenny, where would I put the entrance to my laboratory?"

The gargoyle shrugged his stone shoulders.

"Lapin said the man was paranoid. He also said the laboratory was deep in the ground, so maybe a trap door?"

Stongorr tilted his head. *Perhaps it's outside. Should I have Ogox look?*

"Not yet." She pushed her spectacles up and blew a loose curl out of her face. "I have a feeling it's here somewhere, but where?"

As her eyes moved over the parts of the wall that still stood, her gaze caught on the Looking Glass. Its dull surface reflected the room back to her—or what was left of it. If you didn't know what the mirror was, its plain exterior would be easy to overlook. Which was most likely the point.

The reflection snagged her attention. Something wasn't quite right. She stepped closer. "Look!" She pointed at the bottom corner of the mirror. "See that moth-eaten rug—something's peeking out from underneath it."

She watched Stongorr walk over to where she indicated. He patted with his clawed foot and then stopped. *This feels different.*

She turned around and looked at the room. The floor under his claws was the same worn stone that covered the rest of the floor.

She looked at the mirror again and peered more closely. "There's definitely something there."

He prodded the floor again. *Spelled, maybe?*

Of course! Lapin had told her the man was paranoid. She wanted to smack herself for being so obtuse.

She walked over to the rug and motioned Stongorr out of the way before she knelt down. As she ran her hand over the smooth surface, her palm hit rough wood. She felt a prick of pain and jerked back. A splinter was stuck in it. As she plucked it out, a smile spread over her face.

"I must give you your due, Phineas. You were most clever, but it's time to give up your secrets."

I don't think he can hear you.

Citrine ignored the gargoyle and pushed the rug back. Pressing her lips together in concentration, and mindful of getting more splinters, she ran her hands gingerly over the floor. "Don't just stand there. Help me find the handle."

It took several passes by both of them before she found what she was looking for. As soon as she lifted the recessed handle, the trap door wobbled into view.

Old and worn, it was surprisingly large.

Stongorr's snout wrinkled. *It's lucky neither of us fell through that. It looks rotted.*

"Well, we didn't, and we've found the entrance." She took a firmer grip on the handle, braced her feet, and pulled.

Nothing happened.

Planting both her feet, she pulled again. The door came up an inch, but she didn't have enough strength. It smacked back down sending up a cloud of dust.

Stongorr stepped up next to her. *Here, let me, before you burst an internal organ.*

He gripped the handle with his clawed fingers. With little effort, he lifted the trap door. The shriek of metal hinges scraped over her ears, and she grimaced.

Citrine darted out of the way as the door flopped open and landed with a bang on the stones.

A waft of damp, fetid air rose from the opening, and Citrine wrinkled her nose as she peered into the black rectangle now gaping at her feet.

A set of stairs disappeared into the darkness. For the first time, Citrine felt a shiver of apprehension. She knelt at the opening and leaned forward, trying to see where the stairs led and, more importantly, what kind of shape they were in. Lapin's warnings about booby traps flashed through her mind. She sat back.

"This probably isn't safe."

Stongorr didn't say anything.

"Maybe it was foolish to come here alone."

Are you trying to convince me or yourself? The gargoyle raised both stony eyebrows.

She pressed her lips together and straightened her shoulders. "I have to go down there if I want answers."

I didn't say you shouldn't.

"No, but your expression reveals what you're really thinking."

My face is stone. Stongorr turned and scuttled toward the outdoors.

"Where are you going?"

Stongorr kept going without even glancing back. *Unless you are able to see in the dark, you're going to need your pocket lantern.*

Chapter 33

Stongorr returned with two pocket lanterns. Citrine set them on the floor and opened the latch, swinging one of the glass panels open. She tapped the pointed tops, and the pulse of magic from them skimmed over her skin. It didn't take long before a cluster of lantern bugs, like so many tiny lights, flitted into the ruins. Shimmering in shades of white, ivory, and gold, they swarmed into a whirling cloud before dividing and zipping into the open lanterns.

"Thank you for your help." There was a harmonized hum that indicated the swarm's happiness.

She turned back to the gaping hole in the ground. "Well, shall we?"

Stongorr leaned over the opening. *What about the traps?*

Citrine frowned. He was right. Most magic users left a signature, but it wasn't always clear or obvious. Even if she was careful, she could still set off a trap and not know until it was too late.

"We need a spell bee."

Stongorr sat back on his haunches and waited.

Citrine set the lanterns back on the ground. She closed her eyes and hummed low in her throat and then waited. She opened her eyes, smiling. It shouldn't take long. Within a few minutes, a sparkle of movement appeared—but it wasn't a purple-and-yellow spell bee.

Instead, a tiny man zipped through an empty window, his small body glowing softly. Citrine swallowed a groan. It was a sparkle pixie. It wasn't that they couldn't detect spells, but they could be tricky creatures, even the friendly ones. Unfortunately, they could also be very prickly. If she didn't accept this one's help, he was sure to pull some prank on her. With the unknowns she faced below, she didn't need any more complications.

Citrine smiled at the tiny creature. "Hello, there. Thank you for answering my summons. What's your name?"

The pixie doffed a tiny cap. "Well, missus, my name's Bancroft, and I can assist you." His smile grew crafty. "Of course, my help doesn't come for free. We'd have to agree to a price, Lady... what were you saying yer name was?"

Stongorr gave a low rumble, and Citrine shot him a warning look.

She turned back to the pixie. "I'm pleased to meet you, Bancroft. I'm Lady Citrine."

As soon as she said her name, the miniature man's eyes bugged out. He clasped his tiny hat to his chest and bowed deeply. "Citrine? As in the Pearl Queen? That Citrine?"

This time Citrine did smile. "One and the same, I'm afraid."

His cheeks flushed, and he spun away from her. Taking his cap, he smacked himself in the face several times. Citrine could hear him muttering. "Stupid, Bancroft. Sure and trap the Pearl Queen into a bargain. Stupid, stupid, stupid."

After several minutes of this, he turned with a wooden smile plastered across his face. "Of course I can help the Pearl Queen." He forced out a chuckle. "And I was only pulling yer leg about a price."

Citrine bit back a laugh. "I don't expect you to give your help for free. I don't believe that's how your kind work. How about a week's worth of honey nectar and three feathers from my collection?"

Desire warred with worry on his small face. Finally, he shook his head. "I couldn't take anything from the Pearl Queen." He twisted his cap so hard Citrine was afraid he'd tear it in half.

"You can and you will. I won't hear another word about it. Now then, do you think you can detect any magical traps or spells?" She pointed to the opening in the floor.

He gave his cap another twist. "I've an excellent nose for magic." He bowed again, this time sweeping his arm out gallantly.

"There's no need for all that formality. Please just call me Citrine."

Bancroft gave an uncertain nod. He then flitted closer to the opening and took several large sniffs. His face scrunched up. "Are you sure you're wanting to go down there, Your Maj— er, Ma'am? It smells old and... unfriendly."

I told you.

Citrine glared at the gargoyle before turning back to Bancroft. "I'm afraid I must."

The pixie zipped into the opening and then back up. "Then you'd best watch your step. Begging your pardon, Ma'am, those stairs don't look too sturdy to me."

Stongorr spread his wings and jumped into the hole. The gloom swallowed his form, and only the glow of his lantern visible from where Citrine stood.

Several moments ticked by. There were no sounds from below and the light didn't move.

"Stongorr? Are you all right?" Citrine's voice echoed back at her.

Yes.

"How far down do you think it is?"

Hard to say without a measuring stick. Maybe twenty-five feet or so.

That gave Citrine a moment's pause, but she ignored it. She had to get down there to find the answers Zander needed. And the only option was these somewhat questionable steps.

Lifting her chin, she put her foot on the first step and tentatively rested her weight on it. It creaked but held. Holding onto the edge of the opening in the floor with one hand and gripping the pocket lantern in the other, she worked her way downward into the darkness. The pixie fluttered around her head, his glow adding to the light of her lantern, chasing some of the shadows away.

About a dozen or so steps down, she hesitated. To continue, she'd need to let go of the floor above her. She tried to calculate the distance left to the ground beneath her, but the darkness of the tunnel made it difficult to gauge the distance with any accuracy, even with her lantern and Stongorr's.

She looked back toward the floor above her. If Stongorr was right in his estimate, it was probably no more than fifteen feet to the bottom. She bit her lip. If she fell now, she wouldn't die unless she had the very unfortunate luck to land on her head, but she might break a limb.

After another moment of hesitation she made up her mind. She had to get to Sacklepenny's workroom, and this was the only way. She forced her fingers to unclench their grip.

The pixie returned to her and fluttered around her head. Her foot found the next step. When it held her weight, the muscles in her shoulders loosened.

She'd made it this far. There was no reason to think—

A large crack broke the silence and her foot plunged into empty space.

A scream ripped out of her throat and she lunged upward, letting the lantern fall as her hand reached for the lip of the floor opening.

Her fingers slipped over the rough wood, and she grasped at air.

She plummeted downward, her arms windmilling. She landed on Stongorr, who tried to catch her, sending them both sprawling. The force sent her backwards, and her head smacked against some part of the gargoyle and made her see stars.

She laid still for a moment, trying to get her bearings. Above her head, Bancroft flew in dizzying circles.

Are ye hurt? You look hurt. What if you're mortally injured? His voice climbed until it was so high pitched Citrine could no longer understand the pixie.

If I swat it, you can try for a spell bee. Stongorr's voice came from under her right shoulder.

"I'm so sorry, Stongorr. I didn't mean to smash you." She rolled to the side and untangled herself from the gargoyle. "Are you all right?"

I am still in one piece.

Relief filtered through her, and she pushed herself up. Her head rang, and a few dots danced in the corners of her vision. She waited until they cleared.

Bancroft continued to buzz around her head like a drunken light. It didn't improve the pulse of pain radiating from the back of her skull. "I'm fine, Bancroft."

Stongorr got to his feet and crouched in front of her. His blocky head tilted as he stared into her face. He held up two claws.

How many do you see?

She pushed his hand away. "I see two, Stongorr. I'm fine. Both of you stop worrying." She held out her hand. "Here, help me up so we can get started."

The gargoyle pulled her to her feet. The cave swung wildly and her legs wobbled. She steadied herself against the wall and slowly lowered herself back into a sitting position. "All right, perhaps I should give myself a few more minutes." She rested her head on her knees and closed her eyes.

When she opened them again, Bancroft hovered in front of her. His tiny face was pinched.

Crap on a cracker! You're in a pickle now, you are!

Chapter 34

ALICE GRIPPED CHESS'S HAND, her palms clammy. "Let's just keep going. Maybe we'll walk out of it."

Chess nodded, and they pressed forward, their pace faster now. As they walked, the mists swirled out from them like waves of water and then eddied back in, each time higher and denser. Within a few minutes, it became difficult to see where they were going.

Alice looked over, alarmed to realize that Chess was only a dim silhouette. She gripped his hand tighter. He squeezed back.

Wickle sat up on her shoulder and chittered. He pawed at her neck. She reached up to comfort him, and he pressed a tiny foot to her cheek.

Close ears! Close eyes!

As if to reinforce his words, his own triangular shaped ears folded over, and he scampered down her shirt and burrowed into the front pocket. She could feel him shivering through the thick linen fabric.

The sparkling blue haze enveloped the entire pathway. Despite not being able to see the sun, Alice knew it was still shining because it reflected off of the sparkles, making her more disorientated. She stepped closer to Chess, glad he was with her.

"We should keep one hand on the walls," she said, her voice a whisper. The blue nothingness around her could hide anything.

"Good idea."

Together they shuffled to the right until branches brushed against her. She put out a tentative hand, the spiky needles of the bushes tickling her palm. Her chest loosened. This was the same path they'd been walking on. They just had to keep going until they passed through this mist. She straightened her shoulders.

"It's only mist," she said out loud. Her voice echoed weirdly back at her.

Chess gave a short laugh. "Should we start whistling?"

"This is worse than when Miss Starkey would make me go down into the school cellars to get potatoes." The memory of the dark, cobwebby space with its shadowy corners her light never reached gave her courage. There had been nothing down there, either.

Something loomed up out of the mist. Chess pushed her behind him, shoving her into the branches of the hedge. Sharp pine needles scratched at her skin. The shape in the mists swirled and dissolved. Both of them let out a loud breath and then gave nervous laughs.

"Let's pick up the pace," said Chess. "The sooner we're out of this stuff, the better."

Alice couldn't agree more and she started to trot, her hand trailing along the wall. Several more times things loomed up, but it was always the mist, twisting into shapes that seemed real.

A low moan sounded behind Alice and she whirled around, her hand slipping from Chess's grasp. She peered into the haze, willing her eyes to detect movement. The swirls and sparkles were mesmerizing. She reached out her hand. The wall was gone. Panic surged inside of her and her heart beat in her ears. She reached in the other direction, but now she couldn't find Chess at all.

She called his name, her voice shaking. Her words bounced back at her. She reached both hands out, groping for something to hang on to.

"Chess," she said again, her voice cracking.

Then he was there. His solid warmth was under her hands, and she collapsed against him, trembling. "I... I didn't think I was going to find you."

He slid his arms around her waist and hugged her to his chest. She closed her eyes for a moment before pushing away from him, still keeping one hand on his arm. She reached with her other hand, but there was nothing. Panic welled up again.

"Chess, I can't feel the wall."

"There's a cross breeze. I think we're at an intersection."

"Great! Now what are we going to do?"

"We keep moving. We'll have to stumble onto a path sooner or later." He slid one arm around her waist and tugged her close to his side. It made walking more difficult, but after her scare, she didn't want to risk losing him again. They shuffled forward and trying to make their way to the right side. Alice wasn't sure of anything anymore. For all she knew, they were going back the way they came or upside down.

More things swirled out of the mist and something grabbed at her hair. She screamed and batted at it. A hiss came from the left and Chess whirled toward the sound, shoving Alice behind him.

Alice pushed at him. "Keep walking. I don't think anything is there."

Reluctantly, Chess resumed his place next to her and they moved forward again. The haze was now so thick that, even though he was right next to her, she could barely make out Chess's outline. It felt like they had been walking through this blue nightmare for hours. Something brushed between their legs and they leapt apart. Alice cursed herself for stupidity and reached for Chess, but there was only empty space.

"Chess?"

"Alice?" His voice sounded far away.

He couldn't have moved away from her that quickly. She groped toward where she thought he had been, but came up empty again. A man-shaped form loomed up, and she shot forward. But it was only mist, and it swirled away into sparkles again.

"Chess!"

"Alice!" His sounded even more distant this time.

"I'm here. Follow my voice. I'll stand still and make noise so you can find me."

Alice hummed loudly, but Chess's voice got further and further away. What was he doing?

Something brushed against her hair again and she swallowed down a scream. She stumbled backwards and came up hard against prickly branches. She almost sobbed in relief.

But where was Chess?

She called his name again, her voice raw. There was no answer. Alice whimpered and huddled against the hedge wall. Zander's warning that people went into the labyrinth and never came out clawed at her mind.

A small paw patted her face. *Close ears! Close eyes!*

It was Wickle. His presence brought her back to herself. She had nothing to lose. She couldn't see anyway. She shut her eyes, stuck both fingers in her ears and, leaning into the hedge, walked forward. She only hoped that Chess would find his way out, too.

Chapter 35

CHESS COULD HEAR ALICE calling him but he couldn't find her. He heard her humming, but it was getting farther and farther away. He grimaced. Why didn't she stay still? A slender figure loomed up in front of him. The sounds of sobs echoed around him. He lurched toward the person but his hands found nothing, only more mist.

He cursed and tried to retrace his steps.

"Alice!"

Silence answered him.

He ran a hand through his hair. What was he supposed to do now? He couldn't just leave her, but apparently, she had left him. Of all the stupid things! He slammed his fist into his other hand and winced.

Then he heard it. Humming. He moved toward the sound. It always seemed only a few steps away.

"Alice! Alice, stop. You have to stay still so I can find you."

A laugh floated in the blue nothingness. He picked up his pace, going faster and faster. He stumbled and fell up against the hedge. A wave of relief washed over him. He didn't want to admit how terrifying it was to be suspended, not knowing which way was up or down. Using the wall as his guide, he started running now.

The humming got louder and louder as the mist became thinner and thinner. Soon, he could make out shapes and the grass under his feet. By the time he reached a round clearing where several paths emptied, the mist had dissipated completely. The sun peeked out from behind a puff of white clouds, one of its rays landing on a vine of purple blossoms waving next to his shoulder.

He stepped away from the hedge, and his relief threatened to bring him to his knees. Then he saw her. She sat on the golden rim of a deep blue pool, her back to him. Large lilies floated on its surface. As he got closer, a surge of anger almost choked him, but he tamped it down. He was just glad she was all right.

"Alice, why in the world didn't you stop?"

She turned, and Alice's big violet eyes blinked up at him. Why hadn't he realized her skin was so perfect or the blush of her cheeks just the right shade of pink? Her rosebud mouth curved into a smile, and she patted the seat next to her.

In a trance, he sat down and took her hand. It felt cold in his, almost clammy. He shook it gently.

"You said you were going to stand still and make noise, but you kept moving."

She leaned forward and ran her fingers over his cheek and stared into his eyes. He felt himself drowning in their twilight depths. Then she closed the distance between them and placed her soft mouth on his. Every other thought flew from his head. His entire world, his very breath, centered on the spot where their lips met.

He tried to gather her closer, but she clamped his arms down with surprising strength. He couldn't wonder about that because she deepened the kiss. He groaned low in his throat and wanted so badly to pull her into his arms. He tried again, but she kept his arms locked firmly against his sides. But he didn't have time to think about that because her lips parted, and he was lost.

He felt as if he was falling, falling, falling. Warm wetness surrounded him, but he barely noticed. His mind, his heart filled with the taste of Alice. He didn't want to take his lips away, but he needed to breathe. But the idea of parting from her, even for air, repulsed him. Just a few more moments.

A sharp pain burned through his scalp. Alice's lips ripped away from him. Water rushed into his mouth. He felt a throbbing agony slice down both of his arms. A screech sounded so loudly, he thought his ears might bleed. He didn't understand what was happening, and he still couldn't seem to get air into his lungs. His eyelids felt so heavy and his lungs ached for oxygen. Darkness crowded into his vision and then everything went black.

Chapter 36

ALICE STUMBLED AS THE hedge she'd been leaning on gave way to empty air. Her eyes popped open.

The mist was gone. She had come out in a circular clearing with paths branching out from it like spokes on a wheel. A golden-rimmed pool sat in the center, waves lapping over its edges onto the ground.

Unease slithered up Alice's spine.

"Chess?"

But there was nobody here, and an eerie silence blanketed the area. Even the birds had stopped twittering.

A splash drew her attention to the pool.

A creature surfaced. Shimmering pink-and-purple hair streamed over its shoulders and floated on the surface of the water. Its head dipped over something, but Alice couldn't see what it was. The creature seemed oblivious to her presence, and she'd rather keep it that way.

She eyed the distance between the pool and the other paths and then edged toward the opposite side of the clearing. She didn't know where Chess was, but she had no desire to tangle with whatever was in the pool.

A faint groan snapped her gaze back to the water. The creature turned, so it was in silhouette. At first, Alice wasn't sure what she was seeing.

Then it came into horrifying focus.

Clutched in her grasp—it was clear whatever this creature was, it was female—was a man. At first Alice couldn't see who it was because the water sprite had her mouth hooked onto the lower half of his face, her jaws stretched wide, but she knew.

Then Alice recognized the dark leather coat and the mop of black curls plastered to the man's head.

Her heart sped up, and her chest constricted. She had to get Chess away from that thing, but how?

A weapon. She needed a weapon.

She frantically dug through the satchel. Citrine said she'd packed a dagger. Her fingers scrabbled through the dark recesses of the bag.

There.

Her hand closed over the handle of the knife. She set the satchel on the ground. Then she shrugged out of her coat and kicked off her boots, careful to be silent.

So far, the creature had shown no indication she knew Alice was there. If she had any hope of rescuing Chess, she had to take that thing by surprise. She plucked the snark out of her shirt pocket and set him gently in the grass.

"Wickle, what is it?" Alice breathed the words.

Merrow. Careful.

Alice straightened. Well, that wasn't a big help. She eased closer to the pool, the dagger clenched in her sweating hand. She stopped a few feet away and stared at the lapping waves.

Her heart thumped in her chest, and her knees trembled. She hated the water. Always had.

The merrow adjusted her position, and Chess flopped against her green-tinted torso. She didn't have time to be afraid. If she waited, it would be too late. Holding her knife out in a trembling hand, she yelled, "Let him go!"

The merrow unsuctioned her jaws from Chess's face, and Alice's stomach flopped. Puncture marks dripped blood at the corners of his mouth. The merrow turned towards Alice. Her face was small and triangular and dominated by a pair of black pupil-less eyes, her skin the lightest of spring greens.

The merrow smiled, revealing jagged teeth and four long fangs stained red. She tilted her head, even as she held Chess in a loose grip by his collar. His head lolled to one side. He was clearly unconscious. At least, Alice hoped he was only unconscious. From here, she couldn't tell if he was breathing or not.

She pointed her knife at the girl and repeated, "Let him go. I don't want to hurt you, but I will." Her hand trembled, undercutting her threat.

Come in, then, and get your man. The merrow drew a long, clawed finger down Chess's cheek. He stayed disturbingly still. *He's very pretty, though. If you don't want him, I'd like to keep him for myself.*

The words had a lilting, musical quality.

She stepped closer and water lapped on her toes. She tightened her grip on the knife. "Well, you can't. Keep him, that is."

The merrow lifted her other hand and beckoned to Alice. *Then come and get him.*

Alice tried to force herself into the water, but her body wouldn't obey her. The old terror rose up and choked her, clamping her limbs in paralysis. The merrow narrowed her eyes and turned back to Chess.

Good. I need a new toy.

Stretching her jaws impossibly wide, she clamped onto his face again and sank downward.

Desperation broke Alice's paralysis, and she flung herself into the pool. She hit the water with a splash and flailed her arms until she realized her feet touched ground. By this time, the merrow had sunk below the surface, and Alice plunged her hand under the water and grasped the first thing she could—Chess's hair—and yanked with all of her might.

The merrow let go with a loud screech, and Alice pulled Chess's limp body toward herself as she pointed the knife toward the creature.

The merrow circled her, an iridescent pink-and-purple tail fin breaking the surface. Alice clutched Chess to her and turned with the merrow, keeping the creature in front of her. She had to keep backing up because the ground slanted, and her feet kept sliding forward. She didn't want to lose her footing or go any deeper.

Without warning, the merrow propelled her body toward Alice, who shrieked. At the last moment, the creature surged upward and then jackknifed back toward the water, her tail slapping a wave of water over Alice's head.

Alice sputtered and pushed the hair out of her face. By the time she'd regained her vision, the merrow had disappeared from sight.

Alice trembled as she strained her eyes to search the depths where the merrow had disappeared. She dragged Chess toward the edge of the pool. With every step, she expected to feel claws dig into flesh or for the merrow to lunge up at her.

She hauled herself up onto the rim of the pool, almost losing her grip on Chess. At the last minute she caught ahold of the back of his shirt and pulled his face out of the water.

She gathered her feet underneath herself and pushed into a crouch. Using all of her strength, she heaved Chess's limp body over the edge, wincing as his back scraped over the rim.

Only his legs from the knee down were still in the water when something stopped him. Her heart lurched as she searched for the merrow, her hand scrabbling for the dagger she'd dropped.

But it was only the edge of his boot, caught on the lip of the pool. She jerked it free, and he popped over the edge, knocking her onto her rear.

Alice paused to allow her heart calm to its normal rhythm, Chess half sprawled across her legs.

The surface of the pool rippled, and she surged to her feet. Chess rolled onto the ground. With the last of her strength, she grabbed him under his arms and dragged him across the grass until there was a suitable distance between them and the pool.

Finally, she laid him down and slumped next to him. His face had taken on a frightening paleness, and blue tinged his lips. His chest was still.

She pressed her head against his breastbone, the wet fabric of his shirt squishing against her cheek. For a long moment, she heard nothing, and then there was a faint thump.

Alice knew she had to get him to breathe. It was a good thing she and Rommy had spent all those months at sea with Papa James or she wouldn't have a clue as to what to do. Gently, she pinched his nostrils shut and, careful not to touch the punctures, she squeezed his mouth open. Fitting her lips to his, she pushed her breath into his lungs.

Alice continued until her head swam. Tears stung her eyes, but she refused to give up. Suddenly, his body jerked and bucked. She rolled him onto his side as a torrent of water gushed from his lips. He coughed and sputtered and tried to sit up, but his arms were too weak to hold him.

He flopped back onto the ground, and she lifted his head onto her lap. His eyes fluttered open. He frowned as he tried to focus on her face.

She smoothed a hand over his forehead, brushing the wet hair out of his eyes. "You're all right, Chess. Just try to breathe in, nice and slow."

"What... where..." His voice was a raw croak. He stopped and tried again, his tongue sounding thick in his mouth. "You... you kissed me."

Before she could respond, his eyes rolled up, and he slid back into unconsciousness.

Chapter 37

CITRINE WASN'T SURE HOW much time had passed by the time she felt well enough to walk. Bancroft had not helped matters as he buzzed around her head, uttering proclamations of dire outcomes.

Now, as she stood again, he fluttered about, his light winking in and out with his agitation.

Oh, thank the heavens, yer not dead. I thought ye was a goner fer sure.

She bit back her exasperation with the pixie and made her voice soothing. "It was a bump on the head, Bancroft. It just made me a little dizzy. I'm fine now." She ran her fingers over her skull again. The lump reassured her. As her mother always said, better in than out with head injuries.

Meanwhile, Stongorr hadn't moved from her side. Now he looked up at her. *Are you sure about this?*

She smiled at him. "It's only a bump on the head, after all."

It's your funeral. The gargoyle rose from his habitual crouch and started down the path in his rolling, simian gait.

She followed, putting her hand on the wall to steady herself. Bancroft flitted around her head, stopping to bob in front of her face.

Yer not going down again, are you? I don't know that my heart can take that. 'Twas bad enough the first time.

"I'm fine, Bancroft." Citrine's voice held more snap than she intend and remorse flooded her. She held up her finger. The tiny man alighted on it, his body vibrating. She softened her voice. "I'm truly all right. But I need you to focus. I'll get a lot worse than a headache if you don't catch the magical traps that could be ahead of us."

The pixie nodded his head so hard his hat flopped off. He caught it and jammed it back onto his straw-colored hair. *Righto. I'm on it.*

He launched into the air and zipped down the tunnel in a zigzag pattern. Once he'd covered a few yards, he stopped and called over his shoulder, *All clear so far.*

Maybe you should try finding a spell bee again. Stongorr was staring after the sparkle pixie with a scowl.

Citrine hid her smile. "Bancroft will do a good job. He's certainly enthusiastic."

If you say so. The gargoyle turned and trailed after the pixie.

Citrine picked up her lantern where it had fallen—thankfully, it was still in one piece—then followed her friends down the tunnel.

Citrine paused as Bancroft disappeared around a curve to check things out.

I don't like this.

"We haven't run into anything yet."

I know. That's what I don't like. Stongorr paced back and forth, his wings opening and closing.

Bancroft careened back around the corner waving his hat. *I found the first trap, but someone set it off, and there's a huge cave-in, and I don't think we...* His stream of words ran together into an indecipherable babble.

"Slow down. I can't understand you."

The pixie stopped only a few inches from Citrine's face and hovered there, his small body vibrating. With a visible effort, he slowed his words. *There's a cave-in.*

"All right, but I think I understood you to say that someone has already triggered the spell. Can you tell if it resets?"

Bancroft held up a tiny finger and then zipped back around the corner.

The gargoyle looked over his shoulder and then at Citrine. *Are you sure you want to do this?*

"I have to get to that laboratory, but you don't have to stay. You can go wait with Ogox."

The gargoyle glowered at her. *I was only asking a question.* He hunched his shoulders.

Citrine pursed her lips. Now she'd offended him. She put a hand on the stiff shoulder, the skin like warm stone under her fingers. "I wasn't questioning your loyalty, Stongorr. I merely wanted to give you the choice."

He shifted under her hand. *I don't need a choice. I'll stay.* He nodded his head at her and his stiff face lost its scowl.

Bancroft reappeared, his voice chiming double speed. *The spell's used up but there's a pile of rocks. Yer not gettin' around those easily, that's for sure.*

"Nonsense. I'm sure we can move them." Citrine strode forward, the pixie and Stongorr trailing behind her.

She stopped in front of the cave-in. Rocks and debris blocked all but a narrow sliver of the tunnel. She pointed. "I think we can probably widen that so we can get through." She turned to Stongorr. "I'm going to need your help with this."

She set her lantern down and reached for the first rock, but the gargoyle didn't move to help her. Instead, he stared at something at the base of the rocks.

"What is it?"

He pointed, and she followed the beam of light. It took her a moment to understand what she was seeing, and when she did, her stomach gave a queasy turn.

"Oh dear!" She touched the tip of her shoe against a boot. The entire thing clattered to the ground, and she jumped back. The end of a stark-white bone gleamed in the lantern's light. She bent to get a closer look.

"Well, that answers one of my questions."

That this Alchemist is going to try to kill us? Stongorr used a clawed finger to push the boot further away from him.

She rolled her eyes. "No, it means other people have tried to get into the laboratory, but at least this one wasn't successful." She frowned. "Judging by the remains, he came here ages ago. Still, I hate to leave him here."

The gargoyle shrugged. *Whoever missed him is long dead by now.*

The pixie flew closer to the boot. *Crap on a cracker. He's smashed flatter than a pastry crust.*

Citrine straightened. "Well, I suppose there's nothing we can do for the poor chap now. Perhaps when we're done here, we can send someone to retrieve his remains and give him a proper burial."

Stongorr gave the boot one last poke. *At least they won't need a big hole.*

Citrine turned away from the bones and surveyed the opening. It was their best chance of getting to the rest of the tunnel. "Never mind about that. Come help me."

Citrine set her lantern down and together they moved the rocks one at a time.

Chapter 38

ALICE WATCHED CHESS BREATHE, counting each rise and fall of his chest as if her life depended on it. Maybe it did. Her gaze snagged on the dagger lying on the grass. She didn't remember throwing it down. Her only focus had been getting Chess out of the pool before that thing came back for both of them.

He was breathing again. Why wasn't he waking up?

She shuddered at the memory of his lifeless body clutched in the merrow's grip, her mouth clamped over the bottom half of his face. The punctures still trickled a bit of blood.

Her gaze snagged on the shredded sleeves of his shirt. She reached out and slipped back the material and sucked in a breath. Long gashes ran down his arms from biceps to wrist. She looked at his other arm and found it in a similar condition. She picked up the knife and cut away the rest of his sleeves.

She struggled to her feet and walked over to where she had dropped her satchel. For some reason, it felt twice as heavy now. She lugged it back over to Chess and dug out some water. She needed to wash out those wounds. Citrine had packed several canteens, so they should have enough water left if she used this one. The idea of using this pool or any other to refill them made her shiver. She tried to unscrew the cap, but her hands shook so much she couldn't manage it. She pressed them together, willing herself to calm down. Chess was here. He was alive. He'd be fine.

If she'd been only a minute or two later... Her mind shied away from the possibilities.

Her gaze moved towards the pool almost against her will. It's surface lay completely still, but that didn't stop a cold knot from forming in her stomach. What if the merrow came back to finish the job? Could the creatures leave the water? Another shiver ran through her, only partly from her wet clothes. She didn't want to be anywhere near this place once the sun went down.

Unfortunately, they were stuck here until Chess woke up.

Alice pressed her lips into a firm line and managed to get the cap off her canteen. She dug into the satchel again and came up with the cloth that had held food. Pouring water onto it, she cleaned the long scratches on Chess's arms. While ugly, they weren't too deep. She didn't know what she'd do if they got infected. She was a long way from Caterpillar's apothecary.

She glanced up at the sun, trying to gauge the time. Enough had passed that their clothes were no longer sopping wet. Alice made a face. They were still damp and clammy, though.

She rubbed at her arms. She was amazed she'd been able to pull Chess out of the water. If she hadn't... A tremor ran through her body again and she almost dropped her canteen. She screwed the cap on and set it on the ground.

Chess's dark brown skin held a waxy pallor that frightened her. She put her hands over her face, swallowing tears. She felt completely alone. Who had she been fooling? Zander had been right. She didn't belong here, not in the Kingdom of Wonderland and certainly not in this labyrinth. There was no chance she'd get to the crown first. Right now, she wasn't even sure she and Chess would survive long enough to make it to the center.

Wickle chirped and hopped onto her knee.

Alice, all right? Alice, sad?

Alice gave him a weary smile, wiping at her eyes. "Yes, Wickle. I'm all right. I'm not sad. I'm just... I don't know what I am."

Struck by how true those words were on so many levels, tears prickled again and she blinked them away.

Wickle clambered up to her shoulder. He patted at her cheek with a tiny paw. She stroked his bright fur, her nerves settling.

The sun beat down on her head, and the silence wrapped around her. A finger of unease slid up her spine.

She looked at Chess again. Asleep, he appeared younger somehow. She eyed the punctures again. They worried her because, unlike the scratches on his arms, they were deep. She didn't like the tiny dark lines spreading out from them. She still didn't understand how that creature had gotten ahold of him.

Wickle's paws drew her attention again. He ran his claws through the ends of her hair.

Mate sick?

Alice shook her head, almost knocking the little guy off her shoulder. "He's not my mate. He's my... friend, I guess."

Wickle scampered down her arm and over her knee, and leaped onto Chess's body. He scurried up Chess's neck and onto his face. Alice hoped Chess didn't choose this moment to wake up.

Wickle delicately touched one of the puncture wounds on Chess's face.

You fix. Poison.

Alice twisted her hands. "What do you mean, poison? I can't fix that. I don't have any medicine or anything."

Wickle tilted his head.

No medicine. Alice has Healer Gift.

Alice frowned. "I have the Creature Gift, but I've never healed anyone. Well, I've doctored the animals at home, but that's different. I used medicines and ointments and things like that." But even as she said it, she remembered how warm her hands had been on Zander's face, and she'd almost been able to see Chess's shoulder when it was dislocated. But that was ridiculous.

Wickle stomped one of his tiny feet. Alice winced. He still stood on Chess's cheek. She could imagine his reaction if he knew a snark was standing on his face. She bit back a smile.

Alice heal, not medicine.

Alice spread her hands out. "I'm sorry, Wickle, but I don't understand what you want me to do."

Wickle leaped off Chess's face and raced back to Alice. He grasped one of Alice's fingers with both paws and tugged. She didn't know what the ball of fluff wanted, but he seemed distraught, so she tried to comply.

"What do you want me to do, Wickle?"

Use hands. Heal mate.

"I told you... Never mind. Do you want me to put my hands on those wounds or—"

Wickle jumped up and down. *Yes, yes, yes. Heal mate. We leave.* His turquoise fur shivered all at once.

"I'll try, but Wickle, I don't think this will work."

Wickle shook his shaggy head. *No talk. Just do.*

Sighing, Alice got up on her knees and leaned forward. She set her fingers on the puncture wounds. She wasn't sure what she was supposed to do. She just sat there, feeling incredibly foolish. If Chess woke up now, he'd never let this go.

After a moment of silence, a faint warmth came into her palms. Unsure and still feeling ridiculous, she closed her eyes and focused on where her fingers touched Chess's face. She tried to picture the wounds closing up and the skin smoothing over. The warmth in her hands grew.

She opened her eyes and gasped. Her hands held a faint glow, and that glow was seeping into Chess's skin. She slammed her eyes closed and focused harder. Her hands moved, almost without her input, down to his chest. A faint gurgle became audible. She pressed her fingers deeper into his flesh, and somehow she knew there was water in his lungs. She didn't know what a lung looked like but she pictured dryness and ease of breathing.

Suddenly, Chess gasped and sat straight up. Alice fell backward in surprise.

"You're..."

"I'm..."

They both stopped and grinned foolishly at each other. Chess ran his hands over his face and then down his chest. "What happened? The last thing I remember we were kissing, and I didn't want it to ever end."

Chapter 39

ALICE DREW AWAY FROM him and blinked. "Kissing?"

Chess leaned back on his arms and stared dreamily up at the sky. "Yes, you leaned over and started kissing me." His eyes found hers. "It was amazing."

His heart picked up its rhythm as he tried to recall the exact feel of her lips, but his mind felt muddled.

Alice's voice intruded. "I think lack of air is causing you to hallucinate, but I definitely wasn't kissing you." Her cheeks flushed. "Well, I tried to blow air into your lungs to get you to breathe again, but that was only to save your life. It wasn't an actual kiss."

Chess leaned forward, his gaze intent on her mouth. "You can call it whatever you want, but I wouldn't mind a repeat." He reached for her.

Alice rolled her eyes and dodged his grasp. "Maybe I should knock you out again."

Chess shook his head, trying to clear his brain. He ran a hand over his hair, surprised he was shaking. He dropped his hands into his lap and clenched them to still their tremors. It was only then he realized all of his clothes were damp and sticking to his skin. "What happened?"

She explained how she'd found him when she'd stumbled out of the mist.

Chess examined his arms, wincing slightly as his fingers passed over some scratches. "I don't understand. You were sitting right there." He pointed to the pool. "I remember being kind of mad that you kept moving away from me, but I was just so relieved to find you." His voice slowed. "Your back was to me, and when I called your name, you turned and patted the seat next to you. Then, when I sat down, you just kissed me." His gaze returned to her mouth and without thought, he leaned toward her again.

Alice scooted backwards in the grass and shook her head. "It wasn't me. It was a merrow. At least that's what Wickle called it." She shrugged. "Whatever it was, that wasn't a kiss. It was trying to kill you."

He shivered as a memory surfaced from the haze. His lungs constricted, and suddenly it was hard to breathe. He stared at the pool. "I didn't know they could come out of the water."

She held up her hands. "This is your Kingdom; I'm just a visitor. In my world, creatures like that are only a story."

Chess pulled at the clammy fabric of his shirt. "This is my first encounter with one. They're supposed to be very beautiful, but views are mixed on whether they're dangerous or not."

Alice snorted. "I think you know the answer to that one now."

Chess rubbed his hands over his face. "I really thought it was you." Dents on the sides of his mouth stilled his fingers. "What happened here?"

Alice pulled his hand away as Wickle stuck his head out of her pocket and chittered at her.

Alice shifted and stroked the tiny head. "I told you, she had her face suctioned to yours. Her fangs left marks."

Chess's fingers flew back to his face, and he explored the spots more closely. "Her fangs? She bit me?"

"You're all right. I cleaned everything."

The little snark twittered and whistled, insistent about something.

Alice glanced at him and then gently pushed Wickle into her pocket. Chess ignored the creature and turned to the pool again. "What happened to her?"

Alice shrugged and told him how the creature taunted her until Alice got into the pool. "And then when I pulled you away, she dove under the water and disappeared. I had a bad few minutes until I got you out. I was sure she was going to come back and attack us both."

Chess turned her words over in his mind. "Citrine kept saying the labyrinth wasn't about physical strength. Maybe this was about overcoming your fears, and I was just the means to the end this time." He smirked, wondering if she'd remember her earlier words in the garden.

Alice's cheeks turned pink, and she folded her arms. "It wasn't like it wanted that thing to attack you, but I am rather terrified of water. I've always been that way."

"Looks like, in this case, the means did justify the ends, then." He tapped her knee and winked.

She didn't respond to his teasing. Instead, she rubbed her arms, her eyes darting toward the water. "When she dragged you under, I knew you were going to die if I didn't do something." She hugged herself. "It's all just a blur now."

Chess grinned. "Well, I'm certainly glad you conquered your fears, love. I'd be fish food if you didn't."

A smile crept over her face. "I'm rather glad I did, too."

A soft splash startled them both. Faint ripples disturbed the glassy surface. Alice scrambled to her feet and pulled on Chess's hand. He let her help him to his feet. She grabbed her satchel and pulled its strap over her shoulder.

"We shouldn't linger here. Do you feel strong enough to walk?" she asked.

Chess cast an apprehensive look at the pool. "Even if I wasn't, I would drag myself away from here."

Alice paused and looked around. Six paths ran off from the round clearing where they stood. She spun in a circle, her movements jerky. When she looked at him, her eyes were wide, the pupils dilated.

"Which way should we go? Citrine said to turn right, but how do you turn right from a circle?"

Chess moved to her side and pointed toward a path where a vine of purple flowers twined in the hedge right where it emptied into the clearing. "I'm pretty sure that's the one I came out of. I remember those flowers. Do you remember which where you came out?"

Alice glanced around the clearing. Finally, she pointed to the pathway next to the one Chess had indicated. "I think it was that one, but I can't be positive. I was so panicked when I saw you."

Chess nodded. "Both of those are on the far side of the clearing, so if we went right"—he spun around until he faced another set of paths—"we probably need one of these two." He gestured directly behind her. "Which one do you think?"

Alice turned in the direction he had pointed, folding her arms over her stomach. "What if I pick the wrong one?" She gaze swung between the two pathways.

Chess grimaced. The snark crawled out of her pocket and onto her shoulder. It was touching her face with a tiny clawed hand. He resisted the urge to swat it away from Alice.

"Ask who?" Alice stared down at the snark, and Chess wished he could understand what it was saying. It was strange to him that he could understand the giant bug but not the snark.

Wickle chittered loudly again.

Chess rolled his eyes. "Please do not tell me you are talking to that fuzz ball."

Alice glared at Chess. "As it so happens, Wickle is worth listening to. If it wasn't for him..." Alice paused, her eyes darting from him to the snark and then back again.

Chess raised his eyebrows. "If it wasn't for him, what?"

Alice held up her hand. "Quiet."

He sighed, but he kept his mouth shut.

Alice cleared her throat and spoke clearly. "Which way do we need to go?"

Realizing she wasn't talking to him, Chess remained quiet. Of course, he wasn't sure who—

The labyrinth rustled and creaked. Of the two paths he had pointed to, only one of them was open to them now. She headed towards it. "I guess we need to go this way."

The hairs on the back of his neck stood up, and he glanced at the hedges before he followed her. "I hope this isn't some kind of trick."

Another splash sounded behind them. Alice hurried forward. "Whatever it is, it's got to be better than staying here."

Chess glanced back as they reached the path. A fin cut the water. Yes, anywhere was better than here.

Chapter 40

IT HAD TAKEN LONGER than she liked to get by the rockfall, but with Stongorr's help she'd done it. She wasn't certain how much time had passed since they squeezed through that opening. Time was impossible to track down here. She wished she'd thought to bring her watch pin. Citrine wondered how far this tunnel went. In the endless darkness broken only by the small pools of light from their pocket lanterns and Bancroft's soft glow, it was easy to believe the laboratory didn't exist, and this path would spit them out somewhere on the opposite side of the mountain.

The floor continued to slope downwards, and Citrine tried to calculate in her head how deep in the earth they were. Bancroft flitted ahead of her, humming a tuneless melody. They rounded a bend and the tunnel angled downward. He paused, hovering in the air.

Citrine hurried forward to catch up with him. Without warning, something cut across her ankle, and she stumbled forward. The slant of the ground pitched her towards an opening in the tunnel. Her fingers dragged over the rough stone wall, trying to keep herself from falling. Something buzzed across her skin.

Her forward momentum stopped when her knees hit the stone floor with a slap of pain.

Stongorr peered around her. *Did you feel that?*

She nodded and pushed to her feet, her knees stinging. "Yes, and I don't like it. Bancroft, do you sense a spell?"

The pixie licked a finger and held it up. He twisted one way and then another as if testing the weather. Finally, he shook his head. *There isn't an active spell like the other one we passed, but there's something. I'll go check out these other tunnels.* He flitted off before Citrine could stop him

They stood on the edge of a round cavern. Several other tunnels branched off from it, but in the darkness, the entrances resembled blacker shadows.

Citrine backed up. The buzzing feeling disappeared.

You should have tried again for the spell bee. Stongorr's voice was gruff.

"You keep saying that, but he's been very helpful so far."

The gargoyle humphed. *We'll see.*

While they waited in silence, Citrine held up her lantern to get a better look at the cavern. The darkness made it impossible to see anything clearly.

She was debating the wisdom of getting a closer look when Stongorr cocked his head. *I hear something.*

Citrine strained her ears. For a long moment, the silence was absolute. Then she heard it, too—the scrabble of tiny nails on rock.

"What do you think that is?" She shifted so her back pressed against the wall.

Stongorr scowled. *Nothing good.*

Citrine licked her lips. "Maybe we should retreat."

Yes. We should. The gargoyle didn't wait but shuffled back the way they had come.

Citrine hesitated. "What about Bancroft?" The words barely left her mouth when she saw a spot of light careening toward her.

It was the pixie, flying at top speed out of one of the side tunnels. He waved his tiny arms over his head, his voice so high-pitched it was hard for Citrine to understand.

Run! Run! It's lorgs, a whole pack of them.

Citrine nearly dropped her lantern. "Lorgs?!"

Dread pooled in her stomach. There was nowhere to run. Once they got your scent, lorgs were relentless. The size of a small rat, they traveled in packs of thousands. If they caught you, they could clean the flesh off your bones in mere minutes. Phineas wasn't just paranoid. He was ruthless. What was he hiding in that laboratory?

What are you waiting for? The urgent tone in Stongorr's normally gruff voice broke Citrine's momentary paralysis.

She retreated up the tunnel, even as she knew it was pointless. Her mind scrambled for a solution. Even if they could make it to the surface, the creatures wouldn't stop. The only thing that worked was flying. It broke the scent chain, but there was no way they would make it back up to the carriage and get in the air in time.

She hummed low in her throat and tried to connect with at least a few of the lorgs, but there were no clear words to hang onto. It was just a whining wall of sound—a hive mind. There was no communicating with that. Icy perspiration broke out over her body.

The scrabbling behind her got louder, accompanied by excited squeaks. Her lantern shook as she raised it and looked back over her shoulder. The light speared down the tunnel revealing a sight that chilled her. A churning wave of cream fur careened toward them.

They couldn't outrun them. They needed help. As she hurried back the way they had come, she sent out a distress call. She slowed as she concentrated on trying to find help. Stongorr grunted and twisted to look at her.

Keep going.

Her breath came in pants, as much from panic as exertion. "I'm trying... to find help.... If only we had... a few minutes."

Stongorr whirled back and pushed her behind him.

"What are you doing?"

Call for your help. I will slow them.

Citrine's chest constricted. "You can't do that. They'll—

You waste time. He turned his back on her and planted himself in the middle of the tunnel. His wings spread from one wall to the other.

He was buying her those few precious minutes. She stopped arguing and closed her eyes. She hummed louder. Nothing answered as seconds ticked by. Then, over the high-pitched whine of the lorgs, something responded. She couldn't make out what, but help was on the way.

Now they only had to hold the lorgs off long enough for it to arrive.

Chapter 41

CHESS AND ALICE KEPT moving until late afternoon. They made right turn after right turn until they came to another large intersection, this one square.

A small temple-like building sat on the right side of the square. Its walls shone and sparkled in the sun. As Alice got closer, she realized it was made of glass, but strangely, she couldn't see through it. The frosted purple doors to the temple stood open, showing the path picking up again on the other side of the building.

She looked around and spotted another way besides the one going through the temple.

"It looks like we have to walk through that shrine," said Chess.

"There's another path."

"Didn't you say we had to go right?" He pointed to the building. "That way is right."

Alice shook her head. "I don't think I want to go in there."

Chess shrugged. "You're the boss."

Alice turned away from the temple and toward the other path. Unease slithered up her spine, but she pressed onward.

She breathed a sigh once they left the intersection. There was something unsettling about that temple, although she couldn't say what it was.

They had a walked about a quarter of an hour when they came to another crossroads. Alice blinked in surprise.

Sparkling in the late afternoon sun was the same temple they had left not fifteen minutes before. An icy chill made her shiver.

"I guess the labyrinth is telling us something," said Chess.

Alice bit her lip. "Well, I'm not listening."

Again, she took a different pathway. She walked faster and faster until she was running. Chess scrambled to keep up with her.

"What are you doing? We're going back the way we just came."

"I don't want to go into that place," Alice said over her shoulder. "There has to be a way to avoid it."

This time, it took even less time before they ended up in the same clearing. The temple's doors still stood open, the pathway beyond beckoning.

Alice stubbornly turned around, intent on finding a different way, but Chess blocked her. "You're being ridiculous. It's obvious that we have to go through that temple."

Alice shook her head, planting her feet. Dread spread through her, and she didn't think she could move even if she wanted to.

"Come on." Chess tugged at her hand. "The sooner we go in, the sooner we get out." He tipped his head back. "Besides, we don't have a lot of day left."

Alice pulled her hand away and rubbed her arms. "I... I... can't explain it, but I don't want to go in there."

"We don't have a choice." He tugged on her hand again, and Alice reluctantly moved her feet. Each step felt like she was trudging through cement.

When they reached the frosted amethyst doors, she paused again. Her heart was beating so fast, she felt a momentary wave of dizziness. Chess's face creased in concern.

"It's not that far, Alice." He pointed with his free hand. "You can see through to the other side."

Alice took a deep breath and nodded. Grasping his hand tighter, Alice stepped into the temple.

They had only taken a few steps when the doors behind them closed with a loud click.

Alice jumped.

Chess picked up his pace.

They entered what looked like a long hallway. Mirrors lined both sides, even the ceiling. Under their feet, black glass gave the feeling that you were walking over a vast nothingness. The effect was disorientating.

Alice kept her gaze on the open back doors, her hand gripping Chess's so hard her knuckles were white. They were halfway through the hallway when the back doors started to shut. Alice and Chess exchanged a look before they both took off at a run.

They were too late.

The doors clicked shut just as they reached the threshold. Alice skidded to a stop before she ran into them, but Chess couldn't stop in time. He slammed into them and stumbled backward.

Alice lurched toward him, catching him before he fell. Once righted, they clung together for a moment. Then Chess pushed at the doors. They didn't budge. He lowered his shoulder and rammed it into the glass, but nothing happened.

Alice turned to look at the hallway. It had dimmed but wasn't completely dark. She could see replicas of herself and Chess over and over in the mirrors. She stepped closer to the nearest one and tentatively reached out a hand. Her fingertips met with smooth, cold glass.

As she looked into the mirror, it began to cloud over with smoke. Panicked, she turned in a circle, but the hallway was clear. The smoke was inside the glass. As she watched, the cloud started to dissipate as if a wind was blowing it away, leaving the mirror clear again.

Alice gasped when she looked into it. She saw herself in the glass, but she was six years old, and she was back in an alley of London's notorious slums. It was the moment her life changed for the better. Two scruffy boys held her arms while she stared defiantly up at the leader of the gang, a boy named Danny. She could smell the rotting trash and feel the fear that had choked her. But she knew what her six-year-old self didn't. Rommy was coming to save her. She watched as Danny balled up his fist. Here it was. Her sister would come charging into the alleyway.

Danny plowed his fist into her stomach. Somehow, Alice felt it even as she watched and doubled over, crying out in pain. His next punch hit her in the jaw, and Alice's own head snapped backward, though nothing actually hit her now. She crumpled to the ground, her hand against the glass.

"No, oh no." The words wrenched out of her. She scrabbled at the glass, wanting to save herself, but she could only watch in horror as the boy beat her six-year-old self almost unconscious, somehow feeling every blow. The last kick to her back sent pain shooting down her legs.

The glass fogged again and when it cleared, she saw a girl no older than thirteen. Her black hair was matted to her head and her eyes were huge in a gaunt face. She was begging on a street corner. Well-dressed men and women hurried past. The ones that looked at her had expressions mixed between disgust and pity. Alice didn't know how, but she felt the hollow hunger in the mirror girl's stomach. She crossed her arms over her own stomach and moaned.

The glass clouded over a third time. This time, though she recognized that the girl in the mirror was her, she looked very different. Dressed in an expensive but scandalously low-cut dress, she was smiling at a well-dressed man who had a proprietary arm around her waist. The smile didn't reach the mirror girl's eyes. Instead, they looked ancient, and her smile had a hard, brittle quality.

Alice's hand covered her mouth, a sob wrenching from her chest. "No, that's not what happened." She pounded a fist against the glass. "That's not me!"

Distantly, she could hear someone calling her name, but the mirrors all along the hallway began to swirl with pictures, all of Alice at different ages, in different places—some in the slums, some in polite society, some that had really happened, many that hadn't, but all of them unhappy, pictures of a victim.

Alice spun from one to the other. Her breath came in short, choppy gasps. The pictures whirled faster and faster. She gripped the sides of her head as her eyes went from one picture to the other. The reel of images finally stopped. She was back in the alleyway. The two boys gripped her arms. Danny balled up his fists. This time, Alice knew nobody was coming. She leaped forward. There was a moment of resistance, and then she was in the alley. The smells of garbage and refuse assaulted her nostrils. She rushed to her smaller self and stepped in front of her. The boys who looked so big to her six-year-old eyes were only children themselves.

"Get away from her!" she screamed. The two boys, their eyes huge, dropped her scrawny arms and backed away. Then they took off down the alley. She whirled to face Danny, who only came up to her chest. He stuck out a belligerent chin. She stepped forward, her hand pulling the knife at her waist. She glared at him. The boy stood for a moment, and then his face crumpled and he took off too.

She turned around to find her six-year-old self staring up at her with enormous eyes. "Ya saved my hide, ya did," she said almost cheerfully.

Alice gulped down a sob. "I... I guess I did."

"Yer ain't one of them watering pots, is ya?"

"I'm afraid so." Alice laughed, her voice wobbly. She gathered the little girl in her arms and hugged her tightly. The little girl clutched her back. "I won't let anything happen to you," she said into the soft curls, closing her eyes. "I promise."

A hand shook her shoulder, and she opened her eyes. Chess's face loomed over hers, his face crinkled with worry. She was kneeling the floor of the temple, hugging herself.

Both sets of doors were wide open.

Chapter 42

CITRINE BACKED FURTHER UP the tunnel. Her lantern light picked up a wave of churning cream bodies as the lorg pack swept up the tunnel toward Stongorr. Their high-pitched squeaks scraped her eardrums.

The gargoyle's wings beat back and forth creating a wind and slowing the oncoming horde. She only hoped it was enough.

Pearl Queen, my family is answering your call.

Citrine's knees buckled at the sound of the feminine voice. "Please hurry."

Even now, she wasn't who their rescuers were because the lorgs' squeaks and squeals made it difficult to hear clearly. She hoped they would be strong enough.

She knew she should get further away, but her feet remained rooted to the floor, her eyes trained on the gargoyle. There was nothing she could do to help him, but she refused to leave him.

Some of the lorgs had reached him now. His clawed hands moved in a blur of speed as he swatted them against the walls. The narrow tunnel worked in his favor.

It limited the number that could attack at one time. It was all that was saving them from being overrun.

His wings continued to flap, the wind working to slow the pack. A shower of rock and debris rained from the ceiling, peppering her head and shoulders with stings of pain, but she didn't move.

We are almost there.

The distant sound of yips and yodels echoed from behind her, but a bend in the tunnel blocked her view.

Stongorr continued to swat the lorgs, his arms moving in a rhythm punctuated by the soft thuds of the small bodies hitting the stone walls. Occasionally, he kicked out or stomped with a foot. Hope welled up. They were going to survive this.

She twisted, her eyes straining in the darkness behind her. Stongorr grunted and she whirled back.

She stifled a cry as a lorg dodged his defenses and latched onto his shoulder. He reached up and ripped it away. Blood streamed from the wound. Worse, it had given others an opening. A half a dozen more sailed from the rippling mass at his feet, sinking their teeth into his torso. He staggered back a few steps, the rhythm of his wings faltering.

Get back. He didn't look at her, his concentration on the enemy in front of him.

Her feet refused to move. The lorgs just kept coming, clogging the tunnel and piling up on top of each other. Stongorr backed up again, ripping more of the creatures from his body.

The yips behind her got louder, accompanied by snarls. The stream of lorgs swirled and eddied. Several dodged past Stongorr's wings and veered in her direction. She backpedaled, and her heel caught on a stone. She tripped and fell, landing on her back. The breath whooshed out of her, and her lantern clattered to the floor.

She pushed herself up on her elbows. Stongorr let out a roar and beat his wings harder as a group climbed his legs. The wind drove some of them back, but there were too many. They scrabbled up and over the gargoyle. He teetered and fell to his knees, his entire body covered in writhing cream fur. He feebly swiped at them with his claws. One wing drooped and blood dripped from a large rip, making a puddle on the stone floor.

Citrine finally found her feet before the lorgs could attack her. She kicked at one, her foot connecting with a small body.

Then a ripple of shadows streaked by her. One shadow stopped as a lorg launched itself at her face. She threw up her hands, but it never landed. Instead, it squealed and there was a dull thud.

When she put down her hands, the lorg, along with two more, lay at her feet, petrified.

A paw touched her leg, and she lifted her foot to deliver another kick, but a voice stopped her.

Your Majesty, we are here.

When she looked down, she saw the top of a furry head with tufted pointed ears, the muzzle aimed at the ground. The fur was a mix of smoke and silver. The ruff around its neck writhed with tiny granite-colored snakes, all flicking their tongues.

Her legs turned rubbery, and she put a hand against the wall to keep herself upright. It was a skulk of Medusa foxes.

"Thank you for coming." Citrine's voice trembled, and she stroked the matriarch's bowed head.

I am Fiana. My family will kill this scourge. The fox yipped and leapt away.

The rest of her family danced over the backs of the lorgs. Their yodels echoed off the rock walls. The writhing mass under their feet slowed.

But they were too late for Stongorr. He lay still, most of the horde having abandoned him.

She grabbed her lantern and ran forward, but a few remaining lorgs leapt off the gargoyle and headed in her direction. She swung her lantern and kicked out at them. She cried out as one bit into her calf. She grabbed its tail and flung it away from her. It squealed as it hit the wall with a sickening thud, and then lay twitching on the ground. Citrine had no time for remorse. She kicked another one, but they had spread out in front of her, their red eyes gleaming in her lantern's light.

A snarl ripped through the air, and Fiana reappeared in front of Citrine. The creatures realized the danger too late. Their bodies hardened and turned to stone. One by one, they fell, clinking onto the ground.

The matriarch spun back toward the battle.

From where Citrine stood, she could see that the surging mass had been frozen into a terrifying tableau like some kind of strange sculpture. She could still hear snarls and the unique battle yodels coming from further away in the cavern.

She ran to Stongorr and dropped to her knees next to him. He was still breathing, each inhalation raspy and labored. His body shook uncontrollably. She could hardly bear to look at him. The gargoyle's body was pockmarked with bites and missing chunks of flesh. In some places, bone showed through, and one of his eye sockets was only a bloody hollow.

She swallowed down the bile in her throat and forced a smile to her trembling lips. She laid her fingers on the back of his hand, the only place she could find that wasn't bleeding.

"You did it, Stongorr. You held them off until help arrived." Tears clogged her throat.

His one remaining eye cracked open. *Not... more pixies... I hope.*

She breathed out a laugh and it turned into a sob. "No. It was a family of Medusa foxes, if you can believe it. They're incredibly rare."

Are... you hurt? His words slurred. He struggled to keep his eye open.

"No. Thanks to you." She wished she could hug him, but she was afraid to hurt him more than he already was.

Worth... it then. The grey eye slid shut.

"Stongorr?"

He didn't respond. Instead, his chest rose once, and he let out a long breath.

Then his head slumped to the side, and his body went slack.

She shook her head, tears leaking from her eyes. "No!" She shook his shoulder, blood smearing onto her fingers. "No, you can't..." A sob stopped her words.

He was gone. Her head dropped forward, and tears streamed down her face. She didn't even bother to wipe them away.

Citrine didn't know how long she stayed bowed over Stongorr's mangled body, but she realized the yodeling and yips had quieted. Loud crunching noises had replaced them.

A small light flitted up the tunnel towards her. *Yer not going to believe what them foxes is doing. Just munching away at all them petrified lorgs.*

As the light got closer, it slowed to hover in the air. Bancroft spiraled downward and settled onto her knee. He took off his hat and twisted it in his hands as he looked at Stongorr. He shook his head sadly. *That's a right shame, it is. He were a good gargoyle.*

Citrine sniffed. "He was, wasn't he?" She ran a gentle hand over Stongorr's shoulder. "He saved my life. I just wish..." She swiped at another tear, surprised there were any left. Her eyes felt gritty and swollen from all the ones she'd already shed.

Soft footfalls pattered close. Citrine shifted and got to her feet, Bancroft fluttering by her shoulder. It was Fiana, the Medusa fox matriarch. Citrine was careful not to look directly into the milky-white eyes that glowed in the dimness of the tunnels.

"I can't thank you and your family enough for coming to our aid."

The fox moved closer and bowed her head. *We are honored to help the Pearl Queen. I am only sorry we could not save your servant, too.* She nudged Stongorr's shoulder with her long nose. *He died bravely.*

Citrine chin dropped, and she blinked rapidly. Stupid tears. They didn't change anything. "Yes, he was very brave, but I know you got here as quickly as you could. It's a miracle you stopped them at all."

The fox's muzzle wrinkled into a snarl. *Lorgs are a scourge. We take great joy in ridding these tunnels of their presence.* She licked her lips. *They are also quite tasty once petrified.*

Citrine fought to keep from gagging at the thought. Instead, she smiled at Fiana. "Your family has done me a great service, and I won't forget it."

The fox bowed her head once more. *You may call on us anytime, Your Majesty.*

The graceful creature lifted her muzzle into the air and gave several sharp yips. When she turned back to Citrine the snakes in her ruff undulated in a lazy rhythm. *We must go now.*

The patter of soft feet on stone echoed up the tunnel as the rest of the Medusa foxes gathered around their matriarch. Their smoke-like fur blended into the darkness, making them resemble a shadow moving across the carpet of petrified lorgs.

Once they were all gathered together, Fiana yodeled and leapt forward. Together, they surged up the tunnel.

It was only then that Citrine heard a voice calling her name. Ice slid down her spine.

It was Zander, and he was headed right into an entire skulk of Medusa foxes.

Without thinking, she jumped over Stongorr's prone body and sprinted after them, yelling, "Zander! Close your eyes!"

Chapter 43

ZANDER ARRIVED AT THE ruins at dusk. When he spotted the open trapdoor and broken steps, he had been alarmed. Then he'd picked up the trail of Citrine and her gargoyle leading into the tunnels.

The rocky underground path was too narrow for anything but his human form, but he'd been able to let his jabberwock surface enough so he could see where he was going.

He'd walked over an hour, but as he rounded another bend he heard voices. That had to be Citrine. Who else would be down here? He hurried forward, but paused when a yodel floated in the air.

"Citrine!" His voice echoed off the stone walls.

When there was no answer, he moved faster. He'd only gone a few steps more when running footfalls thundered towards him. Above it, Citrine was yelling, but he couldn't quite make out her words.

Zander picked up his pace until he was jogging. He rounded another bend, and a surging shadow lit by a dozen glowing eyes flowed towards him.

He flattened himself against the wall as the shadow raced closer.

"Zander! Close your eyes!" The words were finally clear, but they made little sense. He obeyed them anyway and squeezed his eyes shut.

A dozen creatures brushed by his legs as Citrine yelled out her instructions again.

Then someone crashed into him, driving the breath from his lungs. His eyes popped open, and he looked into Citrine's face. Her eyes were red and swollen, like she'd been crying.

He scanned her, looking for injuries. "What's going on? Are you all right?"

She flung her arms around him, and he hugged her back. Her voice wobbled with emotion. "I'm fine, but Stongorr is dead, and those were Medusa foxes, and I was so afraid. If you'd looked at their eyes you'd be petrified, and I don't know what I'd do if—"

He squeezed her tighter. "Hey, slow down. What happened? Did the foxes kill Stongorr?" He shifted so his body blocked hers and glanced down the tunnel where the foxes had disappeared.

Citrine shook her head against his shoulder, her words muffled. "No, it was lorgs."

A chill slid down his spine. Lorgs were nasty creatures. He'd heard what they could do, and it wasn't pretty. Poor Stongorr. He leaned back so he could look into her face. "Are you sure you're all right? They didn't hurt you, did they?"

Tears streaked her cheeks. "No, Fiana and her family came in the nick of time." She wiped at the corners of her eyes. "But it was too late for Stongorr and..." She trailed off and stared at him.

Then she pushed him away and put her hands on her hips. "What are you doing here?"

Heat climbed up Zander's neck and he was thankful for the dim light. "I... I came to check on you. Lapin said you'd come here. That it was dangerous."

She narrowed her eyes. "But why were you at Lapin's? I would think you'd have enough to deal with at the palace. Especially now."

Before he could answer, a light flitted over and flew around Zander's head in a dizzying circle. Tiny bells chimed in his ears, making him wince. He waved a hand, trying to shoo it away.

"Bancroft, come over here and leave the prince alone." The ball of light zipped toward Citrine and hovered over her shoulder. Once it stopped buzzing around, he realized it was a sparkle pixie.

"Zander, why are you really here? Did something happen?"

He pulled his focus back to Citrine, and swallowed, not sure what to say.

Her grey eyes pierced into his and his gaze dropped first. His ugly words from earlier echoed in his head. "I... I don't know. I mean, when Lapin told me where you'd gone, I knew I couldn't let you do this alone, but as to why I went to Sir Lapin's..." He rubbed a hand on his neck and paced away from her. "I've made such a mess of everything." A bitter laugh escaped his lips. "Lord Beecher let me know just what a disappointment I truly am."

She laid a hand on his arm. "You know that isn't true. He's made an art of raking people over the coals, and he's been doing it since before either of us were born."

Zander snorted. "It doesn't mean he's wrong though, and then... how I treated you. It was inexcusable, the things I said." He risked looking at her. "I just thought... if I could fix one thing today..." He closed his eyes, feeling like an even bigger fool for coming after her. What was he doing here when he had responsibilities back home?

Her hand cupped his cheek, and he opened his eyes. She smiled up at him. "I can't deny that your words hurt me, but you've been under a tremendous amount of strain for a good long while now."

He leaned into her palm, a smile playing on his lips. "Does that mean you'll forgive me?"

She stepped away from him and rolled her eyes. "I'm here trying to help you, aren't I?"

The knot in his chest loosened, and he resisted the urge to hug her again. "What exactly *are* you trying to do down here?"

She tilted her head. "Get into Sacklepenny's laboratory to find the answers you need." She said it as if this should be obvious. "I don't have much time, though. I have to find something before the competition is over."

Zander was still confused. "What do you think you're going to find?"

Citrine leaned over and picked up the lantern from where it dropped when she'd tackled him. "If we can find a way to override your Drifter Gene, or even a more reliable antidote to the Jabberwock's Curse, the Queen has nothing to hold over you."

Warmth spread through Zander's chest. "I don't deserve you."

She gave him a cheeky grin. "No, you probably don't." Then her expression sobered, and she stepped closer. "Whatever else we've been to each other in the past, you're my dearest friend. I won't let anyone hurt you if I have it in my power to prevent it."

Before he could speak around the lump in his throat, she spun away. Her voice floated back to him. "Besides, seeing Lyssandra's face when she realizes she's been thwarted will be tremendously satisfying."

Zander chuckled. "I never knew you were so..." He rounded the corner and almost ran into Citrine. She was standing by Stongorr's body. When she turned to look at him, the sorrow on her face tore at his heart.

Zander moved to stand next to her and put his arm around her shoulder. "I'm sorry. I know he meant a lot to you."

Citrine sniffed and straightened her shoulders. "He was so brave, and he saved my life." Her voice cracked on the last word, and she cleared her throat. "I hate to leave him here, like this. He should get a proper burial."

Zander stepped away from her and shrugged out of his coat. Gently, he laid it over Stongorr's ravaged face and torso. "We'll bring him out when we leave."

She looked at him for a long moment and then went up on her toes, pressing a kiss on his cheek. "Thank you, Zander."

Before he could respond, she drew in a deep breath. "Now, we need to find that laboratory." She walked toward the cavern up ahead. He followed her, trying to avoid the petrified lorgs that still littered the ground.

It didn't take long for them to reach the cavern's opening. He stopped and stared. The entire floor was covered in stone creatures, many broken or bitten to dust.

Citrine pulled on his sleeves to get his attention, and he wrenched his gaze away from the carnage. She pointed to one of the tunnels leading out of it. "It's probably down the same tunnel the lorgs came through."

He nodded. "I'll follow you."

She hesitated and then lifted her chin and strode into the cavern, sidestepping the piles of petrified lorgs. Zander shivered at the sheer number of the things. He was truly sorry about Stongorr, but he was thankful for the gargoyle's sacrifice. Without it, Citrine would be dead.

When she reached the mouth of the tunnel, her voice was brisk. "I think we'll find your answers down this way."

After all of this, Zander hoped she was right.

Chapter 44

CHESS STARED INTO ALICE'S damp eyes and released a puff of air, his shoulders sagging. He had been frantic when she'd collapsed to the floor. She had banged and shouted at the mirrors, but no matter how many times he called her name or tried to get her attention, it was like she was in a waking nightmare. Wherever she was, it was playing out in the mirrors, but all he saw was their own reflections.

"Are you all right?" He kept his voice soft, still afraid she'd disappear back to the tortured place she had been.

She nodded and looked down at her crossed arms. A series of emotions flickered over her face before it smoothed out. He held out a hand and helped her to her feet. She wobbled for a moment before righting herself.

He wasn't surprised when she lifted her chin and straightened her shoulders. "We should leave while we can." Her voice was hoarse but firm.

Chess tentatively reached for her hand, but she strode ahead of him. He looked back over his shoulder at the hall of mirrors. For a fleeting moment, a small girl with

Alice's big violet eyes and soft black curls smiled out at him. He blinked and she was gone.

Alice had already reached the pathway outside, so Chess hurried after her. His thoughts were a tangle of questions, but Alice didn't stop.

He reached out and gripped her arm. "Hey, what happened back there? Are you all right?"

She shook him off impatiently. "Yes, I'm fine." She started walking again and he fell into step beside her. He didn't think she was fine, but she obviously didn't want to talk about it. The snark popped out of her pocket and started twittering at her, but she only patted him absently.

Chess frowned. The shadows had lengthened and the sun was almost gone. How long had they been in that house of mirrors? It had seemed both mere moments and days. The path was dim in the dusk, and the shadows of the hedges stretched in front of them.

Weariness washed over him as he plodded forward. He sighed loudly. Alice turned to him. "What's wrong?"

Chess rolled his shoulders. "It's been a rather long day," he said. A sheepish smile spread over his face at this vast understatement.

Alice frowned at him. "It's hard to believe we haven't even been in here a full day."

Chess started when he realized she was right. Time didn't feel linear in this labyrinth. They kept walking. He reached out and took her hand. She glanced down but didn't say anything—or pull away. After several minutes of walking in silence, he couldn't keep the question back.

"Are you going to tell me what happened in there?"

Alice's eyes slid away from his. "I... I can't. I don't really know..."

Her voice was soft and her expression troubled. Chess forced himself to shut up. He wanted to cajole her, charm her, get her to spill what was behind the haunted expression. Instead, he just squeezed her hand, and they kept walking.

After the third time Alice tripped over her own feet, Chess pulled her to a stop.

"What?" Alice turned her gaze to his.

"We need to rest."

Alice shook her head and tried to continue walking, but Chess's grip firmed.

"If what's ahead is anything like the rest of what we've been through today, we have to rest. We're both exhausted."

Alice twisted around and then looked back at him. "Where do you propose we rest?"

He took in their surroundings. The pathway was empty. There really wasn't anywhere to set up a shelter, but there was nowhere to hide in this twist of paths anyway.

Grinning, he plopped down on the ground and patted the grass next to him. Alice wrapped her arms around herself.

"We need to find somewhere safe."

The grin faded from Chess's face. "I don't think there is such a place in this labyrinth, Alice." He lifted one shoulder. "I think we have to just make the best of it until we reach the center."

He reached up and tugged on her hand, and she let him pull her down next to him without another word.

Chess didn't like how quiet she had been since they left the temple.

He reached out and touched her cheek. "It's going to be all right, Alice. We're going to get to the center, and then this will all be over." He swallowed. "You'll be able to go home." The words felt like sharp rocks as he pushed them out of his mouth.

Alice ignored his offer of comfort. Instead, she dug into her satchel and pulled out another one of Citrine's wrapped bundles, plus a canteen. Chess watched her movements. While they were brisk and practical, her hands trembled.

That disgusting little snark popped out of her pocket, scrambled onto the grass and beelined over to the hedges. Chess's lip curled. He still couldn't believe the thing hadn't poisoned one of them yet, but Alice was enchanted by the thing. He had to admit, the little guy did seem attached to her, but he still wasn't going to trust it. He watched it until it climbed into a hedge before turning back to Alice.

She had unwrapped the bundle and pushed some of the food over his way. Cold ham, rolls, and an apple were sitting in front of him. He tore into the food, his growling stomach demanding attention. After devouring most of the ham and several rolls, he paused and looked across at Alice. She was absently nibbling on one of the rolls, her eyes staring into the distance at something he couldn't see. A slither of unease worked its way up his spine. Had that place of mirrors damaged her somehow? She seemed... different. He saw her again on the floor of the temple, desperately hugging herself, murmuring and crying.

"It was my past," she said, startling him out of his thoughts.

"What?"

"The mirrors, they showed me my past, or what my past would've been without my sister." She shuddered and closed her eyes for a moment. When she opened them, they shimmered with unshed tears. "It... it was... horrible. Rommy was supposed to come, she did come and saved me from Danny and his gang. But... in the mirror... nobody came. Nobody saved me."

Chess set his food down and leaned forward. "But that's not true. What the mirror showed you didn't really happen, right? Your sister *did* come."

"It was so real." Her throat worked and her voice wobbled when she spoke again. "I felt every blow Danny landed on me." Tears clogged her voice. "I was only six. Why would he do that to a little girl? And then later..." A sob escaped. She buried her face in her hands, her shoulders shaking.

Chess hesitated and then reached over and gathered her into his arms, his food forgotten. "I don't know what you saw, but it wasn't real, Alice. Whatever it was, that didn't happen to you. Your sister *did* come. She *did* save you. That little girl was just fine."

For a long moment, Alice couldn't speak. The damp spot on Chess's shoulder grew, but he didn't move, just kept gently rubbing a hand over her back. Suddenly, she lifted her face from his shoulder, grabbing his arms, almost shaking him. "But... but... I think... Oh, Chess, what if it wasn't Danny who beat the little-girl-me unconscious?"

He pulled back a bit so he could see her face more clearly. "I'm sorry, love. You've lost me."

"At the end, I had to go into the mirror and rescue myself. Don't you see?" She shook his arms.

Chess shook his head and a smile ghosted over his face. "No, I'm afraid I don't. Why don't you explain it to me?"

"I... I had to push who I was way down to fit into the polite world my adopted family inhabited. When Papa James first adopted me, I didn't talk right or know anything about getting about in society. It was so hard because they had grown up that way, but to me everything was foreign. I didn't know it at the time, but Rommy and Papa James were considered rather eccentric, so it wasn't even as difficult as it could have been, but I still fought against it. It felt like I had to be someone I wasn't to fit in. Then when I was twelve..." Her voice trailed off, and her face lit with a wondering expression.

"That's why...," she murmured under her breath. She stared off into space until Chess squeezed her hands.

"When you were twelve?" he prodded her.

"When I was twelve there was this horrible incident at boarding school. I ran away. I had decided I was going to go back to London because I couldn't do it. I couldn't be this polite society girl they wanted, and I was letting my family down." Her eyes had a faraway look, and Chess wondered what she was seeing. He waited patiently for her to continue.

After a moment she picked up the story again. "One of the teachers, Miss Woodrow, found me. After she scolded me for running off, she told me even though my family loved me, if I didn't learn to fit in, it would reflect badly on them. She told me the only way to do that was to forget who I had been and become someone new." Alice's eyes closed briefly. "If I tried to hold on to who I had been, it would never work."

She opened her eyes and her expression grew fierce. "Don't you see? I owed it to my family. I didn't want to embarrass them or make them sorry they took me in."

Chess's heart squeezed. "Oh, Alice."

She pushed away from him. "Don't pity me."

"I'm—"

She held up a hand. "No, I can see it in your face. *Poor Alice*. I've had a good life and my family truly loves me. If I would have stayed in that alley, my life would have been over, in every way that mattered."

"Maybe, but you didn't have to stop being who you were to live the life you were meant for. I know that teacher was trying to help you, but nobody should have to do that."

She shrugged. "I don't know, Chess. Maybe I did, at least for a while. I don't know if I could have acclimated if I hadn't pushed down my former self, but now... I've been so... restless. Before I tumbled into Wonderland, I was at loose ends. Everyone wanted something for me that I didn't want for myself, and I felt guilty about it. Now I know why. I had to go back and save my little-girl self. It's time to let her into my life again."

Chess blinked at the blinding smile Alice turned on him. He opened his mouth, but before he could say anything, she threw her arms around him. He decided more talking could wait.

Chapter 45

THEIR BOOTS CLATTERED ON the rocky floor of the tunnel and echoed around them. Death tugged at Citrine's mind. Flashes of Stongorr overrun by lorgs kept trying to play over in her head. She shook the thoughts away and forced herself to concentrate on their surroundings. Bancroft flitted ahead, checking for traps and returning to give periodic reports.

The chances of someone surviving a horde of lorgs were slim, but that didn't mean that their friend Phineas hadn't planted more surprises for them. She was thankful they still had Bancroft's nose for spells. Most alchemists left a signature of their work. Even though she could have checked for those signs, it would have been exhausting work.

And she was already tired.

They reached the end of the tunnel without incident. Instead of making her happy, though, it only increased her unease.

Citrine held up her lantern and stared at the solid rock wall in dismay. "I was so sure this was the right way."

Zander shrugged. "It's fine. We'll go back and try another tunnel."

He was right, but the strain of more surprises was wearing on her. "I suppose we can." Still, logic dictated this should have been the right tunnel. She rubbed at her forehead. With a sigh, she turned around and started walking back up the way they had come.

Bancroft flew up and down the blank wall, and she waved at him. "Come on, Bancroft. There's nothing there."

His zipped in front of her face, his body vibrating. *Sure and you've missed something, Lady Citrine.*

"What?"

He flitted backward, waving his arms as he went. *Have a look and see if I'm right.*

She glanced at Zander and shrugged. "We may as well check out what he's found."

When she got to the wall, Citrine leaned in close, squinting at the rock. "Good job, Bancroft. There is something here."

The pixie beamed at her. She pointed out the faint lines that were just visible in the lamplight to Zander.

He held up his own lantern. "Do you know what they mean? It just looks like squiggles to me."

Citrine pushed up her spectacles, her nose practically touching the stone. "This sign... I believe it's the symbol for a dragon, but I can't make out the one before it."

"You don't think Sacklepenny has a..."

Citrine held up a hand and cocked her head. Her voice dropped to a whisper. "I hear something."

A faint voice—no, *two* voices were coming from somewhere off to the side. Bancroft flew over and settled on her shoulder. Citrine peered into the gloom, but the tunnel came to a dead end and there was only solid rock around them. There were no other paths branching off from it.

I can't believe we almost slept through visitors!

I suppose you thought it was my job to wake you up.

That's not what I said at all. Why must you always think the worst of me, Thalo?

I don't!

You do too!

"What do you hear?" Citrine looked at Zander.

He tilted his head. "Scrabbling, and, I don't know, grunts and grumbles. Do you know what it is?"

They both backed away from the sound and glanced back the way they had come.

"There's more than one of them, but I'm not sure what kind of creatures they are." Citrine frowned. "It sounds like they're arguing."

"About what?"

She raised an eyebrow. "About us, I think."

Before Citrine could explain anymore, an orange snout poked through a gap that neither of them had noticed. It was at head height, and a bump in the rock hid the slim opening from view. Bancroft crawled higher on her shoulder, half hiding in her hair.

Before she could identify what it was, the snout jerked out of view.

Why do you always get to go first?

I'm the one who heard them first, so I should get to see them first too.

Fine, then. Don't mind me.

I won't!

A green snout poked through the hole. Zander pulled Citrine back so they'd be able to run if it became necessary.

A small dragon's head appeared, along with a front paw. The creature wiggled itself free, but before it could pull itself out, there was a yelp.

Ouch! You can't go out there without me!

The dragon looked over its shoulder toward the hole. *I suppose you're right.* There was a humph and then, *Are you coming? They're staring at me.*

A second dragon's head, the orange one again, emerged. Both grunted and strained.

Citrine wondered if they had gotten stuck trying to get out at the same time. She stepped forward and gave a low hum in the back of her throat. Both dragons stopped.

She has the Creature Gift.

Maybe she's just humming.

Don't be daft. Why would she start humming for no reason?

Zander nudged Citrine and spoke in her ear. "Should we leave while we can?"

Citrine shook her head. "They don't seem dangerous just... argumentative. Perhaps they're siblings."

A loud pop caused Citrine and Zander to whip their heads back toward the dragons—but it wasn't two creatures at all. Instead, a dragon about the size of a large dog stood on the floor. One half of its plump body was green, and the other side was orange. Extending from that bi-colored body were two long necks and two snub-nosed dragon heads. The green head had orange eyes, and the orange head had green eyes. Both sets of eyes stared at them.

"What is that? Is it dangerous?"

Citrine gave a rueful smile and whispered so the small dragon couldn't hear her. "I should have known by all the bickering. That's a Tweedle dragon. They do have the ability to breathe out a venomous gas, but they are far more likely to direct it at each other than at us."

Zander lifted an eyebrow. "That doesn't make me feel any better. What if they shoot this gas at each other and it hits us instead?"

She shook her head. "The odds of that happening are extremely low. These two don't seem overly aggressive with each other. Even so, you better make yourself comfortable. This is going to take a while."

Bancroft flitted off her shoulder and slapped his hat on his leg. *I haven't seen one of those in a snark's age.*

The orange dragon snaked its head closer and tried to edge nearer, but the green dragon planted its feet and refused to budge.

What are you doing, Jasper? They could be dangerous.

Oh, piffle. Look how adorable they are, and a matched pair, too.

The green dragon let out a stream of smoke. *You've always had a regrettable soft spot for humans, but we don't know who these two are. They could be up to something nefarious.*

Jasper gave a little hop, almost knocking himself off-balance when his twin didn't move. *We should introduce ourselves.*

When Thalo did nothing, Jasper nudged him with his snout. *Go on. Introduce us!*

They're the ones who intruded. They should introduce themselves first.

Jasper tilted his head. *Maybe they're afraid of us. We are dragons, after all.*

Do it yourself then, if you're so eager. I won't stop you.

The orange head bobbed up and down. *Do you mean it? I truly can?*

I said so, didn't I? I'm not in the habit of saying things I don't mean.

Yes, but sometimes you say I should do things and then when I do, you get all angry about it. Then I have to listen to you lecturing me on and on.

I do not! You're too dense to understand sarcasm when you hear it. Honestly, that's half your problem. If you'd not be so simple-minded—

Simple-minded? Well, at least I'm not a cranky pants.

Citrine decided she better step in or they would be here all day. "Hello, my name is Citrine. I'm the current Pearl Queen." She touched Zander's shoulder. "This is Zander. He's the Red Prince." She gave Zander a look and dipped her chin.

Following her lead, Zander bowed his head toward the small dragon. "I'm pleased to meet you, er, both."

Jasper's green eyes widened. *The Red Prince and the Pearl Queen. Did you hear that Thalo? This is so exciting! I've never gotten to see human royals.*

The green snout wrinkled. *Don't be ridiculous. Of course you have. Don't you remember? Master Sacklepenny had to help the one that was...* He lifted a clawed paw and made a circle motion around the side of his head. *Not that it helped. He lost his mind anyway—and after Master Sacklepenny went to all that trouble, too.*

Jasper's neck drooped. *Oh yes. I think I just blocked that right out of my memory. It was so sad.* His head perked up. *He was a Red Prince too, like this one.* He pointed a claw at Zander who looked vaguely alarmed.

Let's hope he's not just like the last one.

Citrine interrupted. If she didn't steer the conversation in the right direction, they'd never get into the laboratory. Everyone knew Tweedle dragons had the ability to argue with themselves over anything.

"We're here for Master Sacklepenny's laboratory. Can you help us find it?"

Why it's just—

The green neck whipped out and smacked against the orange one. *Shut your snout, Jasper. You can't just tell anyone who toddles along where the laboratory is. How do we even know they are who they say they are?*

The orange dragon rubbed his neck with his paw and glared at Thalo. *You could have just said. You didn't have to hit me.*

You were about to blab everything to these two. How else was I going to stop you?

You always think you know everything, but you don't. We should tell them. It's the Pearl Queen.

So she says. You're far too trusting, Jasper.

Well, who else would she be if she wasn't herself?

She could not be herself.

A pounding began in Citrine's temples. "I can assure you both that I am myself—er, the Pearl Queen. I have the Creature Gift. That should be some proof."

Thalo drew his head back and his orange eyes narrowed. *There are others who have it.*

Who? Who has it, Thalo?

Other people.

What other people?

What, now you want a list?

I want a name. Name one person who has the Creature Gift besides the Pearl Queen? I bet you can't.

Thalo snorted. *Ha! Any of her siblings would probably have it too.*

"You're right, Mr. Thalo. My brother Spar had the Creature Gift, too."

The green dragon shot a smug smile at Jasper. Before Citrine could say anything else, he twisted his head back around and frowned at her. *That still doesn't mean you should go into the laboratory. Master Sacklepenny charged us with guarding it. Why should we let you in?*

"We're looking for information about the counter-curse that affected the previous Red Prince." Citrine didn't want to mention the Drifter Gene to these two.

That seems like a good reason, Thalo. We should just tell her how to open the door. It's right there, anyway.

Now you've done it.

Done what?

Next you'll tell her all you have to do is say 'open for Sacklepenny the Great' to reveal it.

The orange dragon sniggered. *I don't have to. You just did.*

Thalo's orange eyes widened and then he snarled at Jasper. *This is all your fault.*

Jasper's expression crumpled. *It is not! Why do you always blame me for everything?*

If you hadn't been so stupid...

Take that back.

It's true.

The green neck swung at the orange one and hit it with a resounding thwap. Jasper growled in response. Citrine scooted backward as the two heads snapped and snarled at each other. She grabbed Zander's arm and pulled him toward the dead end of the tunnel and stood facing it. Bancroft flitted after them, but more slowly. He seemed to be greatly entertained by the dragon.

In a low voice she said, "Open for Sacklepenny the Great."

Zander quirked an eyebrow. "Really?"

"Shhh, it's working."

The rock wall shimmered and then disappeared, and in front of them was a large wooden door banded with iron crossbeams. Dust and cobwebs clung to its surface. The hinges creaked as it slowly swung open, revealing Phineas Sacklepenny's laboratory.

Chapter 46

Citrine paused as Bancroft flew into the room before her. He buzzed several laps before he zipped back to her. *All clear, it is. No traps in here.*

Citrine smiled at him and held out her hand. He alighted on her finger. "Thank you for your service, Bancroft. You got me here, and I am grateful to you. I don't have your payment with me, but if you go to the Pearl Palace, someone will see that you get it."

He pulled off his hat and twisted it between his hands, his head drooping. *I don't deserve no payment, Lady Citrine. I didn't get ya all here safely.* He slapped the hat against his leg. *I'm right sorry about yer gargoyle.*

Citrine shook her head. "I'm the one who tripped the wire, Bancroft, and I'm the one that asked him to come along. You bear no responsibility in this."

I can't rightly gainsay the Pearl Queen, but I'll skip yer payment, if it's all the same to you.

She hesitated and then nodded. If it made him feel better, she wouldn't force him to accept the nectar or the feathers. He stepped off her finger and bowed deeply, first to her and then Zander before he zipped past her and into the tunnels.

Citrine watched him until the darkness swallowed his light. Then she stepped over the threshold of the laboratory and looked around. Two long workbenches ran parallel to each other in the middle of the room. Various bowls and implements, along with several opened notebooks, pens, and inkpots, cluttered their surfaces, as if Sacklepenny had left in a hurry and thought he would be back soon. The thick layer of dust that covered everything said otherwise.

Although it was clear it had started out as a natural cavern, Sacklepenny had made improvements to it. Niches had been carved into the walls, where lanterns still stood dark and shuttered. Shelves were set into the rock walls on either side of the room. One set held numerous books and notepads. The other side held a jumble of jars, beakers, and vials, all filled with ingredients and potions.

An overstuffed armchair sat in a corner, a tufted footstool in front of it. An open book and a pair of reading glasses lay discarded on the arm of the chair, and a pile of papers and what looked like an old sweater covered the seat.

Citrine stepped toward the closest workbench and turned the page of an open notebook. A rustling sound startled her, and she whirled toward it.

Much to her amazement, the papers on the chair slid to the floor, and the sweater uncurled and shook itself.

"What is that?" Zander moved closer to her and held his lantern up to illuminate the chair seat.

A small owl blinked up at them and said in a cranky voice, *What a rude question. I'm not a what. I'm a who.*

Citrine stared in disbelief. She had thought library owls were extinct. In fact, it was one of her great sorrows that she'd never have one nest in her library, and here this one had been burrowed in Sacklepenny's laboratory for over a hundred years.

Look, Thalo, it's Perkins! I thought he was dead!

Do I look dead, you idiot? The owl stretched his wings and shook himself, and then stepped off the chair.

His small round body sat incongruously on long, stork-like legs. Citrine bit back a smile, afraid of offending the creature, but Zander wasn't quite so diplomatic and chuckled.

I fail to see what's so funny, young man. In fact, I'd like to know what the two of you are doing here, and why you brought those dunderheads with you. The owl jerked his head toward the Tweedle dragon, who was currently arguing with itself over what to explore first and thus didn't hear the insult.

The owl stalked toward them. He stopped a step or two away and blinked up at Citrine and Zander. *Well, I asked you a question. Are you going to answer me or just stand there like a couple of statues?*

Once again, Citrine made the introductions. When she was finished, the owl snorted. *At least you can understand me. Phineas had to wear a charm, or nothing I said got through to him.*

"How fascinating. I had no idea that was even possible."

Perkins gave a fond smile. *Phineas was only a human, but he had a very strong Alchemy Gift. And he applied himself. There's still a few of the charms around here somewhere.* The owl blinked and shook his feathers out. *You still didn't say what you're doing here and why—Here now, don't touch that. Do you want to blow us all to kingdom come?*

The owl scurried over to the dragon, who had risen onto his hind legs. One head was sniffing a stoppered bottle, and the other was nosing a basket of dried ingredients. He pecked the closest head, which happened to be Jasper. Startled, the dragon dropped back down, dragging his other half down, too, and shook his head.

Ow! That really hurt. What did you do that for?

How many times did Phineas tell you both not to touch things in here?

Both heads hung low, and Jasper scuffed his foot on the stone floor.

Go stand over by the door and stay out of trouble while I deal with these two. The owl fluffed his feathers until he looked twice his normal size and scuttled back toward Citrine and Zander, muttering under his breath, *And to think I woke up from my lovely nap for this.*

Citrine straightened her shoulders. Enough was enough. They needed to find answers, and watching these creatures, funny as they were, wasn't getting her any closer to her goals.

"My friend and I are looking for information about how Phineas figured out how to break the Jabberwock Curse."

The owl peered at her and then looked at Zander without blinking for a long moment. *Hmmm, the Jabberwock Curse, you say? Does someone need the antidote? I can tell you how to break—*

Citrine held up a hand. "No, I know how to break that curse. I was just hoping to find out—that is—" She glanced at Zander, and he gave an almost imperceptible nod. "I want to find out more about the Drifter Gene, and I was hoping, if I could see how Phineas figured out how to break the Jabberwock Curse, it could give me the clues I need."

The owl lifted a shaggy eyebrow. *Clues, hmmm, and just why do you need clues? The Drifter Gene was banned decades ago. With all the culling that happened, I'm surprised it still exists in the human population.* His large topaz eyes turned to Zander again.

Citrine started to twist her hands, realized what she was doing, and rubbed them along her trouser legs instead. "But it hasn't. Died out, that is" She hesitated. "Though it has been much longer than a few decades. I'm afraid you've been asleep for rather a long time."

The owl blinked up at her and then ruffled his feathers. *I suppose you want to tell me how long it's been. Well, I don't particularly care. Time's all the same down here anyway. Now out with it—what kind of clues are you looking for?*

"I'm hoping to find some answers for those who have the gene."

Are you an Alchemist?

Citrine shook her head. "No, my twin gift is the Scholar Gift."

The owl stretched its wings and preened its feathers. The minutes ticked by in a thick silence. Citrine resisted the urge to shift from one foot to the other. Zander reached out and took her hand, giving it a gentle squeeze.

Finally, the owl nodded its head. *I suppose since you came all this way and had to deal with them, I can help you.*

He flapped over to the bookshelves and began running his beak over the spines. Periodically, he pulled out a book or a notebook until he had a pile at his feet.

There, that's all Phineas had on the matter. If you don't find your answer in those, it's not in here.

Citrine walked over and scooped up the pile. She set it on one of the worktables and set the lantern next to it. The owl made his way to the doorway. He poked at something just out of sight, and the lantern in the niches glowed to life.

Citrine smiled at the owl. "Thank you, Perkins."

The faster you're done, the faster I can get my peace and quiet back. Although his voice was gruff, he didn't look upset. *Now, if you don't mind, I think I'll do some reading. I haven't been awake for this long in several decades.* He climbed back into his chair, turned once and then twice before telescoping down into a round ball of feathers. He pulled the open book on the small table into his lap and popped the reading glasses on his beak.

Citrine drew the first book toward her and opened to the first page. "I hope that's a good book. This could take a while."

Perkins humphed but didn't look up from what he was reading.

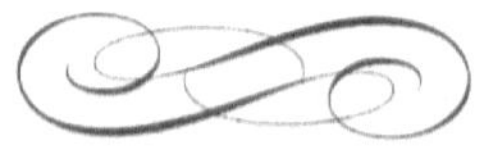

Zander wandered around the perimeter of the room. He studied the jumble of bottles and baskets. He was amazed the dry ingredients hadn't turned to dust a long time ago. Maybe Phineas had put some kind of preserving spell on them.

A soft snore jerked his attention away from a bottle that held a thick bright-blue liquid. The Tweedle dragon, tired of standing by the wall, had slumped down, and both heads rested on the floor. Soft wisps of smoke rose first from one set of nostrils and then the other.

While he couldn't understand what they were saying, it was a relief not have to listen to them bickering. He didn't know how Citrine stood it. He glanced over at her, and a smile curved across his face.

Her spectacles had slid to the end of her nose. As he watched, she turned a page in a book and then started flipping furiously through a notepad. She turned to the very back and ripped out an empty page and made notes with a pencil nub.

Warmth spread through his chest. She had come here for him. She kept saying they couldn't be together, that their duties were too important... but then she did this.

He turned back to the shelves. A jar of iridescent powder caught his attention. Even in the dim light, it sparkled. He picked it up. The label had half peeled off the side, but when he smoothed it out, bold, black words were still legible: *Fae Dust*. He gave the jar a shake and the contents twinkled back at him.

A sharp peck on his leg made him jump, and he almost dropped it.

Perkins glared up at him. He clacked his beak and ruffled his feathers, and then looked expectantly at Zander, who shrugged. The owl let out an exasperated huff and pointed at the jar and then back at the shelf.

Zander held it up. "Do you want me to put this back?"

Perkins rolled his eyes and shooed his wings at Zander. Zander replaced the jar on the shelf. The owl shuffled until he stood between Zander and the shelves of bottles and jars, and then he glared, folding his wings.

Zander felt his face flush as he moved away. He was a prince, and he'd just been banished to the corner like a child. The owl watched him until Zander reached the other side of the room. Only then did he climb back into his chair and resume his reading.

Zander reached into his pocket and pulled out the Timepiece and flipped open the lid. The tiny labyrinth unfolded, and he studied the contraption. It surprised him how much of the brass had turned to gold already. He wished it was clearer how much time was left in the competition.

He hoped Alice was all right. He squeezed the watch, and the gilt edges bit into his palm. If she lost... No, he couldn't think like that. She would win. She had to.

Zander glanced over at the armchair with longing. It was too bad the owl had reclaimed it. With a sigh, he put his back to a blank space of wall and slid down.

Citrine was still flipping back and forth between the book and the notepad. He leaned his head back and let his eyes close.

Chapter 47

THE NEXT MORNING, ALICE and Chess got started early. Chess had agreed to take turns keeping watch, but Alice was pretty sure he had taken most of the night. At least, it hadn't felt very long from the time her watch started to when the night began to fade.

Despite not knowing if they were even going in the right direction, there was a lightness in her step. Alice didn't understand exactly what had happened in the temple of mirrors, but she felt different. For the first time in a long time, she felt at peace inside of herself. She slid a glance at Chess, still embarrassed at the way she had blubbered all over him and then thrown herself into his arms. He had simply held her.

It surprised her he hadn't tried to make the moment into something more. If she was completely honest with herself, she wouldn't have minded, but this wasn't the right time for romance. Of course, it would never be the right time with him, would it? Once this was over, she was going home. She'd have to leave him behind. That thought was surprisingly painful.

She glanced at him again and her stomach fluttered. There was no denying he was handsome with his silky black curls and smooth brown skin. Her eyes slid over his sculpted features and full lips. The sun caught the long lashes that framed those blue eyes of his.

Chess glanced at her and caught her staring. Alice's cheeks heated, and she hastily cleared her throat. "How much further do you think it is until we reach the center?"

Chess smirked, and she thought he would comment on her attention, but for once, he let the opportunity to tease her pass. "It's hard to tell. The boundaries of the labyrinth cover several acres, so going by that, we should be close. But there are so many twists and turns, it's impossible to tell how far it actually is."

They came to another place where the path forked, and they turned right. "I hope we're actually going in the right direction," she said. Tipping her head back, she scanned the tops of the hedges. They were at least ten feet tall, if not higher, so it was impossible to see much besides the paths immediately in front and behind them.

"Do you think there will be some kind of final test?" It was a question that had been nagging at her.

Chess shrugged. "Didn't Citrine's book tell you anything?"

"It just said that the tests wouldn't involve physical strength."

Chess reached across and took her hand. Alice wondered if she should let him. At home, holding hands would have been scandalous, but they weren't home. And she rather liked the feel of his calloused palm against her own. She let their arms swing companionably as they continued walking.

The roar startled both of them, and they leapt together. Wickle poked his head out of her pocket, chittering nervously. Alice turned slowly in a circle, her heart pounding in her chest.

Chess's hand went to his dagger, his eyes scanning the pathway before and behind them. Silence fell like a blanket. After a long, tense moment, a bird twittered in the branch near Alice's head and another one answered.

She looked at Chess, her eyes wide. "What do you think that was?"

"Nothing friendly, that's for sure." He grimaced. "It didn't seem close, but sound carries strangely here. We should be on our guard."

The peaceful companionship of earlier evaporated. Alice chided herself for letting her guard down. She wasn't here to flirt with Chess. She was here to win a crown so she could go home. With a start, she realized she hadn't given Zander even a passing thought since she'd awoken, despite the fact that she was doing this for him.

"Do you think Zander's still angry with us?"

Chess's mouth tightened. "He has no right to be angry with you."

Alice frowned. "If I lose, he'll have every right."

Chess stopped and looked down at her. "Do you regret coming in here?"

"No, but if I'm honest, if you weren't with me, that bug would have probably squashed me in the first few hours."

"Well, the merrow would have finished me off, so I guess it's a good thing both of us are in here." He smiled down at her.

"I'm glad I'm not in here alone."

He reached out and tucked a wayward curl behind her ear.

There was a rustle and creak, and then branches pushed into her back. She stumbled into Chess, who caught her. Alice's face heated, and she hoped he didn't think she'd done that on purpose.

She straightened and started walking again. Chess fell into step beside her, their shoulders now brushing in the narrowed path.

"Do you think the Queen'll accept it, if I win?"

Chess lifted a shoulder. "Probably not, but it won't matter. The Commander is loyal to the crown, whoever wears it."

Alice peered up at him. "He's your father. Why do you call him the Commander?"

Chess rubbed the back of his neck, avoiding her gaze. "I don't know. It's just the way I think of him, I guess."

Alice hesitated. Her curiosity wanted to ask about his mother. Besides telling her that his mother had left when he was young, Chess never mentioned her, almost like she no longer existed or something, but...

The roar sounded again, and she leaned into Chess. He put a protective arm around her shoulder, and they both scanned the surrounding trail. Again, there was nothing. After a moment, they resumed walking, but Alice couldn't quite push away the dread that coiled in her belly.

They made another right-hand turn, and Alice frowned. The path ahead of them was darker, the hedges leaning inward, their branches reaching.

"That doesn't look promising."

"No, it doesn't, but we can't go back the way we came."

He was right. They pressed onward, their progress slow as branches snagged at their clothes. At one point, Alice's hair became tangled in a vine, and she had to stop Chess from cutting her free. Citrine's warning about taking anything from the labyrinth echoed in her mind.

The further they went, the narrower and more crowded the path became, until it forced her and Chess to walk single file for the first time since they had entered the labyrinth.

Eventually, the branches almost completely obscured the way ahead. Chess pushed them aside and disappeared through the foliage. Alice squirmed after him. The path spit her into a clearing and she bumped into Chess's back. When she tried to move around him, he put out an arm, forcing her to a halt. She followed his gaze and bit back a gasp as she took in the scene in front of her.

Chapter 48

SOMEONE WAS SHAKING HIS shoulder. Zander blinked his eyes open, his mind groggy. Citrine leaned over him, her face alive with excitement.

"I think I found something, Zander."

He shook his head, trying to clear the cobwebs. "Found what?"

"Come see."

He sat up, his arm stiff from where he'd used it as a cushion on the hard floor.

Citrine grabbed his hands to pull him to his feet. Once he was standing, she towed him across the room to the nearest workbench and pointed to a page in a small book. "Right here, in the last notebook. I had about given up hope, but it talks about someone 'slipping off their Alchemy Gift.' If someone can do that, it's logical to conclude that it's possible with the other Gifts as well."

Zander leaned closer to where she was pointing and tried to make out the messy writing. "Does it say how to do it?"

Citrine clutched at his arm. "No, but don't you see? Now we have a trail to follow."

Zander wasn't sure why she was so excited. If they didn't know how to get rid of his Drifter Gene, knowing it was a possibility only frustrated him.

Citrine pulled the notebook over and pointed to some archaic scribblings he couldn't read. "Phineas put this formula down, but I'm not an Alchemist so I'd need to find someone to help me with it." She pointed to more writing. "The interesting thing is, he has this information about Fae artifacts." She frowned. "I'm not sure what this symbol is, either. I think if I figured that out, this would all make sense. "

She drew a finger over the flower with an up-side-down triangle at its center.

Zander squinted at it, something tugging at the back of his mind. He tapped the page. "I've seen this before, but I'm not sure where."

Perkins' scratchy squawk made them both jump. He had arisen from his chair again and was standing behind them, his neck stretched to see the notepad. Zander edged away from the owl, not wanting to get pecked again.

Citrine responded to something the owl said. Not for the first time, Zander wished his Gifting was different.

Citrine tapped his arm to get his attention and pointed to the strange flower. "Perkins said this is a symbol of the Fae Regent."

"That's why it looks so familiar. It must have been on their correspondence with my father."

The owl nudged them, and Citrine and Zander moved to give him room. The bird stepped up to the table. His stalk-like legs made him just tall enough to read comfortably.

"Do you know what it all means?" Citrine pointed to the notepad.

Perkins tilted his head one way and then another. Finally, he squawked.

Citrine turned to him and interpreted. "He said that for this formula, we'll need one of the royal Fae artifacts." Her mouth turned downward. "But he doesn't think they'll want to help, and he's probably right. You know how they are about visitors now, and I'm not sure they'll even let outsiders handle one of their artifacts, never mind use it."

Zander's stomach sank. He shouldn't have gotten his hopes up. If Alice won, he had no doubt the Queen would try to make good on her threat to tell everyone his secret. He'd have to banish her somewhere. He wasn't sure he could trust the citizens of Wonderland to believe he wasn't a danger, even though they'd known him, had watched him grow up.

Citrine's touched his arm. "Maybe Chess would—"

"I can't ask that of him. He won't admit it, but he's never gotten over his mother leaving. Besides, we aren't on the best terms at the moment."

"Chess isn't one to hold a grudge. He'll want to help you."

"I don't know..."

"Even if he's angry with you now, he wouldn't want the Queen to reveal your secret and use it to get on the throne."

"I suppose you're right." Zander's mind flashed back to how wrecked Chess was after his mother left. "But I still don't want to ask him."

Citrine rubbed at her forehead. "I still don't understand how the Queen can pull off these complicated spells and curses. Even with a powerful Flora Gift, it makes no sense."

Zander tilted his head. "You know, Chess and I wondered if she was an unregistered Alchemist."

Citrine scrunched her nose. "Why would she hide that, when she must have spent most of her life hiding her Drifter Gene? There's no reason to do that with Alchemy, too."

Zander shrugged. "Maybe she wanted to be underestimated?"

Perkins had been watching them, his head swiveling back and forth. Now he clacked his beak and twittered at Citrine.

She covered her mouth to stifle a laugh, and her eyes lit with amusement.

Zander crossed his arms. "What?"

"Perkins said that there are certain things that can boost power."

"What's so funny about that?"

"He also mentioned that"—she lowered her voice to sound gruff—"'that dunderhead of a prince almost broke a jar of it earlier.'" A snort of laughter escaped before she could swallow it down again. "What in the world did you get into? He's quite indignant about it."

"It was a jar of Fae dust. I didn't know there was anything special about it." Even as he the words crossed his lips, a puzzle piece clicked in his mind. He whirled toward the owl. "What is that Fae dust made of?"

Perkins let out a hoarse whistle and then several lower coos.

Citrine frowned and turned back to Zander. "He said that its made from Fae wings. I guess they're ground into the dust, but what does that—"

Zander grabbed her arm. "I need to go back to the palace right away."

Citrine frowned. "But why..."

He shook her arm. "Don't you see? The Queen asked for her flower maidens the night I got back."

"I'm still not sure..."

He leaned closer. "The flower maidens whose wings are clipped every year."

Her eyes widened. "Zander, you don't think she's using..."

His face paled. "Yes, yes I do. And I left those girls at her mercy." He turned away, unable to meet her gaze. "They're under my protection, and I just abandoned them. I left all my responsibilities because some old windbag said a few cutting things to me. I don't deserve the throne."

She walked over to him and looked him in the eye. "You expect yourself to be perfect and never make any mistakes. It doesn't work like that. If you continue to hold yourself to that kind of standard, you'll never be able to stand under the pressure."

"But I'm going to be the King. My mistakes don't just hurt me."

She shook her head. "Nobody's mistakes just hurt themselves. That's true whether you're a prince or a peasant, and mistakes aren't all bad. When I'm researching or studying a subject, finding out what *isn't* the answer often points me where I need to go." She put a hand on his cheek. "Besides, if you hadn't come here, you would have discovered nothing about spell boosters. I've never heard about them before now. Have you?"

"No, I suppose I haven't, but still..."

"Zander, you can waste time recriminating yourself, or you can stop the Queen."

Without thinking, he pulled her into his arms and hugged her tightly. After a brief hesitation, her arms slid around his waist and she hugged him back. They stood that way for a long moment, and then Perkins squawked.

They pulled apart, and Citrine raised an eyebrow. "Apparently, Perkins doesn't have much patience for all this mumbo jumbo, as he calls it."

Zander shrugged. "He's not wrong. We need to return to the palace."

"But what about all this?" Citrine swept out an arm to encompass the books and papers scattered in front of her. "I can't leave until I find the answers, otherwise my trip will be wasted."

"Well, you can't stay here."

Citrine lifted her chin. "I don't see why not. I remember the way out."

"Do you also remember who died in those tunnels?" He regretted the words as soon as they left his mouth.

Citrine turned her head away and blinked rapidly. "Of course, I do," she snapped. "But that doesn't mean I'm going to leave when we're so close to answers."

Zander crossed his arms. He felt like a bully, but he couldn't let her stay down here in this creepy laboratory by herself, and he had to get back to the palace before the Queen hurt any of the flower maidens. He didn't know what happened if you sheared off too much of their wings. He put a hand on her stiff shoulder and tried again. "We can come back."

She shrugged him off and paced away from him. "But it's all right here. We have the answers. I just need a little more time."

"I know…"

The owl turned to look first at him and then at Citrine. His sigh ruffled the loose papers on the table. Then he clacked his beak and waved his wings at the piles of books and papers. Zander tamped down his impatience.

Citrine must have liked what the owl had to say because she whirled around and clasped her hands. Then she rushed over to the bird as if to hug him. The owl backpedaled, so instead she just reached out and ran her fingers through his top feathers. The owl blustered a bit, but Zander could tell the old fellow was pleased.

Zander helped Citrine scoop up the papers and books she wanted. The owl tapped a clawed foot. Once Citrine had packed the things she wanted into her bag, he made a shooing gesture with his wings and stalked back toward his chair. Even Zander didn't need an interpreter for that. Citrine grabbed his hand. Together they hurried out of the laboratory, only taking time to wake Jasper and Thalo on their way out.

Chapter 49

THE BUTTERFLY FLUTTERED ITS iridescent wings gently back and forth, stirring up a wind that pushed Alice back a step. She stared in a mixture of horror and wonder. The insect's wings were easily eight or nine feet across. With each flutter, the sunlight filtering through the branches changed the wing's color from deep blue to turquoise to bottle green.

The cocooned bundle hanging from one of the branches wiggled, and she could make out a pair of dark brown eyes. She knew the moment the person saw her because the eyes widened and the wiggling became more pronounced.

Alice took a step forward and Chess's grip on her arm tightened. "Don't attract its attention." His voice was barely a whisper.

"But—" She gestured at the person hanging upside down, his booted feet sticking out of the top of the cocoon. "That has to be Leander. We can't just leave him."

Chess frowned at her and put a finger to his lips, nodding toward the nearest pathway, but Alice ignored him.

The butterfly skittered forward and grasped the cocoon with two stick-like legs. It hissed and pulled one of its legs protectively in toward its middle. The man began to buck frantically, his voice muffled by the cocoon. The butterfly still managed to turn the bundle this way and that in its sticky grasp, despite its injured leg.

A long, thin tube uncurled from underneath the butterfly's chin. The man became even more desperate as the tube gently probed here and there along the silken threads that bound him. Alice didn't know what the butterfly was doing or why, but she had no doubt that time was running out for the man in the creature's grasp.

Before she could think better of it, she darted into the center of the clearing. Behind her, Chess groaned. Startled by her sudden appearance, the butterfly dropped the cocoon. It swung wildly back and forth from its branch.

The butterfly spread its impressive wings and stared down at Alice. It tilted its head, and its almond-shaped black eyes bore into her.

She swallowed, not sure what to do. Her last encounter with an insect hadn't gone too well. She reminded herself not to mention the Mirror World to this one.

"Erm..." Alice licked her lips, searching for something to say.

The bug's antennae waved back and forth. *Who are you, and what do you want?*

"I... That is..."

Oh, for goodness' sake. The butterfly folded its wings back and shook its head. *I'm just sitting down to eat, so if you don't mind, state your business and be on your way.*

"D... d... dinner? I didn't know butterflies ate—well, that is, I thought you drank nectar. From flowers."

Well, yes, we do drink nectar, but don't you eat as well as drink?

"Er, yes, of course."

Why wouldn't we do the same? The creature turned its attention back to its prey.

Alice wasn't sure what to say to that. Chess stepped up behind her, and his warmth at her back gave her confidence.

"It looks like your, um, guest isn't too happy to be invited for dinner."

The butterfly snickered. *They never are.* It reached out and swatted the cocoon so it swung back and forth again. It narrowed its eyes at the bundle. *And this one injured me.* Its wings opened and closed. *It's not often I have a chance at this much meat in one day.* Its gaze narrowed on her and Chess.

She slid backward a step. The word *meat* coming from the insect made her stomach turn. "We're just passing through."

Humans never just pass through here. Why are you really here? Is it the monster?

"Monster?"

The butterfly waved its good leg in the air. *You know, all the roaring.* It gave a delicate shiver, causing its wings to ripple. *It's quite put me off my appetite; otherwise, I'd be done by now.* The tube under its chin extended and curled up again. Alice repressed a tremor.

"Actually, now that you mention it, I believe your dinner guest is my competition."

The insect leaned closer. Alice fought the urge to back up again. *What kind of competition? It's so boring in here. Any entertainment is welcome.*

"We're competing for a crown to decide the new ruler of the Kingdom of Wonderland." Alice put a finger on her chin, her mind whirring. "I'm sure the Red Prince and the Red Queen would appreciate you letting him go." She gestured toward the other champion who had gone still, his dark eyes trained on her.

Why should I let a free meal go? For that matter, I could wrap up both of you for later. The butterfly took a menacing step closer.

"Oh, you wouldn't want to do that! The royals would be most put out if they had to find two new champions."

Two? The butterfly jabbed a leg toward Chess. *Is he extra?*

Alice shook her head so hard her hair flew around her face as she clamped a hand on Chess's arm. "No, he's here to... to..." Panic blanked her mind.

Chess stepped forward, subtly pushing her behind him. "I'm here to see that the competition runs fairly. Just think of me as the official." He gave the butterfly a small bow.

Alice stepped around Chess. "I'm sure whoever wins will be very grateful that you allowed their champions to go through the labyrinth unharmed. It would be a great deal of trouble for them to redo the competition."

The creature's eyes narrowed. *Just how grateful do you think they'd be?*

Alice scrambled to come up with a reward that would appease the creature, but came up empty. She cast a desperate look at Chess.

He didn't disappoint her. He smiled up at the creature. "There's a whole dungeon full of prisoners that nobody knows what to do with. I'm sure they'd be happy to turn them loose in here."

The insect waved its legs, keeping the injured one tucked up against its body, and hissed again. It was difficult to discern its expression, but its antennae were rigid and stiff. *How do I know I'd get any of them? This is a big place, and I'm not the only one looking for his next meal.*

Chess chuckled. "I can see your dilemma, but if you let us pass, we'll be happy to share how very helpful you've been."

"And if you let him go, they'll be even happier," Alice added.

Chess shot her a look.

The bug looked from them to the cocoon. His wings fluttered back and forth, causing the branches to sway and dip.

A human in the hand is worth two in the bush, as my grandmother always said. The insect nodded to itself. *You two may go, but I'll keep this one for my dinner. After all, he did try to kill me. Besides, if one of you wins, they won't have to redo the competition, now will they?* The long tube under his chin extended and flicked the cocoon, which resumed its frantic wiggling.

Alice's stomach turned queasily. The idea of leaving anyone to this kind of fate made her want to throw up. There had to be something she could do.

"It's not really a competition if there aren't at least two participants," she said.

The butterfly made a tsking sound. *I think I'm being more than fair. You can't expect me to give up a good dinner with only your promise of a future one.*

Alice's mind scrambled for something that would change the butterfly's mind. "I can heal your leg!" She wanted to suck the words back in as soon as they left her mouth. Just because she'd healed Chess that one time didn't mean she could do it again.

Chess shot her a look. "What are you doing? If you don't do what you promise, it'll eat both of us!" he whispered furiously.

Alice ignored him because she had the butterfly's attention. The creature had turned away from its meal and was staring down at her with great bulbous eyes. Alice swallowed. "I can see your wound pains you, and I can fix that, if you promise to let us all go in return."

How do I know I can trust you? The bug swatted the cocoon again, sending it swaying back and forth. The person inside groaned. *This human tried to run me through with his puny sword.*

"He was wrong to do that, but I give you my word that I only want to help, not hurt you, You'll need to give me your word that you'll let us go, including him." Alice pointed at the man in the cocoon.

He gave me his word, too, and then almost cut off my leg.

Alice clenched her fists. Of all the stupid things to do. Of course, Leander was certainly paying for his stupidity, and there was still no guarantee he'd get out of this alive.

Chess's lips brushed her ear. "Tell it that you are friends with the Pearl Queen."

She took a step closer to the giant butterfly. "I realize you have no reason to trust me, but I am good friends with the Pearl Queen."

The creature tilted its head, its wings relaxing. *Well, in that case, I agree. Everyone knows the Pearl Queen is a friend of all creatures and utterly trustworthy.*

Alice's shoulders inched down from her ears. "If you'll just lower yourself down, I can reach your wound to heal it."

She bit back a scream as the creature's good leg snaked out and curled around her waist, hoisting her in the air. "I... I think this would work better if I were on the ground." Alice had to push the words through chattering teeth.

I can't get down that low. This will have to do. The tube under its chin unfurled and almost touched Alice's leg. *Unless you are going back on your word.*

Alice shook her head. "No... no, of course not." She tried to ignore the fact that her feet were dangling in midair. "If you could bring me a bit closer? I can't quite reach from here."

She bit back her cry as the butterfly jerked her through the air, her stomach sloshing in protest. It was difficult to find her composure when in the grip of a giant bug, but she drew in a deep breath. Holding out her hands, she placed them on either side of the gaping wound, careful to avoid the green ichor that oozed from it.

She closed her eyes and felt her palms warming. The wound glowed in her mind's eye, and she pictured it knitting back together, the pain leaking away. She held the picture of the healed leg in her mind for a long moment and then opened her eyes.

And breathed a puff of air. The leg looked completely whole. Her whole body slumped in the bug's grasp, and a wave of weariness washed over her.

The butterfly turned the limb this way and that. *What do you know? It's completely better.* It stretched out its leg and then folded it closed. *There's no pain at all.*

Alice smiled. "I'm glad. Now, we really need to—"

The bug pulled her closer, and her stomach lurched again.

"Will you please stop doing that?" she snapped.

The bug's eyes widened. *What am I doing?*

"You're jerking me around without any warning, and it makes me feel like I'm going to be sick."

It pulled its head back, and its tone turned stiff. *Oh, I didn't realize.*

The butterfly sounded put out, but it moved much more slowly as it brought her closer to its face to examine more closely.

Now she was the one that felt like a bug under the microscope. A giggle escaped. Her propensity to laugh at all the wrong times was going to get her into trouble. She clamped her lips shut over another gurgle of laughter.

I think I need to keep you. What if I get hurt again? You'd come in so handy.

"But you promised you'd let us go," Alice protested. She crossed her arms. "I would be very disappointed to find out you weren't an insect of your word."

I'll let the other two go, but I think I'll keep you. You never know when more humans will come along and stab me with their pointy sticks.

Her fear forgotten, Alice scowled up at the bug. "I demand you put me down this instant and let us all go like you promised."

Oh, stop fussing. I only promised not to eat you all. You're safe enough. It would hardly be in my best interests to eat my pet healer, would it?

"That's not what you said. You said you'd let us all go, and I am NOT a pet."

The bug gave her a shake that made Alice's head rattle. *I hope you aren't implying that I'm lying.* The beak-like mouth clacked. *I'm still hungry, you know. I never did get to eat.*

Before Alice could think of a reply to that, Wickle popped out of her pocket and chittered loudly at the butterfly.

The insect drew back, throwing up its arms to shield its face and letting go of Alice in the process.

Her scream trailed behind her like a ribbon as she plummeted to the ground. She managed to land on her feet, but she hit the ground so hard, she bounced backwards. She landed on her hip and then her shoulder, pain blooming in each spot.

Before she could stop the stars circling her vision, Chess was next to her. "Are you all right? What happened? I couldn't see from down here."

"Wickle happened." She tried to get to her feet but couldn't quite manage it.

Chess put his hand on her shoulder. "Give yourself a minute."

Alice shook her head and then regretted it. "No, we need to get out of here." This time, she was able to get to her feet. Chess steadied her.

The butterfly had scuttled back into its cave-like nest of branches. Only the top half of its body was visible, but it was watching them.

It stepped forward when Alice stood up. Wickle was watching, too. As soon as the other creature moved, he scrambled out of Alice's pocket and down her leg. Trundling across the space, he hissed at the butterfly, his puffed fur making him twice the normal size.

The butterfly retreated again. *I hate snarks. Nasty poisonous creatures.* He waved one of his stick-like legs. *Shoo! Shoo, I say!*

Alice turned back to Chess and gestured toward the cocoon, now hanging still. "Can you cut him down? We need to get out of here while we can." She jerked a thumb in the bug's direction. "Apparently, I did too good of a job healing its leg. Now it wants to keep me as its pet healer."

Chess's eyebrows climbed. "When we get out of this, I think we need to have a conversation."

The ground under their feet trembled as the bug stomped one leg, trying to smash Wickle, who darted out of the way.

"Never mind about that. Let's just get out of here."

Chess drew his dagger and slashed at the sticky stem of the cocoon. The ground continued to shake as the butterfly renewed its efforts to kill Wickle. Alice bit her lip. She didn't want anything to happen to the little snark, but without his interference, they'd never escape.

Finally, Chess got through the fibrous strands, and the cocoon thudded to the ground. Leander groaned.

Wickle let out a loud hiss, and Alice realized the butterfly had only narrowly missed him. The snark opened his mouth, his jaws stretching wide. Long fangs extended outward, making his face resemble a snake, ready to strike. He let out a surprisingly loud snarl.

The butterfly screeched, the sound like nails on a chalkboard, and scuttled backwards.

They needed to leave.

Now.

Chess apparently was of the same mind because he picked up the sticky bundle and slung it over his shoulder. "I've got him. Let's go."

Alice called to Wickle and scooped up her satchel where she'd dropped it. Chess was already jogging toward the path on the other side of the clearing.

With a last loud hiss, Wickle beelined toward Alice, his little legs churning up dust. The butterfly, realizing both its healer and its meal were about to escape, darted forward, its beating wings giving it alarming speed.

Wickle jumped onto her trouser leg, and she put on a burst of speed as he scrambled up her body and tucked himself back into her pocket.

Chess had reached the pathway, and she sprinted toward him, even as the ground shook under her feet. She stumbled and nearly fell but didn't dare look back. The insect was gaining on her.

She waved her arms. "Go! Go!"

Her only hope was that the path ahead would be too narrow for the giant insect. Her feet pounded as she exited the clearing. She hadn't gone more than a dozen steps when there was a loud creak and rustle.

Alarmed that the butterfly was on them, she twisted around.

And gasped.

A solid wall of hedge met her eyes. She could still hear the insect hurling insults and threats on the other side, but the branches muffled its voice.

She slowed and tried to catch her breath. "You can stop... running."

Chess came to a halt, panting from his burden. He shrugged the cocoon from his shoulder and let it slide to the ground. Another groan escaped from the person inside.

Alice ran a hand over the branches. "Thank you." The branches and leaves swished and crackled under her touch.

Chess grinned at her. "Well, that was unexpected." He gave the closest branch a friendly pat before he turned back to her. "Now that we don't have a giant bug trying to kill us, I think you've a few things to tell me, love."

Chapter 50

CITRINE STOOD OUTSIDE OF her carriage. Zander had put Stongorr inside, still wrapped in his jacket. She was thankful for his help. After death, the gargoyle's body had returned to stone. Without Zander, she doubted she would have been able to get herself, never mind Stongorr, back up to the ruins.

Telling Ogox that his brother was dead was the worst of it, though. Even now, his wings drooped, weighed down with sorrow.

"I think you need to go home, Citrine." Zander's expression had turned determined.

"But what about the competition? And Alice? What about the flower maidens?"

Zander tucked a wisp of hair behind her ear. "I'll send a raven with updates, but you'll be safer at home. I have no idea who will win or what the Queen will do if she loses."

Citrine crossed her arms. "I'm not afraid of that woman."

"Well, you should be. Besides, you have a much better chance of finding answers at your library than at the palace."

Citrine pursed her lips. He wasn't being fair now. "I have Phineas's materials. I don't even know if there's anything at home that could help me." Even to her own ears, she didn't sound convinced.

He took her hand. "I promise I will let you know as soon as the competition is over. Besides, you need to oversee Stongorr's burial, and Ogox looks like he's taking it pretty hard."

Citrine sighed. "I suppose you're right. I've been gone too long as it is."

His mouth curved in a half smile. "I'll miss you, though."

Her heart fluttered in her chest. Before she could think better of it, she threw her arms around him and hugged him tightly. His shoulder muffled her voice. "You be careful. Don't let that witch hurt you."

His cheek rested on her hair. "I won't."

She knew she should step away, but she clung to him for another long moment. He was the one who finally broke their embrace.

"I have to get back." He put his hands in his pockets.

She nodded. "Please be safe, Zander."

He winked. "Don't worry about me!"

She stepped back. He shifted into his jabberwock form and leapt into the air. He soared into the sky.

When he was just a speck, she climbed onto the carriage steps. Ogox turned his blocky head toward her.

The Pearl Palace?

"Yes, Ogox. It's time to go home."

Chapter 51

ALICE HELD UP HER hand to stave off Chess's questions. "Later. We need to free him first—unless you want to carry him the rest of the way?"

Chess crossed his arms and stared down at the cocoon. "We could just leave him here."

Alice rolled her eyes and rummaged through her bag. Pulling out her dagger, she began the work of cutting the cocoon away from Leander's face.

When Chess made no move, she pointed the tip of her dagger at him. "Aren't you going to help?"

"I wasn't joking about leaving him. I don't think this is a good idea, Alice. If the situation was reversed, he wouldn't have thought twice about leaving you to be that bug's dinner. You got him out of there. He can figure it out from here."

Alice stopped what she was doing and stared up at Chess. "How can you say that?" She gestured at Leander. "Look at him. There's no way he can free himself. Leaving him would almost be worse than being eaten. At least that would have been over faster."

Chess crossed his arms. "Look, it's a case of survival. It's him or us."

A mixture of dismay at his words and shame washed over Alice. How could she have forgotten in less than a fortnight that no matter how charming or handsome he might be, Chess had already demonstrated his priorities?

"I don't know why I'm surprised," she muttered under her breath as she turned back to her task. The fibers were tough, but because they were so close to Leander's face, she couldn't just slice them open.

"What's that supposed to mean?"

Alice didn't look at him as she worked the tip of her dagger under another few fibers and cut them apart. "Just that you've already proved what you'll do to survive."

"You say that like surviving is a bad thing."

She cut through another cluster of fibers. "It is if you're the means to the end."

He frowned. "And what 'means' am I supposed to be getting now? I went against my best friend to get you in here."

Her eyes flicked up to his face. "I'm not saying I don't appreciate your help, but the truth is, you're the reason I'm here in the first place. I didn't fall into Wonderland on my own. You pushed me." She sat back and waved her dagger in his direction. "And don't think I've forgotten how you just left me at Caterpillar's, either. That almost ended with me losing my head."

Hurt and annoyance flashed over his face. "Zander would have died if I hadn't—"

She cut him off. "I know, but that only proves my point. You left me because Zander's survival was more important." She reached for the pieces that still covered Leander's face.

Chess put his hand on hers and she stilled. "Alice, you have to know you're important to me. I already told you I was sorry for bringing you here without asking." His mouth twisted. "I didn't realize you held grudges."

She shook off his touch. "I'm not. I let myself get caught up in... I forgot who you really are."

"And just who is that?" His expression was tight, and there was a spark of temper in his eyes.

"More than the charming flirt, that's for sure."

He smirked. "Surely everyone's opinion of me can't be wrong."

He was deflecting again. She searched his face, not sure what she was looking for. Maybe the truth. "Then they're fools not to realize how dangerous you truly are."

His eyes narrowed and the hairs on the back of her neck stood up. "And just why does a girl from the Mirror World think she knows me better than the people I've been around all my life?"

Alice refused to let him intimidate her. She shrugged and turned back to her task. "Maybe because I *haven't* been around you all of my life. Look, we need to win the crown, but I have to be able to live with myself afterwards. I'm going home, Chess, and I don't want guilt following me there."

Chess stared at her for a long moment. Then, without another word, he pulled out his own dagger and began cutting at the sticky stuff around Leander's legs. She worked her fingers under the edge of the cocoon and tugged off the material covering Leander's face, wincing as it pulled at his skin.

He blinked, some of his blond eyelashes sticking together from stray bits of cocoon. Alice reached out and tried to wipe it away so it didn't get into his eyes.

"Are you hurt anywhere?"

He worked his mouth back and forth. "N..." His voice came out in a croak, and he tried again. "No, I'm all right—now. I didn't think..." His voice choked up, and he turned his head, trying to hide the moisture gathering in his eyes.

Alice reached into her bag and pulled out a canteen. She held it up so Leander could drink. He downed several long swallows.

When he finished, she screwed the cap back on and returned it to her bag. "I can't imagine what an awful experience that was for you, but that creature won't be coming after any of us now." She gave him an encouraging smile.

By this time, Chess had freed the other champion's legs. Leander moved them experimentally, and there was a loud pop as his knee cracked.

"How long have you been in this... stuff?" Alice pulled some of the sticky strands off her own shirt.

Leander had regained his composure. "I'm not sure. Since last night? Maybe?" He moved his head back and forth, stretching his neck.

Alice nodded. "We've only been in here since yesterday."

Leander swallowed and closed his eyes for a moment. "It seemed like a lot longer." When he opened them, he smiled. "I have to thank you for your help. I truly thought I wasn't long for this world."

She patted his still bound shoulder. "You're safe now."

She started to work on the cocoon around his upper body, but Chess stopped her. "We need to talk."

She looked between him and Leander, and found the latter was scrutinizing them both with more shrewdness than was comfortable. Reluctantly she stood up and let Chess pull her to the side.

"I know you don't agree with me"—he held up both hands— "and I wouldn't *dream* of suggesting again that we leave him here. But I don't trust him, and you shouldn't either."

Alice tilted her head. Chess had a point. "So, what do you propose we do?"

"He can walk on his own now, but I think we should keep his arms bound—at least until we can get rid of him."

Alice turned the idea over in her mind. On the one hand, Leander was probably anxious to be freed completely, but on the other, he *was* the Queen's brother. While she didn't view Leander as an enemy just yet, that didn't mean he felt the same way. Alice didn't want to be stupid just to prove a point. "All right. We'll leave it for now."

Chess tight posture loosened. "I didn't think it would be that easy."

Alice raised an eyebrow. "Just because I don't want to leave him to die a terrible death doesn't mean I'm a ninny."

Chess hooked his finger around a stray piece of cocoon and pulled it from her cheek. "I never thought you were, love."

His touch left a trail of heat on her face. Flustered, she turned back to Leander. "We should get going. I don't want to be in here any longer than I have to."

Chapter 52

WHEN ALICE REACHED OUT to steady Leander for the third time in as many minutes, she looked over at Chess. He was walking just ahead of them and had hardly said two words to her or Leander in the past couple of hours. He didn't seem angry, exactly, but she couldn't help wondering if she should have kept her thoughts to herself. She missed their earlier camaraderie.

But how real had it been? Yes, he'd helped her, even if it meant going against Zander, but was that because he cared about what happened to her, or was it because it was the best way to get rid of the Queen?

As if feeling her gaze, he twisted his head to look at her. "What?"

"Maybe we should stop." She nodded at Leander.

After his initial protest, Leander had trudged next to them without complaint. The cocoon's sticky strings glued his arms to his sides and bound his torso from waist to shoulder. His stoic acceptance was beginning to make her feel guilty.

"We could all do with a rest, I think."

Chess frowned. "It's only a few more hours until the sun will set."

"Actually, I need to, erm, see to some personal needs." Leander's tone was polite, but two slashes of pink darkened his cheekbones.

Alice felt a pang of sympathy for him. He was probably miserable. "Of course, we'll just wait here while you, er, see to things."

Leander frowned. "I'm afraid, bound as I am..." His face turned redder still.

Alice looked at Chess. He smirked. "Don't look at me, love. I'm not playing nursemaid to a bloke."

Well, now what were they going to do? She certainly couldn't help the man. But if they freed him—he'd been cooperative up until now, but that didn't mean much. Without the use of his arms, he was almost helpless. He was dependent on them, as his current request demonstrated.

"On my word, as a gentleman, I will behave honorably." Leander's expression turned pained. "But I... things are a bit urgent at the moment."

Oh dear. She didn't trust him, but he must be desperate if he'd been tied up since last night. Besides, it almost felt like cheating to keep him trussed up like this.

They all stopped in the middle of the path. Leander leaned against the hedge, his head hanging down. Alice sidled over to Chess and whispered, "I think we have to free him."

A number of emotions flitted across Chess's face, and then he lifted one shoulder. "If that's what you want."

Alice bit her lip. "We can't leave him tied up forever, and if we don't free him..." She wrinkled her nose.

"Are you trying to convince me or yourself?"

She poked his arm. "I'm trying to figure out the best thing to do, under the circumstances."

"*If* you're asking my opinion, I think it's safer not to free him until we reach the center."

Alice twisted her hands together. What if they freed him, and he turned on them? Supposedly, one champion couldn't hurt the other, but there were always loopholes to these things. But not to, seemed unnecessarily cruel.

Chess touched her cheek, interrupting the spiral of her thoughts. "Whatever you decide, it'll work out." Her eyes flew up to his, startled. He tucked a curl behind her ear. "You might not think much of me, but you can trust yourself. You've got good instincts."

"Chess, I..."

But he'd already turned away. He strode over to Leander and drew his dagger. He raised his arm, and the other man's face twisted into alarm. Chess brought the sharp tip down on the edge of the cocoon, and in one powerful movement, he cut it in two. The other man sagged in relief, and Chess pointed his dagger at Leander.

"You can thank the lady for your freedom and your dignity." He bared his teeth in a jagged smile, and Leander visibly paled. "But don't think I won't finish you if you harm a hair on her head. Are we clear?"

Leander drew himself up. "As a gentleman, I'm aware of what I owe the lady." He pulled at the sticky strands as he extricated himself from his bindings. "Besides, if I harm her, I'll forfeit the competition."

Chess snorted. "Good to know where we stand."

Leander didn't respond. Instead, he quickly walked back the way they had come and disappeared around a curve in the path.

Alice dropped her satchel on the ground and pulled out several packets of food.

She straightened. "Can you stop pacing? You're making me dizzy."

"He's been gone a long time." Chess stopped and chewed on his thumb. "Maybe I should go after him."

"He *was* in that cocoon since yesterday. I'm sure he's, well..." She trailed off and her cheeks heated. "Besides, even if he takes off, will it really matter at this point?"

She shoved down her doubts. She'd made the decision to free him, and she couldn't regret it.

Chess shifted. "I suppose you're right. It would save us from..." Footsteps crunched on the path, and they both turned toward the sound.

Leander approached, his hands tucked into his pockets. He stopped in front of Alice. Taking her hand, he bowed over it and kissed the knuckles. "I must thank you again for your kindness."

He straightened and smiled down at her, still holding her hand. He looked a lot like his sister, with his pale blond hair and dark eyes, but his features were more sculpted than delicate.

Alice used the excuse of getting out the food to extricate her hand. "I'm sure you'd have done the same if our situations were reversed." She actually didn't know any such thing, but it seemed wiser to start off with at least the appearance of goodwill.

She handed him some bread and cheese and then sat down. He dropped down next to her on the grass, his knee almost brushing hers. Trying to ignore her unease, she held some of the cheese out to Chess, but he waved away her offering.

"I'm fine. I'll eat when we stop later."

"Are you sure? It'll be a few hours until it's dark."

He lifted one shoulder. "It's best if one of us keeps watch."

Alice frowned. His tone sounded... off, but she didn't press.

"Far be it from me to seem ungrateful to either of you, but how is it that there are two of you in here?"

Alice turned back to Leander. "It was rather an accident."

His brow furrowed. "I was under the impression—but perhaps I misunderstood—each of the royals could have but one champion." He lifted a dark golden eyebrow, his eyes wide.

"The labyrinth wouldn't let Chess leave." Alice took a bite of bread, chewed, and swallowed. "It seems to have a mind of its own."

"I've noticed." One side of Leander's mouth tipped up. "Of course, I shouldn't be surprised that Felinas has managed to get himself stuck with a beautiful girl." He glanced at Chess, who was standing a few feet away with his arms crossed. Then he leaned toward Alice. "He does have quite the reputation as a ladies' man."

Alice suppressed a stab of irritation. "I wouldn't know anything about that." She took a rather aggressive bite out of her cheese.

Leander frowned. "I'm sorry. I didn't mean to offend."

Alice raised her eyebrows. "Then what did you mean to do with a comment like that?"

Leander startled, and then his expression melted into one of contrition. "I see I *have* put my foot in it. Please accept my apologies. I'm afraid my thinking is still a bit muddled."

Alice took another bite of cheese and bread and decided to let him off the hook. "You did have a terrible ordeal."

The tension in the man's shoulders eased, and he put a hand on Alice's arm. "You are very kind." He smiled. "And charming."

Before Alice could pull away, Wickle popped out of her pocket. Leander threw himself backward, scuttling away like a crab. She heard Chess stifle a laugh.

"That's... that's..." His finger shook as he pointed to the blue puff of fur.

Alice patted the little snark's head and frowned at Leander. "You're scaring him."

"But..." Leander blustered, apparently speechless. "That's—those—they're poisonous."

Alice shrugged and cuddled the little creature, who had crawled out onto her palm. "Maybe, but he's not done a single thing to make me feel afraid. He's been a good friend."

Leander was on his feet now, so Alice pushed the last of the bread in her mouth and stood up, too. She took a swig of water before stowing it into her bag and slinging the satchel onto her shoulder.

"Are you ready?" It was the first thing Chess had said since they'd started eating. Alice couldn't help but notice the smirk on his face as they started walking again.

Chapter 53

CHESS TRAILED BEHIND ALICE and Leander as they continued down the path a few hours later. Alice knew he was keeping an eye on the other champion. She couldn't disagree. While Leander had been charmingly grateful—he'd thanked her no less than a dozen times for saving him—as the twilight deepened, she couldn't quell her unease that he would try something underhanded.

Leander's voice broke into her thoughts. "I can see why Lyssa likes you."

Alice wasn't sure what to say to that, since his sister had tried to kill her. The polite responses rose automatically to her lips. "She made quite an impression on me, too."

Chess snorted behind them, but she resolutely ignored him. It wouldn't hurt to get more information out of Leander about his sister.

Leander gave a half smile. "You don't have to be polite about it. I know she nearly separated your head from your shoulders. But with Lyssie, that doesn't mean she doesn't like you. It just means you weren't expedient."

He sighed. "It's not her fault she's the way she is. Our father instilled a certain ruthlessness in her."

"And he didn't instill that in you?" Alice asked.

"He didn't have the chance he had with my sister. He sent me away to boarding school when I was eight." He shook his head. "Lyssie never got that chance."

"Your father sounds..." Alice trailed off, afraid to offend him.

Leander frowned. "He's dead now, but he was utterly without any softer feelings, and I'm not sure an actual heart ever beat in his chest. He certainly didn't love his children. They were merely another possession he could use."

"Oh... I'm sorry." Alice didn't know what else to say, and an awkward silence hung in the air.

She wasn't sure why Leander was suddenly sharing confidences with her, and the sudden intimacy made her uncomfortable. She adjusted the strap on her satchel to hide her discomfort.

Seemingly aware of her unease, Leander lapsed into silence again. They made another right turn. Alice noticed these were coming much more frequently.

After a few moments, Leander touched her arm. "I'm sorry. I seem to have made you uncomfortable. That wasn't my intention." He licked his lips and his eyes darted around as if he feared someone overhearing. "It's just... you need to understand my sister. She's... Her feelings for a person don't matter. If you stand in her way or fail her"—his Adam's apple bobbed as he swallowed—"she'll eliminate you."

Alice's mind raced. She already knew the Queen had no compunctions about killing people, but was he referring to her or himself? If he lost, would the Queen eliminate him too?

"I know you probably find it odd, me speaking to you this way, but you seem like a nice person." His expression was troubled. "You've been kind to me, and, well, it would be a shame if after all this you got yourself killed."

"Thank you?" Alice heard the question in her own voice, but what was she supposed to say to something like that?

"Lyssandra is... That is, sometimes I fear she isn't well." Leander clasped his hands behind his back, his brow furrowed.

"I'm sorry. That has to be difficult—for both of you."

Leander nodded. "It is." He glanced at her and then down at the path. "The truth is, this isn't something I wanted, but"—he shrugged—"after our father died, it didn't seem wise to upset her."

Alice caught the odd emphasis on the word died. "Did he pass away recently?"

Leander shot her a strange look. "I thought someone would have told you. He had an... accident... right before we came back here."

Suddenly, the pieces clicked. The Queen had killed her own father? No wonder her brother felt like he had no choice. She wished she could ask him about his Gift. If the Queen was his twin and had the Drifter Gene, did that mean he had it, too? But if he did, why would he be afraid of her?

Chess suddenly pushed between them and put a hand on her arm. "Sshhh!"

"Wha..."

He clapped a hand over her mouth and pointed at the hedge. A fuchsia growth bulged out from the branches. She realized as she looked closer, it looked like bubbles stuck together. She could vaguely make out shapes moving inside of it.

Leander's eyes widened when he caught sight of it, and he crowded her over to the far side of the path.

She found herself sandwiched between the two men. "What in the world?" Chess's palm muffled her voice.

Wickle popped up from her shoulder and placed his own paw on her cheek. *Snark hive...*

She pulled Chess's hand away from her mouth. "Is that your home, Wickle?" she asked in a whisper. She would be sad to see him go, but if it was his home... He shook his tiny head back and forth.

Not my clan.

They eased down the path as quickly and quietly as they could. After they had put a suitable distance and several turns between themselves and the snark hive, they came to another intersection, the first in a while. A tall tree grew in the center. Chess drew to a halt just outside the circle of its branches. "I think we're far enough away. We can stop now. It's too dark to go any further."

Leander stepped away from her, and she breathed a sigh of relief. His confessions about his sister had only increased her unease.

Chess moved away from her too, and Alice rubbed her arms, the leather under her fingers somehow comforting. She needed to talk to Chess about Leander. If she'd learned anything from helping Tom in the stables back home, it was that a fearful animal was the most dangerous of all.

Chapter 54

ALICE SAT ON THE ground between the two men and handed out the food. There wasn't much left, maybe enough for a few more meals. Chess had been tense and irritable since they'd stopped. She wished she could get him alone to talk to him about Leander and his sister. She didn't like the idea that Leander could be desperate.

Another roar split through the moonlit night, and she jumped. "Do those sound louder to you?"

Chess nodded. "We need to be alert. I'll take watch."

"We can all take a turn," said Alice.

"I said, I'll take watch," Chess snapped and nodded at Leander. "He's still the competition, in case you've forgotten." He leveled a hard stare at the other man. "I still don't trust you."

Leander held up both hands. "I completely understand. If I was in your place, I'm sure I'd feel the same way, especially with someone as lovely as Alice to protect."

Alice resisted the urge to roll her eyes. As if she'd be taken in by all the flattery. Chess scowled at them both. Apparently, he thought she could.

She turned to get the other canteen, but Leander grabbed her satchel first. "Here, let me get it for you." She wanted to snatch her bag away from him as he rummaged around. He finally pulled out the water and unscrewed the lid.

When he went to hand it to her, he fumbled it, but managed to catch it awkwardly. "Oh, I'm so sorry. I don't think I lost too much, though."

She pressed her lips together to keep from snapping at him. Instead, she gave him a tight smile. "Maybe just let me get it next time."

He passed it to her, and she took a long drink. Her throat was dry from the bread and cheese. For some reason, the water tasted extra good tonight. She took another long drink.

Leander took it back from her and screwed the lid on again.

"Aren't you thirsty?" she asked.

He shook his head. "No, I'm fine."

Wickle poked his head out of her pocket and chittered at her.

Mate unhappy.

She had long since stopped trying to explain to the little snark that Chess was not her mate. "It's fine," she murmured to him.

Don't like yellow-haired man.

Alice wasn't sure if Wickle was saying he didn't like Leander or if Chess didn't like Leander. It didn't much matter, though. She patted his fuzzy head. She couldn't very well discuss Leander or Chess when they were sitting right next to her.

Wickle clambered out of her pocket and landed nimbly on her knee.

Watch yellow-hair.

With this cryptic warning, the snark leaped off her leg and scuttled up into the hedges to find his own supper.

Don't worry, Wickle, I'm just as worried as you are, Alice thought. She looked over at Chess. He was frowning as he bit off pieces of food, and when she glanced at Leander, she found he was watching her. She shifted uneasily.

A wave of weariness washed over Alice, and she yawned, her jaw cracking.

"I guess I'm more tired than I thought."

Leander patted her shoulder. "Maybe you should lie down and get some rest."

Another roar echoed in the night, and Alice hugged herself. "I don't know if I can sleep if that goes on all night."

Leander gave her a strange smile. "You'll be just fine, I think."

Another wave of tiredness threatened to drag Alice under. Suddenly, she could hardly keep her eyes open. "I'm sorry, but I can't seem to stay awake."

Chess tilted his head. "Are you all right?"

His face blurred, and she blinked. "I'm fine. I just need to..." She yawned again. It seemed too much work to stand up, so she crawled over to the base of the tree. She barely got her satchel under her head when her eyes fluttered shut and she sank into a deep sleep.

Chapter 55

ZANDER HAD BEEN TEMPTED to stay in his jabberwock form so he could get back to the palace faster, but in the end, he decided it was too risky. He'd stopped at Lapin's to pick up Verros, informing the rabbit that Citrine had headed home.

Although it only added a few hours to his journey, he'd had to fight the temptation to push the griffon too hard. He hoped he hadn't made another mistake by stopping.

Verros landed on the front lawn of the palace, but before Zander could dismount, the doors flung open. The Commander strode down the steps, his face a storm cloud.

Zander slipped from the griffon's back before his uncle reached him. The man stopped in front of Zander and said nothing for a long moment, the muscle in his jaw ticking.

When he finally spoke, he didn't shout, but his voice vibrated with anger. "Where have you been?"

Zander kept his chin level, conscious of the soldiers lining the doors. "I went after Citrine. I realize…"

"No, I don't think you realize anything at all." The Commander's hands flexed open and shut. "You left the Council waiting to run after a girl. I'd expect something like that from Chess, but not you. That is not the actions of a soon-to-be king. Do you have any idea how hard it was to calm Lord Beecher? He was calling to dethrone you. You're lucky that the Queen is such a poor choice, or he might have gotten his wish."

Zander swallowed. "I'm aware of his opinion of me. He made it quite clear before I left."

The Commander's eyes narrowed. "Please don't tell me you let that old man's blustering make you run away with your tail between your legs. I know my brother raised you better than that."

The words hit Zander like punches but he refused to look away. "I made a mistake, but I think—"

"That's the problem, Zander. You didn't think. You just ran off without telling anyone. You ignored your responsibilities, and I had to clean up the mess."

"I'm sorry. I know I left you in a bad spot."

The Commander put his hands on his hips. "Yes, you did. I had to cover for you with that baron from the Northern Estates." He leaned in close and pointed a finger in Zander's face. "You do not want to make enemies with that group of noblemen. They may live far from the palace, but they have a lot of influence."

Zander's temper sparked. He drew himself up. "I don't plan on it. You're upset and you've a right to be, but I've apologized. I will not stand here while you scold me like a child."

"Then stop acting like one. I'll gather the Council." His nostrils flared. "We'll meet at noon. That gives you about an hour to clean yourself up and get your head together." The Commander whirled on his heel and stomped toward the palace.

A groom approached, and Zander handed Verros's reins to the young man. Then he set off after the Commander.

"Wait!"

The Commander paused by the fountain and turned back. Some of the clouds had cleared from his face, but Zander knew he'd have to earn his way into his uncle's good graces again. Suddenly, he had more sympathy for Chess.

"Look, I know I shouldn't have run off, and I apologize again for putting you in the position of covering for me." He shifted, his gaze taking in the rainbow water that spurted in graceful arcs. "But I found out something important while I was gone."

The Commander lifted both eyebrows. "Well, what is it?"

"Citrine and I went to Phineas Sacklepenny's laboratory."

"What's so important in there? I thought the place was in ruins."

Zander waved a hand. "Citrine was looking for something, but while we were in there, I found this jar, and it had sparkly dust in it." Zander lowered his voice. "It was ground up Fae wings. Perkins told us that it boosts spells... and curses."

The Commander tilted his head. "Who's Perkins?"

"He's a library owl—but never mind about him. Don't you see what this means?"

The Commander shook his head. "No, I'm afraid I don't—besides the two of you needing your heads examined."

"The Queen has always had her flower maidens around. In fact, the first thing she did when she returned here was ask for them again."

"I'm afraid I still don't know what you're getting at."

Zander bit back a growl of frustration. "Don't you see? Every year, they get their wings trimmed. I think she's been using the trimmings. How else has she been able to do such complicated magic when she has a Flora Gifting? She's not even registered as an Alchemist."

The Commander frowned. "I hope that isn't true. It could cause some serious repercussions with the Fae. The flower maidens have become a touchy subject with them in recent years."

Zander glanced up at the soldiers. "The Council will have to wait. We need to get the flower maidens away from the Queen. She was going to have their wings trimmed again, and it was just done in the spring. She could hurt them."

"How do you know that?"

"Citrine told me. I guess one of the maidens said something when she came to help her and Alice get ready for the ball. This can't wait."

He started forward, but the Commander put out a hand to stop him. "You can't just march up to the Queen's door with armed men. She'll interpret that as an attack."

Zander crossed his arms. "Well, she wouldn't be wrong. Those Fae girls are under my protection—or they should be, anyway."

The Commander's face smoothed back into his normal neutral expression. "I appreciate your desire to protect them, but you can't go off half-cocked." He shook his head. "You need to learn to stop and think rather than react. You've already got one mess to clean up. Don't make another one."

Zander ducked his head, a flush working its way up his neck. "You're right. I'm sorry. I'm just worried about those girls. If the Queen gets desperate..."

The Commander clapped him on the shoulder. "I know, and we'll take care of this, but let's get some information first, all right?"

Zander nodded, and the two of them walked up the steps and through the front doors. Their feet echoed on the marble tiles.

"Do you know how many maidens went to the Queen?" the Commander asked.

Zander shook his head. "No, but Anders will."

Before he could ask for his steward, the man appeared at his elbow. It was disconcerting how he seemed to know what Zander wanted before Zander did.

The steward bowed. "Your Highness, I am happy to see you back." He nodded at the Commander. "Did you require my services?"

Zander smiled at the wispy man. "Yes, I need to know how many of the flower maidens went to the Queen."

Anders paused, his eyes rolled up toward the ceiling. "I believe three of them went the first time."

Zander's stomach clenched. "The first time?"

"Yes, Your Highness. The Queen came earlier today and requested more attend her."

Zander exchanged a glance with the Commander. "How many more went over there?"

"You had left orders that only those who were willing should go over. When I had the housekeeper ask, only one volunteered, I believe."

Zander's shoulders slumped. "That's better than I was fearing." He turned to the Commander. "But we still need to get them away from her."

The Commander tapped a finger on his chin. "We can't force things. You're in a very precarious position right now, and you mustn't give her a reason to accuse you of any underhanded behavior."

"But she's using living beings to fuel her spells. That's not just wrong, it's illegal."

"We don't have any real proof. We'll keep an eye on her, but right now, you need to meet with the Council. Then you need to see Baron Belier."

"But..."

The Commander held up a hand. "One fire at a time, Your Highness."

Zander knew he was right, even if the idea of leaving the flower maidens at the mercy of the Queen made him queasy. He let out a sigh. "All right. We'll wait for now, but we can't let any other flower maidens go over there."

The Commander nodded. "I'll send word to the Council. We'll make the meeting this afternoon instead of noon." He quirked an eyebrow. "Try to get some rest before then. You'll need all the energy you can muster to face Beecher."

Chapter 56

ALICE WOKE TO THE sound of buzzing. Her head felt muzzy, and when she opened her eyes, things blurred. She shook her head, and her stomach lurched. It was still dark, but dawn wasn't far off.

She tried to push herself up, but her arms wouldn't move. Panic washed over her, and she struggled. "Chess!"

A hand cupped her cheek. "I'm afraid he can't help you, Alice." It was Leander. He was crouched next to her.

"What have you done to him?" Her voice came out high-pitched and tight.

"I'm afraid I had to get him out of the way."

"Is he... dead?" Alice could hardly bring herself to ask, and her breath came in gasps.

"No, no. I just knocked him out. It's a blessing, really." He gently brushed her hair from her eyes. "I'm truly sorry about this, Alice. There should have been enough of the plant I gave you to make sure you slept through this part. It wasn't my intention to make you suffer." His brown eyes were warm as he smiled at her. "My sister was right. You are delightful. I wish things could be different." He pressed a kiss against her cheek and she jerked away. "I'm afraid I have to go. Lyssandra is most impatient for her crown."

"I saved your miserable life," she gritted out between her teeth.

"Yes, you did, and I am grateful. Which is why I wanted your death to be painless, but you woke up." She tried to kick out at him, but he'd trussed up her legs too. He easily avoided her feeble attempts. "At least it'll be quick. From what I've been told, snark poison acts almost instantaneously from one bite, and we have an entire hive here."

Sudden panic gripped her. "Where's Wickle? What did you do to him?"

Leander's lip curled. "I have no idea why you care about that disgusting little creature."

Tears welled in Alice's eyes. "You didn't hurt him, did you?"

Leander was silent, and for an agonizing moment Alice thought he wasn't going to answer her at all. Then he blew out a breath. "I suppose it would be unkind not to tell you. He got away from me before I could finish him off." He shrugged. "He disappeared into the hedges and is probably long gone by now."

Alice let her head sag onto the ground as relief washed through her. Things were bad enough without Wickle being an innocent victim in all of this.

Leander picked up her satchel, revealing a bright splash of pink lying a few feet from her. "Time's getting away. I need to get going." He leaned over and touched one of the vines that choked the bottom half of the hive.

His lips moved but the words were too soft for Alice to hear. After a moment the vines slithered to the ground and the buzzing in the hive increased.

Leander straightened. "I am sorry about this. It's been my pleasure to know you." Then he gave the hive a vicious kick and sprinted up the path.

Alice squirmed, trying to work her arms free, but Leander had bound them tightly. The buzzing in the hive became louder and more high-pitched, and she watched in horror as something round, pink, and fuzzy tore through a large leaf plastered over an opening. It was a snark, and it wasn't alone.

The snarks poured from the hive opening: pink, baby blue, yellow, mint. They tumbled over each other in their united purpose of reaching the nearest threat—her.

Alice wasn't going to give up without a fight. She gave one last futile tug on her arms, but that was hopeless. Instead, she rolled onto her side and worked her way into a kneeling position—but with her legs tied, she couldn't stand up. She could finally see Chess, though. He lay facedown, unconscious beneath the tree. With any luck, the snarks wouldn't notice him.

Right now, they seemed pretty focused on her as they swept toward her in a single-minded swarm. She gave a last glance at Chess and sent up a prayer that he'd survive.

Alice closed her eyes against the chittering, chirping, hissing hoard and braced herself.

A high-pitched chittering squeal made her eyes pop open, and she swayed in relief. Wickle stood in front of her, puffed to twice his normal size. The mass of snarks seethed in a neverending mass of color, but they were no longer moving forward.

Chittering and hisses filled the air. One snark, pink and slightly larger than the others, confronted Wickle. Wickle stomped his foot. They were twittering so quickly, Alice could only make out snatches of the conversation.

Friend

Enemy... hive... danger

Friend. Help us.

Finally, the pink snark deflated. It turned and made a series of high-pitched whistles. The rest of the snarks settled, their movements slowing. Alice stayed very still, watching warily.

Wickle cheeped twice and the pink snark, along with a smaller mint one, scuttled over to where she knelt. Alice leaned backward. She trusted Wickle, but she wasn't so sure about these other ones. They wheeked up at her and gave a few hops. Alice tried to shuffle away on her knees but didn't get very far.

"Wickle, no offense intended, but I'm not sure I want your friends too near me."

We help. Unbind you.

"Are you sure about this? They were just ready to kill me a few minutes ago."

The pink snark hopped up and down and cheeped. The voice was feminine. *Lilo sorry. Thought enemy. You not enemy. Not hurt.* The creature blinked its enormous eyes up at her, and a smile crept across Alice's face. Now that they weren't trying to kill her, it was impossible not to melt just a little.

"All right, Lilo." She stumbled a bit over the unfamiliar name, sounding it out as lye-low. "I suppose it was
an honest mistake." The one called Lilo scrambled up
her trouser leg and onto her arms, while the mint one
and Wickle tackled the bindings on her legs. Despite
Lilo's assurances, Alice held very still as the three snarks
chewed through her bindings. It seemed to take forever,
and Alice tried to think of something else besides how
close the poisonous fangs were to her skin. After what
felt like hours, but was surely just minutes, her arms
were free. Three pieces of vine lay at her feet. She bent
over and picked one piece up and examined it. It was
fibrous and tough, but already the green had faded into
a dull brown. Leander must have cut this down. Citrine's
warning floated back to her: never cut any of the plants
in the labyrinth. A wintry smile curved her lips. Too bad
Leander didn't know that.

With the small herd of snarks milling around her feet,
Alice hurried over to Chess. He was still out. She knelt
next to him and gently examined the back of his head.
Her fingers found a slight indent among his curls. She
could feel dampness, and when she lifted her hand there
was a dark smear on her finger that had to be blood, but
she was relieved when she realized there didn't seem to
be too much of it. She ran her fingers over the wound
again, and her eyes drifted shut. A picture of a small
crack formed in her mind.

She gasped, and her eyes flew open and filled with tears. She was the one who'd insisted they free Leander. Now, Chess was paying for her decision. The tears spilled over and dripped down her cheeks. She couldn't leave him here, but every moment she sat there, Leander was getting closer to the center of the labyrinth and the crown. It was still dark, but she didn't think dawn was very far off.

A roar shook the air, and the snarks drew closer as one unit, clustering around her. Her mouth twisted into a snarl. She hoped whatever the center contained, it would defeat Leander.

Wickle jumped onto her lap, hopping from one foot to the next.

Head cracked.

She stroked the little creature. "Yes, I know, but I can't fix that. That's a very serious injury. I can't just leave Chess here, but if I don't keep going soon, Leander will win."

A loud sigh issued from the ball of fluff, making the fringe above his eyes blow upward.

Heal mate. Have Healing Gift. Use.

"But this is serious, Wickle. An injury like that can kill you or leave you unsound in the mind."

Healing Gift strong. Heal mate.

"I can't, Wickle. It's too... complicated. What if I do it wrong and cause more harm?"

Wickle stared at her and shook his tiny head.

Mate dying. Try.

Alice swiped at the tears on her cheeks. She once again placed her fingers on the wound and let her eyes close. Pushing away the panic, she concentrated on the picture of the crack in her mind, imagined it knitting back together. This time, she felt warmth leave her hands and go into Chess. Slowly, the picture of the crack changed. It melded back together until there was only a tiny ridge where it had been. Under her fingertips, she could no longer feel the dent that had been there.

When she opened her eyes, Chess was still not awake. The night sky had lightened enough that she could see the pallor on his face was gone. His warm brown skin had its glow back. She traced a finger over his cheek, relief making her shoulders sag. A wave of exhaustion washed over her, and her head swam. She needed to go after Leander. She couldn't sleep, not now...

Without her permission, her body sank next to Chess, and she curled into his side. Her last thought was how strange they must look. Two people sleeping in the middle of a pathway, surrounded by an endless sea of poisonous pastel balls of fluff.

Chapter 57

CHESS OPENED HIS EYES and squinted. The sun was up and beat down on his face. He turned his head to find Alice only inches away. She was sleeping, her breath steady and rhythmic. Her black curls tumbled around her face, her thick lashes a crescent fringe on her cheek. He let himself take her in, the high cheekbones and full mouth set in a heart-shaped face.

He wasn't sure why she was next to him, but he lifted a hand and gently touched her cheek. Her violet eyes blinked open sleepily, and a smile curved over her face. This close, he could see silver flecks in the blue-purple irises. It would be so easy to lean in, to close the distance between them. He shifted onto his side, propping his head up with his hand. Alice's face was soft with sleep, but he noticed the purple shadows under her eyes. As he leaned forward, her lashes fluttered closed again. His lips almost brushed hers when a loud cheep sounded in his ear. He startled and pulled back. His eyes swept past Alice, and he let out a yell, sitting bolt upright, his heart hammering in his chest.

A sea of snarks surrounded him and Alice. Hundreds of eyes watched them, and soft murmurs of twittering and tweets filled the air.

"Alice, I want you to sit up very slowly," he said, his lips barely moving.

"Hmm?" Alice rolled over onto her back and stretched her arms over her head.

He hissed in a breath when her arm brushed several of the snarks. They surged backwards as a group. She reached out and ran her fingers over several closest to her, smiling.

"What are you doing?" Chess's voice was low. "There's a whole hive here. I don't know how we're still breathing, but we have to get far away, as quickly as we can without startling them."

Alice let out a bright laugh. "We're fine, Chess. Wickle explained things to them. They're harmless."

Chess pulled in his legs and swiveled to take in the numbers. "You'll forgive me if I don't believe you."

Alice pulled herself up to a sitting position. As soon as she did, several of the snarks hopped onto her lap. She picked up a small mint-colored one and held it to her cheek. It trilled happily.

Chess grimaced. He had never heard of anyone who liked snarks, never mind cuddled them. He absently rubbed the back of his head where the memory of pain lingered. "What happened? How did we end up taking a nap with a bunch of snarks in the middle of the pathway?"

The smile fled off Alice's face. She stared down at the creature in her palm and stroked its back. "It was Leander," she finally said.

Chess hit his fist against his thigh. "I knew we couldn't trust him. I suppose he's responsible for these?" He swept out a hand, indicating the furry creatures all around him.

Alice nodded and swallowed. She still wouldn't look at him. "He drugged me, but I woke up. He'd already knocked you out." She shivered. "He was so calm as he explained how we would die... I think he might be mad." She peeked up at him, her face drawn. "He took the satchel, too."

Chess stared at her and then put a hand to the back of his head again. "I guess I got lucky if he hit me hard enough to knock me out. I don't even feel a lump."

Alice shrugged and looked away again. "I'm sorry, Chess. This is my fault. I'm the one who insisted we free him."

He rubbed a hand over her shoulder. "It's not a crime to have a soft heart, Alice. He used his sob stories to lure you in."

Alice blinked. "But he didn't..."

He held up a hand. "It's fine, really. We all make mistakes."

Her brows drew down. "You're wrong, though. It was his sob stories that made me worried."

"What do you mean?"

She ran a hand over the green snark sitting on her leg. "He seemed afraid of his sister. I don't know if that was a show because he thought it would make me trust him or if it was real, but it made me nervous."

Chess tilted his head. "How so?"

"At home, the worst animals to deal with are the ones that are afraid. They're unpredictable. The worst bite I ever got was from a stray cat that was terrified."

Chess rubbed a hand over the back of his neck. "I don't know if it matters if he's doing this for his sister or because he's afraid of her."

Alice hopped to her feet. "I suppose you're right." She held out a hand, and he let her pull him up.

Then she walked over to the pink hive and squatted down to examine it. The sea of snarks got louder and milled around her feet. With a grunt, she set the hive up and fingered the top, where Leander had obviously broken it off.

"I don't think you're going to be able to fix that," he said.

"I was hoping to restore their hive before we left. It doesn't seem fair that Leander used them and then left them homeless."

Chess moved closer. "I don't think it's something you or I can fix. Besides, the snarks are hardly helpless. I wouldn't waste too much worry on them. They'll be fine."

"We don't know that," she said.

"Alice, you're losing focus here. Leander has hours on us, and the center of the labyrinth has to be close now. We—*you* can't afford to worry about this."

As if to back up his words, a roar shook the air around them. The snarks churned closer to Alice, cheeping and chittering.

"You're right. We need to go." She looked down at the snarks, who were now swarming over their own hive. It took only a moment before they hoisted it up so it was floating on a sea of tiny backs. Alice leaned over and patted a pink snark. "I have to go now, Lilo. I wish you the best of luck, and I'm sorry about your hive."

The pink snark cheeped twice, and then the swarm moved away in a rippling pastel wave.

Alice watched them go for a moment before she straightened and began walking. Chess fell into step beside her. He reached for her hand, twining their fingers together as they hurried toward the labyrinth's center.

Chess only hoped they got there in time.

Chapter 58

ALICE FELT A SENSE of urgency as they hurried down the path, even as she was conscious of Chess's hand in hers. The idea of going home and leaving him behind made her chest tighten, but she didn't have time to think about what that might mean. There were bigger things to worry about right now. If they lived through this, then they could talk about what lay between them. Until then—

The roar that tore through the air made the hairs on the back of her neck stand up. Her footsteps slowed momentarily, but then the urgency washed over her and she picked up her pace again until she was almost running. Chess didn't ask her why; he merely squeezed her hand, matching his pace to hers. She gave him a grateful smile.

They were no longer choosing turns, but rather the path twisted in on itself, winding tighter and tighter. The hedges seemed to lean inward, making the sunlight dim and casting shadows on the path under their feet. An opening in the hedge appeared, and when Alice stepped through it, she found herself on a circular pathway. The next roar made her clap her hands over her ears. Whatever was making the noise was here, somewhere inside these pathways.

Alice and Chess both stopped and looked around. It was only then that Alice realized that it wasn't one circular pathway, but three circles set inside of each other. They were designed in such a way that there was no clear line of sight to the center of the labyrinth. Instead, sections of hedges blocked the view from one path to another, only giving glimpses of what lay in each subsequent layer.

Her stomach dropped with the realization that this was it. They were at the center of the labyrinth. Alice wasn't sure why she felt so surprised, like she had stumbled on this place when it had been her destination all along.

Unease crawled up her spine at the stillness that blanketed this area of the maze. No birds chirped; no insects buzzed.

And there was no sign of the other champion.

"Where do you think Leander is?" Her voice was barely a whisper in Chess's ear.

Chess put his finger to his lips, and that's when she heard it too: the rustle of branches. It was coming from behind a section of hedge. By unspoken agreement, they both drew their knives and walked toward the sound. Chess skirted the hedge and motioned for Alice to follow. Chess peered around and then turned back toward her, lowering his knife.

"He's not going anywhere."

Alice frowned and peered around the hedge. Leander was there, all right, but vines held him snug against the branches of the hedge. His sword lay on the ground by his feet.

"Where do you think that came from?" she asked, pointing at it. "He didn't have it on him earlier."

Chess shrugged. "That's a good question. Maybe you can ask him while he's indisposed."

She couldn't help a sense of smug satisfaction as she patted a nearby branch. The labyrinth didn't like cheaters.

She and Chess stepped around together. Leander's eyes widened when he saw them, and he began struggling. As soon as they stepped into view, the vines let go, and Leander dropped forward onto his knees. In a blink, Chess was on him, his fist slamming into the other man's nose. Leander staggered back and clapped a hand over his face.

"You're not allowed to hurt me!"

Chess grinned. "I think that only applies to the champion. I'm not the champion."

While he was distracted, Alice hurried over to pick up his sword.

Leander's mouth curled into a snarl. "That's mine."

"Where did it come from?" Alice held the sword with both hands, its weight pulling at her arms.

"I lost it when I ran into that stupid butterfly. When I reached the center, it just appeared on the path."

"You'll have to excuse me if I don't want to give you a deadly weapon right now," Alice said.

Leander shook his head. "You should both be dead. I don't understand how you survived."

Chess pushed his forearm against Leander's throat and slammed him back into the hedges. "That's not the question you should be asking, Leander. The question you should be asking is how you are going to survive, because I promised what would happen if you hurt Alice—and I always keep my promises."

Leander eyed Chess with disgust. "Don't be so stupid, you half-flit mongrel. You can't kill me."

Chess leaned forward and Leander choked. "You're wrong about that."

"Tell him," Leander gasped to Alice.

Alice tipped her head. "Tell him what?"

"He can't kill me!"

"Hmm, it rather looks like he can." She turned to Chess. "You can, right? Kill him, I mean."

Chess bared his teeth in a simile of a smile. "I believe so, yes."

"No, you fools." Leander's words came out with effort, and Alice wondered why he wasted them on insults. "If... you... kill... me... the... crown will be forfeit."

"Then it's already forfeited because you tried to kill both of us," Alice said.

"Not directly," Leander said.

An anguished bawl of sound came from behind them. All three of them turned their heads, and Chess loosened his hold on Leander. Leander took the opportunity and pushed Chess away. He wiped his nose with the back of his hand.

"It doesn't matter," he said, a sneer sliding across his face. "You'll never be able to beat the beast that guards the crown."

Alice stared at him.

"If you don't believe me, go look for yourself. You may as well give me my sword so I can finish him off and claim that crown. Unless you want to die today, that is."

Alice lifted the sword and pointed it at the advancing Leander. He stopped and held up both his hands. "Go on, see for yourself."

Alice waved the sword in his direction. "I will."

She carefully backed away from him and moved to the next opening in the hedge and stepped through it. Behind her, a loud breath huffed out. Slowly, she turned. Air escaped her lips in a surprised puff. Her knees threatened to buckle, and she grasped a branch for balance.

Just visible through the final opening in the hedges at the very center of the labyrinth stood a creature for which Alice didn't have a name. It had the head of an enormous bull with horns that twisted out of its head into points that glistened in the sun. A gold circlet sat incongruously on its head, the ruby in the center winking at her. The head sat upon a man's body that rippled with muscles. Its bulky arms ended in hands tipped with razor-sharp claws. If it had ever worn a shirt, it was gone. A pair of ripped trousers clung to its hips, and its feet were bare.

Alice raised her eyes back to the creature's face. It was staring right at her, smoke rising from its nostrils that were pierced with a golden ring. A bellow made Alice flinch backward, automatically bringing up the sword. The creature's mouth twisted into a snarl, and lowering its head, it charged right at her.

Chapter 59

ZANDER SAT AT HIS desk. He was expecting the Commander any minute. He flicked open the Champion Timepiece. It unfolded with a click. Most of the brass had turned to gold.

The door opened, and the Commander strode in. He stopped in front of Zander's desk and gave a brief bow. Then he leaned forward and looked at the watch. "I think at least one champion will reach the center today."

Zander clicked the button on the side and watched as the maze folded back inside. Then he shut the lid and laid it on his desk. He stared at it. "Do you think Alice has any chance at all?" His voice dropped. "Do you think she's even still alive?"

The Commander lifted one shoulder, the gesture reminding Zander of Chess. "If she wasn't, one side of the Timepiece would still be brass."

Zander's shoulder muscles loosened. He needed her to win. His meeting with the Council yesterday hadn't gone well. Beecher bellowed so much, he'd hardly been able to go over any of his points.

The only one definitely willing to stand up to the Queen if she won was the Duchess. The rest weren't willing to commit. "Do you think it's possible to bring charges against the Queen if she wins?"

The Commander tilted his head. "I'm not sure—"

A knock sounded on the door. Zander and the Commander exchanged glances.

Zander said, "Come in."

The door creaked open to reveal Anders standing next to a flower maiden. She was tall and willowy like all of her kind. She had light brown skin, and her eyes and hair were the same pale yellow. Zander didn't spend any time with the Fae maidens and so he wasn't sure who this one was.

"Your Highness, Miss Buttercup wishes to speak to you." The steward raised both eyebrows. "She says it is of the utmost importance, but if you are too busy..."

Zander stood to his feet and waved the girl in. "No, that's fine."

Anders dipped his head. "As you wish." He withdrew and disappeared down the hallway.

Zander turned his attention the flower maiden. Her name sounded familiar to him, but he couldn't remember why. The girl bowed her head and curtsied. Even when she stood, she kept her head lowered.

Zander rounded his desk and walked over to her. "What did you wish to speak to me about, Miss Buttercup?"

The girl's cheeks flushed. Her voice had a musical lilt to it. "I am sorry to bother you, Your Highness. If it wasn't truly urgent, I would not have intruded."

He smiled at her, and tried to put her at ease. "You're under my protection. If there is something amiss, I want to hear about it."

She lowered her head again, her long hands twisting together. "I am sure you have many important duties."

"Yes, and one of them is to help you, but I can't do that unless you tell me what the problem is."

She kept her eyes trained on the floor. "The housekeeper asked for more flower maidens for the Queen."

Zander leaned forward. "And?"

Her hands continued to twist nervously. "My sister was the one who volunteered, even though I told her not to." Buttercup's lips thinned. "I... I haven't been able to speak to her since."

She finally looked up, her eyes wide, the vertical pupils slitted. "I am worried for her."

Zander frowned. "Did you go to the Dower House to check on her?"

The girl shook her head, her hair lashing around her face. "Oh no, Your Highness. That would be most unwise."

Zander tilted his head. "I'm not sure I understand."

She glanced down again and seemed to struggle with what to say. When she looked up, her expression was set. "Fae can communicate... in our minds." Her hands fluttered as she tried to explain. "I do not know how to describe it, but I attempted to reach my sister, and..." Her breath hitched. "It was just blank space." Her face crumpled as she blinked back tears. "I believe something very bad has happened to her."

Zander looked at the Commander, who nodded. Then he turned back to Buttercup. "I can see why you're worried. I will definitely..."

Three loud chimes interrupted him. He turned to his desk. The watch flipped open and the maze unfolded. He hurried over and picked it up. The only brass left was at the very center.

The Commander looked at him. "The champions have reached the final test. I'll call the Councilmembers."

"Will they all make it in time?"

The Commander shook his head. "Probably not, but they should know to be ready. Besides, you can't leave any of them out or you'll have more problems on your hands."

Zander rolled his eyes at the thought of Lord Beecher. He hoped the old man would decide his gout was a good reason to stay home.

"Your Highness?"

His face flushed, and he turned back to Buttercup. "I promise you, we will find your sister, but right now, we have pressing business that can't wait."

The girl curtsied again. "Thank you, Your Highness." With a last hopeful look, she slipped out the door.

He turned to the Commander. "I suppose it's time."

The Commander nodded. "Are you ready?"

Zander grimaced. "Does it matter if I am or not?"

Then the two of them walked out of the study and headed for the labyrinth.

Chapter 60

ALICE COULDN'T HELP THE scream that tore from her as she pressed backward into the hedge. The creature raced forward, its muscles bunching, but when it reached the opening, it was slammed to a halt. It staggered backward and shook its massive head. Its breath came in smoky gasps and its eyes glowed red.

It backed up for another charge and again slammed into the invisible barrier. Her terror ebbing, Alice looked at the beast, and something tugged at her. She narrowed her eyes and stepped closer, her movement slow and careful.

The bull-man now stood completely still, watching her. There was something about his eyes. Alice took another step closer. The thing's muscles bunched, and it shook its head. The red glow dimmed and for a fleeting moment, Alice saw a man's tortured gaze. She blinked, and it was gone. The beast was back.

Shaken, she slipped back to where Leander and Chess waited. Chess had released Leander, but he was keeping a close watch on the other man.

"What... is that thing?"

The smirk on Leander's face made her want to slap it off. "Minotaur."

At her confused look, he rolled his eyes. "Didn't they teach Greek mythology at whatever pathetic finishing school you attended in the Mirror World?"

Alice huffed out a breath. "Of course I know about Greek mythology. What I want to know is, how did King Minos's minotaur get from his labyrinth in Greece to the Kingdom of Wonderland?"

Leander gave her a slow clap. "Well, bravo for you and your progressive education."

"If you're done insulting me, maybe you can explain why it's here?" Alice crossed her arms.

"It doesn't really matter, since I'm going to kill it." Leander reached over and pulled the sword from Alice's limp grip.

Chess stepped forward, and Leander gave him a disgusted look. "Oh, do stand down. I already told you, neither of us can injure the other or we'll forfeit the crown." He gave Alice a dismissive look. "And only one of us is capable of killing that thing, and it's not you. Really, it's quite unfair that you were allowed into this competition, anyway. You're not remotely qualified."

Alice narrowed her eyes. "I was qualified enough to get you away from that butterfly, wasn't I?"

His face flushed. "I suppose, but this requires a whole other level of skill that you don't have."

Leander hefted the sword and turned toward the center as Alice grabbed his arm. "No, wait. There's something... not right about this. That creature, I think..." She paused, trying to explain what she felt, what she had seen in its eyes.

Leander shook off her hand. "Enough stalling. You've lost, and I'm going to win."

"No, Leander. I think there's a person in that thing."

Chess stared at her, and Leander snorted. "Nice try, Alice, but you're not going to trick me out of that crown."

"Will you please listen? Just now, I saw something in its eyes, like a person looking out from behind the bars of a cage. It was fast, it was hard to tell, exactly, but I really don't think you should kill it."

Leander looked at Chess. "Perhaps the stresses of the labyrinth have sent your lady friend around the bend." He huffed out a laugh. "A person, indeed."

He turned back toward the center, determination settling across his features.

Alice let out a cry of frustration and stomped her foot. "I should just let you charge in there and get yourself killed, Leander, but I'm not like you."

Leander's lip curled. "No, you most certainly are not."

"Look, you pompous idiot, nothing in this labyrinth has been about strength. Think about it. I didn't save your miserable hide by defeating the butterfly. I had to outwit it. It said you attacked it. I assume that's true since it was injured, or am I wrong?"

Leander opened his mouth and then shut it. She raised an eyebrow. "I think this is the same thing. I don't know who set this labyrinth up, but the labyrinth itself is part of this."

Chess looked at Alice, his eyes bright. "You're right, Alice. Nothing we've faced has been about strength." He swung his gaze to Leander. "I think you'd be a fool not to listen to her."

Indecision flickered over Leander's face, and he lowered his sword until the point rested on the ground. "I admit, you've made an interesting observation." Then his eyes narrowed. "But that doesn't mean I'm going to let you win. That crown belongs to my sister."

Alice resisted the urge to argue with him, knowing she wouldn't get anywhere. Instead, she gestured toward the center of the labyrinth. "I think we need to observe him a little more so we can understand how to approach him."

Leander didn't answer, but instead lifted his sword and strode forward. He stopped only a few feet from the opening into the very heart of the labyrinth. The minotaur had sunk to the ground in a crouch, his clawed hands combing through the grass. At their approach, he sprang to his feet, his nostrils flaring. He lifted his head and let out an ear shattering bellow. Alice and Chess clapped their hands over their ears. Leander didn't move. He stared into the creature's glowing red eyes. It backed up and charged toward the opening, again getting slammed back by the invisible barrier that kept him secure in the center.

Alice had to give Leander credit. He didn't even flinch. His eyes ran over the bull-man coolly as it repeatedly charged, only to get slammed backward each time. It only shook its head, steam rising from its nostrils, backed up, and tried again. Even though it was terrifying being this close, Alice felt her heart wrench, watching it. After a particularly hard charge, she again got a glimpse of a man's gaze, hollow and desperate.

"You're wrong." Leander's voice snapped Alice back from her thoughts. He gripped his sword more firmly. "Maybe the other obstacles in the labyrinth weren't about strength, but clearly, this one is." He gave Alice a brief smile. "I admit you've been more of a challenge than I expected, but there can be only one winner, and I'm afraid that's going to be me."

He set his face, lifted his sword, and charged forward. Alice lunged to grab his arm, but her fingers only grazed his sleeve. The invisible barrier opened for him and he was through. Alice thought she saw the beast smile right before it charged.

Chapter 61

LEANDER LEAPED TO THE side as the beast charged by him. A smile hovered on his mouth and he crouched low, balancing on the balls of his feet. His sword gleamed in a sudden ray of sunshine. Alice gripped Chess's hand, her breath caught in her throat.

The bull-man whirled, its clawed hands flexing. Instead of charging, it surveyed its opponent. Alice didn't like the gleam of cunning in its eyes as they glowed a darker red. Leander circled warily, the two opponents assessing and weighing each other.

"I'm right here, Beast. Come and get me." Leander beckoned with one hand, his other holding his sword at the ready.

Steam rose from the creature's nostrils and it lowered its head, apparently unable to resist. It charged across the circle, its feet churning up the grass. Leander leaped out of the way again, using his sword to swipe at the bullish man. A long line of red opened on its side and it bellowed. Alice could hear it huffing from here. It didn't wait but charged again, so fast Leander couldn't quite get out of the way this time. It knocked into his

shoulder, spinning him sideways. He regained his footing with lightning quickness, but not before the creature
had swiped a long claw over his chest. Even from where
she stood, Alice saw how deep the slices went. Leander
staggered slightly, but righted himself.

His lip curled, and he didn't wait for the creature to
attack but went on the defensive. He was wicked quick
with his sword, and soon the brute was bleeding from
several slashes to its upper body. However, they didn't
faze the monster. It lifted its snout in the air and roared
and beat one fist on its chest as if challenging Leander.

For the first time, Alice saw a flicker of doubt on the
other champion's face. His lips pressed together, and
he launched into another flurry of attacks. The creature
swung its colossal head, and the tip of one horn pierced
Leander's shoulder. He screamed in pain and jerked
backward. His left arm now hung limp by his side.

Alice huddled next to Chess, her heart in her throat.
The monster stalked closer. This calmer version was,
if anything, more terrifying than the blindly charging
creature of before. It showed cunning intelligence that
chilled Alice to her core. She could see it had a similar
effect on Leander. Even from here, she could see the
sweat on his face and the hard swallow. He lifted his
sword and danced out of the way of the beast's next
swipe, which seemed almost haphazard.

The creature followed him around the circle leisurely.
All the while, blood dripped down Leander's injured
arm. He lunged several times, but his sword came up
empty. He couldn't risk another full-on attack, not with
one of his arms out of commission. The creature toyed

with Leander, feinting in and out, almost seeming to taunt Leander to attack.

Leander swayed on his feet, but pulled from some deep well of strength. He lunged forward again, and his sword found purchase, piercing the beast's shoulder joint. It let out a loud bellow, its eyes glowing blood-red. Steam billowed from its nostrils and it charged again. This time, Leander was too slow, and the massive head hit his chest with a resounding crack. The blow threw Leander against the hedge. He managed to keep his feet as he ducked downward and slid out of the creature's way just in time, as it swiped a clawed hand at his gut.

Leander put on a desperate burst of speed and ran toward the opening near Alice. The air seemed to stretch, and Alice's gaze met his. His face was bone white and terror lurked in his eyes. The invisible barrier bounced him backward, and the beast caught him in his massive arms.

Alice turned her head into Chess's shoulder, but she couldn't block out the crunch of bones, the ripping of flesh, and Leander's high, thin scream. It cut off suddenly, and an eerie silence fell over the labyrinth.

Alice tried to lift her head, but Chess pressed it more firmly into his shoulder and turned away himself. "No, you don't want to see that."

A roar broke the stillness. Alice's body trembled and Chess tightened his arms. "We're done. You can't go in there," he murmured into her hair.

Alice swallowed down the bile that had risen in her throat. She pushed away from Chess and, steeling herself, turned toward the center. Her eyes were drawn to the bloody heap that had been Leander. Her gaze caught on the glint of a sword on the far side of the circle. It took a moment for her to realize Leander's hand still gripped the handle.

She turned and staggered several steps, desperately trying to keep down the contents of her stomach.

"I told you not to look." Chess put an arm around her and pulled her toward him. She turned again, and Chess let out a hiss of exasperation. "Why are you torturing yourself?"

She put out a hand to quiet him and turned her eyes back to the center. This time, she kept them steadfastly away from Leander, or what was left of him. Instead, she focused on the minotaur.

It stood at the center, chest heaving. The red glow had faded from its eyes and when its gaze met hers, she saw something akin to horror flash in the hazel irises.

She stepped closer, something pulling her toward the creature even as her body trembled.

Chess grabbed her arm and whirled her around. "You can't go in there, Alice. That thing tore a seasoned warrior to pieces. You have no chance. Zander wouldn't want you to do this. I don't want you to do this! There has to be another way."

Alice pulled her arm away and lifted her chin. "You're right. There is another way."

Chapter 62

CHESS WAS ALMOST DIZZY with relief. He tried to turn her away, but she resisted. She walked out from underneath his arm and started toward the center. He grabbed her arm to stop her.

"What are you doing? I thought you agreed with me."

Her brow wrinkled. "I do, but..." Her eyes widened. "Oh, no, Chess, you've misunderstood. I still have to go in there."

"No, you don't." Chess loomed over her, and even as he did it, he felt like a heel.

She straightened to her full height. "You can't bully me into quitting."

Chess ran a hand through his hair. "I'm not... All right, I am, but you saw what that thing did to Leander. You can't expect me to watch it tear you limb from limb."

Although she kept her chin high, a tremor rippled through her frame. "I'm not going to fight it."

He threw his hands into the air and stalked away from her. "Oh, great! What are you going to do? Talk it to death?"

"Don't be ridiculous."

"I'm not the one who's being ridiculous, Alice. That thing is a menace. It's not going to give you some riddle to solve or listen to anything you have to say. As soon as you step past that barrier, it's going to attack you with the aim of killing you." His voice cracked on the word *killing*, and he cleared his throat.

Alice's face softened, and she put her hand on his arm. "I understand why you don't want me to go in there." She gave a rueful laugh. "I'm rather terrified myself, but there's someone trapped in that beast. I've seen glimpses of him looking out." She leaned closer, her expression earnest. "I don't think it's a monster at all."

He shook off her hand and let out a puff of air. "Are you will to bet your life on that, Alice? Because I'm not. I won't let you do this."

Alice's eyes narrowed, and she bristled. "This isn't your choice, Chess. I thought you believed in me. You certainly said as much to the prince. Or were those just empty words?"

"You're not being fair, Alice. Just because I don't want to watch the woman I—that is, I can't stand idly by while you get torn to pieces." He ran a hand over his face. Determination settled over him. "I won't do it."

She lifted her chin. Her eyes glistened with unshed tears, and her voice sounded choked. "There's no other choice. We can't stay in here forever. One of us has to defeat that thing. Please don't make me do this without your support."

The way her chin trembled ripped at his heart. "Then let me do it instead." He gripped her shoulders. "Don't ask me to watch you die."

The tears spilled over, and she put a hand against his cheek. "You can't know what it means to me that you'd offer to do that."

He turned his head and pressed a kiss to her palm, his eyes closing. "I have a feeling there's a *but* coming with that statement."

Her laugh hitched. "Oh, Chess." She looked up at him, her lashes still wet. "As much as I don't want to go in there, it has to be me. Don't you see? *I'm* the champion, but I'll always remember you were willing to go to my place."

He knew she was right, but he couldn't speak past the lump in his throat. Instead, he cupped her face in his hands. They stared at each other for a long moment, and then he did what he'd been longing to do for days now. He lowered his head and captured her soft mouth with his. After a brief hesitation, she sighed and melted against him. When her hands crept up his chest and curled around his neck, his control frayed. He gathered her closer, wrapping one arm around her waist and letting his other hand delve into the silkiness of her hair, deepening the kiss. The labyrinth faded away as he tried to memorize the feel of her lips and the way her slim body fit perfectly against his.

He wanted to hold onto her forever, but finally, she pushed him away, her laugh shaky. "No fair trying to distract me."

He blinked rapidly to clear the moisture from his eyes and gave a half smile. "I thought it was worth a shot."

They gazed at each other for several long moments. The words *I love you* hovered on his lips, but he knew if he spoke them out loud, he'd never let her go. She fixed her eyes on him with a pleading expression.

"If... if I'm wrong, will you go back to the Mirror World and get a message to my family?" She stared down at their hands, still clasped together. "I... I wouldn't want them to wonder what happened to me. It would be better for them to... know." She wiped at a stray tear that tracked over her cheek.

He wanted to plead with her not to do this. He wanted to pull her back into his arms and distract her for real, but she was right. She had to go in there. He forced his lips into a smile. "Nothing's going to happen to you, but... I promise anyway."

She smiled, her dimple peeking out at him. "I also need your help with something else."

The lump in Chess's throat felt like a rock. "Anything you want, love."

Alice lifted her palm, and Wickle popped out of her pocket and jumped nimbly into her hand. She held the snark toward Chess. He backed up a step and put up both hands.

"Now, wait a minute."

Wickle chittered at him, his big eyes staring at Chess. A shiver worked its way up his spine.

Alice's expression turned apologetic. "If... if something happens to me, he'll be stuck in there... with the monster." She laid her cheek against the snark's head. "I can't do that to him."

When Chess still hesitated, her eyes narrowed. "He saved us both from that snark hive. You owe him." She raised an eyebrow. "Besides, you just promised you'd do anything."

Chess let out a sigh and reluctantly held out his hands. She passed Wickle to him. The snark hardly weighed anything. She ran a finger over the tiny head. "You stay with Chess. I'll be back in a little while... I hope." The last words were said under her breath.

Her smile, when she looked up at him, almost blinded him. "Thank you, Chess."

Standing on her toes, she pressed a soft kiss to his cheek and turned toward the center and the waiting monster.

Wickle squeaked in alarm and hopped up and down in his palm. He looked at the snark and gingerly patted it. "I know, mate. I don't want to see her go in there either, but we don't have a choice."

As Alice slipped through the opening, Chess did something he never thought he'd do. He cuddled the snark to his chest.

Chapter 63

ALICE WALKED TOWARD THE entrance to the labyrinth's center. Terror pooled in her belly, and her hands and feet felt numb. She wanted to see Chess one more time, but she was afraid if she looked at him, she'd lose her nerve.

Just knowing he was back there, willing her onward, helped her hang on to the shred of courage that kept her feet moving forward.

She stopped at the entrance. The minotaur stood in the very center, his dark gaze trained on her. He huffed loudly. Her skin prickled, but she didn't look away. Instead, she held the beast's gaze as she moved forward. She hesitated at the opening, knowing once she passed through, she would seal her fate, whatever that might be.

Alice lifted up a silent prayer that Chess wouldn't have to make the trip to the Mirror World to tell her family of her grisly death. Her knees almost buckled at the thought of what might happen in the next moments. With a last shaky breath, she walked through the invisible barrier and into the labyrinth's center.

She slid into the space and along the hedge. The creature turned his massive head to follow her progress, but it didn't make any move toward her. Alice pressed her trembling lips together and focused her mind toward the creature, avoiding looking at Leander's remains. The creature took a step toward her, and she resisted the urge to back up. Instead, she kept her voice low and soothing.

"I know you aren't a monster, not really."

The beast snorted loudly and she jumped. Her breath lodged in her chest somewhere, but she made herself breathe in and out slowly, trying to still the frantic pace of her heart.

"I'm not here to hurt you. I'm here to help you."

The minotaur tilted its head and stalked toward her. She stood very still. Unlike most of the creatures in Wonderland, his thoughts were closed to her. As he got closer, emotions rolled off of him and slammed into her—confusion, fear, anger. They pulsed around her like a choking cloud, but somehow she knew if she could get past that cloud, she'd find the problem. Her eyes slid shut, and she latched onto those feelings, following them deeper into the creature's mind.

She felt the minotaur's presence even though he wasn't touching her. His musky odor enveloped her and made her stomach churn. But she kept pushing deeper.

She felt the brush of his chest as he leaned closer, and her eyes flew open, her heart hammering in her chest so hard black spots danced at the edges of her vision.

He was barely half a foot away from her. His massive body blocked her view of the rest of the circle they stood inside. Her body froze into numbness as he snuffled her hair. She squeezed her eyes shut as the snout moved to her neck, the golden ring brushing against her skin. She could barely make herself breathe as he moved closer still, his massive muscled chest pushing into her, shoving her into the hedge. Branches scratched at her back, poking through her shirt, but she barely felt them. She kept her body still. Slowly she lifted her hand and let it rest on creature's chest.

His skin twitched under her fingertips and he reared back, snorting.

Alice stayed very still and kept her hand in contact with his chest.

"It's all right. I want to help you, to take away the pain."

The creature let out a bellow that blew her hair back, even as it shook his head. The lethally sharp horns danced in front of her face, and steam billowed from his nostrils. Alice shrunk back into the hedge and lost contact with the beast.

His eyes glowed red, and she knew if she was going to reach him, she needed to do it soon. Moving very slowly, she touched him again. He snorted but didn't pull away. She let her eyes drift shut, focusing on the where the pain originated. Her hand moved of its own accord and settled on the minotaur's snout. She opened her eyes, and the golden hoop that pierced his nostrils drew her attention.

Alice's stomach sank as she realized what she was going to have to do. She gently touched the scratched hoop with a fingertip, noting it was locked in place by a clasp held shut by a tiny screw. The beast reared its head back, growling low in its throat. Alice swallowed hard. There was a very real chance she'd get herself killed in the next few moments. Fine tremors shook her entire body, and she pressed her back into the branches, trying to still them.

The minotaur reached out and touched her face with one long claw. Alice flinched. The creature's snout wrinkled. Alice brought her focus to his eyes, which were hazel again.

She spoke past trembling lips, her voice wavering. "I know you're in there. I can help you, but you have to let me."

There was intelligence shining back at her. She slowly lifted her hands again.

"I have to take this out." She gestured to the golden hoop. "But I'm afraid it's going to hurt more before it's better."

The creature pulled away and turned its head to the side. She gently reached over and place a hand on the hard cheek, turning his face back toward her. It gripped her arms in meaty hands, grunting. She felt the tips of his claws, reminding her of Leander's messy end.

Alice stared into the creature's eyes and the word *help* formed in her mind.

And suddenly she knew with certainty. There was a man somewhere inside this monster, and he had been cursed. If she removed that nose ring, she could break the curse.

"I can free you, but you have to fight the monster. Can you do that?"

Hope flared in the beast's eyes and he jerked his head in a nod. Alice took a long breath and let it out slowly. She reached up and steadied the hoop with one hand. Saying a last prayer, she grasped the tiny screw that held the latch in place between her fingertips and tried to turn it. It stayed stubbornly still.

Pain lanced through her arms as the creature's claws pierced her skin. She gritted her teeth and kept going, focusing all of her attention on the tiny piece of metal between her fingers until finally it began to turn. The creature's eyes started to glow red again and steam curled from his nostrils and over her hands.

Alice knew her time was up, and her fingers grew clumsy as she worked frantically to get the ring open. The tiny screw finally fell out and she flicked open the clasp that locked the hoop in place. The creature bellowed, his breath rancid in her face. In desperation, she wrenched the sides of the ring. With an audible click the hoop came apart and she pulled it out of the monster's nose. She let her arms fall to her sides, the blood-smeared hoop still clutched in one hand.

The minotaur roared in pain as he wrapped his arms around her in a bear hug, crushing her into the hedge. She squeezed her eyes shut as a branch poked painfully into her back and another tore at her hair. Her ribs creaked as he squeezed tighter.

Alice knew she was going to die. Tears leaked from her eyes.

Then the pressure was gone. When she dared to look, a gaunt man was on his knees in front of her. The crown that had been on the creature's head lay in the grass between them. He was staring at his hands, turning them this way and that. He patted at his shrunken chest and then put his hands over his nose and mouth. Something like wonder sparked in his hazel eyes.

He turned his haggard face up to hers. When he spoke, his voice was hoarse and barely audible. "Thank... you."

Chapter 64

ALICE HASTILY SHOVED THE battered hoop into her pocket and, gathering her wits, dropped down next to him, her hand on his back.

"Are you all right?"

The man looked at her blankly for a moment, his eyes unfocused. Fear slithered up Alice's spine, and she breathed out a sigh of relief when the man's eyes came back into focus. He frowned.

"I'm... I'm not sure."

Standing, she put a hand under his arm and helped him to his feet. He turned in a slow circle, his face turning pale when his gaze snagged on Leander's body. He swayed precariously, and Alice steadied him. A low groan wrenched from him that made tears well in Alice's eyes.

"I... Did I...?" He couldn't finish the sentence. The haunted look on his face tore at Alice's heart. She simply nodded once. The man covered his face with both hands, a keening noise escaping through his fingers.

Not knowing what else to do, Alice put a hand on the man's shoulder. "It's not your fault. I know it's awful, and

I can't begin to imagine how you must feel, but... it's not your fault. Whoever did this to you, that's whose fault it is."

He took his hands away from his face and stared at them. Emotions flickered over his face like the film reels back home. He shook his head, anguish twisting his features.

She took his elbow and turned him away from the carnage in the grass, feeling her own stomach churn at the sight of Leander's face, frozen in a tortured scream. It would likely haunt her dreams for a long time to come. She couldn't imagine how it would affect the man next to her. She reached for the first thing she could think of to distract him.

"What's your name?"

He slowly lowered his hands and looked at her blankly. His mouth opened and then closed and then opened again. "My name?" His voice was slow, like it was still trying to find its way out of his throat.

She smiled at him. "I'm Alice, Alice Cavendish."

He put a gnarled hand over hers, and one side of his mouth attempted to curve upward. Alice appreciated the effort. "I'm afraid... Do I know you? My mind, it feels quite out of focus."

He stumbled over the words, but Alice waited patiently for him to finish before answering. "I'm afraid not. I'm a visitor here, from the Mirror World." She paused, almost afraid to push him. "And your name is...?"

"Za... ne?" He said the name as if it was unfamiliar. "Zane. My name is Zane." He looked at her, and again, something about him seemed familiar. Her mind niggled with a memory, but it wouldn't quite come into focus.

"Do you know what happened to you, how you got here?"

He looked around, his eyes searching for something—maybe an answer? Alice wasn't sure. She waited while he gathered his thoughts. Finally, he shook his head, putting a hand to his forehead. "No, I... I don't know what happened." Panic flashed across his face and he clutched at her arm. "How long have I been in here? What about the Kingdom?"

A sense of déjà vu swept over Alice, but she focused on trying to reassure the man. "I'm afraid I don't have the answer to your first question. I've only been here a few weeks myself." She patted his hand. "As for the other, everything is just fine." She didn't see the need to worry this poor man over the recent turmoil.

Suddenly, the man straightened, his eyes darting right and left. "My son, how is my son?" He swayed, and Alice was afraid he was going to topple over. His breath hitched as he clasped his hands together, pleading with her for answers she didn't have. "Please, you must tell me how my son fares."

Alice gave him an apologetic smile. "I'm so sorry. I'm sure your son is just fine, but I don't know—that is, we need to get you home. I really have no idea who your son is."

The man pulled his head back, his forehead wrinkling. Something about his expression reminded her of someone. "But you're a visitor here from the Mirror World." He blinked against the sun. "You did say that's where you are from?"

Alice tilted her head. "I'm afraid I'm not following you."

The man looked confused. In the silence that followed, Alice became aware of Chess calling her name. She looked over to see him at the entrance. She waved at him to come in, but he shook his head, pushing his hands against the invisible barrier.

"The crown!" he shouted. "Pick up the crown."

Alice gasped at her oversight. She had been so distracted by this poor man, she had completely forgotten why she was there in the first place. She leaned over and picked up the crown from the grass. The gold circlet was surprisingly heavy for such a simple creation.

Chess came crashing into the circle just as Alice turned to the older man. "I'm sorry. What were you saying?"

The man reached a trembling hand out and touched the crown. "How did my crown get in here?"

Alice blinked at him. "What did you say?" Her heart began to beat frantically in her chest.

"That's what I've been trying to tell you," Chess said, his voice strained. "That's the Red King."

Chess skidded to a halt and then fell to one knee and bowed his head. "Your Majesty."

"Chess?" The King looked from Chess back to Alice. He surprised Alice with a rusty chuckle. "I should have known I'd find you with the pretty girl."

Chess got back to his feet. "Do you remember how this happened, Your Majesty?"

The confusion slipped back over the man's face, and his smile died away. "No, son. The last thing I remember is sitting in front of the fire with my wife." He shook his head and his expression hardened. "I don't know who did this, but they will pay."

He stepped toward Chess. "You must tell me. Is Zander all right?"

Chess nodded. "He is, and that's thanks to the young woman next to you."

The King swung his gaze to Alice, but before she could respond, there was a loud rustling and creaking.

Alice exchanged startled looks with Chess as the labyrinth folded back to form a straight pathway to the outside. The King put a shaking hand over his mouth. "I didn't think—that is, the few fleeting moments when I overpowered the monster, I never believed I'd be free." He shook his head again, and tears welled in his eyes.

"If I may?" Chess moved to the other side of the King. The man nodded absently and allowed Chess to take his arm.

Alice looked back at Leander's remains and her eyes found Chess's. He grimaced. "We'll send someone so he can have a proper burial."

A shudder ran up Alice's spine, but she straightened her shoulders. As she turned to leave, something brushed her leg. When she looked down, she saw Wickle clinging to the fabric of her trousers.

No leave me.

Oh dear. She'd completely forgotten about him. He should probably stay here, but she didn't have time to deal with that right now. "Come on, then," she whispered.

The snark scampered up her body and tucked himself into her pocket. Maybe Citrine would know what to do with him.

Chess turned to look at her. "Are you coming?"

She hurried over and took the King's other arm. Together, she and Chess escorted the King down the pathway and out of the labyrinth.

Chapter 65

THEY WERE ONLY A few yards away from the outer edge of the labyrinth when two groups of people came into view. In one group was the prince, flanked by the Commander, several members of the Council, and a small contingent of guards. In the other, the Queen stood with her own guards.

Alice knew the moment everyone spotted them because there was a hush of silence and then exclamations of surprise from the prince and those around him.

Alice's eyes went to the Queen's face. She didn't seem nearly as surprised as everyone else. The woman's eyes flitted from Alice to Chess to the King. Then her features arranged themselves into an expression of joy and disbelief.

She lifted the hem of her skirts and ran toward them, tears sparkling in her big brown eyes. As she approached, one crystal tear ran down her perfect cheek. She trained her gaze on her husband and covered her mouth with both hands.

"My darling, how is it... How can this be? I thought..." She slid her arms around the older man's waist and nestled into him. The King slowly embraced his young wife. His eyes closed, and a sigh escaped his lips.

Zander strode toward the Queen, the others following in his wake. He stopped only a few feet away. "Father." Emotion choked the single word.

The King lifted his head, a genuine smile curving his lips. He gently set aside his wife and turned to his son, holding out his arms. The two men embraced for a long moment. When they stepped apart, the Duchess dipped into a low curtsey before she spoke.

"Your Majesty, I am delighted to find you still among us. Although, I have to admit to being puzzled about where you've been all this time. And forgive me, as I mean no disrespect, but are you quite all right? You're not looking well at all."

Before the King could answer, Lord Beecher banged his cane on the ground. "I say, it's a relief to see you again. It's been nothing but poppycock and foolishness the last few weeks, what with jabberwocks and curses and competitions. I'm too old for all that nonsense."

While the Councilmembers were speaking, the Commander motioned several of his guards forward, but it was the Queen that Alice was watching. She saw when the other woman realized her brother wasn't there. Lyssandra's eyes glinted with cunning before another mask slid into place.

Her face crumpled, and looking wildly around, she started toward the labyrinth. "My brother. Where's Leander?"

Chess blocked her path, taking hold of both her arms. "I'm afraid he didn't make it." His voice was gentle. "Trust me, you don't want to see him that way." Alice wondered if the Queen cared about her brother at all or if any of her grief was real.

The Queen tried to pull her arms away and started to scream. "No! No! I want to see him." She sagged against Chess, tears cascading down her cheeks, her words becoming incoherent.

The King's face creased into a worried frown, and he stepped toward his distraught wife. "I'm sorry.... I didn't mean..."

Zander stopped him, his expression pained. "No, Father. Please stay away from her."

"But she's... I must go to her."

Zander shook his head. "A lot has happened since you've been gone."

The King's face creased in confusion. "How long has it been?"

Zander's expression turned grim. "Over a year. The entire Kingdom, as well as myself, believed you dead. We've been mourning you all this time." He ran a hand over his face and weariness settled over the lines of his body. "I'm afraid that your wife, the Queen, has been behind all of this. She's the one who told everyone you died from a terrible disease while I was away. She's the one who said she had your body burned on a funeral pyre before I even returned home because of a contagion." His lip curled, and his eyes found the Queen, who was still in the midst of a hysterical bout of crying. "I'm afraid she's the one who is responsible for whatever happened to you in there." He gestured toward the labyrinth.

The King shook his head, his face crumpling. He suddenly looked like a very old man. Alice's heart squeezed in sympathy. "I don't understand." He twisted to look at his wife. "She couldn't possibly..." His voice trailed off, his expression lost.

Zander took a breath. "She's also the one who cursed me, and if it wasn't for Alice, I would have lost the throne and probably be dead by now."

The Queen let out an anguished cry and rushed into the space between the two men. She gave several shuddering breaths, as if trying to stop her tears. She cast an accusing look at Zander.

When she spoke, there was a convincing wobble to her voice. "Please don't listen to him, darling. He's not himself, and hasn't been since we thought you died. When he found out, he was mad with grief, as is understandable given your close relationship. When he learned about the change in the will"—she spread her hands—"he just disappeared into the mountains. I had no idea what had happened to him."

She lifted her trembling chin. "It was difficult, but I carried on as best I could." She gestured toward Alice. "And then he showed up with this girl and some crazy story of being cursed. You know I'm not an Alchemist. How could I curse anyone? In his confused state, he was susceptible to this girl's manipulations. I can't pretend to know what her true motivations are, but she clearly wielded some kind of influence over him in his confused state. She *is* from the Mirror World." She gave a delicate shrug, as if this should be explanation enough.

The King looked from his wife to his son, and back again. His face clouded with bewilderment. Doubt shimmered in his eyes.

"I still don't understand. How did I come to be in the labyrinth? How was I turned into a monster?" The King's body trembled as he said the word, and his eyes turned glassy and unfocused as if reliving the horror of the last months. "How..."

The Queen placed a tiny hand over his mouth. "There's time enough to find the answers to your questions, darling, but right now, we should get you back to the palace." She framed his face between her hands, her expression tender. "You're looking too pale by far. I can't imagine what you've experienced."

"You mustn't believe her, Father." Zander's voice was firm and even. "She's responsible for all of this. I'm not positive how she's able to cast these complicated curses—Citrine and I found some things that might help to explain it—but she's dangerous."

"Don't forget she has the blasted Drifter Gene as well." Lord Beecher harrumphed. "Nearly took out the entire ballroom last week."

The King's eyes widened, and he turned to his wife. "Curses? Drifter Gene... Why...?"

The Queen's eyes filled with tears again and she looked down. "I... I never meant to deceive you, but my father"—her body quaked—"he made me promise to hide it from you." A sob escaped, and she pressed a hand to her mouth. "I was so afraid..."

The King automatically put his arms around her and rubbed her back. His face was haggard. "I... I don't know..." His voice faltered as he looked between his son and his wife. He seemed to use all of his strength just to stay on his feet.

Silence stretched over the lawn. Then a cool voice said, "I'm impressed with your acting abilities, Your Majesty, but how can you lie so blatantly? We were all at the ball when you showed your true colors." The Duchess crossed her arms and stared at the Queen.

There was a jingle, and the Commander stepped next to the Duchess. "I'm sorry to tell you the Queen isn't being honest with you, Your Majesty."

Chapter 66

THE KING DROPPED HIS arms and looked at his wife, pain and disbelief written across his features. Zander saw the moment when the Queen realized her husband no longer believed her. He had to give the other woman credit for her ability to improvise so well.

The Queen's expression twisted as more tears fell down her cheeks. She covered her face with delicate hands. The Commander hesitated, looking between Zander and the King. When the King didn't say or do anything, Zander nodded his head even as his eyes didn't leave his father's face. He hoped his father could withstand all the shocks hitting him today.

The Commander stepped forward to take Queen's arm, and when the King didn't protest, she turned a stricken face to her husband. She held out her arms. "You know the Duchess never supported our marriage, and Zander's always resented me." She lifted her chin and looked sorrowfully over at him. Zander resisted the urge to roll his eyes at her theatrics. "It's understandable. He loved his dear mother, and I'm the intruder." She drew in a shuddering breath, her voice hitching. "I never thought he'd turn on me like this, though." Once again, she lowered her face into her hands, her sobs the only sound.

Watching her like this, as if from a distance, Zander experienced a clarity about his stepmother that brought a flush to his face. How could he have ever been taken in by her delicate damsel act?

Apparently, his father didn't have that clarity because doubt crept back into his face. Zander shot the Queen a withering stare. "Enough, Lyssandra. Most of the court witnessed your treachery. You can cry all you want, but neither your pretty face nor your tears will change the fact that you cursed both my father and myself with the hopes other people would do your dirty work and kill us."

The King, already confused and weakened by his ordeal, looked at his wife. The anguish in his father's face made Zander want to turn away. "Why, Lyssie? Why would you do this? I gave you everything. I... I loved you."

The Queen's face cleared as if someone had turned a switch. The tears dried up, and her mouth twisted into a snarl. She gave a bitter bark of laughter. "Everything? You treated me like I was some kind of pet, patting my head as if I were a particularly daft child. You didn't love me. I was just a pretty bauble to stave off the loneliness of old age. But I won't be under any man's control—not anymore." Her expression turned fierce, and she swept her hand out. "If you think I'm going to meekly allow you to put me in a cell, you are stupider than I thought."

Zander wanted to shield Alice as the woman's venomous gaze fell on her and steam puffed from her nose.

The King took a step back, shaking his head. "I... I..."

"Oh, shut up, you old fool." The Queen threw back her head and her body stretched and elongated. A long red tail slid across the ground. In less than a minute, the Queen stood before them in her jabberwock form, her ruby scales glinting in the sun.

The King staggered back and Alice grabbed his arm to keep him from falling. He shook his head. "No... you can't..." His voice trailed off.

Time slowed for Zander. Alice tried to pull his father backward, away from the red dragon, but shock bolted the King to the earth, his horrified gaze glued to his wife.

The Queen reared back, and fire flickered in the back of her throat. He had a split second to decide. In slow motion, he saw the fire erupt from the Queen's jaws, and Alice pull her arms back to shove the King.

Zander's body started shifting form before he had fully decided what he was going to do. By the time his jabberwock emerged, the King was lying in the grass and a burst of fire was racing towards Alice.

Zander leapt over Alice and shielded her with his body. Heat washed over his right side and wing.

He had no time to consider the consequences of his decision. Behind him, pandemonium erupted. Screams and shouts echoed while feet pounded across the ground. The Commander shouted at his men. The grass crackled and caught. Zander spread his wings and spouted his own stream of flame. The twang of arrows rang out, and the red dragon let out a roar as several landed with dull thuds in her body.

The queen snapped at Zander. He dodged, almost stepping on Alice in the process. She tried to move out of his way, but another blast of fire kept her pinned behind one of his massive legs. More arrows twanged through the air.

His father laid on the ground in a daze. If someone didn't move him, he'd get burnt or crushed—

His moment of inattention cost him. The Queen's long neck snaked forward. She closed her jaws around his shoulder and wrenched her head to the side. Zander bellowed as agonizing pain bloomed across his right side. She spit the chunk of flesh she'd ripped away into the grass.

He staggered backward, and she lunged toward the King. Zander whirled in her direction, ignoring the pain that pulsed through him. The Queen's head darted forward, but Alice stepped in front of the King's prone body.

Zander sprang forward even as he knew he wouldn't get there in time. The Queen knew it, too, and her reptilian lips curled up in a hideous smile.

Suddenly something blue popped out of Alice's pocket and hissed at the Queen. The Queen reared back, and Zander saw his opportunity. His snaked his neck out and slammed against her. The Queen staggered sideways.

Being smaller and more nimble, she managed to evade Zander's next attack. A maniacal laugh scraped across his ears. *You've lost. Everyone knows your precious secret now.*

Zander slashed a taloned foot at her and grunted with satisfaction as a long gash in the Queen's side spurted a fountain of blood. Out of the corner of his eye, he saw Alice trying to pull his father out of the way, but she was struggling to move his bulk.

He tried to follow up on his advantage to give Alice more time, but the Queen twisted away from him. Using her spiked tail, she lashed it across his face. A spike tore open his cheek, dangerously close to his eye. Zander roared and blew a river of fire at the other jabberwock. The Queen ducked just as another volley of arrows thunked into her side. She lurched sideways and shook her head. Blood streamed from a dozen wounds along her body.

Her leg muscles bunched and she spread her wings. Zander leapt toward her. She couldn't get away. Not now.

He landed on her back, but she bucked wildly underneath him, throwing him to the side. He rolled across the grass, barely missing Chess, who was helping Alice move the King.

The Queen's jaws snatched up something in the grass a few feet from where the King lay. It glinted gold in the sunlight. His father struggled to sit up, and one of her clawed feet whipped forward and slammed him back into the ground. More arrows flew through the air, several finding her neck.

She roared and shook her head before she vaulted into the air. Zander spread his own wings, intent on following her. He wouldn't let her get away this time.

Then the Duchess's scream rent the air. "The King! He's dying! Someone fetch the palace physicians!"

The Queen flew away even as Zander's body twisted and shrunk back into his human form. He ran to his Father. Alice was already kneeling next to him, holding his hand.

His father's eyes widened and his face turned even paler. Then his eyes rolled up in his head and he went limp.

Chapter 67

"OH DEAR!" ALARMED, ALICE pushed Wickle back into her pocket.

"I told you everyone hated snarks," Chess said.

Alice glared up at him. "You're not helping." She nodded at the Duchess who looked on the verge of fainting. "If you want to do something useful, get her seated somewhere before she falls down. We don't need any other injuries."

Chess hesitated and then moved over to the other woman. Alice turned back to the King and leaned over him. His chest rose and fell in fits and starts, and his face had lost all color. Alice knew she needed to stop the river of blood dripping from his arm onto the grass.

Tentatively, she laid her hands on the gash. She let her mind focus in on his wound, and her eyes drifted shut. Even as a distant part of her registered the sounds of people drawing near, she concentrated on his injury. A picture like a burst pipe popped into her head. It needed to be mended, or the King would bleed to death.

She sank deeper into the picture, carefully imagining the walls of the pipe curling back into place, melding together. The gush of blood gradually slowed until it was a trickle, and then stopped all together.

A great wave of exhaustion swept over Alice, and she might have laid down on the grass next to King and gone to sleep if someone hadn't put a hand on her shoulder.

She blinked open her eyes to meet Zander's stare. He had returned to his human form. There was a gleam in his hazel eyes as he knelt next to her. Blood dripped from his cheek, and a bruise was forming along his jaw-line, but he otherwise seemed to be in one piece.

"You saved him, Alice." Zander hugged her to him before letting her go. "I don't know what I'd have done if I lost him again so soon after..." His voice choked to a stop.

He swallowed several times before he spoke again. "How do you have the Healing Gift and none of us knew?"

Alice felt as if she were pushing her words throughs syrup. "Because I didn't know. At least not until Wickle showed me."

"Wickle?"

"Brace yourself. A snark has attached himself to Alice." Chess had wandered back over. The Duchess stood off to the side, no longer looking quite so white. "I suppose the little guy's not quite as bad as I originally thought." He quirked an eyebrow at Alice and absently rubbed at the back of his head.

Before anyone could question her further, the King blinked open his eyes, his gaze bleary. He scanned the faces looking down at him.

He frowned at the blue fluff ball that poked out of her pocket. "Those are poisonous."

Alice resisted rolled her eyes. He was the King, after all. "Yes, so everyone keeps telling me, but they are also sweet and wonderful, and he helped save your life." She gently stroked Wickle's head, and he closed his eyes, trilling softly.

The King let out a shaky breath. "Thank... you, my dear."

Then his gaze moved to Zander, and his eyes welled. Alice drew back to give Zander room next to his father.

The King raised a trembling hand, and Zander gripped it. "I'm sorry. I should have told you, but I was afraid..."

Tears leaked from the King's eyes. "I'm sorry... you felt you... couldn't tell me. Did I..."

"No, it wasn't you, Father. It was me. I was a coward." Tears dripped off of Zander's chin, and Alice wanted to herd everyone away from the two men. It didn't seem right they were having this conversation with an audience, but nobody moved.

"No, this is... my fault. I should have... told you. I didn't think... Your mother worried, but we never saw any signs."

"Are you saying Mother...?"

The King shook his head. "No, it was her mother, your grandmother, that had the Drifter Gene." He struggled to get up. "Here, help me."

Zander put an arm around the King's shoulders, and the King sat up and then wobbled to his feet.

"I'm afraid this will cause you problems," Zander said and gestured to the ring of people who silently watched them with wary expressions. Alice's eyes immediately cut to Lord Beecher. The older man scowled and opened his mouth, but the Duchess elbowed him so hard only his cane prevented him from falling into the grass.

The King put a hand on Zander's shoulder. "You're my son. The people know you. We'll work through it."

Alice hoped, for Zander's sake, that was true. Zander took the King's arm, and they walked toward a carriage waiting on the far side of the green, everyone trailing after them. Alice fell into step with Chess and followed. Her foot hit something hard in the grass. When she looked down, a flash of red caught her eye. She bent over and picked up the forgotten crown. Its ruby glistened in the sun. She ran to catch up with Zander and the King. When they paused, she held it out to Zander.

"I think this belongs to you."

Chapter 68

Two days later, a knock on her bedroom door startled Alice. She glanced at Wickle, who sat on the bed. "Who do you think that is?"

Wickle hopped up and down. *See! See!*

Alice laughed as she hurried to the door and pulled it open to reveal Chess, leaning on the doorjamb. His lips quirked into a smile as his eyes studied her.

Alice fought the urge to smooth her hair. "What are you doing here?" Her voice came out more sharply than she intended. This was the first time she'd seen him since they'd left the labyrinth.

He straightened. "A little bird told me you were leaving later today." He lifted a shoulder. "I wanted to catch you before you left."

"You're not coming to the Looking Glass with us?"

He shook his head. "No, I'll let Zander and the King see you off. I'm not great at goodbyes, anyway."

Alice shifted. She wasn't sure what to say. She searched his face, looking for the man she'd come to know in the labyrinth, but his expression gave nothing away.

He gestured. "Can I come in, or are you going to keep me standing in the doorway?"

"Of course." Alice moved back to let him inside. She had been hoping to see him for the last couple days, but now that he was here, she didn't know what to say.

Chess grinned and pointed to Wickle. "Are you taking home a souvenir?"

She shook her head. "No, he'll have to stay in Wonderland, but I haven't had the heart to send him away yet."

Chess patted the snark's head with one finger, and Wickle cheeped happily. "You should take him with you. I bet that sister of yours would love him."

Alice rolled her eyes. "Oh yes, it would be such a wonderful idea to take a poisonous animal back to England with me." She tickled Wickle under his chin. "Besides, it doesn't seem right to condemn him to a life without any of his own kind."

Wickle hissed. *Go with you.*

Alice ignored him and turned her attention back to Chess. "So, do you know how the King is doing? Zander told me the palace physicians were optimistic about his recovery, but he's been so busy, I haven't talked to him since yesterday morning."

Chess shrugged. "He's doing well enough. The palace healers have given him a clean bill of health. I'm sure it will take time for him to fully recover, though."

Alice moved toward the French doors. Sunlight spilled through and made a golden square on the floor. "What do you think the Council will do about Zander, now that everyone knows about his jabberwock? I know he's been really worried."

Chess leaned against one of the posters of the bed. "To be honest, I'm not sure. The people love him though, and the King will support him. Besides you don't have to worry about all this anymore. You're going home."

She nodded but a sudden lump in her throat made it hard to speak. "Yes, I suppose I am."

He shifted, and one side of his mouth curved up. "After all you've done to make that happen, you don't sound too excited."

Her eyes prickled with tears. "It's just, I'll miss... everyone." She glanced at him. "I didn't even get to say goodbye to Citrine."

He shoved his hands in his pockets. "With Citrine, you never know. She might show up at your door when you least expect it."

Alice gave a laugh but her voice wobbled. "I hope she does."

His eyes glinted. "You never know."

The tension in Alice coiled tighter. After everything they had been through, she hated this awkwardness between them.

She was leaving in a few hours, and she'd probably never see Chess again. She didn't want her last memory of him be this stilted conversation.

She turned to him. "Why did you come, Chess? Surely, it wasn't to ask me about Wickle."

"I told you, I couldn't let you waltz back to the Mirror World without a word."

She smirked. "No, I don't suppose you could. We both know silence isn't your strength."

He chuckled and then his expression turned serious. "Actually, I wanted to give you something—if you'll take it, that is." He reached into his pocket, and her heart began to race. Was he going to ask her to stay? Would she if he did?

He stepped closer until only a few inches separated them. "I know you have to go home, and I'm happy that you're finally getting what you've wanted since you got here. It's my fault that you've been kept from your family for this long."

"Chess, I didn't—"

"No, let me finish." He met her gaze, his blue eyes burning with an emotion she was too afraid to identify in case she was wrong. "I should have never dragged you here against your will. I took away your choices, and for that I'm truly sorry, Alice." He paused and cleared his throat. When he spoke again, his voice was rough. "But I'm too selfish to say I'm sorry for our adventures together."

Alice's lips parted, but before she could speak, he continued. "You were right when you said you didn't belong here." He took her hand and pressed something smooth into her palm and then curled her fingers around it. "But if you ever need me, you can reach me with this. Just hold this, picture me, and call my name. It should work even in the Mirror World."

She opened her hand and looked down. A round piece of greenish-blue quartz lay in her palm, one side polished so that it resembled a tiny mirror. She looked up at him. Words crowded into her throat and stuck there. Tears welled in her eyes. "I don't know what to say."

"You don't have to say anything." He closed the space between them, but the kiss she anticipated landed on her cheek. Before she could respond, he stepped away.

Then, he winked at her. "Don't be a stranger, love."

He sauntered out the door, pulling it shut behind him with a click. Alice didn't realize she was crying until a tear dripped onto the shiny surface of the stone.

Chapter 69

ALICE STOOD IN THE ruins of Sacklepenny's home with Zander, the King, and the Commander, along with several of his soldiers who served as protection to the small group. Alice tried not to think about Chess. She had put the stone in the pocket of her gown, and she kept touching it to make sure it was still there.

She kept remembering their last conversation and felt torn. She needed to go home, longed for it, and it was unrealistic to believe anything could work out between them. They belonged in separate worlds, and yet, she couldn't help wishing things were different.

Alice turned to the small group with her. The King had made a remarkable recovery in such a short time, and if his eyes sometimes seemed haunted, Alice didn't feel like she could blame him after all he had been through. Despite the sadness of leaving, it warmed her heart to see Zander and his father reunited. It was clear their bond was strong despite what Lyssandra had done to sever it.

She turned to Zander. She still felt a mix of feelings for him. While she understood why he'd done what he'd done, and he'd apologized, she couldn't forget he'd almost forced her into a marriage neither of them wanted. She knew his troubles were far from over, though, and she couldn't bring herself to hold a grudge. So when he bent down to hug her, she returned the embrace.

When he pulled back, he smiled at her, his eyes crinkling at the edges. "I can never repay you for what you've done for me. I won't forget it."

She squeezed his arm. "I hope everything works out for you and your father. You'll make a great king someday."

The King smiled in agreement. "We'll be forever in your debt, my dear." His eyes fuzzed and then cleared again, like a ghost was walking on his grave.

Zander took her hand and walked with her toward the mirror. "Are you ready?"

Alice looked behind her one last time. Then she squeezed his hand back. "Yes, I think I am."

She stared at the Looking Glass.

Zander gestured. "Remember, hold your destination in your mind, and then walk through."

Alice nodded. She was going home. At last. She stepped up to the mirror, and Chess's face flashed in her brain right before she stepped through.

Walking through the Looking Glass felt like pushing through invisible gelatin. Alice popped out into another forest. Birds twittered, and insects buzzed in the sunshine.

She looked back. The group she'd left in Wonderland shimmered in the air, like a faded painting. She watched as the picture rippled and dimmed. Her eyes roved over each face until they landed on the King, who stood removed from the others. A gasp escaped her lips. Just as the view was almost gone, his eyes glowed a familiar but unwelcome red. She took several steps toward the portal, but her hand passed through the space as it winked out. The Kingdom of Wonderland was gone.

Her heart thudded in her chest, and panic clawed at her throat. Something was wrong with the King. She should warn them, but how? Then she remembered the stone Chess had given her. Scrabbling in her pocket, she whirled around and collided with a solid wall of muscle.

She stumbled backwards.

"Well, what do we have here? You're far from home, my sweet."

She looked up at the person standing in front of her. Although his face was handsome, his skin was blue, and he had two small horns poking up from a sheet of silver hair that fell over his shoulders.

Alice's stomach sank. It looked like she wasn't home, after all.

Look for *JABBERWOCK'S CROWN*, Book 3 of *THE LOOKING GLASS CHRONICLES* in SPRING 2024.

Wondering how Prince Zander ended up cursed? Find out in Jabberwock Prince, your free gift for signing up to my newsletter. Just scan the code below.

One secret may cost him everything.

Prince Zander thought he had years before he would ascend the Kingdom of Wonderland's throne.

But then he is summoned back to the palace and finds his father dead. Before he even has time to mourn, he's informed that the Queen will be the interim ruler until his 21st birthday. Which is news to him.

Suddenly, he is thrust into a cat and mouse game with his stepmother. And she knows more than she's saying.

If he doesn't thwart the Red Queen's schemes, he won't survive long enough to blow out his candles or claim his crown.

Acknowledgments

Once again, I'd like to take a moment to thank those that helped me get my book into the world. Even though writing is a solitary job, there is a small, but mighty team that helped me get this story to you, the reader. First, I'd like to thank my beta readers who were the first eyes to see these words. Emily Bontrager, Amanda Sutton, and Steph Hesseling gave me invaluable feedback. Thanks, ladies – without you, this story would not exist in its current form.

Another invaluable set of eyes was my editor Jody Skinner, of Skinner Book Services. She did a stellar job. Not only was she easy to work with, but her eagle eye caught a lot of important things I would have completely missed, including historically appropriate language and snagged plot lines. Finally, what's a book without its cover? Elona Bezooshko from Psycat Studio created my gorgeous cover and she also redid the cover of *Jabberwock's Curse*. If you haven't seen it, you should check it out.

I also want to thank my students who offered many possibilities for naming my snark. A special thank you goes to Carter Johns who came up with the name Wickle which was a perfect fit.

Of course, I also want to thank my family – without their support I couldn't do what I do. I also want to thank my mom, Mary Ann McColm, who always listens to all my plot snags and character questions without complaining – and she isn't really a fan of fantasy. Thanks, Mom! You're the best!

Finally, I want to thank you, my reader. Without you, Alice, Chess, Citrine, and Zander would just be ideas in my brain, but when the magic of a reader's imagination is added, suddenly they leap off the page and exist in the world. I'll never get over the magic of that, and I am mindful of how blessed I am to be able to write stories and bring them to you – so thank you!

R. V. Bowman

About the Author

R.V. Bowman spends her days teaching high school students in an effort to instill a love of reading and writing. By night, she hits her keyboard to write fantastical tales full of magic and heart. She is also the author of the middle grade fantasy trilogy, *The Pirate Princess Chronicles—Hook's Daughter, Pan's Secret,* and *Neverland's Key.*

She currently lives in Northwest Ohio with her husband, The Coach, two sons, and a nosey dog named Sherlock. You can find out more about her and her books at www.rvbowman.com or follow her on Instagram under the handle @r.v.bowmanfantasyauthor.